PENGUIN BOOKS

manners

Robert Newman is a stand-up comedian.
Manners is his second novel.

robert newman

manners

PENGUIN BOOKS

PENGUIN BOOKS

Published by the Penguin Group
Penguin Books Ltd, 27 Wrights Lane, London W8 5TZ England
Penguin Putnam Inc., 375 Hudson Street, New York, New York 10014, USA
Penguin Books Australia Ltd, Ringwood, Victoria, Australia
Penguin Books Canada Ltd, 10 Alcorn Avenue, Toronto, Ontario, Canada M4V 3B2
Penguin Books (NZ) Ltd, Private Bag 102902, NSMC, Auckland, New Zealand

Penguin Books Ltd, Registered Offices: Harmondsworth, Middlesex, England

First published by Hamish Hamilton Ltd 1998
Published in Penguin Books 1999
10 9 8 7 6 5 4 3 2 1

Printed in England by Clays Ltd, St Ives plc

This book is dedicated to
Gavin Hills
1966–1997

Contents

BOOK TWO

acknowledgements

Special thanks to Hannah Griffiths, Anya Waddington, Louise Moore, Georgia Garret and Johnny Geller for all their help, support and advice with the book.

Martine, Andy Weatherall, Mai and Eddie Walsh and family in County Tramore, Vince Power, Tania Harrison, 'Alfie' Hitchcock, Wil Sanders, John 'Digger' Gardiner, James Midgley. Paul 'Woody' Woodward, Becky Reisenman, Maria Johnstone and all the L8 people from then, Mark Freeman, Mum and Ann, cousin Helen, Ami, Kate Samano, John Bond, Jessica Ward, Simon London, Wendy Rimmington, Hannah Robson, Nick Hornby, Emma, Jeff and Lynn, Mehmet Dilloo, Agnes Brittain, Michaela Betts, Jim and Stan, Sam Arnold-Lawrence, Adrian Chapman, Justin Irwin and Astrid Williamson.

And to the police officers of different ranks in different reliefs around the country who took me out on patrol, gave me their time and trust and without whose help this book would've been impossible.

I found Roger Graef's *Talking Blues* a useful source, too.

Book One

*We were not meant to stand alone. We need to belong –
to something or someone . . . Duty and conscience have no
meaning if there is no sense of commitment to others, and
others to us. 'Think of a person', said Rawls, 'without any
sense of justice. He would be without any ties of affection,
friendship or mutual trust . . . He would be less than human.'
The interesting question is, then, not why some of us are
criminals, but why more of us are not, in a world where so
many of the connections which underlie that sense of justice
are being broken down.*

*The workplace has been the central community in the lives
of many in this century . . . That 'many', however, is now less
than a third of all adults. The organizational society removed
from many of us the need to belong to anywhere other than
our workplace. As a result, when we leave it we have nowhere.*

The Empty Raincoat – CHARLES HANDY

*Even here in the heart of great, hand-made London we were
forced to raise our minds for the instant from the routine of
life, and to recognize the presence of those great, elemental
forces which shriek at mankind through the bars of his civilization, like untamed beasts in a cage.*

Sherlock Holmes and the Five Orange Pips – SIR ARTHUR
CONAN DOYLE

*And is evil just something you are?
Or something you do?*

'*Sister, I'm a Poet*', MORRISSEY

beat surrender

I go over it again and again but it keeps coming out the same. Lee Andrew is still there at the end.

One a.m. Three hours ago it was just another late, an ordinary home beat on the Holloway Road, Kyle Trevorrow and two others tidily skipping a low wall out the park.

'Got any sharps?' I ask, running the quilted lining of his coat through both palms.

'No.'

'What were you doing in the park?' I smile.

'Short cut,' Kyle replies. Front pockets, back pockets. Kyle Trevorrow is just a scally – ten-bob deals of wiz and puff, boosting car-stezzies, Taking and Driving Away. A very different order from Lee Andrew.

'Where you going now?' I ask, stepping back.

'Party,' says Kyle.

'Eh?'

'A party.'

'Where's that?'

'We're just gonna find out now.'

'Yeah?'

'Yeah,' he says.

'OK.'

The three black kids walk away. Then I'm . . . then I'm back at the nick. (There's ten minutes I can't remember here but I'm confident no one died.)

Go up to the canteen for 'lunch' at ten p.m. The happy van

5

(Territorial Support Group) are in. I nod to a couple of them and sit on my own eavesdropping, hoping to hear cretinisms to tell Kieran when he gets back. We collect playbus sayings and repeat them to each other like they were profound philosophies. Each quotation is always appended with the phrase '*Cuppa tea? Cuppa tea?*' (To be said in an Arthur Mullard voice.) Tonight I glean a classic which I can't wait to share with Kieran when he comes back from his course:

'Nah, the reason I shouted out "*Balls of Steel*" wasn't just 'cos I was excited – it's 'cos it's the name of the new AC/DC album.'

Excellent!

(The zenith of me and Kieran's running gag was one home beat when we saw a Royal Variety Sunshine Coach stopped at the lights on the Seven Sisters Road. I was looking at the cerebral palsy adolescents helplessly gurning out the window when Kieran supplied the subtitles: '*Everyone else in the division is jealous of us. Cuppa tea?*' Unforgiveable of course, but pissed myself all the same.)

I enjoy a very pleasing beef and onion pie, a bag of crisps and a coffee, but the mention of AC/DC reminds me of a small thing that's been niggling away at my mind all evening. Walking past a clothes shop earlier on I heard 'Geno' playing, but ever since I cannot for the life of me think what the name of the lead singer was. Can't leave it alone either like a loose tooth. I picture his face, I picture the Lyceum gig – all trombones and leather box-jackets. I try running sentences like 'When *Celtic Soul Brothers* was released Dexy's Midnight Runners' frontman [*blank, blank*] said that –'. But it's no good. I've had a complete brainstorm, forgotten one of those things you think you'll never forget. Next it'll be Joe Strummer that goes out the fucking window! And then where will I be? Or rather who will I be? Will I have forgotten John Lydon's name by the time I die?

'Look out arteries!' says Mickey, setting a white paper plate bearing an uncompromising Cornish pasty down on the table.

'Hi, sir.'

Mickey, the duty inspector, sits down opposite. His blue uniform jumper is stretched tight over fatherly pot-belly. I roll up the sleeves of my jumper to cover the holes at the elbow. I put in an order for a new black V-neck six months ago when this one started falling apart. But there's people been waiting over a year for body-armour and radio-packs and handcuffs that lock. If people are still waiting on radios then jumpers is, is . . . Mickey's thick black belt has all sorts of shit on it. I'm tempted to have him relieve me of my Dexy's conundrum, but guess he wouldn't know, him being late forties or whatever he is with his pointy brown beard with flint-chips of grey. Is it Kevin something? Kevin . . .

'Going out on your own?' he asks. Even Mickey lowers his voice when the playbus are in the canteen. We all do. I think this is because when they go quiet – to concentrate on digestion, say – you're worried that to them your conversation sounds like: '*Ooh, when I saw the Issey Miyake winter collection I almost dropped my slice of Battenburg.*'

'Just till Kieran gets back from his course, sir. Probably.'

'Why's that?'

'I don't know. I think the sight of an officer on his own at night reassures the public. I mean, if they see you and there's always two of you and you're always in a car and . . .'

'Yeah, yeah – but that's not the reason though.'

'I don't know . . . In the day I'll go out with someone, it's just at night.'

'Ah, *macho*.'

'No.'

'No?'

'No.' I don't want to tell Mickey that I feel more alert and switched on alone at night because you don't want to give the impression that you're not a team player. And the truth is I do like the collaborative side sometimes. But at night I've felt that the other officer gets in the way of something (Kieran exempted when we're both on a late). I am, however, bothered by the fact that I don't really have an answer.

'No, I was just asking,' he says, and takes a sip from his tea. What I really want him to say of course is 'Well it certainly seems to work, you're getting the results, John.' But he doesn't. And that's not a point I can make myself, either. There's a sort of etiquette whereby you never blow your own trumpet. The only thing you can ever do is tell an anecdote about an arrest you made and in passing describe the good thinking you were doing, but just as a description of what was going through your mind at the time type thing. 'When I first started on home beat it used to be more common than not.'

'Where was this, sir?'

'Bow. I was on me tod on about me first night and, er –' Mickey stops. His radio pack stands upright on the table and he turns up the dial to listen to something. There's such a frequency about this in canteen talk that no one ever says 'excuse me' or 'one moment'. You just gently fade out of the conversation like you were listening to a little portable conscience. It not needing his attention right here and now he turns the volume back down low and meets my eyes once more. 'And it was me first ever night beat and I get in a fight with the local head-villain. I seen a crowd all gathered round, so I think, "Ooh, I better have a look here," an' this guy was beatin' up a black man with an iron bar, I stepped in and he turns on me, I dropped him and 'cos he was the big boss I got quite a lot of respect from the local faces arter that.'

'I think I'm hoping to impress them with my sprinting speed.'

'Good idea.' He hears something, turns up the radio again, thinks about it, turns it down on low again.

'Is it all right if I don't wear my Gelex, sir?' I ask. 'I wanna obbo the robbers in Miranda Park.'

'It mus' be Thursday.'

'Yeah,' I laugh.

Thursdays all the Irish lads off the building-sites get paid. One or two car-teams in the area like to watch and wait across from the Archway Tavern to see who's going home scuppered, alone or both. They roll them in a choice of the same two or three tight spots. Everyone's been ordered to wear the bright yellow Gelex since the 'RA's last big bang, the idea being to reassure the public with a visible police presence. But the day-glo yellow makes it impossible to keep a low-profile watch on those who watch and wait. With your normal dark uniform you can get right up on someone before they see you.

'No, sorry, John. Oh, and I forgot to tell yer, Kieran's not on a course. He's moved to another division 'cos he hates yer.'

'No, he's in love with me but he's trying to fight it. He's terrified by the strength of his own emotions.'

'He's transferred to the Shetlands.'

'Actually he's gone to sort out his drug problem, sir, but he didn't want you to know.'

'Thanks for telling me,' he says, getting up.

'I was just gonna take it off when I got there, sir, only when I'm actually in the park. So, you know, I'll still be reassuring the public and that.'

'You ain't very reassuring the best of times,' he chuckles. 'Keep it on!'

'All right, sir. See yer.'

'Yeah, ta-ta,' he goes, with his back already to me.

It would've been so easy for it not to have happened. How easily Mickey might have said, 'Well, you can *forget* to put your Gelex on.' Then I'd have been standing in a shop doorway in sight of the Archway Tavern, instead of where I was.

He walks out the canteen and I go over to the vending

machine for a Twix. The women in the TSG are all hard-faced blondes. They're pretty scary as well. One of the women, a sort, too, smiles up at me, perhaps longing for intelligent company after her years in the armoured van among the riot squad, but then again she may just be staring me out. Suppose I'd chatted with her? Killed a few seconds, minutes? Then I wouldn't have been exactly where I was, when I was; the tiniest movements of the nerve-endings in my arm would have been different; perhaps I would have taken a left turn rather than a right and never seen Lee Andrew's van, and then, and then. 'Hello, I'm John,' I might have said to her, or 'Busy night with you?' or 'Hello. My name's John.' But I don't talk to her. I go for a bifta.

Contrary to the fags-and-black-coffee cliché, I'm about the only smoker in the division. The canteen's No Smoking so I have to go and stand in the little room with arcade games – *NBA Basketball*, *Space Invaders* – and puff away, looking at everyone else through mesh-glass like I'm in a decompression chamber. I screw the butt down into the burnt, tin-foil ashtray where it lies next to my bifta of an hour ago when I was just starting my innocent late.

There's two flights of steps going down to the cells. If only I'd slipped on the cell steps and broken my collar-bone. (But the TSG were having their tea-break.) If I'd broken my collar-bone on the steps then I'd still be a good man. But instead the night carries on with vicious precision accurate to a millionth of a second.

Outside the dungeons, squatting against the wall, Big Stuart looks up: 'Ten minutes it took us from there to there,' he says, raising a hand off his knee to point out a ten-yard stretch of corridor. His shirt is torn at the shoulder and he holds an epaulette in his hand.

I peek in the cell. A wizened man about forty with a wire-wool beard and wearing a flea-bitten parka. Bald except for long, crazy wisps of grey hair below the hat-line and a peaked sore on the top of his grimy dome. Alone in his new cell he acts out slow-motion replays of punches he's thrown, gurgling in glory. Clocking me he stops, lifts his chin and waves me away like a lord: 'Move along, it's all over, move along, nothing to see here, nothing to see.' Then mutters, 'You missed it mate, heh-heh. You missed it.'

When I turn back Big Stuart's waiting with a see-what-I'm-up-against face. 'I tell yer,' he says, 'it's true what they say about nutters having superhuman strength!'

Let me stop this time and ask him what the nutter's in for. Let me stop and stand still for no reason and have Stuart look at me a bit strangely.

Out in the car park I walk through night drizzle on to the street, putting my hand up my jacket sleeve to roll down the arms of my jumper. For the next half-hour I prowl all the back-doubles. In an alley off Central Road I notice Lee and Tony Andrew's *Repairs and Alterations* Toyota Hi-Ace parked up. Lee Andrew. Tony Andrew. Andrews? Andrew. Lee and Tony Andrew and four other slags walked into an electrical repair shop and raped the sixteen-year-old Indian girl who'd been left in charge while her parents were out to lunch. Knew who they were, too scared to say. A shining, Kieran said. A shining he told me then is when your new gang member bloods himself by organizing a gang-rape for the others. 'And', he added, 'the Andrews are expanding their slagbase.' Central Road. Check my watch and file and store. I cut through the Derwent Estate and up a side-street, remembering more about the Andrews.

Another time, they waited in a van and abducted two girls walking back from a gig. The Andrew brothers and team drove them half a mile, then broke into an office-furniture warehouse where the attack took place. If I keep following the side-streets I should come out by that road that leads to St John's Road.

The girls positively identified Lee Andrew right down to the blue bug-eyes and light-brown hair, and got his nose exactly on the E-fit. They even picked out his picture from the North London Slag Directory despite the fact that he's got long hair in the photo. But the girls were too scared to go to court. Once they checked out of the rape-suite they were never coming back, I was told, not for all the tea and Chocolate Hob-Nobs in China. I cross Drayton Park. Cut through the Holloway Estate, over a little bank of grass and on to Massie Street. Hear something on my PR and turn it up:

'*Sexual assault, Ley's Leisure Centre, six suspects IC1s. On foot going north at the end of Central Road . . .*'

'Can you tell us where there's a minicab office around here, please?' asks the girl in the red and black stripy tights and a bobbly white synthetic-wool coat. I give her the international hand gesture for 'Shut up a second,' press my ear to the radio. Crackle and static. I point towards the minicab office. Control repeats the same message only this time adding, ' . . . *mid- to late twenties . . .*'. My mind is already racing and not until I've run two blocks do I realize that I've sent her the wrong way. 'Fucking pig.'

Central Road, Lee and Tony Andrew's van. IC1: white males, mid- to late twenties. You could get six in that van. Helpless pinned woman. Scarved-up cheers. A tin-can taste from the sump of burnt lungs slows me to a trot. I push-button the PR and ask Control for details of the victim.

'*She's the aerobics teacher working at the gym and it appears the assault took place in the, er, ladies' changing-room.*'

Oh no. The place where she felt most confident, compromise of shiny-clothes and sweat and making yourself pretty. The forever association of sweatiness with this . . . Was it broken up before – Shut up! – Sick pulse pounding too much at the thought of it to think clearly . . . Think clearly. If this is Lee

Andrew he'll go home, get changed and go out again (why, the night is young!). So. OK. Right now we are both in the same night air. Fibres from the aerobic teacher's lycra still speckle him like dandruff in a warehouse party's ultraviolet. If I can take him prisoner now . . . if I can head him off . . .

'Control? Me again. What *end* of Central Road's that? Do you mean the Farringdon Road end or the other one?'

'*The top.*'

'Do you mean the top as in the north or the top of the hill?'

'*The top of the hill, I think.*'

What will Andrew's rat-run be? No longer heading for Central Road now, I thread an alley, grapple up a creosote fence into a builder's yard. Hopping and jumping across spotlit log-piles and loud plank stacks I glimpse a sudden canyon, a shocking drop. Railway tracks run far below on its valley floor. A great bite out of London, this hidden quarry.

I jog under the cement pillars of the Breaconbridge Tower where the Andrews live and out into a long dead-end street. He'll stay off roads to avoid squad cars and the TSG van. There's a chance he might use this restricted access one though if he isn't going to duck and bob the whole route. Walking now to get my breath back, I follow the tedious blind curve of towering brick like a city wall, where a huge, dead factory runs alongside this deserted street. I hear my footsteps like they're another man's. Lee Andrew comes marching round the corner in black, knee-length leather coat, looking over his shoulder and not a gelled hair out of place. He nano-hesitates, keeps right on walking towards me.

'Oops!'

'There's nothing on me,' he says, hand on heart and smiling. He halts at three paces and holds his arms out crucifixion-style in like a stop-and-search mode.

'You're nicked, Lee Andrew.' Let him know I know what he's done.

My guts sink: he's going to fight. When someone squares up for imminent violence with you there's a sort of obscene intimacy. In a stand-off comes vile, sonar knowledge, a penetrating, instantaneous exchange of core secrets; there's like an overload of physical awareness, a sickening glut of it, a super-vividness about, say, the shape of his head. I have an imprint of his physicality on my jelly self even before it's kicked off. Horrible.

We stare some more.

Kevin Rowland.

I can see him doing mental arithmetic.

He shoots off to my right. Gets past me. British Bulldog. I chase after him, build to a sprint. He stops, spins and I'm running full-face into the rings on his fist. I tear the tendons of my neck trying to avoid the bomb-blast. His fist crashes into my ear. Deafening rather than crippling me. If he'd caught me full-face then my head would've joined the helmet now rolling into the street.

An upper-cut clatters my teeth and I sort of fall straight down like a detonated high-rise.

Roll away, scrambling up just out of reach of a vicious kick. My heart sinks as it whirrs past me loud like a fluting kite. Staggering up to my feet I throw something approaching a left hook but it skims past, perfectly describing the shape of his head, smoothing his bristly side-crop.

His underarm punch shows me how it's done, landing in my guts like instant cholera. No! This can't happen! This can't be! Is a decision made below the level of thought on which my soul swings my whole being around, aligning itself to a new shape like iron filings under a magnet? It is the only way to ... win? Survive? All my fury, hate and evil enter me. A deal with the devil. The most vital decision I will ever make? Feet find primal steps, ancient steps, and with an open left hand in front of his face, I whirl my shoulders, throw my lurching weight into jerking a short, dervish right as hard as I can. I let go the very thing you must never let go to feel his nostrils hot on my knuckles. His head bumps back and up. The only clean blow I land in the whole fight.

I don't see the kick until my kneecap burns. I howl, hopping, limping back (who would think a soft Nike could cause so much pain?), my hand out to stay him. He steps in and drops me with a solid hayraker. Fall on to my good knee and PHHTURRPP! take a faceful of trainer. I grab the crook of his knee.

Now suddenly at the same time I'm doing all the following things:

getting punched on the top of my head

pulling his knee towards me

and rising . . .

I step in, still holding his leg off the ground, and trip his other foot. He goes down, I fall on top of him. Yes. His multi-gym strength whirls me on my back with him on top. No.

Scuffling and wrestling, him trying to get a clean blow, me trying not to die. To press the panic-button on my PR will cost me a clean blow from him. I will have to use the hand that's holding him off.

'10-9 – Acklam Street!'

BANG! The back of my head cracks on to the road as he hits me under the eye. I reach up and try and pull his head down towards me, to lessen the distance between us.

Floor fighting's a bitch. It's all instinctive struggle, tuning into the sound of each other's breathing, distribution of each other's weight and movement until suddenly I'm check-mated: one arm stuck behind my back under both our straining body weights, my other arm pinned to the asphalt by his foot. It crosses my mind to say 'I give'.

I gag as his forearm lithely finds my throat and tries to push down on my windpipe. That's the pipe that carries oxygen from the air to my brain and body. I feel him relaxing as if to compose himself for the killer push, breathing heavily. I nearly puke with his coat sleeve on my throat. I'm being killed here and now, but it's not my life that passes before my eyes, just his freckles, his aftershave, the cold leather sleeve.

He relaxes even more. Too casual. Maybe there's a way out of this. Maybe if he thinks I'm out cold . . .

He slumps heavily on me. A weird, long noise comes out his mouth, unblocking the drain. He is still and heavy. Very heavy. I lift the hand which had been sanding my knuckles on the road and find it to be as light and cooperative as a lost child's. I roll out from under him and straddle him, my shins pinning his upper-arms like kids playing in the rec. He lies more perfectly still than anything I've ever seen.

My thumb on his carotid artery. No pulse. Delayed reaction from the one blow I landed, his nose is too high in his head, higher than it was. Too high, a different face. I tighten thumb and finger on his throat and punch the slag who's died and left me in a street with all the hate of the night. The world and its witness come round the corner, a mob of feet and sirens, van doors and shouts. I hit him again. Blind with tears I'm punching his lump-face slower and slower and slower and slower. Two TSG lift me off the dead man.

vigil

Lots of people talking at me in the TSG van, and then on some steps, and in the nick, but all I'm thinking is: why did it have to happen? Why did it happen to me? Why then? Why wasn't I somewhere else? It would've been so easy for me to be somewhere else. If just five minutes in my twenty-seven years had been spent doing one thing instead of the other.

Mickey drove me home. And now I'm here. Just me. It feels audacious that I'm allowed to be alone in my flat tonight, that I'm allowed to do all the small things everyone else does: I turn the tap and water still comes just like it would for any rate-payer.

I clean my teeth which hurts swelling mouth and wobbly gums. There is blood in the sink and spits of caramel and wafer too. Not two hours ago I got a Twix from the vending machine. 'Twix or Crunchie?' I remember having to decide back then. I waited for the crane to shuffle forward, I bent down and lifted the Twix out the flap. And at that point I could still have done anything with my life. I could have walked out the door and gone to live in a beach-hut in Thailand. I could have done anything and gone anywhere. But now all spheres of movement are gone, leaving just . . . this, and whatever this holds, allows, dictates.

I stare at a jutting right-angle in this bathroom wall. I tread on unremitting floor-tiles, then wood. The world is made of hard edges among which I have no place. A detachment in which I feel dangerously exposed, like a live crab unshelled and shuttling careful-careful around. Light switches are connected to dangerous wires and high-voltage sub-stations of muzzled, terrible fury (like the thicket of massive electrodes south of Birmingham I see on my way to see Beverley – can't think about her yet). This flat is a collection of pipes and wires concealed by plaster and tacked-on wooden boards which nature will destroy.

I am now a man putting the lid back on the coffee, a man putting his hand on the side of the kettle to see how near it is to boiling. *A* man. I hear my shoes tread on the floor, hear the delicate tap-tap as I set my lighter flat on the formica table. I imagine very clearly, it seems, what everyone else is doing now and elsewhere: there will be youths still out on the streets discussing what happened; Kieran in bed maybe; Mickey driving home; Mrs Andrew is just having the bad news broken to her.

Strangely, the only friendly things in the world are my busted lip, the bulging bruise under my eye and my grated face: pain gives my self some definition when the world would take it all away. Yet each time I'm aware of these wounds – the bump of veins pumping, the graze contracting right now as I open my mouth for a cigarette – I'm brought back again, brought up face to pulpy face with where I am, with what has happened, with what I've done.

What I've done, what has happened tonight is hugely present and yet each time I go over it I remember less and less. And so I sit in this hard, straight-back Shaker chair, picking bits of cracked, black formica from the table. Sit and wait.

Outside a group of people on the corner are chatting after-hours. I'll never know them, they'll never know me. I will die and it won't matter a shiver.

Tomorrow I have to go in and see the bosses. I should be preparing what I'm gonna say in my defence. Not just sitting here. But my head is all atomized to fuck, whizzing too fast to engage.

All I get is flashbacks; pelting memories which share the same spectral clarity of bathroom and floor and the tip-tap of my lighter on the table, and seem to reveal new connections between events. Before tonight my past life was like a shed skin, but now it's come back like someone claiming a bad debt, like repossession bailiffs who want you out by morning.

A bluebottle rattles against the pane on the sill, dying in impotent fury. One minute stunned, groping, the next frenetic, upside down. A long night's work ahead of him.

In another world I'd be able to do some simple penance, to run about the forest and gather stuff, find hidden sacraments and, once my task was done, be accepted back into the tribe. Or I'd have to make some kind of symbolic sacrifice. But here and now I just sit in this chair, staring at the table, still picking and peeling off the black plastic coating in little snappy bits. The congealed spastic glue underneath looks like a septic wound.

The noisy fridge gnashes and lows and wails and simmers and buzzes and drones.

In the nick tonight someone handed me a safety-pin to hold my shirt together. Sitting back down now with my coffee, its cold metal sticks in my tum and reminds me of a latchkey, of Mum and me, and . . .

No. Try and think in a straight line, get your defence together. Maybe all these random memories that seem so important are nothing more than that deliberate jabbering you do to get an ugly thought out of your head. Is that what all these memory flashes are about – evasion? Returning to a past full of possibilities now that I'm in a present that has none? It's comforting, certainly, now that everything's come on top, to crawl back to skiver afternoons, when I was seven or eight and we were curled up together on the couch, Mum and me, and feel as safe as I did then. But it's not escapism. These memories pelting the back of my eyes all seem instantly relevant to what happened between me and Lee Andrew two hours ago, like I can't know exactly what happened tonight without looking at my whole life. And not a trawl for mitigating circumstances, either. They all seem more like incriminating *prosecution* evidence: secret stores of anger, the hate-stash and all like my life is a guilty secret, suppressed evidence ... *previous*.

A life for a life.

The burglar alarm of one of the shops has been howling away for a while. It keeps going off of its own accord, its siren wailing louder and louder the more it's ignored.

return to the flightpath estate

The time is 1976, we are in the front room of 47 Tower Road. Present in the room are John Manners and his mum . . .

I've just taken my bike apart and now I can't put it back together again. I'm getting more and more het up, about to throw what my mum would call 'a paddy'. She looks at me, nodding slowly to herself, in that particular manner which means peace is on its way. Without a word I go and sit at the kitchen table. She runs me a beaker of lemon squash. Popping the loud-as-BOO! cap from tinted-brown-plastic jar of her prescription tranquillizers, she goes, 'One for you, one for me.' I feel the large dryness of her fingers in the wetness of my mouth and the shiny-smooth capsule on my tongue like communion wafer.

We sit curled in each other's arms on the orange woollen sofa, watching this programme called *Yoga with Lyn Marshall*. Lyn Marshall has long, blonde hair. She demonstrates yoga on green mats against an orange background along with a Japanese Zen-master who has black-framed glasses like a deposed dictator.

'Inhale,' says the Japanese man, while Mum sucks deep on her Dunhill Superking, 'And . . . exhale!' he says, disappearing behind a cloud of smoke in the shape of an expanding lotus lily.

She never minds me skiving because it means she doesn't have to trek out for bifters. She doesn't like going outdoors in case she gets lost, and also because, she says, 'there's too much

21

of it' – 'it' meaning outside, which for her just goes on and on.

Yoga with Lyn Marshall is followed by *Playschool* (which we are both too old for but watch all the same). Then she gets up and stares rigidly out the sitting-room window.

Through the square window is an endless sprawl of houses just like ours for miles around. Light and roomy council terraces, all brand new bricks and white, wooden slatted panels on the front. Some windows still have yellow glass-crayon crosses on the pane and bits of Cellophane in the sill. Garden-shaped plots of mud, learner street lamps and seeded verges. Everything new, trim and shiny and full of possibility as the hundred children just moved in. The streets and estates are triumphantly named after what they destroyed: Meadow Roundabout, Cherry Tree Estate, Five Elms Flyover.

I've got into the habit of going back five steps when I've gone round a corner. I'm checking on a theory: am I in an experiment that everyone knows about except me? Hypothesis: given a particular society and told it is normal, how long will it take nine-year-old John Manners to cotton on? Am I the guinea pig in an experiment to test human gullibility? Every time I turn the corner of my street, I go back five steps to check if they've flipped the switch and the 'houses' have rolled over to reveal how people really live. They all emerge from their real dwellings grinning and chatting to each other. They suppose they'll have to tell me soon. Isn't it amazing that he still hasn't tumbled. How much longer will it take him?

My desk-sergeant dad had died when I was too young to remember him. Driving home pissed from the police social one night, his Vauxhall Viva got stuck in the snow. He struck out for home on foot, passed out face-down in a snowdrift and suffocated. I remember being proud of the fact that my dad had been a policeman if only for the fact that other kids' dads never seemed to know what exactly their job was. Other kids' dads knew *where* they worked: Roche Chemical, Vauxhall, the airport; they could narrow it down to shopfloor, machines or assembly, but they hadn't the foggiest, it seemed, of what they actually did. And then, in the middle of secondary school when for most of them it suddenly became what they *used* to do, the same dads would say defiantly and definitely what it was they once did: I made cars, I had to make sure all the different chemicals went to the right places.

It was about this time that the Great Experiment got stuck. One day they couldn't press the switch and flip the houses over any more, and now none of them knew quite what to do. They were left where I was. The mums and dads looked stumped as if they'd mislaid something, but as if the really worrying thing was that they couldn't remember what it was they had mislaid.

When the Great Experiment was still up and running, they used to lean casually against a kitchen fitment and tell their sons, 'Well, if John gets three pound pocket-money' (police-widow's-pension bonanza) 'go and live with him, then.' And smiling, say, 'No, you can't have a bike/skateboard yet.' But now the Experiment had crumbled they set their teeth in determination that their children *would* have a bike or skateboard or three pound pocket-money. They lost confidence about what to put in sandwiches, how late to let my friends stay out, how much to insist on homework, which rules to enforce. Now they all seemed to be watching each other, and had more time to do so.

The time is eight-twenty a.m. in the front room of 47 Tower Road. Present is John Manners, back from his paper round.

I'm staring at the picture on the wall. An oil painting of the dark and moody man with shiny, black, greased-back hair and sideboards who understands all the things about my mum that I don't. He is dressed all in white, white flares and a white cape

23

studded with emeralds. Hawaiian flowers are wreathed around his neck. He stands on two twinkly stars in the warmth of outer space, from where he holds out a hand with rings on his fingers. His eye-level in the painting is Mum's height, not mine . . . when she's in the room, that is. But she hasn't got up this morning.

I knock on her door. No reply. Enter.

There is a thin cord of goo between her bottom lip and the pillow. On the other end of Mum's bedside phone the ambulance man asks me to read out the labels of the little jars I find among crumpled tissues by her bed. Long words for a twelve-year-old but I make use of Meaty Mrs Beaty's English tip about how you shouldn't be frightened by long words because they're just short words stuck together. The temaz and the zep and the pam.

Our school was integrated with another and they still tried to tell us they hadn't changed the essentials. But they were like bad liars in the interview room changing their story on the hoof. 'Er, did we say the Napoleonic wars were the most important thing in world history? No, what we, er, meant was, ah, that the American Indians, their terrible plight you know, and colonialism, that *that* was the most important thing.' Ho-hum, we went, and didn't give a shit about either.

At break we all stand round in a circle, hands in pockets, and talk in level voices about violence:

He was just standing at the urinal and this geezer slashes his dick with a Stanley knife and he just dies of shock.

Why?

No reason. He just did it.

And there was the same randomness about how every Saturday in the Arndale Centre another shop would have shut down, and there was no reason, it seemed, about whose dad became the next lay-off from Vauxhall, Roche or the airport.

. . . Yeah, the Cherry Tree went over the George and they

climbed the wall into where everyone drinks outside and the people couldn't get away 'cos of the wall and they beat them up, to like a pulp . . .

. . . and Sham 69 at the Conway Hall – all these skins were rushing the punks and the bouncers said 'Shut the doors,' and some skins were trapped between the two doors and they were just slaughtered . . .

. . . and this kid Sandy Doolan from New York, he's the hardest kid at St Joe's and he wrapped some barbed wire round this kid's head and he was just banging his head again and again against the concrete – bang bang bang.

Colin Sparrow and Robert Gower were playing headers and volleys in the rec. I repeated this last one like I knew Sandy Doolan, like it was first-hand. Colin Sparrow turned to me and said, 'And you think that's good, do you? You think that makes him a man.' I was ashamed. I knew what Colin Sparrow was saying was what I really thought. I'd just needed to hear someone else say it. I'd been caught out on the wrong side. They carried on playing and when Robert Gower skied the ball over the bar I went and got it. Colin Sparrow was a big, quiet seventeen-year-old. And a police cadet.

Tomorrow is my thirteenth birthday. Mum and a coach-driver called Kenneth are posing for pictures outside the registry office. On the grass beneath their feet my dad is represented by a thin and threadbare covering of snow.

My stepfather Kenneth is, if not the most evil man in the world, then surely among the most evil coach-drivers in the world.

'How old do you think you'll be when you can have me?'

'Eighteen . . .?' I mumble-whine.

'Eighteen! Six, seven years' time! I'll be an old man by then. But you'll never be able to beat me. You know why? I've killed people. That's why. And I can take pain. And that's another reason,' he says, pointing at my nose, 'you're what we used to call in boxing a "bleeder".'

He makes a big show of looking after my mum like it's my fault the nervous state she is in – like he could ever've got a shag off someone so fit if she wasn't a basket-case.

He is one of those cockney wankers who thinks that criminals are gents. '*Ronnie Knight? I had a drink with him in Torremolinos*'. All that shite and Kray bollocks. Then again, he may be winding me up because he knows what my dad did for a living. Just like how he winds up me and my *Misty in Roots* album by doing a 'darkie' dance in my bedroom doorway, or by going, 'Goo on, mah sone' when a white South African soldier clubs down a Soweto runner on the *News at Ten*.

Oddly, he was never violent when he'd been drinking. In fact he was weirdly gentle then. One night he came home from the pub and rang the bell because I'd accidentally put the mortise on. (He'd been on my case about that before, as well as an unconscious habit I'd got into of leaving a room with him and my mum and turning out the light as I did so as if they weren't there. 'Oi!' they'd go.) I let him in, nervously spilling loose shekels all over the noisy floor. I can't remember how I did this, whether I jerked my hand out of my pocket in my haste to open the door, or whether I knocked a stack of coins off the side, or how it happened. I just remember all these coins on the floor which were mine and what happened next ... Squatting down, face flushed with drinking, he strangely picked them up for me one by one, and then handed them to me like a humble man with his overbearing boss! Strange, strange, strange.

Thinking back now, maybe I gave him funny looks. Because when his fists were clenched in my bedroom and he was building up to it, he'd say, 'I've been in the war! I'm clean! I earn £10,000 a year! I'm clean, I shower twice a day! I've gone three rounds with the All-England Amateur Boxing Champion!' And the next thing I know I'm on the carpet and he's kneeling on me, with his tongue between his teeth and trying to land one which will sound like the one he has in his mind. Clean. But not being able to and getting madder and madder. And my mum in the doorway saying at first 'Leave that poor child alone!' but then changing her tune to 'It's your own fault, John.' At the container depot I once saw him punch a man in the face and then, pointing with the index finger of the same hand, say, '*Manners!*'

There was a lucky, lucky star over my childhood, however, and Kenneth was only around for a few years. Kenneth got a new job and him and Mum moved up north. I wished just he'd gone and not Mum as well, but it was like I'd struck a deal in some smoke-filled room of my soul. I was always cutting deals then: if I catch the bread knife I've spun in the air my mum will cheer up; if I go back and touch the lamp-post with my left hand (now that I've touched it with my right) then I will be the first Englishman asked to play football, say, for Brazil *and* England and will have to make a speech saying, '*Much as I hate to disappoint one of you, I have, reluctantly, to make a choice. I wish I didn't, but what with my Formula One commitments [wise nodding from assembled dignitaries] and until I can stand down as President of the United States and Prime Minister of England, I must, I have to say, choose between one of you two great nations. And when I say that my choice has been much influenced by my growing friendship with Emerson Fittipaldi, you will know what my final decision . . .*'. Would I want Kenneth to leave even if it meant Mum went with him? I must've asked myself in that smoke-filled deal room. On balance this was better. I was free and went to live in a nearby village with my nan.

Nan lived in a grey-white prefab. Four rooms in all – her room, my room, bathroom, and the sitting-room which had a kind of kitchenette against the back window. Nan always pronounced it priffib, like triffid, and the whole thing stood not much taller than a grown man. There was an odd contrast between the ErectorSet walls and the ancient, loving detail of the well-stocked garden which ran round the front and side of it. Painstakingly nurtured and weeded, her garden had bits of wooden fence made into little archways with pretty red and yellow roses growing up them, which I had to stoop through even at that age.

Spook Wood has creepers on that you could swing from like Tarzan. I can jump from the second-floor scaffolding on to the builder's sandpit below, but Alex and Sean can jump off the third. The cool way of walking is to have your thumbs hooked into the pockets of your jeans. Dingo and me glue our names in glitter on the back of our Harringtons.

One schoolday just after I bought The Clash's *London Calling*, I stood on the top field after Upal had been beaten up. Upal, who everyone said was an untouchable in Indian culture (even though, looking back now, he must have been Sikh not Hindu anyway). Dirt-poor, strange-smelling Upal, with a milky cast in one eye. That afternoon he lay on his back, his unravelled purple turban strewn impossibly long on the top field. I stayed behind after everyone had gone but I never helped him up or offered a kind word. Just stood there and watched him lying on his back loudly sobbing out and crying, 'Not again! Oh God! Not again!' to the God who wouldn't hear his outcast cry.

When I was a puny thirteen-year-old mod-punk-prat I used to have these long arguments with eighteen-year-old skins at the Youth Centre. I knew that at school these same skins had black friends; I knew that they'd only get up for Prince Buster at a dance, and so, as an idealistic little Clash fan, I couldn't understand their C18 shit, or why Vimhead had marker-penned Bad Manners down the back of his sheepskin in vertical columns so that it spelt BM in bold across the shoulders. And so, sitting on the table football, we'd have these long, interminable arguments that never got anywhere until one night I understood that we were arguing at cross purposes. Black and white wasn't the issue; hate was the issue. They had all this hate and they'd found somewhere for it to go. I gave up arguing with the skins after that and started going to a different youth club.

The burglar alarm outside has stopped howling. I get up and make a coffee.

Liverpool University, PPS (Politics, Philosophy, Sociology). A breakdown but 'considered honours'. Smoke rises out of Luton crematorium chimney scattering Mum's ashes to the four winds (in accordance with the agoraphobic's last wishes).

They couldn't believe their luck at the interview. Here was I, a graduate but whose dad was a cop *and* who wanted to start as a Permanent Beat Officer rather than on the much-sneered-at Bramshill Special Entry which whisks top-notch wankers into Inspector in five years.

All through the interview I felt like a liar, a guilty fraud. Yes, my dad was a cop, but I knew and they didn't that he'd had no influence on me at all. They didn't ask how young I was when he died. The sense of fraud and deception may also have been just fear of authority. But it was to do with something much deeper too and maybe there was even a glimpse of it when, the interview having subsided into chit-chat, I made a little joke. It came in a long pause during which the three interviewers were looking at me, each waiting for the other to speak:

'All right,' I said, 'I did it.'

*

Outside my window I hear the steel roller-shutter of the late-night corner shop rattle down. They bang the steel lock into place. Clunk.

I got off to a flying start in my chosen career, so they gave me a lot of autonomy. Six months after I transferred down to the Met., me and Kieran got Special Commendations for pulling some Senagalese women out of an arson attack. (The papers said it was a race thing but it was the mad old dad come back to destroy what he could not possess. We reckon he'd skipped the country but the terrified women couldn't be persuaded he wasn't still around.)

The Special Commendations were given out at a big dinner for cops, firemen, nurses and coastguards in the Dorchester Hotel. The Home Secretary – I still can't bring myself to say his name – stuck the medals on. I'd been watching him out the corner of my eye pinning the sport-shop Your-Inscription-Here-type medal on everyone's left breast along the line to my right. We'd all been told about protocol for him, but no fucker had told him about protocol for me. I can't stand being touched by someone I don't know. (I don't know why. Handshakes are OK. But not shoulder-jostling on the tube – none of that sort of thing. Or doctors, dentists, tailors. None of that. No one, for example, has ever slapped me on the back. Luckily, they just know.) I hadn't even thought about this aspect of the ceremony – that it would involve physical contact, the pinning-on bit with the flat of his hand fidgeting around all knuckly fingerly on my breast, and I still hadn't thought about it until the back of my hand had knocked his wrist away from me in a sudden flinch and my left hand was stayed in mid-air like 'Off!'. A hard-knotted little hiatus followed, then he put the free gift in my hand with a country-vicar smile. (Luckily Kieran was a few people up the line as they'd stood us, so I didn't spoil his day, I think.)

*

Outside the shopkeeper kicks the steel roller-shutter to check it's locked. Clunk. Locked securely into place for the night ahead.

Looking back at the award ceremony tonight I feel fitted up by life just like I did about the Great Experiment when I was a boy.

The fridge finds another gear, one lower, as if the God of Indesit is satisfied for the moment.

I sit as still as this hard-backed wooden chair. It is right to sit in darkness and see haphazard bits of street-light and night cross the table-top and my folded, harmful hands. The light and shade that I don't control, and to which I am irrelevant. To know for the first time properly that nature doesn't give a fuck if I live or die.

The burglar alarm shuts off. I hover, suspended on a new silence, scanning for the next memory on the night-dial.

stay free

I was out on my first home beat after the commendation
when I saw Mick Jones off The Clash. Excellent! Mick Jones!
Mick Jones off The Clash! Mick Jones that sung 'Stay Free',
my favourite-ever Clash song:

> *I practised daily in my room,*
> *You were down the Crown planning your next move –*
> *Go on a nicking spree,*
> *Hit the wrong guy,*
> *Each of you get three*
> *Years in Brixton.*

I was twenty-four, he was down the Angel with his girlfriend,
a tall, worried-looking blonde. I crossed the street grinning in
my uniform. 'Hiya Mick, The Clash changed my life!'

'Oh no!' he said without stopping, 'Where did we go
wrong?'

Fuck you too, I thought, stranded on the pavement.
Fuck you too. Should've stopped and searched the druggie-
cunt.

Couldn't listen to any Clash after that. He'd no idea what
he'd done. Up till then I'd played The Clash as much as all my
other tapes and CDs put together. But after that, I couldn't
listen to them or even hum them. Why did he have to say that?
Why couldn't he see that maybe I was trying to be the better
cop? What my motives might be? Fucking slag.

I remember at school all the black kids used to let on to me and I never knew why. Still don't. I told Beverley about it once, and, typically skew-whiff, she said it was a spiritual connection. By which she meant I think that I was probably less hard-faced than the other white boys, or looked at black kids less coldly. Maybe I under-estimate how off the other white boys were. Even little black first-years I didn't know would say hello. Wish I could have told Mick Jones that maybe there might've been something of that in the weave of my blue uniform. Or Upal on the top field. Or Colin Sparrow. Or the feelings I'd had at the Dorchester the week before.

I never get offended when some civilian calls me a fascist pig – unless he used to be in The Clash – because I know that their souls would be even worse if they had to do only six weeks of the duty I do. It has to happen. It's just how much of your powder you can keep dry. That's all. And if there was one thing above all else that stopped my cynicism curdling into fascism it was the eight- to thirteen-year-olds I met on Liverpool Summer Action before I transferred down. I feel this memory is coming to me for a reason: logging itself somewhere as a stave against the despair that will soon crash in on my head.

How did I get from there to here? So isolated. Few cops are single. And I couldn't get off my high horse and make friends with any colleagues save Kieran. But with the Liverpool kids life was more collective than I've ever known. Then again, it led to something else though, didn't it? Something that might have been a warning of all what's come on top. The nearest I came before tonight to 'doing my legs'.

The force were running Summer Action, sponsored by Midland Bank and some charities/trust funds. We took Liverpool kids who wouldn't otherwise get a holiday to Anglesey or the Lake District.

Carri-mats and sleeping bags in the Llangoed church hall, Anglesey, and a big old army tent pitched in a farmer's field a mile away for the brave to sleep in. We glued together a huge bouncy inflatable at the church hall.

The kids had a song they sang as we drove from canoeing to pony trekking:

> *I'll sing you twelve-oh,*
> *Red fly the banners-oh,*
> *What is your twelve-oh?*
> *Twelve for the chimes of the Kremlin clock,*
> *Eleven for the Moscow dynamos*
> *And ten for the works of Lenin*
> *Nine for the nine bright satellite states*
> *And eight for the 8th Red Army,*
> *Seven for the days of the working week*
> *And six for the Tolpuddle martyrs,*
> *Five for the years of the Five Year Plan*
> *And four for the years it's taken*
> *Three, three the rights of people,*
> *Two, two the workers' hands working for a living-oh,*
> *One is workers' unity and evermore shall be so.*

A visit to a theme-park called Camelot based on the Arthurian legend: Merlin's Dragon, space rockets and the OK Corral; a barbecue on the beach; a play written and performed by some of the kids.

The harder kids resisted the whole deal for a couple of days. Didn't we know they were adults? That they'd had to be adults for years? So you had a couple of days of throwing rocks at cows, of running away, or shoplifting from a village shop which didn't slip your Twix and change through a flip-flop security hatch in the steel-mesh. A couple of days of spitting in your face, pointing at you and saying, 'Don't talk him he's a fookin' scuffer!'

But then they became kids again. I remember the curious way Perry, a long-chinned, pale-skinned black kid with bags under his eleven-year-old eyes, said 'wheee!' as he rode a BMX down a footpath. Curious because it had the self-consciousness of a married man sliding on an iced-over path in front of his wife, like '*Look at me, I'm a big kid.*' Instead of throwing stones at cattle, they started fighting over who got the right to take the cows scraps and leftovers. 'Eeee!' they'd go, every time the full nine yards of the cow's tongue sanded tiny palms clean of trifle. Tony Clanton and Perry spent long hours leaning on the five-bar like farmers, staring at the unstressed movements of the Fresians. Perry got all steamed-up in the high-pitched wail of complaining scousers when one of the herd had a limp and nothing was done about it day after day.

Working with these kids made me feel complete, strong, whole. Before I first worked with them I was in the worst depression of my life (although I think there's a bigger one on the way). Yet as soon as I was a helper – as we were called – all my insecurities and gaps disappeared. I had a definite outline, a working self, I knew what to do in situations, I had a purpose: I felt I was making a difference. I could see the results of my work. And was it something to do with being able to get through to the wildest kids that had made me go and become a police-officer? Thinking I'd be the cool cop.

I did Liverpool Summer Action for two summers. And what with it being the same kids both years, plus the winter project in Aigburth, plus seeing them or their families as a CBO when I was still in Liverpool, we got close. Me and the Clantons, especially.

The thing I was proudest of was when one of the coordinators said at a planning meeting of all the helpers, 'John is the key to the Clanton family, he's the can-opener.' I was the only one who could form a relationship with the Clantons, who were the wildest family. I wanted to adopt them but I was single and boiled my dinner in a bag.

The Clantons: Tony, Robbie, Jamie and Tina.

The first time I saw Tony, Robbie and Jamie, they tore into the hall and threw themselves on the folded inflatable singing 'We Are Family' with fists in the air.

Tony had a husky twenty-a-day voice. A twelve-year-old skinhead with facial sores. A lot of knowledge in his face. Too much too young.

We were on a beach having a barbecue and toasting marsh-mallows round a fire and singing 'You'll Never Get To Heaven'. The slow integration of the Clantons began with Tony looking down at the sand, grinning to no one and adding a verse of his own:

> Oh, you'll never get to heaven in a biscuit-tin,
> 'cos a biscuit tin's got sponkies in.

And then a curious mixed smile – part I've-been-cool-and-naughty and part what-a-twat-I-am-to-actually-join-in.

Another time, I was driving the shaky Ford Transit when Tony leans over from the back and asks, 'What time is it, John?'

'About eleven.'

'So it's about one o'clock in Liverpool now then?'

'No, it's eleven there too.'

'No, it can't be. It's about two hours different.'

Robbie looked like how the lead singer off of UB40 perhaps looked when he was eleven (if he was also a hyperactive, freckle-faced skinhead).

Jamie didn't have the guile of his two older brothers. Tony and Robbie had blond no. 2 crops; Jamie, though, had a blondy-brown fringe of greasy Three Stooges hair on a Munster face. Where Tony and Robbie had a containment in their movements, trim in Adidas, Jamie was chaotic, walked with his feet splayed, saggy-arsed in grubby cords and a lop-sided grin. His voice was shriller and louder, too, which would earn him the occasional punch from one of his brothers.

The youngest Clanton was Tina. Nine years old, Tina was usually found hunching one shy shoulder after another as if someone were going to hit her. In more outgoing moments she'd be gnawing her fingers, with her long blonde hair hanging over one or both eyes. Beautiful with a wide nose and mouth like Lauren Bacall (crossed with the lead singer of UB40!). The other helpers called her a 'limpet' because she always wanted to be carried or to sit on my lap. The little she said was in a heart-stopping, sing-song whisper of a voice. An aerated, dreamy lilt which snagged on the scouse hard 'c's and 'k's and sounded like someone spinning a bright copper cog. Once when I was giving her a piggy-back, the soft, quiet voice in my ear said, 'I can read that word.'

Her grubby finger pointed down at the large white letters painted on the car-park Tarmac we were walking over.

'Go on then.'

'A-L-L-O-W-E-D. Allowed.'

'How do you know that word?' (She had problems spelling her own surname.)

'It says that by ours. NO BALL GAMES ALLOWED.'

Another time, Tina was sitting on my lap one night in the back of the crowded van as we returned from the chippy. She was looking at a thicket of white moths against the night.

'The moths look like they're dancing,' she whispered.

'Tina, you're an angel.'

'What's that?'

She was a tough kid, too. She'd never wail when one of her brothers walked past and gave her a dig in the face or stomach. Just lower her head and bite her lip.

'Where's Tina?' I joked one morning to a blonde curtain of matted hair where an eye peeped out over her cornflakes. (Breakfast served on three long trestle tables.) That same afternoon Tina took to the smooth floor of the roller-rink like a duck to its skateboard. Her shoulder-length fringe blew up and away from bold, assured eyes and a quiet, confident smile at thirty miles an hour.

Day Two I drove the leaky Transit full of singing kids to the swimming-pool.

We're off, we're off, we're off in a motor car,
Sixty coppers are after us, we don't know where we are.
Turn round the corner eating a Christmas pie,
Along came a copper I punched him in the eye.

I went to tell me mother, me mother wasn't in,
I went to tell me father, he kicked me in the bin.

We're off, we're off . . .

I was so proud of our children when we hit the swimming-pool. How fearless they were on the boards, how completely they took over the place, how quickly Robbie Clanton got thrown out. (For diving in from the balcony of the cafeteria.)

Laughed out loud seeing Leanne Evans in her costume. Costume slightly too large.

Turning around and around with Anna and Tina in each arm, wet bodies, slippery as soap, as alive as mice. Laughing close in each other's faces I wondered whether this was extreme happiness or just a self-conscious replica of that slow-motion frame. But there was a hypnotic field-effect keeping us chuckling in each other's wet faces, turning and turning. And though I was aware of it being a time-stand-still moment, time standing still all the same.

The intense light, the bright-coloured swimsuits, the yellow armbands, the red and white life-belts and sky-blue diving board. All the beautiful, energetic bodies, tiny legs, bombing or on the side shivering with hunched shoulders and elbows, excited yelps, shouts echoing round the baths, wave upon wave.

The little pelvic hollows where a municipal swimsuit didn't fit. One scrawny, wizened-faced boy in baggy nylon football shorts and whose name I can't remember dropped off the top boards as if he was dropping into a sofa. I stood in the shallow end watching Leanne Evans star-diving into the five foot. Jumping off the side in her stripy all-in-one, arms and legs out like a starfish, tiny little nates.

'Having a good look?' probed Sarah, one of the helpers.

'Eh?'

'Staring at semi-naked little girls,' she said, with a sharky inquisitor's smile. Arch. Float if I'm guilty, sink if I'm not.

'Yes,' I said, turning to her but then looking down at the water and then the big windows. 'Not like that, but . . . but their bodies *are* beautiful.'

'You like looking at their bodies?'

'But it's not a *sexual* thing! I don't want to have *sex* with them.'

'Lots of paedophiles don't actually have sex with their prey, or don't actually penetrate.'

'What the fuck are you using a word like penetrate for? In this conversation. How did we get here?'

One of the kids swam up. Little Annie with her granny face (grey-eyed and washer-womany for all her slender, chirpy frame). She sensed a spat and turned and swam off again. I watched her confiding importantly in the other kids not to come near, with the respect for adult rows an alkie dad had taught her.

'Well, would you look at the boys like that?'

'Like what?'

'Well, would you say their bodies were beautiful?'

'That's not the same, well, no but yes, they've got a certain life . . . but . . .'

'Ah!'

My mouth gaped open and shut like a landed fish. In the

back of my stung mind was a sense that it wasn't anything like lust. It was a cheery benign thing. The freedom of their bodies. The neat compactness. The lack of shame. The quick of life in their bodies. Their faces more individual than adults'. Brighter than adult faces that have had a lifetime of disappointing answers to all those eager questions. And know that the moon is a big ball of dust.

A whistle blew. Robbie Clanton had just dived in off the balcony and I had to accompany him out.

Me and Robbie crossed the car park with wet hair and crisps. Two social outcasts. I couldn't find the van for about ten minutes.

'You glad you're here?' I asked him as we searched.

'It's all right,' he said. 'Your food's shit though.'

'What's your favourite food?'

'Chopped pork.'

'What's that?'

'It comes in a tin.'

'OK, we got an hour – let's go and get some.'

I gave him a fiver of my own money outside Londis.

'I'll be wanting some change and don't peg off to Acapulco.'

When he came out with the tin and my present and correct change, I made a show of patting down his pockets.

'You arlarse,' he said.

There were a few shekels in his jacket pocket.

'Ah, my change,' I said.

'Fuck off, that's mine!'

'I gave you a tenner.'

'Fiver.'

'I clearly remember giving you a twenty. It was purple.'

'Arlarse!' he said as I handed back his few coins.

Driving back to the pool, I saw a gate open and drove into an empty field.

'If you make me a cup of tea when we get back to the hall, you can drive the van now round this field.'

'Go 'ead!'

'But it will have to be a very special cup of tea. You have to soak the tea-bag for exactly fifty-eight seconds, two sugars and plenty of milk and it has to be stirred with love.'

'Yeah, yeah.'

'Yeah?'

'Yeah, I'll make you a cup of tea.'

'How do I have it?'

'Flob in it, wipe my arse on the teabag, no sugars, no milk.'

'No driving,' I said, pretending to be about to turn the van round.

'Two sugars, some fucking milk, fifty seconds . . .'

'No, Robbie, not fifty seconds.'

'Fifty-four.'

I shook my head.

'Fifty-eight.'

'Fight-eight seconds and then you *whip* that tea-bag out. And what do you stir it with?'

'Give me the keys you queer!'

'That's near enough,' I said, sliding off the seat, but holding on to the keys until I'd walked round and got in the passenger side.

Robbie drove the van gently round the field with no hand-brake turns.

One night we had a ghost hunt. We drove to a deserted spot, the van headlights went off, and a Pifco-underlit helper told the kids a ghost story which he said had happened on this very footpath.

The village we were billeted in was haunted by souvenir witches, leering from tea-towels, pub signs and china mugs.

The kids had all seen these as we walked through the village, which helped our ghosts' sheet cred.

On the first ghost hunt me and Robbie Clanton, Jason Macarthy and Donna Craig were the acting ghosts. (It was meant to be Tony too but he had to stay back at the hall with Sue for beating up a 'woollyback' local.) Amazingly I got Robbie to paint his face white, wear a long black robe and paint my face white too. We painted some blood on each other. Robbie got the plastic fangs.

When the four of us got to the ruin just off the footpath where the ghost-busters would come, my kids were too scared by the ruin to haunt it. This was strange as two of the ghost-children – Robbie and Donna – had burglary convictions back in the ghost town.

On the last day we had a party with games like *Port! Aft! Starboard! Bow!* The kids charged into wall after wall – Aft! Starboard! Starboard! – not wanting to be the stranded, picked off last. And the next morning we drove them back to stranded Liverpool.

On the morning of their departure I crouched down in front of this shivering gawky kid whose name I forget. He was seven or eight with slightly goofy teeth and brown hair. A shivering outsider, he had seldom mixed in with any of the others, and once when we were all walking back in the early evening sun from a kickabout, I watched him, alone, thinking he was unobserved. As cars passed up the hill we were walking down he introvertedly mimed that he was kicking or punching each car.

As we were about to leave, I crouched down in front of him, his sparrow rib-cage in my hand and asked, 'Did you have a good time on camp?'

Eyes staring wildly at the distance, and with shrill panic in his voice, he anguishedly cried, '*No*! It was *crap*!'

Two vans took the kids home, and always the same ritual. As the van left the kids flicked the Vs out the windows. We grinned and flicked the Vs back, so they'd give it to wanker hand or swivel digit as the distance between you grew.

I drove the second van, which included the Clantons, on the drop-off.

Heading for home fourteen kids sang songs as we bowled along.

> We are ace, we are cool,
> We all come from Liverpool . . .
>
> . . . We are the scousers,
> Mighty, mighty scousers . . .
>
> . . . And you'll never walk alone.

The complete hymn sheet. But as the van turned off the A-road and started bumping over the mean, mean streets of home, the songs dropped off like loose tiling.

The kids were silent, watching anxiously, gathering their things. Fourteen individual kids, or sudden families again. Gina Grant talked quietly to her younger brother Joey, making sure he'd got both bags. And that his cozzy was in her bag. After that little flurry of activity, a tense silence again as the kids stared anxiously out the window, hoping to spot home a split second before anyone else did. Worried perhaps in case anything 'made a show of them'.

I dropped each of them all back off again until it was just me and the Clantons. When we got to the Linden Estate where they lived I wondered if we'd done them a favour at all.

Was it cruel to show them how different life could be before throwing them back in the hole? A taste of honey's worse than none at all. Or was it worth it perhaps just to have seen an alternative way of being; something else might do some enriching work, like the rain from two years ago – rain that lies down in the water-table and stops the ground cracking in a dry season.

And you'll never walk alone . . .

They insisted I didn't walk them to the door. (This from the same Tina and Robbie who'd wanted a carry/swing-round/piggy-back all week.) So I just walked them to the end of the street. They walked off about twenty paces carrying their heavy bags back into the real world, heads bowed like name-tagged evacuees returning to the city in 1941. They walked towards the Linden Estate's anti-personnel lights, twenty yards until they were back on the other side of that invisible Check-point Charlie. Then they stopped, turned and flicked the Vs. Like the whole week had been a practical joke they'd played on us. Adult faced again. Throwers of rocks at cows again.

One of the students, Sue Dornan, was from Oxford University on attachment. She arranged a February-half-term weekend down there for about eleven kids who were driven down by me and two women students. Tina turned up with a bandaged hand. She'd picked up some ice on Smithdown Road L8 and it was broken glass.

'What do they do in all those old buildings?' asked Jamie outside one of the colleges.

. . . What's that saying the Jesuits had? 'Give me a child at the age of four . . .' These kids were between eight and thirteen, but it was the same thing . . . Some of those bright Liverpool kids were so obviously university material – although not Jamie! – yet they'd never get there.

Me, Robbie, Jamie and Tina went with Sue Dornan to her Oxford tutor's for 'supper'. The kindly tutor and her husband made me and the Clanton kids twisty pasta and those thin, crispy, straggly chips you get in posh restaurants. They let the Clantons light the dinner candles, hold the baby and gave them

Cornettos for pud. How would the Clantons react to this ambience: would the 'cello end up halfway through the Matisse print?

'Can we come again tomorrow?' asked Robbie when we walked home in the night air.

'Depends how much stuff they notice missing.'

'Fuck off!' he scowled.

'Sorry.'

We shared an attic room in Sue Dornan's shared student house. Me on the bed, him on a lilo.

'Can we go there again tomorrow?'

'No, we're going home tomorrow, aren't we?'

'Before we leave, then . . .'

'They're probably doing something tomorrow. You like it here?'

'Their house was mad!'

'No, it wasn't. It wasn't at all.'

'It was full of crazy things. Big mad fucking violins and off-his-head drawings and pictures, and mad food.'

'Did you like the food?'

'Yeah.'

'Yeah, it was nice. I'm knackered. Good-night.'

'Yeah. Good-night.'

I turned out the light, and rolled over to the wall. In a small voice, Robbie said, 'You wouldn't think I was scared of the dark, would you?'

We fell asleep with the light on.

That weekend was the last time I saw any of the Clantons. The second summer of hate was a few months away. And during that summer's 'mini'-riots, community beat-officers like me were used to point out the known faces and lead TSG divisions through the back-doubles. Liverpool 8 never trusted community police again, and I transferred down to Holloway.

After my transfer I did a bit of work in the local youth club for a while. (Kyle Trevorrow was a member back then, all bumfluff and Tacchini and excited about girls.) But there was nothing doing. These kids were seventeen not thirteen and by then the damage had been done, the cynicism had set in. Like them, I'd inherited a culture I had no part in making but was powerless to resist. I soon jacked it in and my police work improved as a result. At the time I felt that it was because I was no longer splitting myself in two, but now I realize I was better at the job because I *did* split myself in two. I stopped questioning things. I just hunted.

You're meant to look back and sneer at idealism, to give yourself the wanker gesture out the back window of the National Express Adulthood coach. But I look back on it as something fine that I lost, pratty but fine. And now after seven years in a black clip-on tie, with a two-way chip on my shoulder, it's gone.

Or maybe it's there somewhere like old rain down in the water-table that stops the earth from cracking in a dry season. Maybe. I'd like to think so. Now it's come on top I'll soon find out.

Now when I try talking to kids on home beat . . . I always get it wrong. When you try and caution them they react like there's another voice in their head that's been on at them for days, and my caution is the last straw. Is their shit fit just a ruse, or is that how they feel? And if so, what is that other voice telling them they're shit? It won't be a dad because there's a dad drought. What is it then?

Three years after I transferred down, during a slack after-noon in Holloway nick I looked up my old family on HOLMES (our computer programme). Robbie and Tony had convictions for train robberies. Jumping a train at a slow corner to boost Giros, cheque books, tax discs, credit cards, driving licences. Spells in Youth Custody for Tony, and Robbie in Risley Remand for three months. I wondered how the hardest kid on the estate coped with lights off at ten. TDA, TDA, TDA (some people never tire of joy-riding). One of Jamie's TDA arrests read 'refused charge due to broken hip and leg'. And then under his distinguishing marks: 'pronounced limp'. Bless you, Jamie. Ah, Jamie you limping fool. Ah well, at least you didn't knock over some stray tot. Ah shit.

Shocked to find that even Tina my angel had form. A one-liner thankfully: shoplifting.

The party of my life and soul, the Clantons took up the whole seventeen-inch computer screen between them. Way to go, kids!

I rocked back in the swivel seat. Looked around. Clicked the seat into upright.

CTRL + DEL

Are you authorized to DELETE this information?

Click YES or NO

YES

Enter officer no. and division code

EH 72

(Superintendent Sandra. A. Rowse. Cheers.)

I walked out into the fine, delicate, pleasant rain (halfway between spitting rain and the gentlest misty spray) and found I was singing under my breath a song I hadn't heard in a long while:

> *And I'll never forget the feeling I got*
> *When I heard that you got home,*
> *And I'll never forget the smile on my face,*
> *'cos I knew where you would be –*

And if you're in the Crown tonight
Have a drink on me.
Go easy,
step lightly,
stay free.

Next morning the Super told me to come along with her to the planning meeting. This confused me. To sit in on a planning meeting was a rare honour. But what was she thinking? Was it just so all the bosses could observe me? All the skippers and Duty Officers and DIs were there. DC Kieran too.

'First up,' she began, leaning forward on the flat of both forearms like a sinking sphinx, chin almost touching the polished wood, 'first up – Arsenal–Tottenham on Sunday. Crowd trouble expected . . . so I thought we'd all go to the seaside instead.' She bounces both palms on the table, sits up straight. Business underway.

Everyone started off trying to look keen and interested but eventually that peculiar committee fatigue took over and everyone was slouching sleepily. She handed out jobs and tasks, and then it was just me and her and the door closing slowly on its weighted hinge. I watched it shut, carpet sealing the sound. She slid me a piece of paper. It was a print-out of the page I deleted.

'Do any of these offenders – Robert Clanton, James Clanton, Tony and/or Tina Clanton have anything incriminating over you?'

'No, ma'am.'

'It'll be better for you if you tell me now.'

'Yes, ma'am. No, they don't have anything incriminating over me.'

'You knew your work was being monitored prior to promotion and all, and that's what worries me. There's something self-destructive in you. You're up for promotion, Acting Sergeant for a few weeks, so you *must* have known your work would be monitored. That's why – I mean, that's almost more worrying than the actual offence. I'm not sure I like police-officers with self-destructive streaks. And using my name, my code – you're very lucky you're still in the job. Because I'm gonna let you stay on, even though if you make a balls-up now it will look bad on me, *I'm* the one that will look bad for *not* sacking you now. You understand? The only reason you're still here is because you can do the job. And because you've been ... I hope you know what you've thrown away, John? And I can't neglect the fact that you have got a commendation ... This is what you call a Bizarre Aberration. That's what it is – a Bizarre Aberration. You'll be on supervised desk-duty for an indefinite period.'

'Thank-you, ma'am.'

I sat in a room of VDUs at the nick. Half the people around me weren't even cops. Non-police-personnel: Johnny Full-Colour-Flow-Chart, Sally Rota-Sheet, Gilbert Standard-Reply-Sender.

I was supposed to be looking for a missing witness statement that's not in the file it should be. (Whoompf adrenalin!) Instead I spent three strange hours looking for my concentration that's not in the computer where it should be, amid an accusatory, wronged and injured blur of miscellaneous witness statements on the microfiche.

All the time I felt the Super was wrong. Why couldn't she see it was just a harmless bit of sentimentality? But was it? Or was it the first evidence of how the job was destabilizing me? Wholeness and division.

*

It was six numb weeks in all on supervised shiny-arse duty, before I was allowed back to full service. I was overjoyed to be back on the job, but now I wish they'd never let me leave the computer room.

the birthday suit

'Shiny-arse.' Numb, shiny-arse in this Shaker chair. Here I sit in my second-hand junk-shop Shaker, wondering whether this stillness is meditative or just hypothermia. I get up from the chair and walk the pins and needles out of my legs.

All the time I've been remembering the Liverpool kids and the Luton kid it's seemed like there was always this fateful dot on the horizon headed my way. But now the memory of Beverley comes, a memory which, like the girl herself, says it is all completely different from the fatalistic way I'm looking at it. There I was all miserable right after being reprimanded for deleting the Clanton file, and there she was down in that car park. She was once a dot on the horizon too, as she filled out the perspective in the low-ceilinged cavern. And I didn't know any different as I walked through the executive car park under the Lower West Stand at Highbury Stadium, where all the police horses in their wrap-around, new-wave glasses were standing down until Arsenal had made their point. Down in the underground car park I couldn't hear the crowd at all. I still didn't know her as I walked under the round yellow lights of the low-ceiling cement with its cathedral hush. Forty horses all in a row. Sleeping Beemers and Mercs absorbed yellow light on waxed bonnet and tinted screen. I smelt the newness of deep-tread black tyres and the odd heap of dry, fawn horse dung, packed so full of high-fibre straw it looked like wattle and daub.

Dismounted police held slack bridles in shiny black knee-high riding boots sculpted to the shape of perfect human calves, boots which did all the standing for them. The talk was quiet, maybe to soothe the horses, or maybe in appreciation of how peaceful it was. The mild echo in this low-ceilinged cement cavern gave a cumulative hum and whirr of upbeat reflection, attenuated tones, far from the sour gripes of the canteen or squad car. An Assistant Chief and a Super in their flat-tops gave me a look for wandering down here, but they were from Kentish Town and so I felt no way. Plus I no longer had to fear doing my legs: I'd already done 'em with the Clantons' file which hung over me like a low ceiling.

No one else around. Just us. Just cops. It was like we'd met in the hushed, smiling benignity of heaven. This was the only time, I reflected, that you could be out on duty and yet there was absolutely no chance of you dying within the hour. Well there might be a pitch invasion that you'd have to clear but nothing's going to happen to you down here. And so everyone was relaxed and nattered quietly. I smiled and said 'hi' to the WPC who was still sitting on her horse at the end of the line.

'Hi,' she replied. 'What's it like up there?' Strong Brummie accent.

'Yeah, it's fine. Hello boy!' I said, lightly stroking the horse's dorsal neck. 'Is he a calm horse?'

'It's a she.'

'Oh right.' Oh shit.

'Yeah, the mares have got the best temperament under pressure,' she grinned.

'What's she called?'

'Spats.'

'Spats?' I pointed a finger accusingly at the horse: 'Fifty quid you lost me at Newmarket! 5–1 my arse!' A few officers turned their heads slowly at my raised voice; turned their heads like grazing horses distantly disturbed. 'Were you at the away supporters' end as they were coming in?' I asked her more quietly.

'No, Plympton Road.'

'The Middlesbrough fans are unbelievable. Beyond white trash, something else.' She frowned at this, not sure what sort of cop I was, and patted the horse's neck on the side furthest from me. 'You know that song they all sing, every team, you know: *We're by far the greatest team the world has ever seen.*' Well, I'm by the away supporters and the Middlesbrough fans re so fucking thick they can't even get that right . . . They actually sing:

And it's Middlesbrough, Middlesbrough FC,
We're by far the best team at football the world has ever
seen.

'Unbelievable. I mean that's a two-line song. How difficult is that?'

And then she smiled, turned my way.

'Yeah,' she said, 'you'd think at least one of them would say "*I was watching Match of the Day last week and we've got the words wrong.*" ' She did quite a good clogs accent with it.

'Yeah, you'd think one of them would've noticed. Hi, I'm John, what's your name?'

'Beverley.'

'What do you do?'

'I'm a police-officer.'

'Yeah, me too.'

'You're not doing much work now though.'

'No, I better be getting back. Have you got like a Thermos or anything?'

'What for?'

'Eh?'

'What for?'

'Well I just wanted a drink.'

53

'Can't you get one out there?'

'Not really.'

She sighed. Looked at me to check something. And then opened a chute in her stiff brown leather saddle-bag. I took a swig of the Bovril; it was laced with whisky.

'See yer,' I said, handing it back.

It's a denigrating act to ask a WPC out when you're on duty, canteen culture and all that, but I made a mental note of the CM 103 on her shoulder, ran it through HOLMES and phoned Beverley Drum at Muswell Hill nick a few weeks later.

'She's left,' said a female voice in the section house.

'What time's she back do you think?'

'No, no, no. She's *left*.'

'What, transferred?'

'No, left the job.'

'Have you got a forwarding number?'

'Who are you, sorry?'

'I'm at Holloway relief, there was just some outstanding business, er, we were both on public order at the Arsenal Saturday, and I just need her to sign a charge sheet,' I lied. Got the number, though.

'Was your hair that colour when you were on the job?'

'No, I dyed it again, I had it auburn before.' Now it was an orangey, blondey affair.

'Why did you join?'

'I always wanted to go on a horse.'

'Didn't you have a pony when you were a girl?' I asked.

'In Chelmsley Wood? No!' she laughed.

'Where's that?'

'Birmingham, clivorr!'

'No, no I just thought, you know it could've been Wolverhampton or Coventry.'

'There was this policewoman who used to gallop her horse

through the park near where we lived which had all these dips in it and I seen her galloping her horse on patrol when I was a kid and I thought, "I'll have some of that! That looks like a grin!"'

'And that's the only reason you joined?'

'No, not the only reason.'

'Of course. Sorry.'

'*And* to drive a car with the sirens going!' She laughed, revolving her chin around while she laughed still looking at me. She was like one of those people who join the army just to drive a tank and leave at the end of the trial period. Beverley joined because she was mad and I joined because I was straight. She joined because it's part of a crazy CV which will probably go on to include being an Angolan People's Front mercenary, circus bareback rider, archaeology volunteer, special-needs teacher, speedway finalist, teaching people to ride elephants in India. She was one of those people who feel that the earth is theirs, while I'm one of those people who feel like we have to do our very best just to be allowed to stay here, who live in fear of being told by a pedestrians' representative to leave the streets, go home and not come out again. It might happen tomorrow. (Me and Lee fall to the pavement together.)

On one of our first dates I learnt, among other things, that:

'Humans think they've invented glue but they haven't. It doesn't work. We haven't invented it yet. Loctite, Superglue, none of those actually stick things together.'

'You can't say we haven't invented it, though.'

'Well, have you ever stuck anything together with them, successfully?'

'No,' I laughed, shaking my head at the merry shite I was hearing.

'Like we haven't invented them trays you make ice-cubes in, either –'

'Of course not!'

'No, right, 'cos you can't get the ice-cubes out without smashing the tray into all little cracked-up bits of plastic, can yer?'

Sitting here tonight picking bits of formica off the table with its wax sealant. The formica cracks loudly. I snap too big a bit off and try and put it back. I give up and go on peeling the formica. I like the cracking sound it makes when I snap off a large slice of black formica from the glue. Maybe I'm just saying goodbye to that other life, now that . . . with what's ahead of me. Tomorrow. Tomorrow morning. At nine o'clock.

Hard to believe it's the same drum. Hard to believe this is the same table where Beverley was once bent over with her skirt around her waist. Hard to believe this septic flat where I hang suspended with all the maggots of bad memory breeding is the same place where I was once grinning from ear to ear with Beverley here, and where I looked like an out-take from a film about a happy man . . .

'It's your turn to get the wine,' I say to her as we lie in bed.

'My turn!' she says.

'Yeah, so I can ogle you.'

'No, you get it so I can ogle you.'

'But it's your turn.'

Beverley brings her face up close, beaming that full-on beam of her beautiful, open, moon face at me. The eyelashes of her small, green, loving eyes look long and nude without her sometimes glasses. But this eye-contact is only a trick! A ruse: she gets up dragging the sheet with her.

'What's this?' cries the king in thwarted fury. She laughs and stands togaed in the middle of the room. 'Off with that sheet!' She turns and walks towards the kitchen. I jump up and unveil the white statue. She runs and hides behind the wall of the kitchen nook. I return to bed with the sheet.

'I'm not coming out till you give me my sheet,' she calls.

'No, I'm really cold, brr, freezing. Lovely sheet. Warm.' She disappears into the kitchen. I lie back and listen to her striplit clankings in the naked kitchen. Alone I notice a smile on my face and realize it's been there for ages.

She peeps out from the kitchen wall, resolutely shaking her head.

'OK, look,' I say, 'I'll turn the light off.' Darkness. 'There.'

Lacking a full moon, all the light-pollution of London can muster, through curtainless, night-blind windows, is barely enough to render her as a vague semi-luminous smudge haze. The ghost pads gently on bare feet towards me. I crack the bedside light on. A glass in each stranded hand, she is trapped and smiling, and giving it that mock-weary head gesture that's like a visual tut.

'Give us a twirl,' says the market porter.

'No.'

'Oh go on, please. Just one.'

'I'll spill the drinks.'

'OK,' I say – all magnanimous concession, 'you can put 'em down first.'

She sets the drinks down and does the Anthea Redfern to my chin-on-the-floor Brucie.

Orange hair. Six foot tall, big, broad, freckly, white shoulders. High hips snow-capped with flesh, the undulating tum, her odd NHS-discount belly-button. Both the stretchmarks on the arse and pale, pale skin she hated and I loved. Powerful thighs, most affecting thick scars on the knee; the strange skin at crotch junction is shockingly soft with a scary thalidomide texture. But there's something else as well. Something that means she is right to be reluctant. Another voice in my head. A harsh, judgemental voice, pointing out where the shape of her stomach and tits does not conform to the pornographic template. All these intruders. All this light pollution from Soho and the West End. And even from places I'd never go but whose glow is on the ether: the astral neon night pollution of seedy shit-holes like Stringfellow's and the Raymond Revue bar.

Standing with the wine glasses by her ankles, Beverley wears her flesh like motley. Feeling foolish she does the twirl too fast, especially the bit with her arse to me. I knew that that was because her arse was the bit she was most self-conscious about, least pleased with. Her arse thrilled me with its shape but she was bothered by these power stretchmarks where the taut skin couldn't take the pace.

I lodge an official complaint. She twirls again, slower.

This is her birthday suit. The phrase birthday suit is on the money because we wear our nakedness like clothes. Some people wear their naked bodies like a comfy, old, familiar tracksuit they can slob unselfconsciously in. Others wear their nudity like ceremonial attire, with the absurd self-importance of Orangemen. To some it's unfamiliar and itchy, a size too big or small. To others – especially girls with small tits – it has all the fun of the dressing-up box. Some women wear their naked bodies like a party frock, others like tomboy mucking-about gear. Some women wear their birthday suit like a reluc-tant ballgown on a riot girl: embarrassed by its extravagance and fanciness, wishing they could play it down, both enjoying and being embarrassed by the glamorous get-up, the effect it's having. Some naked people feel their birthday suit is a hand-me-down. They are always trying to hide the mend-and-make-do and display the hopefully fashionable, nearly new bits. Some women wear their birthday suits *as* a suit: business-like, let's get down to it, with serious face and studied movement. Whereas to others their birthday suit is something they've had to wear as a forfeit, like a career woman in a rah-rah skirt: *not* what she would have chosen herself, you understand. To some it's like their nude body is a shameful shrift they've been told to wear. Not theirs. '*You want fries with that?*' Even if such people have bodies which are, on paper, statistically perfect, their bodies are never, somehow, beautiful, because disowned. Often such people have faces which are tireder, more worn, a shade darker or older-looking than their unlived-in bodies.

Beverley spins round again, slower, as she begins to wear her nudity proper. A transition beautiful to see. And in that transition comes a glimpse of her secret relation to her own body, her face reflective now, abstracted. Birthday suit because your relation to your body comes from the mother and lovers that called you *baby*.

She spins again, fast, confident, swooping to scoop the wine glasses, and coming up out the helter-skelter, jokily half-singing, '*Wonder womaan!*' her arms wide with a slopping glass in each hand. She comes to a stop facing me.

And now she wears her birthday suit like the outlawed colours of a secret corps. A quiet, defiant pride, a pact with subversive acts. The best-kept secret . . .

'How did you get those two bruises on your arse?'

'How do you think?' she replies, grinning. (She was seeing someone else for the first few weeks I saw her. But he didn't last long.)

I think I know the answer even now, but I go, 'I dunno.'

'Go on.'

'You banged into something?' She rolls her eyes to the ceiling. 'Someone . . . hit you?'

'Yes,' she goes, but as if she was saying, '*Doh!*'

'Spanking?' I croak.

'Yes,' she says placidly – an inner secret, approach with care, amused.

'With something?'

'No, I think it was just a hand.'

'Do you like that?'

'Yes,' she says.

'Do . . . you want me to . . .?'

'You couldn't go through with it.' How to get what you want from a man! *'Don't worry about it. I'll go somewhere else!!!'* But still I'm not sure about spanking her. Once you go through that door, says Bluebeard, things will never be the same.

Six weeks without a day apart, but only after the bruises of that other man had faded entirely from sight was I ready to cross the Rubicon. Building to it, that night six weeks later, I ran my palm over both her bare cheeks, grinding my hand into them, harder, there was a real sense of threshold, like a palm signature in the Pentagon to key the sliding door to the Red Button Room. Building and building to it. Like trying to resist a force? Pushing her arse as if pushing something away, or trying to? I felt through her arse flesh the double bone of her pelvis: twin towers of Beaver Stadium.

Two lines, dainty creases like the palm's own fortune lines beneath the buttock. The converging crease-lines in the baby flesh led my mesmerized, smoothing hand like gravity towards the meat of the vagina. My stomach lurched as I pulled back my arm and whacked her milky buttocks.

The most vital decision I ever made?

She gives a little gasp, like an innocent pre-pubescent in a children's home. That's her game. But what's mine? Again I spank her. Little 'innocent' gasps, as if I'm totally in control and she doesn't know what these things happening to her are. But she's deep, deep into the dance. A dance she is an intimate of, and me just a neophyte. Her being totally into it helps me lose myself too. I spank her again, and then again. I feel sick, faint and light-headed but impelled. On, on. Her bottom now is red, but the marks look more like grazes than blotches, it looks more like abrasion than impact wounds.

'In such cases an officer should look for "star-pattern" bruising on the child, corresponding to the five fingers of the suspect adult's hand or fist.'

This is just a play zone to her, but to me it's like a psycho-drama session gone terribly wrong, botched by the bogus group-leader with sham certificate on the wall. The bruises shade from red to mauve as the abandon becomes real violence.

It's been a law with me always to know what I'm going to do next, and now here I am, not knowing what I'm going to do next. Like a strobe or jump-cut filming I find myself with a fistful of orange hair in my hand – FLASH – and her head jerked back – FLASH – find myself whacking her inside thigh – FLASH – find myself slapping a hanging breast – FLASH – FLASH.

Yet still one part of me holding on to restraint. Again like a strobe: recurring interventions or islands of normal vision. Yes, I know what I'm doing, I know it's a game. Yes, I know what I'm doing, I know it's a game.

Resentment fuels me. There she is having thrown off responsibility and rediscovered a child-like absence from self-determination. But for me abandonment means to be abandoned to all the ogrish adult nastiness.

So important to me all my life not to hate women. It's been such a fundamental article of the Manners constitution that I don't hate women. And yet here it is. Here is the hatred of women. Here is the resentment of enslavement to arse and tit – as I slap her full breast and she yelps.

Pandora's box.

I'd never been able to do this before. Maybe because I'd never been this close to someone. You've got to really love someone before you thrash the arse off them. I punch her arse and feel the scallop bone beneath. A different howl from her this time. Her noises were like she had just put herself in perdition. Liar!

'You know what you're fucking doing, you bitch, you fucking deceitful bitch!!!' She moans at this which makes me even more furious. It's easy for you, you don't know what this means to me. I smack her arse and the backs of her legs hard and unleashed as the blows will land. She yelps differently now. 'You fucking two-faced lying WHORE!!!'

I flip her over from her knees to her back, pausing only to mutter, 'Put me inside you.' I stare down at her vagina. What power in her swamp thing, controlling everything. A salivating fury to get inside her, the johnny half masted at full stretch with the raging bloodstorm. Inside her and still urgent. I slap her face and come on hearing the Dolby thwack of palm on hollow cheek. The first time I've ever hit a woman. As I melt what else has melted inside me? What strange death have I died? What new life am I prone and naked to suffer entry from?

As soon as I came I felt ill and scared. Before the blow landed there was knowledge, telepathic knowledge, that this was what she wanted me to do. I was sure of it. From the rummage-sale of her clothes she asked me: 'Why do you always *ask* me to put you inside?'

'So there's no doubt in a court of law!'

For a beat she winced. She looked as if she was about to cry but then rolled over on to her side, away from me, roaring with laughter. A strange, grossed-out laughter, though. She paused in her raucous cackle, thought about it, looked at me, gave another groan and started all over again.

I went out to the late-night shop. My head had blown a gasket. How could life still be the same out here? How could life continue the same?

There I was in the corner shop, passing copper and silver coins to a chubby young Sudanese man. Maybe he knew about all this stuff too, but it didn't unhinge him.

Back at the flat we sat side by side on the floor leaning against the bed, like two innocent children. I found, however, that I couldn't eat anything shiny or smooth. An apple was too much like flesh. I felt too dissolved in flesh, insubstantial. Crisps were good. Unflesh-like. I got to my feet and found relief in touching a crumbly bit of flaky plaster on the wall and the dry, abrasive breeze-block beneath.

'What are you doing?' she asked.

'Stroking the wall.'

'Oh, well, that's all right, then.'

We sat at the table. She'd put on a greying, crumpled Bundeswehr vest of mine, but I still felt oppressed by the freedom of her flesh, the unbound white mound where breast met armpit in creases, by her loose breasts swaying perilously. If only I could tell her to get dressed, to cover up. I opened the back door to make it colder but the night was warm.

Always been a 'no means no' hardliner. But here 'no' meant 'yes'. This was all beyond what I could talk about, so instead I played a game. With a polite, straightforward smile I gripped her naked upper arm and inched my fuming cigarette towards the flesh.

'No,' she said, leaning away, with a questioning smile.

'No?' I asked.

'No!' she said. Her grin now was half 'of course not' and half 'you're mad'.

I tapped the side of my nose and said in the plodding voice of an old, bar-stool cockney: 'I understand the game . . .' I pushed the cigarette towards the flesh again, nodding my wiseacre head.

'Get off!' she squealed, startled, clasping my fag arm and holding it off.

'OK "Get off", yeah, I understand the game! Heh-heh, I got yer drift,' said the geezer as I pretended still to try and burn her arm. 'I understand the game.' I gripped her for another second before letting her go, peacefully puffing away, still in character.

'You're mad,' she said, but her face was smiling so that meant everything was OK. Yeah, it meant everything was fine.

'You're mad.' My stomach is melting lead. I get up to put the kettle on. There is a musty smell of something dead in the fridge even with the door closed. 'You're mad.' I fix a coffee and sit back in the chair hoping to have shaken off the next memory which is coming: the counsellor. No matter what happens tomorrow I'm never going to see the counsellor again. I can't go back there because of something she said to me, once, a few months before I'd killed anyone, when I went to see her about something disturbing I saw just after tea-time on a cool, light summer's evening . . .

Kieran was looking as vexed as he ever looked which wasn't much. He's got one of those patient faces where the natural settling point is sunny. A V-shaped top lip. A face both laid back and alert. Slightly thinning, sandy, light-brown hair, a touch of grey here and there. But he was frustrated by this slow Thursday. Every call out we responded to there'd already be about two other patrol cars and an LDV on the scene! Walking back to the mauve, unmarked Astra Kieran said, 'Where's the breakdown of society when you need it? I should've stayed at Stoke Newington.'

'Yeah?'

'Oh, it was brilliant.'

'Why was that?' I asked.

He shook his head with slow admiration. 'The *quality* of crime.'

'How do you mean?' I asked.

'Oh, *every* night: two rapes, a murder, shootings . . .' he reminisced.

Back in the car we asked Control for anything. Colin Weaver, the Control jockey, read off a complaint from someone on the Derwent Estate about a brown stain on the ceiling that had started dripping gunk into theirs. No response from the upstairs flat.

'Sold!' Kieran told him. 'Over.'

Derwent Estate is red-brick 1950s deck-access flats. We banged on the door, peered through mesh-window into the kitchen.

We both took turns trying to kick the door down and fell about laughing when neither of us could.

Kieran held a finger aloft in a cartoonish, lightbulb-above-the-head gesture. 'Fortunately,' he explained, 'the local community are on hand to help the police.' We left the estate, marched across a few streets to Marlborough Road and rang a bell that said Flat D.

'Who lives here?' I asked.

'A thief.'

A window opened above us. A skinny girl with long ginger hair in a centre-parting leant out in a very baggy T-shirt. I was wondering whether I'd be able to see the white sides of her breasts through the hanging armpit of the outsize T-shirt sleeve. (And I'm getting paid by the government!)

'Hiya, I'd like to talk to Mr Collins, please.'

'I haven't seen him myself for a few days. I'll tell him when I see him.'

'Well have a look in the living-room,' Kieran called up to her, 'perhaps around the sofa area. He's probably there.' She paused. And that was it. That pause was all we needed to see, and she knew it. She withdrew her head out of the up-and-over window, dark glass where it was tilted away from the light. Collins stuck his head out where his girlfriend's had been. A young man with black hair.

'Hello,' said Kieran.

'Hi,' he replied. Kieran banged and rubbed his hands once.

'Don't worry, I'm not gonna come in. Can you bring down a crowbar or something? I've got to get into a flat.'

'I've given it up.'

'Yeah, well if you've sold the tools I'm gonna wanna know who you sold them to, and if you haven't they'll still be there.'

He pulled his head in. Kieran turned to me and said in a quieter, more sardonic voice, as if he was talking to Collins, '. . . you know, at the back of an old cupboard somewhere.'

We waited while they tidied up the roaches or whatever they needed to do in case we asked to come in after all. Kieran was just ringing the bell again after five minutes when Collins came down. He was in grey jogging pants, barefoot and stripped to the waist, with an ordinary screwdriver and a wry grin.

'This is all I've got.'

'Oh yeah?'

'This'll do.'

'Are you sure?'

'Yeah,' he said, grinning for an instant then biting his lip.

'It's not as easy as you make it look,' said Kieran. Collins didn't say anything so Kieran then asked, 'What do I do?'

'I wouldn't know.'

'Do you just put it –' Kieran held the screwdriver in both hands and mimed sliding it between the lock and the frame, 'and then just click the lock up?'

'Is there a mortise?'

'No,' I said.

'It's the other side,' he said.

'Eh?'

'Hinges.'

'Excellent! I'll bring it straight back.'

'Ta.'

'Thank-you.'

'OK.'

The hinges were a palaver but in the end we jemmied them just like Collins had mimed.

The suffocating flat stank of rancid milk. Black, rotten fruit smeared and powdered a glass bowl shaped like a leaf. Flies and bigger insects with see-through wings were zipping audibly around.

'Hello?' I called out as we walked through the flat. I opened the bedroom door and against mouth-stuffing heat said, 'Oh Jesus.'

An old lady lay dead in bed. I noticed the red light of her electric blanket in the curtained gloom. I should have thought before I lifted the electric blanket off her body. Failure to stop at a red light. Dead for a fortnight maybe more with the electric blanket on. The blanket lay strangely sunk here and there and was wet to the touch. There was a sucking sound when I peeled back the gooey blanket. I screwed my eyes and turned my head away at the risen stench, then looked back down at the old, dead woman.

She'd died in her sleep, alone. The electric blanket set to MAX for a fortnight in the sealed and sweaty room had melted all her body fat. The fat had sagged through the soggy mattress, the dripping had strained through the mesh of the bed base's hessian underlay on to the floor, coalesced into a pool of off-white gunk on the thin carpet, glooped heavy, stained and sunk through to the ceiling below.

The nightie was halfway inside the goo where her stomach had been, resting now on her slippery spinal cord.

'Oh God,' said Kieran, kissing his Irish-Catholic fingertips and closing her eyes. He placed his hand a second on the dry land of her forehead.

68

We called up the ambulance and went and stuck our heads out the window. I lit a Camel and looked out at a steep muddy slide of earth, a copse of trees and a gaping black vinyl chain-link fence. When the bifta was halfway down, Kieran asked, 'What shall we tell 'em it is downstairs?'

'What do you mean?'

'Well we should just say a burst pipe or something.'

'Fuck that.'

'You don't want to gross them out. They've got to live there.'

'No way! That old lady was their neighbour. You'd think they might've popped up and said, "Sorry to bother you, but we just thought we'd check you're all right seeing as how your body fat has started dripping through the ceiling."'

'Do you know who your neighbours are?'

'No.'

'Well then.'

'That's not the point,' I said.

'Yes, it is.'

'It's not.'

'What is the point then?'

'What's the point?'

'Yeah.'

'The point is,' I shouted, flicking dog-end out the window and drawing myself up to my full height, *that's my nan!*'

We pissed ourselves, Kieran sliding down the radiator, while I had to put my head on the top of the telly. We laughed like how you used to laugh at school, ab-crunching, face-aching attacks of the giggles at the back of double-maths. We fell quiet eventually, then I heard Kieran's breath catch and we were off again. We sighed to a stop. Kieran cleared his throat – ahem ahem – and we were off again. 'Oh dear,' I kept saying, drying my eyes. 'Oh dear. Oh dear.'

Eventually the thing that sobered me up was how much of

the diseased air of the flat I was sucking in with all this wheezing. Even so when the ambulance men came me and Kieran were grim-faced and not looking at each other for fear of laughing. It must have looked like we were guilty.

You can never tell what's gonna upset you. With every officer it's different. Some officers get very upset at traffic accidents. But this has never bothered me. Well not on that level where it really gets under your skin. But this did.

Beverley came round that night and I couldn't have sex with her.

'Are you seeing another woman?' she casually enquired.

'Yes.'

About a week later me and Kieran were on home beat down the Holloway Road. I'd say Kieran has a better mind than me. For a start he's a DC – only plodding with a street-officer because of Two Year Tenure (two years after promotion CID such as him have to go back on the beat for a year, sometimes two). He doesn't however like to get abstract or theoretical – though I wish he would because he has stronger analytical powers than me. This difference between us has evolved into a particular convention . . . We'll be walking along on home beat or whatever and I'll wonder aloud something like, I dunno, how, say, racism slips into your thinking unawares. And he'll go, 'Yes . . .' only he'll say it sarcastically, mock-thoughtfully, piss-takingly, over-interested like: 'hmmm, fascinating . . .' (I sometimes think that Kieran's ironic 'yes . . .' is because he doesn't think I'm as academically detached as my tone of voice. But maybe I'm reading too much into it.)

Kieran as he often did was getting on my case about my stately pace. 'Do you think you could you walk a bit slower?' he said in the crowded daytime high street.

'I'm going further than you,' I replied. 'My journey is longer.

More is required of me. I'm pacing myself as I walk a closer walk with Jesus.'

'It's my arse, isn't it?'

'Yes, it's your buns of steel. I'm mesmerized by your arse. I can't take my eyes off it. I've no idea what's happening in the street. There could be a murder happening but – would I know?'

'Would you care?'

'Only if you had to run across the road and a lorry temporarily obscured your pert buttocks from me. Then I'd just stand on the pavement and cry.'

'Well in that case you can walk as slow as you like.'

'No, it's OK, I'll step it up,' I said. I caught up with him and after we'd walked for a bit asked, 'Don't you feel inundated with sheer evil and ugliness sometimes so that the whole world seems tawdry and squalid?'

'*Yes* . . .' he said, but he was only half-hearted in honouring the catch-phrase. His next words showed that he knew what I was talking about and that he'd been thinking about it too. 'I wouldn't say the old lady being in that . . . state was evil, though.'

'No, all right, but just how that life can be so . . . you know –'

'We've got a rule now – me and Becca – that I'll always tell her about stuff on the job . . . but I broke it with this.'

'You didn't tell her about . . .'

'The old lady. No,' said Kieran.

'No,' I said.

'Miss Wet T-shirt.'

'You are a cunt! You are a *cunt*! I'm saying that not in passion, just a clear statement of objective fact. You. Are. A. Cunt! And I want you to remember when your children are on your knee saying, "Oh we love you Daddy," that you are a cunt. That is the absolutely central and fundamental part of your character and who you are. It's that you are a fucking cunt. You cunt!'

Kieran laughed a little, but was more puzzled at how cross I was.

'Sorry, I'm sorry,' he said, 'but you wanna take it all on. You can't let it stay in your system. You *want* to dwell on it –'

'I don't *want* –'

'– for some reason of your own.'

I needed to talk to someone about the melted old woman. I had a word with Mickey. 'You should go an' 'ave a bit of cahncelling,' he suggested. Yes, I thought, I could do with some of that cancelling. There's still a bit of a macho thing about it though. Not as bad as it was but it's still there. And what with me being known as a university graduate my Plimsoll-line of ponciness is always bobbing under the briny (however much I like to identify with footballers like Graeme Le Saux or Pat Nevin with their degrees and Joy Division records). There's the macho thing plus 'will-this-fuck-up-promotion?' So I said no.

If you don't fancy seeing a shrink they just put you on to another officer who's had a bad experience himself. I met up in a Holborn pub with a middle-aged DS from City police.

'My friend Pete was about to be married, I was best man. We get a call that a squad car's crashed, we rush over and it's him, it's Pete, and I pull his dead body out the passenger door – chasing a couple of . . . joy-riders, weren't they? Next day I have to tell his fiancée, Ann, and all I remember thinking was I hope I don't get there just as they're pinning up her dress. I had this image in my head that she'd be standing there in the white dress with a seamstress pinning her up. It's funny what goes through your mind.'

'Was she?'

'Eh? No,' he chuckled, 'no, she was just having coffee in a denim shirt. So what happens Monday morning? Never happened before or since, but it happened then two, three days afterwards . . . I get slashed in the neck with a razor and nearly died.' The scar was tiny now but he told me he was in Critical. I believed him, the nick was just above the collar bone, bang on the carotid. It was an ordinary Wilkinson Sword, he said over his fourth IPA, but to this day when he goes into Boots and sees a Wilkinson Sword display or just sees it on sale it gives him a strange feeling.

I left the pub, and felt a great relief looking at a woman's arse in a pair of grimy Levi's. Slightly pissed I rubber-necked all the way home.

'How did it go?' asked Mickey when I got back.

'Oh, it was all right, like, but I didn't really feel anything was said.'

'Well, people who've seen the canceller say they found it helpful.'

'I'll see how I go.'

'OK.'

In recent years they've made it so no one needs to know you've gone. They just leave the address of the counselling service up on the noticeboard. It also comes free – one of those double-edged perks of the job like bingo disability pension and the bereavement rollover.

To my shame, I've been as guilty of macho bollocks in this regard as the dustiest canteen cowboy. Me and Kieran were sitting in the canteen one evening chatting to Perry, a dark, skinny, nervy CBO, and his partner Ellen. Perry asked the table if any of us had ever had to go to counselling for things we'd seen on the job.

'So you're saying you have?' I leered (thinking I was being ironic at the time but really I wasn't).

'Yeah,' said Perry courageously.

'You all right now?' asked K.

'Oh yeah, it was just this accident I was first on the scene for. The ambulance crew got me fucking shovelling bits of human off the motorway. I mean literally shovelling with a fucking trowel they have there. Plus I was first on the scene and it took ages for the ambulance to respond. I was there for about twenty minutes helpless and there was like this man with the fucking steering column *embedded* in his gut.' He paused. 'And loads of other stuff besides.'

I put on a gravelly, low-life pervert voice like Dudley Moore does on one of the *Derek & Clive* tapes. 'Did the steering-wheel go, you know, *right inside,* you know, right in there . . .?'

'Fuck off, everyone knows you're the mental person here.'

'Did it . . .?'

'How do you work with that?' the always-flustered-looking, untalented Perry asked K.

'Well, there's that. But you know what he means, Perry. I mean there's nothing to be ashamed of. You drive past a car crash and you get so fucking turned on, you know, all that twisted metal.'

'And like they weren't expecting it, were they,' I added with a connoisseur's wry cocking of the head.

Perry raised his eyes from the formica, like, 'Have you finished yet?'

'Yeah, yeah, yeah,' he said, 'but it's waiting for you and it's your own fears that's making you –'

'Yeah, sorry,' said Keiran.

'No, you're right, Perry,' I said, suddenly ashamed, suddenly wanting to be on the right side again. (All the while I'd been taking the piss I'd actually been admiring him, especially when he glossed over, *And loads of other stuff besides.*)

'Yeah, well the counsellor,' said Perry looking at Kieran, and winding up his riposte unconfidently but doggedly, 'she keeps saying, "When's Manners coming in?"'

She was in her late thirties, middle-class, no-make-up pretty, rounded. Light-brown, fine shoulder-length hair in a bob. She had small eyes, small nose and mouth in a round, intelligent face lightly dusted with freckles. Her sparse, brown eyebrows naturally petered out halfway. A rounded body with big tits under a loose, white linen grandad shirt. I could see a bit of white bra between the buttons of her loose shirt. It occurred to me that it might do me real good if I could just suckle at her tits for the remaining three-quarters of an hour. That would be truly comforting. 'There's a good boy,' she says, stroking my hair as thick warm milk spills over my greedy lips, 'Mummy's here,' milk dribbling down my gooey chin and out the corners of my mouth. Sucking harder and harder on the barrel peg nipple yummy yummy yummy I got love in my tummy.

Her room had two chairs turned towards each other, water-colours and scatter-cushions designed so as not to induce a homicidal spree, and a glass-top table with a presumptuous box of Kleenex. Some rogue TSG voice in my head wanted to throw the box out the window, like, 'We won't be needing *these*, love.'

Seeing as we only had fifty minutes, it vexed me that she spent five, ten telling me why the session had to stop dead on fifty minutes. Make that forty, then.

We didn't talk that much about the old woman who melted, as it happened. She – the shrink – kept wanting to know why that should have made *everything* ugly, she kept on about why that one scene had made *all* life tainted, what it was in *me*. It was like being in the witness stand when suddenly the attack swivels from the crime to me, and the Crown start digging me out like I'm just as terrible, that the real evil lies in me and my crazy, whacked-out claim of what I saw!

I can't remember much of the session – it was over a year ago – but I remember how she ended it. I remember her last words; what we were in the middle of when the clock that she could see and I couldn't politely clicked. I remember getting these two sentences next to each other:

'I think you're worried you're so angry that you might kill someone. But we must stop for today.'

It had been strange getting up to see her at eight a.m., as I usually did the lates no one else wants to do. When I came home the curtains were still drawn, and I half-expected to find my unexamined self still asleep. Whatever was said was irrelevant back here in the stalled flat. Her long, accepting pauses, I felt then, were as nothing against the one long pause of my charged room.

beverley's new curtains

The struggling bluebottle has been reduced to sporadic buzzing in a moany key between longer and longer silences.

It's weird to look at the phone now and think it used to be all right to call Beverley from it. (Lost in that past when I counted myself among all those people who'd never killed another human being.) Same phone, different life. Then I could phone her even if – and this was the glorious bit – I had nothing to say . . .

'Hello?' she'd say, greeting a mean aggregate of all humanity that always phones us. Some people are hostile, guarded, suspicious in that moment before you know who or what is at the other end of the line, but she was expectant. On balance she had found she liked humans.

'Hi, it's me.'

'Hey, sexy.'

'No, it's John.'

'Oh, I'm sorry. I thought it was my three o'clock.'

'You prostitute.'

'Mmnh-mmnnh,' she mock-moaned.

'You're a disgrace.'

'Why are you going out with me, then?'

'I dunno. It's an extended sympathy shag.'

'Oh, that's all right, then.'

'What are you wearing . . .?'

'You always ask me what I'm wearing.'

'Yeah, it gives me a picture.'

'You an' all.'

'What d'you mean?'

'I had this prank phone call two days ago from these boys saying they could see me walking round the flat with no clothes on.'

A forty-minute response time before I'm pressing her entry buzzer clutching two pairs of thick, canvasy blue curtains, wrought-iron curtain rails, brackets and a cordless drill.

'You're mad,' she said.

'Which flats is it?' I say, looking out the window, hoping they'll clock Eternal Male Protector.

'I dunno,' said Beverley, grinning, 'it could be front or back.' Front or back! Both holes! 'You can see in from both sides. It might not even be – you know they might have just been phoning random numbers and not even live anywhere near here.'

'Yeah, but they know about the curtains.' I went to the window again to see if any men were looking in and getting more and more obsessed each night.

'Well, they didn't specifically say –'

'But if they *can* see you then they'll get obsessed and start brooding on . . . the whole thing.'

'Well, it might not have been that at all: it might have been a complaint. "We can see you naked: please buy some curtains." You know, the Residents' Association.'

'Yeah, case solved. Well done.' I put the bit in the drill.

'Thank-you, officer,' she smiled rawly. I held the drill in my hand next to my shoulder, pointing up at the ceiling like a gun. I pulled the trigger, eyes wide like Driller Killer and it whined frantically, hating to be spinning in mid-air.

The blue curtains gave a strange new vibe to her drum, the afternoon outside stitched into the moody weave.

'I don't have to have them drawn all the time just 'cos they're up, do I?'

'Yeah, except when you go out, when I'd like you to be wearing them.'

She'd got a new job working as a rigger for Neg. Earth, a lighting company for music venues: laying down the rubber-matting for outdoor gigs, hoisting the lighting rig, bolting the follow-spots.

'The job's a grin 'cos if the get-in's early, we finish in time to all go absailing,' she said when I saw her a week later.

How to describe her face? How to describe anyone's? If humans had spent some of the Middle Ages inventing words for types of human faces, we might have had less war. We'd have classified a gimlet-eyed, dewdrop-nose overbite face, say, as a *gammelstad,* and would have recognized it in all races. In a world without war the peaceful Swedes would dominate the discourse and a *sten* or *friggesby, billy-80* or *expressivo* might have been types of face and not furniture and fittings. But the world being what it is, however, the best way we know of describing the human face is a police E-fit. Let us open the blue vinyl ring-book called Caucasian Female 20–30.

Start with Elizabeth McGovern off of *Once Upon A Time in America*. Thin the lips out. Key in a wider nose. Buff that wide nose up till you get a good shine on it. Build up a strong clear jaw and chin. For her flesh-tone factor in a childhood diet of Fray Bentos pies, ketchup and chips under Birmingham skies as your base over which to update on all the different colours she does her hair. For her gait, click on the tall swagger of the toughest girl in the school walking up to the gates of a rival school certain of 'having' their top girl. For the look in her eyes send out the city's photographers to snap people who have just missed what everyone else is laughing at and have their mouths open in anticipation of getting it. Smelt 'em down and mesh 'em all in. For the feeling you get when you see her, merge in a photo taken by a nervous boy-virgin of a girl in a denim jacket at a funfair about to win an Elvis mirror at darts.

That day she was wearing a tartan mini-skirt, army boots and a loose-fit, white T-shirt.

She went to open a bottle of wine. I followed her. 'Didn't you cause a riot on the tube?'

'No,' she replied.

'Weren't you pestered by everybody?'

'No, I sat there and read.'

'That's a very short skirt.'

'It's a short skirt.'

'Suppose someone came up to you and did this.'

'Well, I think I'd notice,' she said as I pressed my palm over her exposed buttock, staring at the black cotton knickers.

'Oh, sorry, miss.'

She carried the bottle through to the table. She looked down to find me lying on the floor staring up her skirt.

'Yeah, I think I'd notice that as well,' she said.

'Are you sure?'

'Get up, you pervert,' she said, smiling down at me. My eyes went from her eyes to her pale skin in shade. The cool scoop above the inner thigh where it turns into buttock, and the slightly creviced black cotton.

The pervert got up. I went round the back of her T-shirt and slid it up over the sheer smooth skin of her hard back. 'Anyone could just come up to you,' I said, bringing my hands round to interfere with her nipples, 'and just do this,' exaggeratedly rippling my fingers so that it became creepy.

'Oh for fuck's sake!' she scoffed, spinning away. 'Like I'd let them!'

'Oh, OK.'

She walked over to me and lazily climbed on to my back. I carried her round on piggy-back as I took the wine glasses to the table where I swung her down as gently and casually as a mum with a two-year-old. Sitting on the chair while I rattled the pack and heard just one answering fag, she put her palm on my genitalia and said, 'Well, suppose I just came up to you and did this.'

'But you wouldn't because my dress is very proper and non-provocative and I wouldn't put those sorts of thoughts in your head. You'd be thinking about good works or religion if you saw me.'

'Not if you were lying on the floor looking up my skirt.'

'Anyway I wouldn't have noticed you.'

She drew my inflating cock out of my trousers and said, 'Have you noticed?'

'At this point I'm just wondering if I did my flies up.' She put me in her mouth as I filled out. 'Madam!' I exclaimed, as if only just having noticed.

She'd bought a new outfit, and took it out the bag with a grin all over one side of her face. I held the tiny silk one-piece in my hand, the size of a hanky.

'It's great,' I said. 'It's staying here!' I went and hid it in a cupboard.

'But if I don't wear it, you look at women who do,' she called out to me. It was true, but I came back with a stupid, fixed grin on my face. A grin I kind of wanted her to dislodge. The fixed, stupid grin didn't feel like my own stupid grin. It felt like some 1950s posh bloke with a pipe who calls his woman honeypie or cherub. One of many ghost faces which come out in the slow exorcism of sexist fear when you're getting close.

I had to leave her then because I was on a late. That night I was walking up the Cally Road by Pentonville. In the same way you flinch before you hear a sound from far-off, my pulse was already lurching noisily even before I heard the sudden shouting and banging in the distance. Where was it coming from? Panel-beating. Joyous, malicious shouting. What was it?

Someone having their head banged against something metal?

I ran towards Market Road with its rows of VW vans that Australians sell after touring Europe and before they fly home. A pack of North London slags were besieging a converted Bedford van. Half a dozen white boys, fifteen- to seventeen-year-olds. Throwing rocks and banging on the curtained windows. Chillingly one of the slags was shouting, 'Have you got any women in there?' But then they saw me and scattered.

A woman looked through the curtain of the silver bus and the bus-door swivelled open. She crouched at the top of the stair, inside where the NZ sticker promised rich and strange delights.

'What if they come back?' she asked.

'No, they won't,' I said, deliberately breezy because fear is the enemy. You have to allay fear because it's the agar nutrient culture of hell.

'But what if they do?'

'They won't.' They wouldn't.

I said good-night and the coach door closed without the hydraulic hiss. Their shadows moved and murmured behind sheets taped over the windows. She was well fit, the New Zealand big-bus spokeswoman. Skinny with short, messy brown hair. Something confident or athletic about her hips which were in a pair of men's boxers, red hearts on white cotton, and with big thick Lapland slipper-boot-type things and a yellow, zipped-up, seventies Adidas track-suit top. I resisted the urge to spend a few hours banging on the bus, despite now knowing that they had in fact got a woman in there.

Instead I headed off back towards the Caledonian Road, past the sickly, citrus smell of all the pulped orange skins in the forecourt of Johnson's orange drink factory. What was it about the silver bus, the converted Bedford, that made them bang on its side panels and shout, 'Are there any women in there?' I thought I knew. It was like that sense when you walk past houseboats and think, 'Wow, who would live here? There's only a thin bit of glass between you and anyone walking along the towpath at night'. But that's true of the houses built of bricks and mortar too, isn't it? What makes the houseboat feel more assailable? Is it the idea that they might not be on the phone? Is it the sense that the neighbouring boats might be unoccupied? Or is it really to do with the fact that somehow there's less of a taboo or less of a force-field about breaking in?

Time was, it would have been less likely for them to besiege a house. Less likely not because a house is bricks and mortar – after all a house is easier to break into than a coach – but because of somehow still-standing bourgeois force-fields, see-thru' shields. And yet tonight on the Rockingham Estate families who aren't 'connected' cower indoors with the lights off, because if the slag youth see the lights on they bang on the windows and on the doors. The families sit in the half of the flat away from the balcony. If they go to the kahzi or turn the bedroom light on so you can see the lights from the balcony it attracts the slags and they're banging on the window. And there's nothing we can do about it. They won't phone us, and when we go door to door they want to show the kids how quickly they shut the door on us.

There are the invisible barriers within yourself . . . In books they say, 'He was blah blah blah but *somewhere inside him was a little voice which knew that he had done wrong.*' I had no faith in that little voice. Could it be heard with all the other noise going on? The boom-boom stezzy within smoked-glass car windows; the loud rhetoric of slag self-justification; or those times when you're talking about what you'd like to do to a nonce, you can feel a distaste inside you when the wicked spirit of hate has possessed you, but engorged with its energy you let it carry you along. But in the UN of the mind that distaste is just a lone, elderly Swedish consul among a thousand

Paraguayan generals. We get used to overriding these voices and the high street looks like a sci-fi film-set after the death of the soul.

And what invisible barriers, I wondered, were coming down the closer I got to Beverley? When women talk about dropping your defences they just mean letting love out. But I knew there were other things pent up behind those defences. Would they also slip through now? I was disturbed by my fascination with the allowed and the not allowed. Looking up her dress and that as if I was just some commuter. I didn't like where this was all leading me.

Our next date was round at mine. It came up in conversation that she was doing one-on-one boxercise training at the gym . . . Sweating intimately with another man. One on one. Him and her. Him on her. Her on him. Just the two of them. He holds her arm or leg or waist to show her another position. How it should be done. Rewarding her with rare praise, she smiles delighted and glittery eyed. The master. All the body blows they pulled I felt with the internal bleeding of a twelve-rounder. And if push came to shove he could smack the shit out of me. I didn't ask 'is he black?' because I wasn't that sort of person. Once. (Most people would be shocked if they ever found out what their real views were.)

She was staying at her sister's in Kentish Town. I was too drunk to drive her home but I wouldn't let her get in a mini-cab, so we walked about a mile, scouring for a proper Joe Baxy.

'For fuck's sake, John!' she said when I walked past a second clapboard and yellow-siren minicab office.

'No.' We walked a bit further, she shook her head and stopped to find the biftas in her bag.

Coming down the other side of the street I saw a community-care crazy fellow, my age, in grey, bobbly track-suit bottoms, brown shoes, a red tie and clean, striped, short-sleeved shirt despite the night. He carried a little pile of litter he'd picked up from the pavement. Crisp packet, Coke can, apple core, McDonald's carton. He looked extremely cross. He had a pinched, lined, black and brown face like he'd lived three lives concurrently. A once-round-the-clock, second-hand, re-tread face. There was a bit of chipboard lying across the pavement. He tried to walk past, but then, exasperatedly, he had to put his pile of litter down, lean the chipboard up against a chain-link fence before picking up his stack of litter again. Half facing away like he was busy elsewhere: kind of doing it as if he wasn't doing it, a part of him barely stopping. All the streets of London to tidy and never a word of thanks. No wonder he looked cross.

'Oh, all right, OK,' I said to Beverley, and put her into the next minicab that came crawling by.

I walked back home in a happy haze and all the *Evening Standard* hoardings knew they couldn't compete.

HOLLOWAY MAN SHOT IN BOTH ARMS . . . ?
RUSSIA 'NO' TO EEC BID . . . ?
TUBE THREAT IN . . . ?
NO, NOTHING.
IT'S NOT IMPORTANT.

Up till then I was the only single cop I knew of. Male or female. None of the other cops in the division are single, none of them. The job is impossible without support. And now I was in love, but with love came . . . other stuff, incessant stuff . . . It was like I'd doubled my surface area of attack, all the things that could happen to her out in the world. Despite her strength and suss all these fears just burst through all the same. If you don't love someone then nothing can happen to someone you love. But now every time I heard the other cops discussing some violent house break-in, or some woman who did parachute jumps now brain-damaged after the attack, here

85

was a new terror. In those moments the fact that it was *possible* that bad things could happen to her became real. And bad men were out there.

a dead man

The first time I saw Lee Andrew was on Fonthill Road only a few weeks before he and I stopped being what we were. Midway through a succession of repetitive home beats me and Kieran were on our way back from an obbo.

(Each time I aim for a memory I come in early; that is, before the actual thing I wanted to fetch my mind at. Is this because that part of me that didn't see disaster coming is fascinated by how time and life are chug-chugging along until you turn the blind corner? Or is it just dawdling to put off the ugly event? Either way, the memory comes in where it wants to come in as I bump, bump, bump my back against the Shaker chair-back like a metronome.)

We'd just spent an hour or so parked up a narrow side-street in the unmarked purple Astra obboing these dealers working out of a fruit and veg. stall. They were selling Es in the post-rain sunshine. We'd heard they were popping Es in brown paper bags to the right customer with some apples or runner beans.

'Lumme!' I said, 'that girl just paid £34 for that cauliflower!'

We'd got into this thing where we'd say 'crikey', 'crumbs' or other innocent, old-fashioned cuss-words. 'Blimey' was another one. Like a used car we'd gone right round the swearing clock: we'd cunted ourselves out. I was actually slightly fonder of these catch-phrases than the K. (He had the charisma to start catch-phrases that the whole division would latch on to. 'Ache' – as in anything involving hassle – was one of his.

And once, after a guilty verdict when he said, 'How did that happen?' this sardonic catch-phrase became used about guilty verdicts from then on. And also for thief-takings made by untalented CBOs.)

'She didn't really have to say much to him, though, did she?' puzzled Kieran.

'No.'

'You probably just go up and say –' Kieran started winking elaborately, "*Can I have* [wink-wink-wink] *five apples please?*" And that's five pills. But then you get some old lady with a twitch come up and go [wink-wink-wink] "*Can I have a turnip please? That one you sold me last week was incredible!*"'

'Yeah, "*That was the best turnip I ever had!*" Crumbs,' I said. Kieran grunted.

We waited some more. Happy now in the sharp, prismatic, glinting rain shards.

'I was driving the other day on the North Circular, and there was this woman in a red BMW and we were sort of level for about half an hour and I felt like we'd been on a journey together me and this woman driving the other car, that we were almost friends . . .'

Kieran started laughing. 'Run for your lives!'

'What?' I asked.

'Run for your lives! "Yeah, I saw these matches in the shop and I really understood how someone becomes an arsonist, you know there they all are all these matches and you can do absolutely anything with them! Anything at all! And then someone went into a house and I really understood how someone becomes a murderer, and then I walked past a bank and I thought it's full of money . . ." Catch on to yourself, won't you?' he chuckled.

His impression of my accent added a yokelly naïve woolliness that made me sound like a Benzedrine Barmy Benny off of *Crossroads*.

We waited some more.

And then, as if on cue with our comedy script a little old lady did turn up. I supplied the sub-titles. '*Don't give me a turnip though, my sister bought one of those and fell asleep with the electric blanket on.*'

K. looked at me like he was looking at a miser who'd just given his watch to a dosser. 'Crikey!' he said. Chuckled, then three seconds later, looking out the windscreen now and thinking to himself, chuckled again.

We waited some more. We were waiting to see who supplied *them*. They spoke to a few other traders and someone from the techno-import 12-inchers shop but that was all. We drove off.

Our way back to the nick took us past the rag-trade wholesalers of Fonthill Road. Two men with short brown hair and bug-eyes of watery blue came out of a shop. *Repairs and Alterations* said the shop's logo over a cartoon man stepping out with a pair of giant shears. Kieran slowed the car and leant out of the window. 'You still around?' he said to the men with unusual aggression.

We drove on.

'Who's that?' I asked.

'Slags,' he replied, 'Lee and Tony Andrew. They deal drugs and knock out fake suits.' Here Kieran put on a cockney sparrer, barrer boy, swaggering, hustling lilt: '*Top quality suits 'ere: Lime'ouse, Jesper Cawnren . . . only cheaper!*'

'I seen their photos up on the board.'

'And they just got refused charge after raping two students coming back from a gig.'

My guts lurched. 'How did they get off?'

'The girls didn't want to proceed. Couldn't face seeing them again.'

'And there they are – walking around.'

'They wrote all over the girls' bodies.'

'What, "whore", "bitch", that sort of stuff?'

'Yeah.'

Familiar icy patches took up position all over my skin, heart zig-zagging the cage, heavy blood throbbing up the sides of my neck. Sexual assaults always have this seismic, sickening, dismaying effect on me in a way that, say, murder doesn't. Slogans: Rape is worse than murder. And yet I have to know all the details and all the details I don't know I make up. There's a terrible complicity in that. I hated Lee Andrew right then and there. We drove round the block to eyeball them a second time. There he was, the scumbag atrocity, walking around free having done that shining and never been caught. If he can do it and get away with it then the world has become a nightmare where there's nothing to stop you doing it and everything is wild, and all the barriers are down and the next woman gets it. I hated him. That look on their faces, like they hadn't done what they'd done, like nothing. Lee was laughing and giving it jest about something on the mobile.

'Which is which?' I asked in a deadly tone.

'Tony the short slag with the bug-eyes and brown hair.'

'And Lee's the large one with the bug-eyes and brown hair.'

'Yeah, Lee's Smoothy Slag and Tony's Runty Slag,' said Kieran. I couldn't join in his japes, but stared at the Andrew brothers with a choking sensation in my throat.

Runtish Tony, older and scruffier, was clearly the dangerous one, however. Gaps in his teeth, prison tats, dirty jeans. The one concession to their schmutter money was a brand-new black puffa jacket. But on him it just looked like he was borrowing it for a day so as not to get identified. He looked more like someone who sold second-hand filing cabinets than Issey Miyake. A squint of continual concentration, of low-down speculation. Energetic, hustling, speaking to a third person in an undertone. A full day on. Busy here, busy there, busy everyfuckingwhere.

Lee was naturally bigger and a body-builder to boot. He looked like one of those white boxers who appears as a *Page 7 Feller*, has his photo took with Linda Lusardi and gets knocked out in Round One. Clean-cut, clean-shaven, gelled-back brown hair, shaved at the sides. Dead Lee had a neat, just-round-the mouth beard. He had a kind of sleeping mouth as if his crimson Cupid's-bow lips were not quite touching. His bulbous nose was flattened at the tip as if he was pressing it against a window. A brown suit over tight, black, shiny V-neck and chewing a fat wad of gum in a wad of jaw. Giving it large: Timberlands, mobile, gangster wannabe.

That was the first time I saw Lee Andrew. The first time I *met* Lee and Tony Andrew is hard to say 'cos I didn't know if it was them or not.

'When you see 'em checking for dealers with the Maglite they're just trying to catch any dealer who's not on the firm,' said Ellen as we walked up the unlit street with gasworks on the horizon. 'Nightforce run the door and just let their own dealers in and take a cut.'

'Who's Nightforce?'

'Lee and Tony Andrew?' said Ellen. 'D'yer know about 'em?'

'Kieran pointed them out to me the other day,' I casually replied. In fact . . . Since Kieran had first pointed them out to me on the Fonthill Road three weeks ago, I'd seen Lee and Tony Andrew all the time, coming out of a shop, parking a car, chatting, sometimes to women.

'Was you eyeballed?' she asked.

'No,' I said with certainty, but in reality I wasn't sure whether they hadn't seen me all the time I was screwing them. Always at the back of my mind I was noting what street Lee or Tony was in and computing whether they'd ever seen Beverley. Clocked her. Got bothered by her swinging gait. Made plans. They could take anyone off the street at any time. They'd done it before. Lee and Tony had done the most terrible thing in the world and here they were walking around free. If they could do it and nothing happen, then, then . . . there was no punishment.

'The Andrew Sisters shouldn't be actually on the door, though,' Ellen added, 'they'll just be around. Keep your face out the closed-circuit when we're queuing in. We just gotta avoid them and go for the vendors and then sweat the vendors later.' We turned into the cobbled slipway that led down to the Drum Club, and now we hear the hot body din of the Drum Club, banging techno bang bang bang, and see the Gelex bouncers.

'How's your footwork?' she asked.

'Don't you worry about me babe – Camber Sands Soul Weekender, Prestatyn '87.'

'Ha ha ha!'

Ellen was wearing a fawn mini-dress and glitter, top-of-the-knee pop-socks. I could smell the delicious scent of cocoa butter which basted her shining brown thighs and bare, Barbasian arms and hands. The soul boy of discretion, I was dressed in Van's, khaki army trousers and some zip-up Ted Bakerage.

WPC Ellen Melvinas was a natural thief-taker. Not only that – more than any other officer I'd worked with – except Kieran – I always had this sense that nothing bad could happen to me when I was out on patrol with her. Something to do with her energy, with the half-smile she had when firing questions at suspects on the street, an intrigued grin which kind of suggested she was thinking at twice their pace. A right old cockney gel.

('I can tell that you come from a family with lots of older brothers, don't you?' I once said to her after a dust-up outside the Rocket on Holloway Road.

'Yeah,' she smiled. 'How d'yer know?' I'd been holding down one hot-head, knee on his shoulder, and looked up while Ellen pushed the other bloke away. He was trying to get past her to have another pop. Then he started winding up to kick it off with her. It was all wrestling with her, very slow, knowing she had extra gears, and then suddenly the bloke's on the floor looking really pissed off with Ellen kneeling on his chest.)

'OK?' Ellen asks me once we're inside.

'Yeah, yeah,' I say.

Ribena her, Beck's me. I spark up and add my smoke to the dry-ice, sweat-steam and sulphurous smog of Marlboro Country. Ellen scopes the room with cop-intensity disguised as an E-stare.

'Right, I'm off!' she says. 'Meet back here.' She gives me a peck on the cheek. Gone.

Germ-free adolescents. Teeth glowing in the UV. A bump at my shoulder nearly spills my beer. Someone chatters to me in Jabberhut then mimes lighting a cigarette. I hand him my bifta to take a light off it. He shakes his head, mimes a cigarette again. I raise no-comprendez hands. He pauses. Thinks. Goes. A girl in snow-camouflage trousers and a pink T-shirt made see-through with sweat (marinate for two hours and allow the breasts to rise) emerges from the steam. She tugs her collar to let the air in.

So this is House. Never danced where most everyone is white before, I say to myself in an effort to lay a straight track of thought over a swirling, tidal-wave swamp of sensation.

They sample an old reggae toaster. A bit of Studio 1 in the bang bang bang.

Early doors so no one's really going for it on the floor yet. Each dancer is just bobbing meditatively, marking time till the pills kick in, nodding their heads slowly as if listening to negotiations between central nervous system and MDMA. The DJ cranks a techno fanfare, but it's too soon and none of the kids get on his bus.

I try to join in, but my feet are heavy because I'm not in the dance. Like a stereo thief at a party I'm outside it all. I always was. Maybe that's even *why* I became a cop, but this thought, too, is bumped and jostled out of hold.

Each time I go to a club I think *this time I'll hang on to myself, my core, or consciousness, hang on to structured thought*, but I always, at some point in the night, lose it. I'm loving it, *the lowest head in the club that night, just polishing steps and keeping out of sight.* Then the next minute, welcome to the theatre of self-hate where I lose it all in a psychic landslide under the rotating lights and bass bins. It all seems mean. Mean-spirited. Brutal. Aggressive. What is it with me? A compound loneliness, a sense that . . . a party to which I was never invited. I'm missing something they've all got in common. A sense of profound rejection, looking up at the podium I feel betrayed, sold out by these girls in shiny mini-skirts.

You have to look away. People don't get it when I talk about the need to overcome lust. And I just feel like a Puritan in black breeches, white collar, black, broad-brimmed clerical hat, long white beard, black buckle shoes. Maybe though these people just aren't players. What happens to me in clubs? I scope and rubber-neck lust at women all day, but in a club I become a Puritan; perhaps horrified to see my own raging desires taken up by a mad army.

Can't see the Andrews or any dealers so I just scope the punters. Two ugly fat white geezers at the bar in white shirts and pleated keks. Keenly aware of being dressed wrong but joking to each other like they're above it all, as if they're a nucleus of calm when in fact they're not. These two regional finalists have bitter expressions on their faces as they scope the women, lowering their expectations. Wow, whichever unlucky woman he gets off with will have to satisfy all that bile.

A South American-looking woman walks by on her way to the toilet queue. Elegant, kindly features. An intelligent, graduate, career woman. They look at her in muted resent-ment. And both pump a swig from their Low-brau. How could she know that she's a walking personification of rejection for them. Her blameless face and white vest on brown skin, carrying a little purse, trousers, no socks, shoes. She's certainly not one of those women who are, in fact, saying 'fuck off' to you in their haughty pose. But to them, it's as if her relaxed hips say, 'Not for scum like you.' The brown, bony peak of her academic shoulders says, 'No chance' to them. Her black-jeaned, red-labelled arse says, 'Well out of your reach!' Her nipples under the vest tell them, 'Get to fuck! Crawl back under your stone!'

Maybe that's why the Andrew brothers' gang wrote all over one of the girls' bodies when they abducted and raped two late-night students. The subconscious justification for every evil act is revenge, a skew-whiff, bent idea of revenge.

And there it is in your own heart: in a dark nook lies a girl passed out on a bench-seat. She lies on her side, knees raised slightly. White knickers visible where her short, shiny cream negligée has ridden up. And a shameful thought crossing my mind, as I walk past her once, twice, the shameful thought which writes its graffiti on the big white wall of the Kremlin until the Thought Police scrub it out and haul you off to the Corrective.

Another beer. Trying not to look at the barmaid because that leads to hunger, emptiness. She bends over in shiny PVC trousers to get some lager out the fridge. Straightens up, sees me, ignores me routinely. I try to be pally with her to say I'm not like everyone here but that's what they all do, isn't it? She wears a super-tight T-shirt with *Babe* written in the Johnson's baby lotion logo. She has brilliant white hair, with a coy, toy plastic slide-grip pushing her collar-length hair into a Berliner side-parting.

What am I supposed to be doing here? What should I be noticing? Where's Ellen? I'll find her and she can give some shape to my mind. I've heard something about they've got a bass level on the speakers here too low to hear but which vibrates some inner core of you. Nudge, shove, angle my way through the bodies. I hate everyone. I can't find her. Two circuits of the club, swimming against the tide, bumped and elbowed because I wasn't in the dance. Can't hear any shape or tune in the music. Just the ugly, cynical 0898 lyrics: '*Come inside. Take me deep, take me deep, take me all the way.*' Two pushing searches through the club must have made me look like a cop with all that linear movement but I wasn't feeling like one with no straight lines of thought in my head. I needed to get somewhere the lights weren't flashing and where the music was less loud to try and regain my rational police head. I went to the bog, not really needing to go.

Sitting on the white sink in the white light was a man with a jacket tied round his waist. His right hand moved to cover what his left hand was holding. Him and this other lad's discussion veered into neutrality as I walked in. I held the door open for some men right behind me, but didn't see them. The man on the sink looked up. 'All right?' he said to one or all of the men coming in behind me. But I couldn't look round and find out who knew who, who was on the firm. Too obvious. At the far end of the bright bogs were some innocent, hot-faced, gog-eyed ravers. The kids were filling mineral-water bottles from the tap which had been plumbed to a trickle so as to keep the profits bar-central.

I queued for a space at the thin beaten-copper designer urinal. My turn at last. Bits of blue copper mould on thin metal hammered into tiny indentations. In mid-stream I hear the creak of a new leather coat as a body moves at speed. My forehead smashes against the tiles, knuckles in the back of my skull. Two hard, downward kicks in the back of my knees like someone trying to kickstart a seized moped. Black leather trainers. A rush of kicks, a punch in the back of my head. A rumble of boots stampede out. Door banging wall banging door.

I lay there with my jaw slumped on the edge of the trough. I was grateful for the cool lemon mint-cake and the white butts which had peeled their brown filters close to my stinging eyes. I heard the door close again.

'Mate, mate, are you OK?' asked one of the gaggle of ravers. The kind kids helped me up. 'Fuckin' 'ell, are you OK?'

The rationed water from the taps won't wash this stench off me. Through a fire exit, on to steel lager barrels, over a tall wooden gate set in a high wall. The reek and pain were worse in the cool air ringing with the tinnitus sound of trebly, high-hat cymbals.

Half a mile away in the Jet garage I upturned a row of green, plastic watering-cans over me. I noticed the twin filing-cabinets of Air and Water. I didn't have a twenty-pence bit so I had to go into the garage and get change. I was expecting the Asian on the till to be difficult with me because of the dangerous state I looked in. Daring him to be difficult. But no.

'For sure,' he said with a kind, reassuring voice. 'No problem.'

I put in the coin; the container's loud juddery-throbbing-knocking was numbed by the ringing in my ears. Stood under the rubber-handled hard jet of coruscating water which I wanted to clean down to the bone, to drill away the ugly event that had happened so quick. Why did it have to happen at all? So quick, why did it have to happen at all? Why couldn't I have been somewhere else?

As the water puttered to a close with a knocking inside the tank I felt the Asian man standing watching. *What you fucking looking at?* I turned to face him. He held a pile of sealed, plastic-wrapped mini-tissues and an Elastoplast Travel-pack. On the floor by his feet was a clean roll of roller-towel cloth.

'If you need to make a phone call, there's one in the shop, OK?' he said.

I nodded a kind of reply, looking away, down. I felt him watching for a bit more. Then he went inside. I couldn't face him again, so I left the soiled roller-towel on the charcoal briquets and walked the long walk home through side-streets to avoid people. Worried about urine in the cuts. It was a weird thing to be beaten up and not know who did it. As if a delegation of humanity had been appointed to cast out the impostor.

My neck is stiff sitting in this straight-back Shaker chair. My hand goes to the scrapes on my face from last night as if they were the scars from that incident at the Drum Club. Like they'd never gone away or as if the body was like the mind and long-forgotten psychic scars were visible. Like the body had as poor a sense of time as the subconscious. Whatever, I feel this memory still hanging around like I didn't get through it by just getting through it. I sip the black coffee with difficulty through my busted lip and sore gums. Swallowing is difficult too after Lee Andrew's arm on my windpipe.

'What happened to your face?' asked Beverley the night after the Drum Club.

'*Fell down some steps*,' I said in a TSG voice. Pacing round her little flat, I issued directives: 'You should put a better lock on here. I'll buy you some security catches for the back window. Where's that fan I bought you?'

'It made too much noise.'

'Aren't you using it?' I demanded.

'No one's gonna attack me.'

'So you're still sleeping with the French windows open?'

'It's fine. And if anything ever did happen to me, I'd never tell *you* anyway.'

'Has anything?' I asked with low, husky urgency like a phone pest's '*What . . . what are you wearing?*'

'John, don't start!'

'Has it?'

'Don't start this shit again!'

*

99

I once heard a woman on Radio 4 say that 'Rape is a way in which all men keep all women in a state of fear.' Then again, rape is a way in which all rapists keep all boyfriends in a state of fear, too. Me and Beverley split up that night. We split up because she walked on her own to the corner shop at night. We split up because she took unlicensed minicabs, because she got the last tube home alone in a short, vinyl lime-green dress. We split up because on hot nights she slept alone with her French windows open. Not much perhaps, but far too much for me. That night when I got out of her how she'd had a narrow escape from a minicab driver, I said 'I could kill him.' I've never thought about that since, seeing as we got back together two weeks later (after I scared myself at a country house).

'*I could kill him.*' At the time I had a belief in acknowledging those feelings – to know that I could kill that minicab driver even though I never would. Being human means keeping those feelings in check. The hippies were all wrong: freedom goes with repression. Even though it feels vital to be that stoked up, that capable of harm, it's all bollocks. Passion and strength are in what you don't do, but then no one ever knows how close they came.

Then again, maybe they do: I'm a scrawny six-foot coward and yet something happens when I'm in a stand-off. Something strange. Like when DS Jason Maddox came looking for me after I'd described him as the worst copper since the war. He found me standing on premises guarding the gate of the squad car park – which was humiliating – pulled me three paces to my right and out of sight of the security camera, giving it come-on-then fight stance. I squared up to him, thinking, 'Oh shit. What am I doing? He's younger, bigger, stronger.' But then a strange calm descended on me and I started grinning mightily with no sense of fear. This is strange. I spend my whole life creeping about terrified that violence is going to happen to me, and yet once within the exclusion zone, the seven seconds to midnight I become this other dude. It's the only time I'm ever totally at ease and cheerily thoughtless, enjoying a sanguine interest in the future like a promising playbill.

I watched his expression go through three spectrum shifts. Fancying it; not fancying it; then breaking into a face-saving leer and walking away. And trying to think back over what happened, all I did was smile.

In civvies with Beverley one night we walked past two guys with gold architecture and prison tats standing outside the Vulture's Perch. One of them was bald-headed with a Virgin Mary pendant and Red Indian crossed feathers hanging round his neck, I remember. They wolf-whistled at her and went 'Carmencita!'. I stopped and turned. They put their bottles down and stood up, screwing me out, ready for the off. As I stared back I felt the same strange merriness on my face, a smile like receiving a guest in my home. They turned away, faking bored expressions, as if they were just leaving anyway.

Afterwards, when I re-inhabited my own body, I thought, *'What the fuck were you thinking? You can't fight! You never could! Second weediest in the school! They could've fucked you up!'* And maybe all that saved me was just them thinking, 'This skinny bastard is so relaxed he *must* have a gun.'

Am I just giving it the big 'un here simply to ward off the fear and humiliation of remembering the Drum Club urinals? (Where I was finally reduced to what Kenneth the coach-driver said I was: 'Piss and breadcrumbs – that's all you are.') Is that what I'm doing here by re-running these other scenes?

In my first year with the Met. there was a summer craze to Do the Bill. A couple of junior slags would taunt or throw bottles at a couple of beat officers and then give it toes. You'd peg after them round a corner, up an alley and into an ambush of about a dozen more scarved-up slags. One night that summer

I was chasing a couple of youths who'd thrown rocks at me from under the spotlights of a steel-mesh-shuttered Tesco. I ran them into the delivery yard and there was the reception committee. Seven or eight older lads. Scarved up. I stopped, stood still, and was surprised to find that same perfect calm envelop me and the same involuntary, chipper grin. Intense fear all the way until I get to the epicentre and then it's this strange, weird ease which descends on me. If I'd pushed it and tried to take their masks off I would've got a hiding, I suppose. But as it was we just stood there for a bit before I turned and strolled back, heart pounding then in case I got rushed from behind. But I didn't. This saving gracelessness has worked for me every time except last night, when whatever bad spirit I host found its mate.

A memory flashes across my mind: the ignition moments in the stand-off with dead Lee.

'There's nothing on me,' he says, hand on heart and smiling. He halts at three paces and holds his arms out crucifixion-style in like a stop-and-search mode.

'You're nicked, Lee Andrew,' I say – letting him know I know what he's done.

In that vile, sonar knowledge you get in a stand-off, what impressions of my soul imprint themselves on his spent and overworked senses? We stare for a bit more and I can see him doing mental arithmetic. What does he see now in that moment before running? Is he scared? Is he running away? (The mental arithmetic of someone in a burning building before bolting for the landing?)

His eyes widen, he shoots off across the road. He's changed his mind. He's not going to fight after all. He's going to try and get past me. To run for it. I chase after him, building to a sprint.

Does he now turn only because I'm gaining? Desperate antelope? Was it calculation that made him run (knowing he was going to stop, swivel and bust a move?) Or was it fear? (Or is this new doubt just an invasion of all the liberals' pro-criminal propaganda?)

The way I've remembered it till now Lee ran from a policeman. But did he see something in my eyes? In me?

Every policeman's favourite advert is that old *Guardian* one:

Skinhead charges at businessman.
Businessman terrified. Clutches briefcase tight.
Skinhead steams right into him and his fear.
Blackout.
Caption: '*Only one paper gives you the whole picture.*'
Cut wide to show pallet of bricks falling from the top of the building right on to where businessman was standing. Skinhead has saved his life.

Cops love this ad. and talk of it like it was still on, because that's how we feel a lot of the time. You're running after some innocent-looking kid and all the goodies and aunties are shouting at you, 'Leave that poor boy alone!' And you can't stop and tell them about the Indian girl sitting over the toilet, scooping cool water over the blood between her legs. And yet now it seems like that 'whole picture' effect might work against me the more I remember of the . . . incident.

My face is throbbing again. I go to the bedroom mirror and check out the grazed cheek and the bumped mouth. This bruise under my eye might become a fat shiner tomorrow. The bumped mouth doesn't look so bad now. I hope it looks worse when I face the board tomorrow. I press my knuckles hard on my lip until my eyes scald.

I take down the full-length bedroom mirror and carry it through to the living-room where I prop it on the floor. I'll rehearse running the gauntlet of press and TV cameras outside the steps of the court come the trial. I get undressed and catch my reflection in the mirror. So these are the boxer shorts I was wearing when it happened. And these are the socks. The boxer shorts I was wearing when it happened were black ones; the socks were navy blue, woollen, hiking socks, it turns out. If I rehearse naked, then perhaps come Judgment Day my threads will feel like armour walking past the jostling booms and arc lights.

Walking back to the door, I think over my approach like a spin bowler. You've got to have an attitude. I walk right out into the hall and turn round. In sequence I try:

Bemused Stroll (too callous).

The Righteous Indignation Strut (too edgy, too violent, too angry).

Heavy, Schlepp-Shouldered Resignation of the Wronged Man (too guilty-looking).

Inspecting an Honour Guard and Nodding with Extreme Rectitude and Upstandingness (mental).

I give up and walk to the mirror to take it from between my legs back to the bedroom wall:

The Naked Defeated Man.

Arrested by this I leave the mirror where it is, step back two paces and take a look. I straighten up, immediately, involuntarily. I cringe under the *generalissimo*'s stare. At first I think my hostile stare is because I'm still rehearsing a look for demonstrators and cameras outside the court. But no. I'm staring at me, and this, I realize, is how I always do: the stern *generalissimo* running a disapproving eye over the slovenly recruit. A look of appeal, girlish or child-like, is held a second in the mirror's gaze. Then quashed.

Extremes. The skin is very, very white, the short, spiky hair very, very black and the eyes are very, very blue. I remember in O-level Human Biology finding out that there was no such thing as a blue iris. Blue eyes mean an absence of any iris pigment, they only look blue from reflecting rhodopsin or something. Like the empty sky poncing colour off the blue sea.

Even though there's not an ounce of spare flesh on my girlish white skin I somehow look like I'm wearing the body of a bigger man. Wide, bony shoulders ride up on one side. Long arms dangle like outsize sleeves by narrow hips and long legs. Varicose veins in the legs are all that will tell the pathologist I was a cop. The *generalissimo* is pleased only by the grazed cheek and the bumped mouth.

I can't stand this hateful scrutiny, but there's one more thing . . . I try out the beatific smile that saved me all those times. How did it look? What's it like? My eyes look like you could bounce stones off them.

The mirror is back in the bedroom on the wall. I go to the back door and turn the key but don't open it. I sit back down in the chair. The coffee was too hot before but now it's too cold. I drink it anyway. It leaks out the side of my fat lip and swollen gum and runs cold down my chin.

kieran's house

I think Kieran was worried about me after I got stoved in the Drum Club urinals. He invited me to dinner round at his a few days later. He picked me up from mine.

'I thought you were bringing Beverley.'

'No.'

As we drove towards his house in Broxbourne near Hoddesdon, it was weird ... we had nothing to say to each other. Odd being so close at work and then, meeting each other outside work, to find it awkward, to be searching for something. Kieran, with a clutch of manila files on the back seat, watched the road intently. I suddenly realized just what different types we were. It almost felt like a casual gay pick-up – a one-night stand where we had nothing to say to each other.

'How's your wife?'

I'd only met Becca once before at the dinner where me and Kieran got our Special Commendations.

As we came through the front door, Becca, bending over a little plastic-nappied baby in one of those walkers, was not as I remembered her from that cocktail-dress night. Her movements were much more lively and cocky. She wore black jeans and her dark-brown, just-off-the-shoulder hair was pinned back above her ears.

'Hello John, sorry about the mess! Say hello, Jack.'

'You should see my place.'

'Ha ha.' No really, you should see it, a septic tank of stagnant time, the bad spirit that hangs heavy over it.

'I hope you like alphabetti-spaghetti and fun-size fish fingers,' she said, coming over to kiss me in her grey sweater.

'Ah, Kieran's told you,' I joked. Ha ha.

'Are they both back yet?' Kieran asked her in that private voice of consulting parents.

'Eric's upstairs, Shannon's on her way.' Parent eye-contact, shared flashes in secret code.

The house was more tasteful than I'd imagined. (How little I knew my partner even though we'd discussed life and love, hate and fear.) I'd expected a Barratt home, but this was a roomy terraced cottage that was more liberal and middle-class than I'd have thought. Oatmeal carpet, fridge magnets and child's drawings, light pouring in from the kitchen window and garden. A little square wooden table. Exposed wooden stairs going up to bed. This was what the squalor patrol paid for. Good on yer, K.

'Are you still working?' I asked her. Becca taught design at a further education college.

'No, I'm just filling in when someone's sick at the moment.'

'Supply teaching?'

'Yeah.'

'It's dat boy again!' cried Kieran, spotting six-year-old Eric on the stairs. He came down the stairs in thick, day-glo green socks and round, brown glasses, dark-haired like his mum. He walked over to his dad, staring at me the whole time like an owl, until Kieran bent at the waist with arms outstretched. Eric giggled and feinted a run-up once, twice into his father's arms then let himself be scooped up. Kieran wiped unsuccessfully at some felt-tip on the boy's mouth, then, pointing at me, said, 'Who's this strange man?'

Eric looked at me – saw Adult Doing Friendly Face – then turned back to his dad, pulling at Kieran's clip-on tie. I was in suspense myself – well, who? – and so when Kieran said, 'It's Daddy's partner at work,' I was awash with love and thanks.

'Hi Eric,' I said.

'Have you come for tea?' he asked.

'No, I've heard that there's a young hooligan here, a terrible troublemaker who's been *so* naughty I may have to arrest him and take him to prison.'

'Nooaww . . .' said the kid, smiling like he's not sure. 'No you're not.' He jerked his head round at his dad like the catcher in a playground game of Frozen Statues.

'I am,' I repeated.

'Who is he?' he squirmed and chortled.

'Let me see – I've got his name written down here somewhere . . .' I put my hand in my shirt pocket and took out a little book of first-class stamps. I underlined an invisible word with my finger as if reading: 'Eric.'

'NO!! It doesn't say that. Let me see!' I put the folded red card back in my shirt pocket.

'No, I'm afraid it's a police secret.'

'You haven't got a piece of paper!'

'That's not you,' Kieran told him, 'you're a good old boy, aren't you? Yeah, good old boy.' Eric slid down, rumpling his saggy trousers and went into his toys.

'Do you want some wine, John or a beer or orange juice?'

'What happened to his face, Daddy?'

'Yeah, wine please. Um, can I use your phone please?' I went over to the wall phone and dialled the number on the blue minicab card wedged behind it and ordered a cab for ten p.m.

'That's so you can drink and don't have to drive me home,' I said to Kieran when I hung up.

'Phone back and tell them half an hour,' he said.

Shannon came through the door and stopped suddenly seeing me, and then immediately did a little parody of stopping short. Shannon was more Kieran's colouring with long sandy hair, and wearing a brown school uniform with a pleated brown mini-skirt.

'Hi Mum, hi Dad, hi whoever you are, I'll find out in a minute,' she said in a mock panic voice as if she had an international conference call waiting, and she boom-boom-boomed back up the stairs.

Kieran popped out to get his files from the car. Becca handed me the wine to open. On the fridge was a child's drawing of a policeman with a very, very tall helmet chasing after a burglar. I was heartened to see that the stripy-jumper, mask and swag-bag archetype was still in existence.

'Did this take Kieran long?' I asked.

'Days.'

Shannon came back down the wooden stairs over-casually with her hair brushed and shiny and wearing a denim mini-skirt, white canvas shoes and a tight, white, long-sleeved top.

Becca shared a rueful face and said, 'Look out, she's got her eye on you.'

Shannon ignored us and went over to Eric who was playing a Casio keyboard with headphones on. He hadn't seen her. She crept down on all fours until her face was right next to him. She waited for him to notice and then the game was that she was trying to put a big, noisy, mauling kiss on his cheek and he was pissing himself and trying to fight her off.

Kieran came back in, took in the scene and said, 'Well, they see us, Becca, and . . .'

Dinner was a five o'clock tea when Kieran was on an early so that he could eat with his family.

Becca made us a lovely stir-fry in a big wok. The baby slept with white stuff on his mouth.

Kieran finished first, and put his face over Eric's plate like a ravenous lion. Eric put up a protective arm and carried on eating with one eye on his dad.

'Do you live in London?' Shannon asked me.

'Yes.'

'Whereabouts?'

'Archway.'

'I've got a friend who lives in London,' she piped.

'Whereabouts?'

'Kilburn.'

'That's not a friend, that's your cousins,' said Becca.

'No, it's a friend of theirs – Monica – and mine. What's Dad like at work?'

'He's brilliant. Your dad's one of the best cops and I am very lucky to have him as my partner,' I said, my eyes smarting.

'Yeah Dad!' she said, looking at him. 'He wouldn't let me do my work experience there.'

'That's not till next year anyway. If then.'

'Well, I've got a new idea anyway.'

'Oh yeah?' said Kieran, picking at Eric's leftovers.

'A new idea for what I'm going to do for work experience,' she repeated.

'YE-EAH?' Kieran said in mock-impatience.

'YE-EAH?' Eric mimicked, delighted that shouting was in, but he couldn't do the mock-shouting and it was really loud. Becca put a hand on his arm while still looking at Shannon.

'Well,' she said, 'I thought I'd go to school for once.'

'Instead of hanging round the town-centre?' asked Becca.

'Taking drugs and shoplifting,' said Shannon like it was a refrain or catch-phrase.

'That's it, you're out of my will,' said Kieran. 'It's all yours Eric. I'm leaving it all to you.'

'Don't get your hopes up, son,' said Becca, 'Mummy will have spent it all.'

'John?' said Kieran, handing me the wine after filling Becca's glass and his own.

'Yes, please.'

'Look at that, kids: manners. Oh shit, sorry,' he said, after the unintentional pun.

'Ooh, Daddy *swore*,' said Becca.

'Why did you say "sorry"?' Shannon asked her dad.

'My surname's Manners,' I said.

'Oh right.'

'Come on then, we're waiting,' said Becca. We were: Shannon's brain was whirring audibly.

'Nothing.'

'That's a relief.'

'Well, I was gonna say you must be descended from the first people to use a knife and fork.'

Becca clapped sarcastically.

'That's very good, John, isn't it?' she said, still clapping. 'Very, very good.'

'Shut up,' Shannon said, clapping back at her and doing a mong face.

Kieran put a last bit of stir-fry in his mouth with his fingers, leant back and slowly raised two fists in the air as if he'd just scored a goal.

'That was fantastic,' he said. 'Right, we're writing a letter to Sainsbury's. Son, fetch me some paper.'

Shannon pushed Eric back in his seat.

'No, let him,' said Becca.

Eric got down from the table and picked up a pink felt pen and some sheets of drawing paper from the carpet floor by a toy garage. Kieran put his plate on top of Becca's. Eric went to hand it all to Kieran, but his Dad just indicated his place mat. The paper and pen before him, Kieran put his hands out and waggled his fingers, then clicked his knuckles but couldn't make them crack.

'Woah-kay,' he said, picking up the pen and saying each word as he wrote: '"Dear Mr Sainsbury, I'm writing to say how much my family and guest enjoyed the stir-fry which we purchased in your shop."'

'Thank-you for selling it to us,' suggested Shannon.

'Yes, very good. "Thank-you for selling it to us. We look forward to thanking you in person when next we visit your shop."'

'Are you the one in the white hat on the cold meats section?' I submitted.

'Very good, John, but a bit long.'

'"Yours sincerely, Kieran Carter" . . .' He passed the paper around and Becca, Shannon, Eric and John were co-signatories.

An envelope was found. I took out my book of first-class stamps.

Shannon wrote Mr J. S. Sainsbury, c/o Sainsbury's Superstore.

'What street is it?' she asked.

'Town centre,' said Kieran.

'Town Centre, Hoddesdon,' wrote Shannon, before using a green pen to draw a wok with sizzle-lines coming off it on the envelope.

Shannon insisted on posting it right away and ran to the door.

'Don't slam it!' said Kieran.

I was very worried that she'd be abducted in her little mini-skirt at dusk. As she got to the door I sprang up urgently, knocking over an empty glass, crying, 'Hold on! Don't go on your own!' I turned to the parents and said, 'I'll watch her go down the street, check she's all right. Can you see the post-box from the front door?'

Kieran just frowned and gave me a wincing look, Becca looked askance at me as if I was halfway through telling her some terrible news. I felt I'd spoiled everything by bringing the sick world into the happy home, like a hypodermic, AIDS-infected needle in the back of a family saloon.

'It's only down the road,' Becca said and time started to flow again.

We were sat in silence when Shannon came back from posting the letter. Detecting the shift in atmosphere she went upstairs. Kieran made coffee, while Becca put Eric and the baby to bed.

They were on the sofa, I was on the comfy chair. Becca had her wine glass while me and Kieran had coffee. Kieran settled into Becca on the couch. Sitting in a chair opposite I felt like they were watching telly and I was the weirdo on *Oprah*. I was worried about the gap between my sock and my trousers but as much as I pulled it the sock wouldn't go any higher and the trouser leg wouldn't go any lower. I was just thinking how it would look were I to stand up, smooth my strideage down and sit down again, when Becca, with that keenness of engagement common to intelligent mothers who miss conversation, asked about the 'zero tolerance' initiative they'd been trying out in King's Cross.

'Well, I passed through King's Cross tonight, as it goes,' Kieran said, ''cos we'd all been at Marylebone, and we see all these squad cars flying around, sirens blaring, and we're like, "Oop, someone's dropped a crisp packet on Gray's Inn Road!" Turning to me he said, 'Do you think you'll stay in the job for ever now?'

'Well, yeah.'

'You've not thought about it?' asked Kieran. 'Since you're not gonna get promoted – at least not like you would've done?'

'What, 'cos of deleting the file?'

'Well, unless there's something else you'd like to tell me about . . .' asked Kieran with a raised eyebrow.

'Er, er, er, no nothing!' I codded, all Ealing comedy like. 'Should I think about leaving? It hadn't crossed my mind . . . until just now.'

'You've not thought about not?' asked Kieran.

'Should I?'

Kieran looked towards his wife as if referring to some past agreement between them, some agreement about what to do in the event of just this conversation – even though that was impossible of course.

'Well, it's not for me to – it's your decision at the end of the day,' he said.

I felt my heart sink. Would he be happier if I did?

'What do you think, though?'

'Well, I think you should think about it.'

'About not staying?'

'Yeah.'

'What – in the division? Or the force?'

'Ah, not the force, the "*service*",' chimed in Becca, happy to be making a cop joke among cops.

'Well,' said Kieran, 'I'm not saying you should or you shouldn't, just that you should think about whether you still want to be in the police . . . ah, *service*, heh heh.'

'Well, you know I'm a good cop.'

'Well,' he looked at Becca again, as if they were crossing another previously agreed contingency marker, 'you are and you aren't.'

'What you on about?!'

'Yes, you're a natural thief-taker and all that, a talented cop, but on another level, temperamentally, you, you're – well, we've discussed it before, haven't we?'

'What, you mean getting too upset by what I see?'

'And everything you see knocks a whole load of chain reactions in your head about all sorts of other shit I don't know about.' Oooh, Daddy swore. I wish we were still at the light stage where that was said. This was a new and shocking region. 'I know what it is, it's like every time you catch a criminal it's like you go "phew I can eliminate myself from the inquiry!"' All the time I thought K. had thought one thing about me, he'd thought something else. I almost felt like crying.

'But you could say,' Becca intervened, 'that perhaps that's what makes, er, John such a capable police officer, because he can identify with things . . .?'

I looked at Kieran who paused and said, 'Yeah, there's that too. I mean I'm just suggesting . . .' I was so relieved he'd said that I regretted having looked at him beseechingly, 'cos now I didn't know whether he'd have said that unprompted. But then I started thinking that every identification with a crime scene is a recognition of some no-go area in myself. I wanted to get right into this thought, but worried that instead of pensive I just looked sad and defeated and so I interrupted myself to say,

'Well, yeah, you're right, I do need to think about it.'

'Yeah,' said Kieran.

'But the thing is the job isn't just what you do, it's what you are.'

'No, I think you'll find it's what you do,' said Kieran.

'But we're the good guys,' I said with a trill in my voice like I was being ironic even though I wasn't.

'No, we're not,' Kieran replied, 'we're no better or worse than anybody else: we murder, commit suicide, take drugs, get in fights, drink-drive. We're embezzlers, shoplifters, wife-beaters, rapists –'

'But on a good day, John,' said Becca, touching a tender hand on Kieran's face, 'he can be the nicest man in the world!'

'I know,' I said, eyes stinging with an inappropriate sincerity.

'And I've been much better lately, haven't I, darling?' asked Kieran. 'And I'll tell you something else – people who do have a fixed idea of, you know, "I am this" or "I'm not that" are the ones who do more harm than they know . . . "I'm not a racist therefore me calling him a nigger doesn't mean anything," or, you know, "I'm not a violent bloke therefore me hitting this bloke round the head with a pick-axe handle means he must have deserved it," you know?'

'Yeah, but if you don't have an idea of who you are you just get slooshed around with the tides of good and evil.'

'Yeah, well, what I do is what I am.'

'Yes. But,' I said, speaking slowly, 'that can easily become what I am is what I do.'

Kieran nodded wisely for a second or two, but then said, 'That's the same thing!'

'How's work?' I asked.

'Just come off a course. Been on loads of courses since promotion. Still I managed to avoid them for years so I can't really complain I suppose.'

'You were on a course a few weeks ago . . . the night that, um . . .'

'No, I wasn't, John. I just changed shifts.'

'Why didn't you tell me?'

'I needed a – you were doing my head in. I had to keep one eye on you, I felt you were headed for something, spontaneous combustion or something, and I needed a break from you.'

They both looked at me. I didn't want there to be an ugly tension in their house. I grinned and said, 'You're lucky: I never get a break from me!'

They laughed, relieved. Becca excused herself and went to bed.

Left on our own we had to fend off an Attack of the Giant Killer-Pauses and so fell to talking shop, discussing the dealers working out of the fruit and veg. stall, naming names of who we knew so far was in the chain.

There came another Giant Pause, but Kieran looked pretty much at home in this one and said, 'Going back to our earlier conversation . . . Your problem is you never had to rebel against a Catholic upbringing. There's no natural sense of right and wrong, any more than you're born with a sense of how to hold a knife and fork properly. It's just taught you.'

'There's just manners?'

'There's just manners. You're on your own, my old mate.'

'What about choices – we all make a choice.'

'Some people don't know there's a choice. Then what?'

'There is an innate sense of good and evil in the human soul.'

'WHERE? You find it for me and I'll believe you.'

'Well, I'm on a case at the moment . . . double-time and all, can't miss out on that, you know?'

'Well, soon as you're through.'

'Soon as I'm through.'

The taxi came early. Kieran showed me to the door.

'Nice to see you,' he said.

'Yeah,' I said, standing out in the misty cold, while he put one sock foot on the other leaning against the jamb. I nodded 'just-a-minute' to the minicab driver. 'You've got a lovely home and a brilliant family.'

'Thanks.'

'Ta-ra mate.'

'Chin up, John.'

'Yeah, see you.'

We shook hands.

'See you,' he said.

I took a couple of steps down the path, then stopped and turned. 'Shit. You're only a couple of years older than me. What was I doing while you were having a family?'

'Wanking into a toilet roll,' said Kieran, and closed the door.

The fridge shudders down from its high-pitched hum to a lower whirr. But my head is still a high-pitched whine with the spin of Kieran saying, 'And I'll tell you something else – people who do have a fixed idea of, you know, "I am this" or "I'm not that" are the ones who do more harm than they know . . . "I'm not a violent bloke therefore me hitting this bloke round the head with a pick-axe handle means he must have deserved it," you know?' Last night's events have driven a wedge between who I think I am and who I am.

Stuck on the fridge is a picture of the 10,000-year-old Iceman they found in a glacier. Oetzi they called him because he was found in the Oetzaler Alps, or 'Tyrolean Man'. A lost Neanderthal wanderer. Thinner than he was but with skin, hair, clothes, tattoos and overnight bag still intact – and blue eyes just like mine. When I cut it out of the magazine I guess I was thinking of my dad face-down in the snowdrift. It's the nearest I've got to a photo of him. The skin around the eye-socket has eroded away so that the blue eyes look furious or horrified.

How weird that me and Kieran were having that discussion about quitting then, as if we somehow knew what was going to happen, as if what's just happened was somehow in the air even then.

Something smells dead and bad in that fridge.

'I felt you were headed for spontaneous combustion or something,' he told me that day. And, weirdly, the very next weekend became a crucible of what he'd said. Was this because I wanted to have it out with myself? Or was I just locked into a flightpath? Looking at it now, the weekend after was a warning, especially the strange way it all ended when I was invited to the country house.

country house

'Why did you invite me along?' I asked as Amy did eighty-five round the North Circular on our way to the country house.

'I like you,' she said. 'You're a real person.'

'What's that mean?' I grimaced, hearing my own remoteness in the compliment.

'I don't know,' she chirruped. I stared out the window. The blurry lamp-posts flicking by knew what she meant. It meant she saw me as a 2D figure representing lost virtues like theme-park actors living in a medieval hamlet. I was not of her world, her interest was only a day-tripper's curiosity. It meant, in fact, that she saw me as *un*real. The strummed lamp-posts wanted to vibrate into each other and not be single posts.

Amy was an actress I met when her house was burgled. She had the clear, Teflon skin of the young and privileged. Her cropped, hacked-about hair made it look as if the burglars had stolen her long, blonde tresses. In the ransacked flat we fell to chatting. She asked a few questions to which my answers were, in effect, 'No, I am not a moron,' and now that Beverley and me were apart I gave her my 'direct line' (home number). But there on the North Circular I began to wish I hadn't. Like all middle-class people she had no idea how routinely rude she was under all that 'niceness'. I put a cassette in the car stezzy.

'What's this?' she asked.

'A Northern Soul compilation.'

'Oh, Northern Soul,' she said, the way posh people do, knowing the name of everything but the meaning of nothing.

The words floated off her lips. Whenever middle-class people talk about working-class culture, they say it without the emphasis of meaning in the way a Gerry spy would say Baker Street, whereas a Tommy would say *Baker* Street. Oh, Northern Soul, she said. No, Northern *Soul*. It's the same when they meaninglessly say Oh, yeah the Sex Pistols, punk. They say it not knowing the significance. It's pronounced *Sex* Pistols or the *Pistols*, it's pronounced *punk*. When I told her about shocking things I'd seen or heard about on the job, they just registered vaguely on her peripheries. Oh *that* stuff.

'Just then, all out of the blue it seemed then, she queried, 'Have you ever hit a woman?'

'No. No *way*.'

'Why not?'

'What do you mean, "Why not?"'

'Ha!' she laughed to herself.

'What?'

'Men always make out that it's such a terrible thing if a man hits a woman but that's sort of sexist, like we're totally victims.'

'It *is* a terrible thing.'

'You've never hit a girl?'

'No! Of *course* not.'

'Donovan used to hit me,' she tested.

'I feel physically ill now.'

'Why?'

'What do you mean, "Why?"'

'It's not such a big thing.'

'Yes it is. When did he hit you?'

'It was only twice, I think.'

'Why?'

'Well, I dunno. But the rules are all changed when you're really close with someone. It's all – you're into a strange area . . .'

'No. They're not. They can't be.'

'All right, then, how many prostitutes have you been to?' she asked me.

'None!'

'Really?'

'Yes, *of course*!'

'Tod sees them all the time,' she said with a triumphant smile, triumphant in her equanimity, triumphant because this didn't bother her a jot.

'That's a truly wicked thing to do,' I said slowly.

'Why?'

'I think it's a class thing. You just don't have any moral sense at all.'

'Any guilt you mean.'

'No. No morals.'

'What's the difference?'

Amy wanted me to confirm her belief in male corruption. If all men were corrupt then that made everything simpler for her emotionally. I knew my own corruption too well to stick around and have it confirmed.

We left the road signs and were on to the biro directions: by a bridge by a phone-box by a green gate by a tree.

At the house, they were playing a late-night game of football in the headlight beam of car parked on the lawn and an outside light lost behind thick, fluorescent ivy. Four boys and five girls, laughing and shouting. Rees, whose house it was – well, parents', but they were away – came over and shook my hand – 'Hello, nice to meet you!' – and then as the ball came near, ran and lifted the woman on the ball off the ground, placed her to one side, and then ran on with the ball. By her retaliatory tackle from behind I guessed it was his girlfriend. We joined the losing side straight away. Five minutes later, after I'd missed a preposterous overhead kick, I lay there with the damp grass under my winded back and felt like I'd been there a week.

Amy had, alas, told them I was a cop and so I arrived bristly with imminent conflict in plus-fours I'd bought from this second-hand shop as a kind of a defensive class joke. (Police officers inhabit a class void: no one ever says 'an officer and a gentleman' about even a senior cop.) But as soon as all of us were sitting at the battered, old wooden table in the candle-lit kitchen, I found I liked this lot. They were interesting people and not really what you'd call posh at all. They were just people who go to art-house films and talk about film directors like old friends who've gone wrong, who keep making mistakes they could've saved them from. All a little older than me they were just graduates – and after all, so was I. And maybe it was time for me to get some new friends now I'd sensed me and Kieran were just colleagues, really. We waited for the kitchen fire to heat us up.

Rees the host was handsomely receding at the temples of a black quiff, and wore an Aran roll-neck and battered black leather coat. And that's Tom in the roll-neck and Graham in the duffle-coat. All the men looked as though Jack Hawkins was waiting for them up on the poop-deck.

Tubby Graham had a lovely Tyneside voice that seemed to come from his chest, and a twinkly intelligent look behind his specs. A beautiful half-Indian woman with oriental eyes and delicate features called Harriet. Angela appeared, at first, not so much a person, more the personification of glandular over-activity. High gums, rabbit eyes, oily skin, Angela Hyper-Thyroid had a posh speech impediment, too. Her saliva-shiny lips said *v* instead of *th*. I liked her. She was open and she couldn't say 'fairer than that'.

There were two people there, however, I didn't like. Polly had let-it-breathe grey strands in her black hair. There was a dragging heaviness about her, a stone in a stream. Pear-shaped herself, she wanted everything around her in her own image and would know no rest until she had made it so. I heard her humming, but she was so ineluctably sour that it sounded like sardonic humming, a parody of facile joy. (Everything she said had a sneer riding on it. She didn't even know she was sneering. She thought she was merely being pointed or droll. There was just a range of sneers to choose from. Tom, New Age Tom, wanted to drag me down to his stillness. He kept looking at me with a patronizing: 'Hey, why are you flying around?' look; a smug 'There's nothing to be afraid of' look. In the cold living-room side-by-side on flowery armchairs, he was chatting to Harriet. Dumping a red plastic clothes-basket full of logs by the fireplace I overheard him say in tones of universal sympathy, 'Of *course* he's getting all these bad things like the migraines. I mean that's because he's staying in this space where he doesn't have to be positive, and what happens when you're in a small, cramped space with no windows? You get a headache.'

It was that simple. Tom, for all his talk of the spirit, was actually a materialist with his belief in instant earthly reward, in good fortune to the good, bad fortune to the bad. For all his talk of the spirit he had a bad spirit, selfish and subtly bullying as he kept staring at me in that pious way. This house was such a buzz, however, that even my unease with him still had the colour of happiness like the small ache of going out to get the logs in for the fire.

I left them to it and went into the warm kitchen where I sat in on a conversation between Graham, Rees, Nick and Amy about *Steptoe & Son*.

'That's why it's called *Steptoe & Son*, even though they are both Steptoe, because it's about the two sides of us, the child and the parent,' said Graham.

'No, it's just the name of the company. Steptoe & Son!' said Nick.

'But it could've been *Steptoe & Steptoe*, but it isn't because it's about how we've got this harsh parental voice in our heads which is about fear and telling us we're no good, and we've got this weak, aspirant voice – and it's about that conflict . . .'

I wasn't sure if he was serious, so I just said, 'I find it too painful to watch sometimes. I'm like "No! Don't take your dad on your honeymoon with you!"'

Graham looked at me. His look seemed to suggest that my strict professional self was tyrant to child Harold, so I laughed when Rees said, 'So, what about Cannon *and* Ball?'

'No, actually I think you might have a point,' said Amy, 'but would you say that the reason it's called "step – toe" is because they're always stepping on each other's toes, or the father is always stepping on the son's toes?'

'I'm not saying that they thought of all this consciously but, yeah,' he grinned, 'there might be summat of that.'

'Bullshit!' cried Nick, triumphantly, and Graham started laughing so maybe he wasn't serious after all.

Rees got out a tin Woodbine box, and turned to me: 'I was gonna build a spliff, but if it'll embarrass you . . .'

'No, no that's very civil of you, but I was about to crash now anyway.'

Amy led me up and along a tiny corridor to my room. 'Here we are!' My room was a thing of wood. Dark, wooden floor, wooden wall-panels, ceiling and headboard. 'This is the haunted room, I'm afraid,' she said. 'Good-night!'

'Good-night!'

'Sleep well! See you tomorrow.'

Sorry, ghost, I thought, unlacing my boots, but you're stacked up in a holding circle in the sky. You'll just have to join the queue. I'm sure you're a scary ghost and everything, I said to the room, but I've seen a woman melt, like. Sorry. I threw the boots across the room. Kenneth told me he'd come back and haunt me, too.

Woke early among mahogany bedposts after mahogany sleep, and went for a walk around the gardens (wearing ordinary black Levi's now that I was part of this). A lawn bit. A small, walled vegetable garden. A covered swimming-pool seen through the mossy windows of a brick conservatory with proud, 1872, iron plumbing. A mazy walkway and sleeping flower-beds. Ploughed and frosty fields stretching beyond the thin, rusty, knee-high fence.

Hands in pockets, I touched my knees on the rusty wire. Ever since getting here I'd been able to hear myself think as if the frost-flat fields were a sounding-board. But over a noisy, japey breakfast, I felt the same, could still hear myself think. The sounding-board was also to do with being mob-handed and not detonated into the ones and twos of north London. The fact that I had gone straight up to bed last night, I reflected, looking out over the silent fields, rather than hanging around and trying to get off with Amy, had to do with the sounding-board, with being able to hear other voices apart from greed and desire, fear and fuck-it. I hadn't even tried. Why not? Because it felt wrong, that's why. Wow! That's a new one. I'd always wanted to think that and mean it. And here and now I did. It felt wrong because I was part of something bigger than just me, or because I was living collectively.

Maybe the reason a break or a holiday is stimulating might just be as simple as smelling new smells, or being in a different-shaped room. Maybe that was why it felt magic here, I thought, washing up to Al Green on a cassette player in the kitchen . . . Echoey water-polo in the steamy glasshouse pool, the women topless or in T-shirt and knickers. The pepperminty smell of their spliff; the tap-tap of table-tennis and stone-tiles. A pyrex baking dish put in to soak, and walking mob-handed down to the sea for a swim in sheet-lightning. Harriet-on-Sea, her green T-shirt clinging to her goose-pimpled dark skin as the sea crashed. The water drying in patches on her thighs, not wanting to leave.

On the last evening we went into town to buy some chips.

I'd only been at the manor two days but Highway Code Town felt a world away. As we drove back in the dusk, I looked down from the high lane at a passing pub. The Beer Garden seemed like a prison association area. A young, married couple sat in flummoxed silence obediently eating their hot meal. No one said monogamy would stand alone. Once it was part of something else, but now it wandered around killing time. The husband in freshly laundered denim sat at a slatted table and stared at the ice-cubes dissolving in his last bit of orange juice. His special treat! His evening! How small our pleasures are, for that is my life too. And one day I'll have forgotten – or have had to forget – that it could ever be bigger, vivider, like it was here at this country house. I began to feel a bitter envy of my warm and lovely host. If it wasn't for a burglary and a show-off nod to the books on Amy's shelf I'd never have got my foot in the door, never known about all this. The others could have this 100-mile soul-service whenever they wanted. I would have to accept a bribe from the Russian mafia before I could ever make this a regular part of my season.

When we got back to the swell house, I realized why I hadn't tried to get off with Amy the night before. Here there were other shapes in the world apart from her breasts. It was like a feeling I had had at weddings and christenings, a feeling that I was somehow a bit further from crime and pervy thoughts. A better self due to the setting.

I left the others to go and watch the Prince Naz fight in the 'lounge'.

'That's your idea of fun, is it?' asked Tom as I wandered off. 'Watching two half-naked black men hitting each other, all sweaty and bloody?'

I sat in the cold front-room with a bowl of rhubarb pie and custard on my lap. The Prince had dispatched his challenger while I still had the tough edges of pie-crust to try and rive with my spoon.

'How was it?' asked Harriet, as I walked in with my begging bowl.

'Excellent, thanks.' I felt a vacuum in the room and knew they'd been talking about me, but they picked up on an earlier conversation: pitying poor lost film-directors again. I wondered whether most modern conversations sound like fake, cover-up conversations. They have the same earnestness about nothing as when you pretend you were engrossed in something before the man you were slagging off walks in.

'He's just repeating himself,' said Nick, lamenting the plight of some billionaire director.

'I haven't seen the film,' I said, 'but I saw an interview where he said about the old-style gangsters: "Morality doesn't enter into it." I couldn't believe he said that.'

'Why not?'

'You can't say that conventional rules of right and wrong don't apply just 'cos that was the Bronx and it's survival.' They went quiet: the cop was talking as a cop. At last. 'And all that bollocks about the old gangsters having a code of conduct, he was saying, and the new ones don't . . . If you're a working-class shopkeeper in the 1930s getting your face slashed 'cos you won't pay protection, it still hurts even if it's done by a man in a trilby. Scorcese just means gangsters were once white and now they're black. It's a foreign code to him and so he thinks there's no –'

'If you're saying all modern gangsters are black . . .' snorted Polly, with a head-shaking jangle of her ear-rings. She had these long, dangly, deliberately unsexy ear-rings – I fucking hate them. Hate them. I hate them. The long, spindly, metal, ethnicky ones. I fucking hate them. Ear-rings inlaid with, of course, *turquoise*. What else? Turquoise will always find its way on to a person of bad spirit, like dots on stale Mother's Pride.

'Do you believe in censorship?' asked Amy.

The conversation now felt like the US visa waiver with its Yes/No tick-box: *Are you entering the USA to engage in acts of terrorism? Yes/No.* I hated the fact that my acceptance at the dinner table depended on a Yes/No tick-box. Are you homophobic? The correct answer is no. Peasy. Peasy and dismaying. As a cop you see all these people with their attitudes all present and correct doing terrible things. But with a sigh, and a sense that everyone else was somehow sitting on the other side of the table, I said, 'I thought that film *Wild At Heart* should've been banned or cut, and *Cape Fear,* too.'

'Why?'

''Cos they had women being raped and enjoying it.'

There was a pause now. I stared at the sunken plunger of the cafetière, its solid metal core inside the coiled spring. I knew by the thickening blood in my neck veins choking my voice while I said this that it wasn't the voice of love, but the solid voice of hate coiled in self-righteousness, plunging you down and blinding you to detail with blind grains at the back of the eyes.

'Mind if I roll a joint?' said Tom to big laughs.

'Go ahead,' I said, 'but you were giving it the high-horse about boxing and yet there's plenty more black people killed as a result of drugs than ever killed in boxing.'

Polly tried to drag me into a black hole of her own making: 'Again you're saying most drug dealers are black . . .' I wanted to say the next bit and so raised my voice over hers, knowing that was a pc black mark against this PC.

'But the way, er, liberals talk about the police is twenty years out of date; you've got Chief Constables talking about legalizing drugs –'

'Are you in favour of legalization?' asked Harriet.

'No, actually,' I said, laughing at my contradiction.

'You've just contradicted yourself,' contradicted Heavy Polly dismissively. Ah, Polly. I thought I'd find you here, waving your little linesman's flag. Of course you're pointing out the regulation lines because stale shapes are all you know.

'Surely, it's people's choice – alcohol's much more dangerous. Surely, it's personal freedom,' repeated Glangela looking at me in the eyes beseechingly like she was my friendly defence attorney hoping to lead me into saying the right thing, wanting me to agree. Throughout all this Graham didn't say anything but was watching me with a scientist's curiosity. I kept checking him out but he was just turning his cigarette packet over and over. Waiting?

'With drugs, though,' I said, 'you've got to ask "whose freedom?" I mean, not the people who live on the estates.' Graham was still staring at me like a scientist watching an experiment: drunk cop flailing around in the ideological bins. When was he going to talk? What did he have? A pair of kings? Two aces?

'It must be difficult,' said Tom slyly, 'not to be racist if you only ever come into contact with black people through crime.' Ooh you subtle, tricksy New Ager, but I seen you clip-clopping round the hill a mile off!

I wasn't about to say what I really thought any more than the accused woman in medieval times would turn to the Witchfinder-General and say, '*I'd like to take this opportunity to read some lesbian love poetry I recently wrote.*' There's no Yes/No about it. Are you a racist? No is no answer. We live in a racist society and so, whether we like it or not, all kinds of racist stuff is going to get in there, going to pop up in your mind. Now, I believe that if you say it isn't there it gets stronger, it festers in the dark. But if white people were to talk about all the shit in our heads then we might get somewhere. What I really thought was, yes, it is hard to keep alive the sense of why they're doing what they're doing. Impossible, I've found. All the accurate reasons for why black crime is high give way and one day you find a terrible word on your lips, in your heart. But instead, all I said was, 'Well, I think the British situation is different from the American situation in that most of the time when people in this country talk about race they're really talking about class.'

'You're obviously a sensitive policeman yourself,' said Harriet, 'but it's just that we've all met, at one time or another, a few really obnoxious policemen and they're the ones you remember, I suppose.'

'Yeah, but imagine the sentence you've just said only with the word black instead of police . . .' A couple of other people came in with different points, and I felt my *coup de grâce* was in peril of not being seen for the matchwinner it was, and so I intoned, '"*It's just, you know, we've all met a few really obnoxious blacks and they're the ones that stick in your mind.*"'

That got their attention because, but for the spin, it was what they'd always wanted to hear a policeman say. Nervously, I was drinking two shots of whisky to one of everybody else's.

'I'm glad you mentioned *class*,' said Graham at last, emphasizing '*class*' to rhyme with 'flat' and 'cap', ''cos it's still different rules for different classes . . . The financial markets are above the laws of property. If ah smashed up a factory ah'd go to jail . . .'

'Yes, we're being reduced to piggy in the middle more and more, but what you've just said – that's just what villains say – "It's all right if we do it, 'cos they're doing it too," like it's some kind of justification. But what *I'm* saying is you shouldn't be allowed to do either and that both are immoral and both should be illegal.'

'But they're *not* both illegal,' laughed Graham. 'It's a casino economy, the money market's destructive speculation – that's like anarchy, legitimized anarchy. How do you justify being a policeman in defence of that? The City's out of control, smashers and wreckers, trashing lives – out of control.' Holding lighter and fag-packet in one hand he made like a window-wipe gesture with them as if to say, 'It's so simple, why can't you see it?'

I took a swig with the others all looking at me.

'You all want me to say something eccentric,' I said, 'and so here it is . . . Policemen are seen in polite society as sort of throwbacks and yet I feel that in one way the police are perhaps the more truly modern people. People no longer feel that any feelings are "beneath us" because all that American psychotherapy culture locates *all* feelings as being beneath us, you know, subconscious. In the sixties repression became a dirty word and it was all about going with your feelings . . . We've forgotten how to be the master or, uh, mistress of ourselves, we blame everyone else . . . And I think a police officer – not by any higher virtue but perhaps just through a professional manner and seeing the consequences – has relearnt the forgotten art of mind over matter, how to master emotions, to draw arbitrary lines and say, "Over this I do not go."'

'Tell that to a black man arrested in Stoke Newington!'

(Or to Lee Andrew I think now from here in the darkened vigil suite.)

'Other people have their belief systems, too,' said Harriet.

'Yeah, except no, actually they don't because they're always moving the goalposts. They're stuck in the hippy idea that we can't deny instincts, and so are morally easier on themselves than a police officer is.'

'No,' said Graham, '*you're* moving the goalposts. You can't be moral working for an immoral system unless you wanna end up a schizophrenic!'

The greasy smell of the roast chicken started to make me feel ill in my forehead. I'd lost the thread of the argument so I just picked up wherever. 'People who slag off the police have got no street-suss. They go: "How do you know he's a dealer?" But everyone on the estate knows he's a dealer, just like you know the man standing outside the grocer's shop is a grocer.

These liberals are the same people who think boxers are forced into it, because they never grew up with people who *loved* to fight and whose Friday night was a failure if they didn't.'

And now you're moving the goalposts of this discussion,' said the smug little four-eyed, brain-box lefty. 'You seem to think you're the last moral man in the land, that you're the only one who's not got a shortfall between beliefs and action – that's hysterical. In a utopia maybe law and morality would be the same thing, but you are, let me point out to you *by the way,* on the side of *in*justice because the law is opposed to social justice.'

'Well, not all the law.'

'Well, which laws are you gonna defend?'

'I can't just pick and choose.'

'Right! So don't come the Mr Morality then!'

'You're just like the Nazis saying, "We were only obeying orders,"' said roly-Polly.

Jesus, why not just up the ante, I thought. 'Well, I think you get into dangerous ground,' I said, 'when you say I'm gonna arrest for this and not for that. I mean then you *are* a fascist because you're sneering at democracy.'

'No you're not, you're the opposite: you're listening to your conscience.'

'No, there's too much right-of-the-individual shit,' I said. 'There's no collective responsibility. *I'll leave the kids so I can be happy.* For example, I feel very strongly about sexual assaults. Now suppose there's another officer who thinks these are just tiffs or human nature or . . . or there's no such thing as date-rape. Then what? You have to subdue, no, not subdue, subordinate your individual impulse to the collective idea, I mean that's what it's all about, that's what crime is . . . I mean, not listening to the civic, shared law.'

'Whatever that law is?'

'No . . . well . . . I . . . er.'

'The law isn't social justice,' said Graham.

Before I came here I thought I'd impress them by having political views they might find surprisingly leftish. I thought I'd get to say that we are the feminist's army, we are the footsoldiers of the women's Reclaim the Night march. They turn up once a year and we safeguard them all year, but that was all gone and torn up now as well.

What I really wanted to say to them earlier on was that the reason *Guardian*-reading, middle-class liberals like you are anti-police is because you know we're really there to protect *you*, and to admit that would wreck your radical self-image – you seeing yourselves as somehow the counter-culture. But now things had changed and those words weren't available any more, somehow didn't apply, and the more it went on the more old certainties didn't apply and the more confused I got. Besides they'd all shuffled out to the front-room now. I felt that Graham had shown up that my self-image was frozen years ago when I was a better man. There was me thinking that because I knew the words of 'Red Fly the Banners' that somehow made me the people's cop – so much so that I didn't need to go out and actually *be* the people's cop.

Alone, I sat in silence and finished off my drink. I felt that everything was torn to bits. In shreds. I lined nine or ten bottles of leftover red in a row among the dinner wreckage. Each sounded a different note when I dinged them with my fork. Next I arranged them in ascending pitch like a xylophone. I sat there alone, drinking red wine and ding-ding-dinging with my tuning fork until they all chimed the same.

Yes, there's a stillness, a containment about many policemen – but not this one.

Ten green bottles, all of them empty.

I thought of going to rejoin the others but suspected they'd all be having a smoke and so I decided as it was still around ten to find a nearby pub. I borrowed someone's coat off the back of a chair and left alone like a lecturer.

Usually I get terrible 'drinker's remorse', wincing and jolting as ECT memories of the night before lash through me. The furious police-state clampdown after a night of harmless revels, fearing what the vacuum of its flouted authority invites. Usually I get terrible drinker's remorse, but not that morning. Something about this magic place had given me a pardon. I came down for breakfast next day around eleven feeling well-rested and good. All the others were standing in the big kitchen where we always ate.

'I was listening to the World Service last night,' I said, speaking slightly posh. 'I kept the volume down very low but I do hope I didn't disturb anyone . . . ?'

They were all standing and looking at me with frosty expressions. They all had their coats on, too. It seemed, at first, like some kind of visual pun.

A dog barked far away. There was something wrong with the sound. Too clear, too loud. I looked at the window. Smashed. All the windows smashed. Shattered tusks of glass sticking in the razor frame. I looked at the wonky, splintered back door. It was hanging on only by the top hinge, like Exhibit A held between thumb and forefinger of Counsel for the Prosecution.

I looked at the accusers. I looked at Amy but her face was just like the others. Then I followed her gaze down to the well-swept black grate of the dormant fireplace in which lay a healthy pile of moist and glistening human shite.

I ran out the door, which was surprisingly difficult to get past.

Out in the woods I pondered my next move. What I wanted to do was just leave, but there was no way to.

I tried to remember the night before. I couldn't. I walked along the lane.

Car coming. I ran, found a gap in a hedge, escaped into a field until it went by. Not them anyhow. On the road again, walking, walking.

Two cyclists went by, a man and a woman. I smiled and said 'hello'. They smiled and said 'hello' back. I enjoyed the illicit feeling of innocence: for all they knew I was just a saintly rambler. Not evil. Listening to the retreating sound of their wheels as the woman behind the man free-wheeled buzzily, I remembered spokes. Spokes. And then I remembered I'd been drinking at a lock-in in an isolated pub and that one of our number was in a wheelchair. Silvery wheelchair spokes. Remembered other faces. A man with a beard, a woman with a shiny Japanese Kimono top over black leggings. Yes, I definitely remembered fancying her. Then I remembered that I'd driven home drunk in charge along rural lanes, just like my father on his last journey, except in an internal blizzard.

My groan echoed off frozen trees and iced puddles. Oh no – *I'd walked to the pub.* Hot prickly sweat on a cold day. What car? I felt the keys in my pocket. Gaps in the memory. Maybe . . . maybe one of those decent sorts at the pub must have, er, maybe, er, *lent* me their car. Yes, that must be . . . Now there was a way out of this: I could just get in the car and drive off.

I warily approached the front of the house and there was my escape vehicle blocking the drive. The steam coming out of his mouth meant Rees was saying stuff. I nonchalantly entered the sky-blue three-wheeler. I turned the ignition. The engine made a funny noise. Oh no, don't say it won't start. I don't want to have to face them all. But then I cottoned on that this was a battery-powered car. It had started. Holding the hand throttle like an indoor motorbike, I accelerated mildly up the road.

*

Outside I hear the ferrety dustman who goes ahead of the truck, taking all the black plastic bags out of their cubbyholes, dustbins and wheely-bins, and stacks them on the kerb ready for the lorry.

I get up and go into the bedroom.

The mattress is bare. The orange sheets I stripped this morning or rather yesterday morning lie balled on the floor. I remember now. I was going to put the sheets in the machine when I got home from work. Nearly made it.

When you strip the sheets in a rented flat the mattress is a forensic scientist's lab top: blood, fluff and semen of the long-gone stranger. You see that it's not your mattress, but the mattress of the last few tenants and the next. Stripping the sheets is the nearest you come to moving out without moving out. Apart from laundry day, you only ever see a bare mattress in the street: after eviction, repossession, a fire, or final and total disgust at the seedy slab.

Beverley haunts me in these sheets. She helped me choose them. The orange sheets make me think of the life I might have led with her, a crusty Turin shroud of better things. Changing these sheets always brings regret, but as they say you makes your bed . . .

She'd left a message with her new Birmingham number just before I'd gone to the county house and said to call if I wanted a chat when I got back. And, what with one thing and another, I did, as it went.

saint beverley's day

The following Sunday she arrived on my doorstep. Hips, tits, lips, power. Six feet tall and carrying a mini Gladstone bag like some funky niece of Miss Marple's here to make it all OK again. Her eyes flashed like she'd just emerged from a dip in the winter Thames. She'd dyed her outgrown bob a deep, warm purple with streaks of blonde at the front.

My hands on her high-rise, power-cambered hips at the front door, I wondered what sort of a kiss she'd give me, what our status was. She kissed me on the mouth with her lips slightly parted.

On Saint Beverley's Day sins were washed clean. On Saint Beverley's Day, in the general amnesty of her presence, I always felt mad as in exciting rather than mad as in a sick menace to society. So I didn't have to think about how the country house had gone off, didn't have to give it another thought. Although I should have done.

That afternoon in a junk-shop, she told me, she'd found a 1950s book: *Cooking with the Stars – Hollywood's Favourite Recipes*. She was cooking us *Ava Gardner Tuna Marinade*.

In first dusk I lit a church candle; she stabbed the cork into the wine with a knife. The back door was open on to the yard. Peace settled like evening cinders of the sweet-smelling garden bonfires two blocks away. Above the mouldy garden wall appeared, for one night only, pink clouds on a grainy blue sky.

We ate opposite each other. I sometimes get tense if people

137

sit opposite me, directly opposite me, but that evening was in many ways . . . my night off.

I was proud that I didn't need to ask how she had her tea because I knew: 'Lots of milk, lots of sugar, lots of tea,' of course. I went through the Gateway bags.

'Oh you stupid fucking cunt!' I cursed myself.

'What have you done!' she asked.

'I've forgotten the fucking milk. I'm such a fucking stupid fucking cunt.'

'You stupid fucking cunt,' she mimicked like a gleeful four-year-old who doesn't know what the words mean.

'No,' I continued, refusing to lighten up. 'I'm so fucking stupid.'

'People are,' she went on. She had lighter and bifta poised in each hand. From the delay before sparking up, I knew I was going to get one of her weird and wonderful little philosophies. 'It's just I been thinking,' she began in the sing-song voice that always went with them, 'humans, we're much more crap than we admit, and if we admitted it – it's like, look at that salt pot. They have to make it with a tiny hole in the top because we're clumsy and knock them over; same with sugar in caffs. And we have to have a big napkin over us because after years of food-fork practice we still can't always get our mouths in one.'

'It's a tricky bastard.'

'Innit! We expect to do things that we've never been able to.'

'Go on, what else?'

She thought for a bit then said, 'Well, carpenters are the best we've got at handling tools. Their hands are covered in black fingernails, stab-marks, missing fingers. There's usually a cut on their forehead. No one knows how to run the government, that's way over our heads, but if they just came out and said, "We've come up with this plan, probably be a disaster but, you know . . ." then that'd be no pressure.'

'Yeah, that'd get voted for,' I said.

I looked at the steamed kitchen windows, and felt a peace which, like condensation, was always waiting in the air to appear. There was a well-sprung feeling in my hand slowly gripping the bottle, lifting it, pouring it, hearing the wine make its noise like a top-dollar rockery.

Talking to Beverley I invented a communication device and called it language. There wasn't much to it really, I just suddenly hit on the idea of using ordinary household words to express thought and feeling. (Maybe I'd have a crack at ice-cube trays or glue next.) With others I always heard myself reciting, speechifying and getting more and more lonely as my stock fillers drove out meaningful contact. This feeling reminded me of something I once saw on the job. I was called to a house after a neighbour reported noises. I rang the bell. A pensioner in his NHS glasses with milk-bottle lenses and a sad, tired face came to the door. No, there was only him at home, it must have been the people upstairs, he said, and closed the door. Miserable bastard, I thought, and rang the top bell. No answer, walked away. Next day I discover there'd been two youths in the kitchen holding his health visitor hostage, while a third was out caning her Mastercard.

But with Beverley it always felt like my first-ever conversation.

'How was – where d'you go again?'

'Holland,' she said. 'Bostin'!' She'd been rigging up the scaffold, rolling out the rubber-matted floor for a big grungy festival-thing over there; and being ogled at by Vikings in the beer tent, no doubt. Vikings lacking criss-cross slashings over their bloated, red faces. 'The plane, right,' she started, 'I hadn't been in a plane since I was a kid, and you know when you look down from a plane just on take-off, when it's still quite low when it's just taken off, everything down below looks so peaceful, like a model city. You know, there's all these toy trucks and cars all moving calmly and slowly, a little blue lorry waiting all patient for a little white car at the roundabout. Neat rows of, you know, the freight things they put on the back of artics. All in a neat row. Everything spaced out all orderly.'

'Yeah, it's probably 'cos from up there you can't sense eye-level vibes and force-fields. Can't see lorry drivers scowling or hear the horn.'

'No . . .'

'No?'

'No,' she chuckled.

'Oh OK, then.'

'I'll tell you what it is – it's because it looks like everyone's involved in the same thing, you know what I mean? It looks like people all work things out together, as if that's how we sorted things out rather than by sending letter-bombs to the council. It's like all the citizens got together and they decide, "OK, we'll put the petrol storage towers here, and, tell you what, why not bung a few dinghies on the reservoir? That might be nice for a few people." And it's like one farmer says to another, "What are you growing in that field? Green? OK, I'll grow yellow in this one."'

'A model city.'

'Yeah, but that people-together tip you get looking down at the town from Economy is not, it's not –'

'Down in the din it's all being broken apart.'

'Yeah.'

She settled on a high stool and looked at me appraisingly.

'You look exhausted,' she said.

'Lates.'

'No, no, that's not what I meant.' She took her time looking down at the floor to one side of her, and then straightening up again in a neck-rolling, aerobic way until her head was right way up and settled again. 'I mean, uh, totally mentally, physically and emotionally exhausted.'

I started telling her about a recent Public Order where they were all protesting about a man who'd died in custody. (It wasn't even in our nick; the death had occurred – surprise, surprise – at Stoke Newington.) 'They're all shouting and spitting at you, at me, like I'm a bad man because I'm a policeman, and you know *they're* slags – half of them. It's all about how we can't control *ourselves* and commit these acts, like we're bad or hollow characters, and yet as they stood there so close to me' – I held my hand up with the palm six inches in front of my face – 'and yet all the time they don't know just how *much* character it's taking me not to . . .'

'You should go on a holiday.'

'*Holiday?*' I said, like, 'What have I got to do with holidays?' I felt like Hitler in the bunker if Eva Braun had suggested an ABTA-approved adventure package on the island of Cos to take his mind off work. But that, of course, was the point. I told her about my weekend break in the country. (Except I left out the bit about the disabled car, which I'd left outside the local train station, hoping the police would find it and return it to the housebound man.)

'But you're so deliberately awkward,' she said. 'When you're with cops you have to be all Karl Marx and when you're with the country house lot and you have to be Mr Defender of the Status Quo.'

On Saint Beverley's Day I allowed myself to think it might be that simple. 'I've got you a present,' I said.

'Oh aye.'

'It's in the freezer bit.'

She opened the fridge and then the freezer flap and took out a heart-shaped red rubber ice-cube tray. She looked at me, then went over to the sink and pushed the ice-cubes out – pop-pop-pop.

'Oh this is great,' she said. 'From now on people will be able to have ice in their drinks!'

And then she smiles, comes my way and her hot breath on my fag-ash lips blows the coals.

'What's that all abaht?' I TSG-ed.

'I always feel very safe with you.'

'That's odd, 'cos I don't.'

'What, with me?'

'No, with me.'

After sex I felt connected to the world, to her, to myself. (And that state of affairs couldn't be allowed.) She left her book behind that night, in that other life. I get up now and with bruised hands take it from under a sprawl of cassettes, which slide off noisily in this silent flat. Hard to turn the pages with these swollen fingers, but flicking through her cookbook now I find:

> Shrimp Salad à la Benny
> One of the meals that I enjoy most is my Sunday night supper and here is a meal I always look forward to.

Some people walk through life hearing foreboding strings accompany creeping film-noir shadows on the stairs; others hear a light-comedy film score. And here we were going out with each other again. Going back out with her, it seemed like all the stuff in my head I thought was fixed was just furniture. Bad things were no more likely to happen if I was off-guard, looking forward to shrimp-salad supper every Sunday. I could change the soundtrack to flutes, kazoos and Tubby the Tuba any time I wanted. But try telling my subconscious that.

Me and the Bevster were always splitting up and then getting back together again. All the time that Beverley was showing me one way, a part of me pulled the other.

*

Outside the dustcart comes along now. A dustman roars, 'Whoa!'

After the controlled explosion at the country house I had an extreme swing back towards her. A week. Two weeks. Until another extreme force swung me back again, and away.

A binman bangs the side of the dustcart, shouting, 'Go! OK! Off you go!' and the cart drives off. Six o'clock and all's shite.

I get up and fix a sugary coffee. Outside I can hear the quick tut-tut-tut of early high heels on their way to work. A car starts and I hear the first front doors closing.

I lie down gingerly on the couch. My ribs ache from a kick or punch I got there. The soreness of my busted, fat lip comes in waves. It hurts now. My body feels drained. It could do with sleep to go about its repair and regeneration. But my mind is separately alive like a blue control room.

I lie for a bit with my forearms over my eyes, pushing the lid-black to orange smash. A memory flashes. I pull my arm away and shout, 'No! Wait Bev! No!'

I met her off the train. Watched them all coming up the platform. All the male passengers were sparking up post-coital biftas, all looking slightly shagged-out as if their journey had been one long, exhausting, racketing orgy. I stared out the other men walking up the concourse, chatting with her in extreme gratitude at the hundred-mile blow-jobs she'd given the lot of them.

Her ragga-style hot-pants were shape-shagged, frayed and run ragged by trying to hang on to her hips and arse. Gym-knicker blue good-God and held up by a thick black belt with bits of leather crumbling on to the buckle. Her black hold-ups left a freefall of exposed pale thigh flesh until my eyes crawled into the fraying hem of her shorts. That gap of upper-thigh which always gets such a hold on a man, like a bedroom door ajar. As the navy hem of her shorts rode the crests of her buttocks I felt – as always when we were in public – that there'd be a riot. But there never was, just the riot inside of me.

'I like your leather jacket,' she said. 'Is that new?'

'No.'

We went and sat in a cramped Italian café. I said something nasty then couldn't listen to what followed. I tuned out the better to concentrate on getting a handful of grains back into the sugar holder. It was quite difficult – you have to go really slow but if you keep your hand steady and make sure the sugar grains come down that deep palm-line about a finger-tip's distance beneath the little finger it can be done. I poured another handful of sugar into my palm. While all this was going on we may have been splitting up. I may have been the one to chuck her. I can't remember.

'The closer I get to you,' she was saying in a wild voice, 'the more you panic, terrified that I'm gonna find out that you're some kind of bad person, rotten to the core.'

The sugar was flowing less freely now from my palm. But by taking a bigger handful I was able to get a good steady stream into the silver hole. I spilt more this way, but I was playing the numbers game: more grains actually going in the hole, but more grains being spilt.

She hadn't said anything for a bit. Then she started again: 'You're always going on about downsizing, when you have to cover for someone else all the time or can't get a new radio-pack . . . evil capitalist downsizing, all that . . . yet that's exactly what you're doing with me. In fact it's *exactly* like downsizing.' I heard the rattle of her metal coat buttons on the table-top as she leant across the formica. 'Because it's like the quick hit, the short-term profit the banks make when they pull out of a business or whatever and flog it.'

I couldn't see how the analogy worked. Clearly hanging out with me had had some effect: her insights were now as showy and hollow as mine. Yes, it was certainly time for her to go.

I crane-winched my head up to look at her for a split-second, then wished I hadn't bothered as there were tears in her eyes. 'How's it the same?' I managed to say, dredging words up from the silt.

'Because', she insisted, 'you'll get a quick hit off the rejection if you leave me, you'll feel impregnable and streamlined, all set free from your past, your weaknesses, all the "so terrible" things I know about you, all the non-perfect stuff, but it will only last a few weeks . . .'

How did she get to that? You chat about X and you chat about Y, go shopping together and go to the cinema and – WHOOMPF! – they've seen into your nuclear core! How do people break in like that? Was this a secret knowledge she had in her head all the time and never told me, or did she just hit on it in this crisis? I tried raising my hand a little higher to let the grains fall further, more noisily. This was more successful for a couple of seconds, but the next palmful of sugar missed completely, sliding off the silver nozzle-cone on to the table. I wiped the damp crumbs away to start again. Hand lower this time.

'This is what happens when I cook for you,' she said strangely, her voice breaking as she stood up. What the fuck did that dinner two weeks ago have to do with anything? I rubbed the last clump of moist sugar off my palms

I sat for a bit more after she'd gone. '*But it will only last a few weeks . . .*' Why don't you just put a curse on my future while you're about it? A curse on my future.

An Italian shouting 'Hey!' behind me on the High Street. An Italian *padrone* at my side waving the bill, about to speak, changing his mind.

A humid night midway through my first late back I went to a disturbance in Mercer Road. A fat boy – only about eighteen – had gone back to his ex-girlfriend's. She wouldn't let him in. So he tried a Holloway serenade: crying and throwing dustbins and stones at the windows! Shouting and bawling until she came down to talk to him.

I took him for a walk round the block. Before and after the harsh stuff about what the law could and would have to do if he came round bothering her again, I let him talk and gripe and get it all off his flabby chest. On one level I knew exactly how he felt; on another level, looking at this snotty blubbering fatboy in search of a mum, I was with the girl. Surprised by fury, I wanted to smack his face off and run away.

end of vigil

I get up and open the curtains. Night has left new litter behind in the yard: a crinkly, thin, plastic shopping bag, some chip paper and a beer can, like driftwood stranded high and dry at low-tide.

Most of us have no-go areas. Hollow ways and gristles of hate that can escape notice for a lifetime. Life doesn't always find you out but in my case it has. Under cover of darkness, last night, I kept thinking '*Why me?*' Right from when Lee Andrew decided to stop breathing my first thoughts were, '*Why me, why did this have to happen to me?*' When I first got back here tonight, last night, I felt that this disaster was like a dot on the horizon that had always been coming towards me throughout my life. But now I know different. *I* was the dot on the horizon, hurtling towards the future. Because it wasn't something that *happened* to me, it was something I did. *I* happened to Lee Andrew.

Everything I've remembered tonight seems like another link in the chain. If I hadn't done this or that then I wouldn't have been there at the end of Lee Andrew. This night's vigil has revealed that it could *only* have happened to me. And it's not down to arbitrary things – like getting the Twix or whatever. Last night happened because of deep decisions made in the very core of me. If I hadn't done my legs by deleting the Clantons' file, then I'd have been a DC and on a different rota last night. All the destabilizing things I saw, and crossing the threshold of violence with the bruises on Beverley's arse.

The compound panic of loving her when all around me I saw the terrible things that happen to somebody's loved one. It could only have been me. A lifetime forged the vicious will that killed the man. I wish I'd come to some other conclusion during last night's vigil. Now that I have to go in to meet my unmakers.

The bluebottle is dead. Daylight has finally reached the north-facing shadow of my back yard. The searchlight day has arrived to examine all God's creatures and pronounced this bluebottle dead. I flick the insect to the floor.

The front door closes behind me. The whippy morning wind reminds the cuts on my face of Lee Andrew's cold leather sleeve, his rasping coat. Walking to the nick I sign a petition against animal testing and answer all the clipboard survey questionnaire. A hundred yards on I give a fiver to a beggar.

After dawdling on the pavement on the way here, I'm whooshed straight through to the planning room. Never got my feet under the long, polished table here before. A slight feeling of having bombed my way to the conference table. There was three of them just like there was three when I first joined: gatekeepers of my beginning and my end. The Super, our DCI and with them the Assistant Deputy Chief Commissioner with his medals sewn on his uniform. For seven years I've hoped to get my police work noticed by them, and now finally I have.

'The first thing I need to know', asks the Chief, 'is why you were hitting him when he was on the floor?'

'I know it looks bad, sir, but he was already dead.' They look at me, look at the table, look at each other. *Maybe if I pretend to be out cold.* Maybe that was what *Lee* was thinking, not me?

'It's gonna be very difficult to convince a jury it was self-defence, John,' says the Super.

I nod but don't say anything. When I spoke just now my

voice sounded different – deeper, clumsier coming through swollen gums and fat lip, and from Lee Andrew's arm on my throat last night. The voice of a neanderthal to whom speaking is new, or a morning-after Dr Jekyll, still stuck with Mr Hyde's night teeth.

'During the fight, were you fighting as a policeman or a man?' she asks.

The inquisition goes on . . . inquest . . . deceased . . . other words too, but I find it difficult to follow. My only clean blow killed him. It must have had a delayed effect. Looking back on it now it was like the Benn–McClellan fight. Nigel Benn is losing heavily in the later rounds but he'd fired a punch in the opening round which, like a dum-dum bullet delay-kicks in and McClellan, on the offensive and winning, suddenly collapses into a coma.

A silence. A long silence. Why aren't they talking? I remember now. The Super is waiting for me to respond to what she said. Think hard. What did she say? I remember now: suspension. That is the word that has been hanging invisibly in the air for some time.

I turn to the Assistant Deputy Chief Commissioner. 'What's your name, sir?' I ask. He drums his fingers gently on the table without moving his thumb, each time more slowly so that on the last roll his fingertips don't make a sound.

'Alan Randall,' he eventually replies.

'I've got a medal, too.'

Here I am, back in the Shaker chair. Just me and time and what will time do to me now?

Book Two

The Marquis de Sade . . . uncannily glimpsed the whole subsequent development of personal life under capitalism . . . The capitalist principle that human beings are ultimately reducible to interchangeable objects . . . [and] the subordination of all social relations to the market . . . stripped away the remaining restraints and mitigating illusions from the war of all against all. In the resulting state of organized anarchy, as Sade was the first to realize, pleasure becomes life's only business – pleasure, however, that is indistinguishable from rape, murder, unbridled aggression. In a society that has reduced reason to mere calculation, reason can impose no limits on the pursuit of pleasure – on the immediate gratification of every desire no matter how perverse, insane, criminal, or merely immoral. For the standards that would condemn crime or cruelty derive from religion, compassion, or the kind of reason that rejects purely instrumental applications; and none of these outmoded forms of thought or feeling has any logical place in a society based on commodity production.

The Culture of Narcissism – CHRISTOPHER LASCH

How can you imagine what particular region of first ages a man's untrammelled feet may take him into by the way of solitude – utter solitude without a policeman – by the way of silence – utter silence . . .? These little things make all the great difference. When they are gone you must fall back upon your own innate strength, upon your own capacity for faithfulness . . . You are being assaulted by powers of darkness.

Heart of Darkness – JOSEPH CONRAD

Psychosis is the final outcome of all that is wrong with a culture.
JULES HENRY

'Felt more like a policeman the other day than I did when I was a policeman.'
JOHN MANNERS

If a craftsman creates something beautiful, but does so on external command, we may admire what he does but despise what he is.
WILHEM VON HUMBOLDT

distress restrictions

Three a.m. Has been for weeks.

Been suspended nine months. Nine months out and still no trial date fixed. Nine months date still suspension fixed. Still. Trial suspension out fixed. Nine months. No out date trial fixed suspension. Out fixed date suspension trial. Nine months.

Suspension. Neither one thing nor the other. A mid-air feeling, not earthed. A bit of a distance between me and everything. Nothing looks quite real. I don't feel that normal interaction with the world, with things.

Can't sleep, can't read, can't listen to music.

I'm so tired all the time but I can't sleep. So tired. Every few days I get a clutch of ragged, merciful sleep.

Can't read. The words seem like the chatter of another life form. Irrelevant. Nothing to do with me. In an old magazine article lying around I tried to read some piece about manic depression, but she was writing in the clucky Esperanto of those who've already decided to live another day. Couldn't take it in. Something strange: reading the article, first one, then another, then every single word looked as if it was spelt wrong. Surely that's not how they are, how they've always been?

Can't listen to music. Makes me edgy and empty. Can't watch TV. Well, not properly. Channel-hop, three channels a second with the dibber. This goes on for hours. I flash through the friezes like a runaway train passing a station, a hundred stations. Me, the cable and the night. Sometimes I'm just sitting there slumped in front of the telly and it's so difficult to move that it crosses my mind just to piss where I'm sitting. So far I've resisted the urge.

Hope is an exhausting emotion and waiting-rooms are tiring places.

Waking up now I'm relieved to find that the depression and emptiness I was begging sleep to carry off has gone. But as always in the hour or so it takes me to get dressed (if I haven't slept in my clothes) and clean my teeth (for their full day's grinding ahead) and spill coffee on myself the black mood returns like an expanding hot stain. A sinking and rotting in the guts immobilizes me. And then – as now – I have to just sit there and suffer all these thoughts of suicide and despair and regret and failure and the ugliness of the world to come at me. It's like being on Public Order at a demo or riot when you just have to take the shit: a lightning-rod for all the ill-will in the world.

Late afternoon now.

Hard to get outdoors. I haven't got out the house for a couple of weeks now – when the milk ran out I did without.

House arrest. Solitary. I can't even talk to Kieran because of him being a defence witness.

At the start of my suspension I used to go driving. Though I had nowhere to go, the atmosphere of the car – all purpose and meaning – gave a partial relief. But now I've spent that reserve of purpose and my aimless journeys have left their spirit in the car's interior like a flat battery. A few months ago I sat in the car. I put the key in the ignition and jiggled the gear stick. It wobbled like a loose tooth, like it was broken. I pulled on the steering-wheel, but hadn't the will to make that extra effort to heave it through the steering-lock. I took the key out.

Time for a walk.

Been slobbing round the house in the same old grubby

strides. But I'm not gonna get changed because the light's already failing and I don't want to miss all the daylight again. (Been trying to get it together to go for a walk for a few days.) Flick tiny salt 'n' vinegar crumbs from the creases in my lap. There are some splashes of toothpaste or milk at the top of the leg. I check with the mirror that the white stain doesn't look like spunk (or that it isn't spunk). For the last few days I haven't bothered to get changed out of the comfy old shirt that I've been sleeping in. The collar's a bit rumpled, but I put on a tie which straightens that out and a jacket which covers the stain at the top of my strides.

I hit the street at the first attempt and head up into Archway in the fresh open air. Walking.

I feel curiously detached under this low-watt sky, perhaps because of not getting changed: it's like I've still got my indoors head on. A wonky, loose paving slab knock-knocks as I walk over it.

I've got to relearn just how to walk in the street: where to look, how to avoid bumping into people and a whole load of pedestrian etiquette besides. Outside Archway tube I walked smack bang into the *Big Issue* badge-vendor, knocking a whole stack of *Big Issue*s out of his arm and on to the pavement.

'Sorry mate, I'm really sorry, I was miles away . . .'

'Fuck's *sake*!' he says, giving me a black look before bending down to retrieve the magazines which have slipped right under the railings, spilling into the gutter.

I turn off into a quiet side-street, my pace slackens. Numbers painted in white on black plastic dustbins, sleeping policemen whose high humps have, by some later council edict, been shaved off so they are half-height. Halfway down the street a high window open despite the cold has old-school funk blaring out. Inconsiderate but not my concern. Not any more. Not for the time being.

Holloway Road's sealed off. Once again a chunk of the city

is brought to a standstill and everyone is made just that bit more tense and uptight by the same, small group of committed Irishmen who work for Murphy's.

The Cancer Research Shop is so small it's like a shrine to the unknown family. Here is the dead man's overcoat, his wide-lapel jackets. Here are his knackered shoes for you to walk a mile in and know what life was like for him. His ties. The board-games the family liked to play, the albums you thought no one would ever have bought. A strange weird extended family whose money ran out in the late seventies, early eighties. They were stuck in time and life wiped them out. The musty, loser smell gets to me and I jump out the shop as fast as a booster.

I feel like a killer in these black leather gloves. No one else is wearing gloves. Then again I am a killer. In the New Year the court will tell me whether I'm a good killer or a bad killer. I'd like to know. It's all gonna be out there, the talk, but the answer is in a tiny inward balance in my mind or soul. And even I don't even know.

All the etched, grey, skew-whiff faces of the poor on Junction Road: old faces fucked this way by cheap teeth, that way by troubles.

The fact that I don't have anywhere to go in particular starts to slow me down. Crossing to the traffic-island by the Archway roundabout, feel like I haven't everyone else's energy as they dash across.

And so I stand where I am. Try to make up my dwindling mind whether to just buy milk, fags and go home or whether to carry on walking up Archway Road and get the milk and fags on my way back. Just then a student with pale skin in Levellers chic approaches. 'If you've come to stop the road being built,' I think, 'I'm afraid you're a bit late, Mr Cunt.'

Light brown tatty dreads, an orange nylon rucksack – full of juggling clubs, no doubt. He wears one of those stupid fucking Persian hats they all get on their year off in Goa: his little reality trophy. But all my prickliness melts as he walks up, smiles and becomes the first person to talk to me for seventeen whole days and nights.

'Excuse me officer, am I going the right way for the Forum, please?'

'No,' I replied, 'you wanna go back down that road you just came from, and then it's about, er, half a mile on your right.'

'Back down there and on the right? Thanks.'

Oh Jesus, that felt fucking *good*! Off up Archway Hill, my steps resprung with real purpose now. Not breaking my brisk stride I pull the chinstrap down, humming. I pound up Archway Hill in the chilly sunshine on and on, stronger and stronger, the rocket-shaped shadow before me travelling over the pavement like a guided missile.

the doorman

Uniform back from the dry-cleaners. Felt more like a policeman the other day than I did when I was a policeman. Sometimes then I just felt like a security guard for all God's share-holders.

It's funny what they take away from you and what they don't. They take your warrant card but not your uniform; they take your nightstick but not your handcuffs.

Up at six a.m. Out the flat at seven. A cold, sharp, bright morning.

Walking, walking. Walking sorts out my head. I vault the railings at Euston Road. For the last eight months I've been so tired but now I've got all this energy to burn.

On the corner of Marylebone High Street and Baker Street stands a stocky, fifty-year-old down-and-out wearing a black dress-shirt and black bow-tie. A full head of fine, straight, ruddy-brown hair slicked back perfectly and still slightly wet.

He is with three standard-issue dossers. Not yet ready for the day the Night Shelter has issued them, they sit on the pavement in their filthy rags. But not him. He stands in black frilly shirt, bow-tie, and the cheap grey suit he folds under his pillow in the pissy Night Shelter and presses smooth with violent dreams.

His sand-blasted, ruddy face looks somehow like it used to be redder – suggesting that he's beaten the bottle and been on tea and tap water for some time now. A sand-blasted face, cold-shaven with some long-service, chipped, white plastic Bic and a bit of dry soap.

Maybe the black dress shirt and dickie bow is because he was once a bouncer. He has the face for it: a boxer's face, the boxer who refused to go down . . .

He stands with purpose against the day, present and correct as the world goes to its work. The entry for self-respect in the city's encyclopaedia.

But doesn't he know? Doesn't he know there's no way back for him? What's he gonna do? Stay standing and wait for a change in the world? That, my friend, will take longer than the collective lifetimes of all the dead men whose overcoats your slumped pals are wearing. Stay standing though you're gonna have more months than hot dinners?

Like all true heroism, it is unspectacular and long term and with nothing really to show for it among the Wonderbra billboards and radios booming from warm cars. It wins whatever obscure point heroism wins somewhere in the collective soul, and registers itself only in something beautiful about the man, for anyone in the mood to notice.

I keep walking. Fifty yards up Baker Street a young man in full nineteenth-century, stripy-cuffed police uniform stands outside the 221B Sherlock Holmes Museum. He grins sheepishly when our eyes meet. I do a kind of mock puffing-up my chest as if inspecting the parade, pretending to show the lanky, saggy-shouldered geek how to do it. He's not to know I'm off-duty. Way off.

'It's all changed mate,' I tell him, 'it's all changed.'

Then again, perhaps not. It hasn't changed because police work brings you into contact with the primeval, the primordial. You can hear it in atavistic terms like Caucasian – as if we were all still walking round the Mesopotamian Basin with clubs like the nightstick they took away from me. You can hear it in the pre-Roman geography of *West Mercia* or the Cambrian topography of *Thames Valley* (from whose limestone they exhume the remains of a Piltdown Woman, skull smashed with a rock, feet in Reeboks).

Night patrol brings you up against the evil beyond the edge of civilization. Only it's not as cut and dried as the first Roman wall built hard against the marshes of West Mercia. There's no simple geography. You can't separate it into areas, into individuals – it's happening within and without everyone all the time. That's why when the Super said, *'During the fight were you fighting as a policeman or as a man?'* I wanted to say that no one is a policeman in a fight. They weren't invented then.

london damage control

Cranking up Lever Street, nine a.m. I stay out of division on my patrols: don't want to be eyeballed by police or thieves, friends or enemies, don't want to have to explain why I'm in uniform.

An engineer sits on the pavement. He has lifted a hatch out of London and his feet dangle in the hole above yellow plastic pipes and black cable. He sits in front of a green telecom cabinet, open to reveal clutches of delicate wires the colour of hundreds and thousands, where the exchange flex meets distribution wires. He clips his red phone to a series of wires, listening, listening . . . each wire a distilled hum of the talk of the town, the parish wail, the mean pitch of a thousand calls. He looks stressed-out, lethargic, his movements are heavy. Too big a responsibility for one man, all this. All this spiritual monitoring, listening, adjusting. He runs dirty thumbs over tired eyes. And it's only nine o'clock.

The sign on the busted black gates says LONDON DAMAGE CONTROL. Its derelict forecourt is overwhelmed with the backlog: chunks of plaster from a wall, empty plastic bottles, sweet wrappers, an old mattress, a cement-caked, punctured wheelbarrow full of filthy clothes, a smashed and splintered beer crate, worn-out engine parts and a perished fan-belt.

I pick up the pace. A few blocks further, in a side-street of council terraces, I spy a ground-floor window full of handwritten notices. Three sheets of A4. I stop to read the block-capital green felt-tip:

> YOU WATCH AND YOU WAIT AND WHEN I GO OUT YOU BREAK IN AND ROB. YOU WAIT TO SEE WHEN I GO OUT. I HAVE TO SIT IN ALL THE TIME. I AM TRAPPED IN HERE AND CANNOT GO OUT!

Sellotaped above this is another sheet of paper with more green, felt-tip block capitals:

> THREE TIMES YOU HAVE BROKEN IN. STOP WATCHING AND WAITING TO STEAL FROM ME. YOU DO NOT NEED TO STEAL. GET A JOB. I HAVE ASKED THE COUNCIL TO MOVE ME BUT THEY DO NOT LISTEN. NOR DO THE POLICE.

I knock at the door. No answer. I bang on the window, wincing in case she thinks I'm them. I stand in front of the double-thickness net curtains. If she's in, and not hiding behind the toilet, she will make out the conehead alien silhouette of a standing police-officer come to save her.

She lifts the bottom square of the nets. To do this she has first to pull out a drawing-pin holding it to the sill.

She opens the jemmy-scarred door, saying, 'That was quick. For once.' She lets me in, looking out defiantly at the steps immediately opposite. 'That's where they congregate – on those steps, and that's where they live too.' We go in through the kicked-in door of her ground-floor flat.

She looks much less vituperative than her notes. Much less mad, too. She glances at me with an easy smile and raises her hands a few inches off the arms of the chair in a little gesture of resignation. She is about sixty, magnified eyes behind tinted-frame glasses. Her pretty, clear-skinned face has wrinkles in strange places. I wonder what possible expressions could put vertical lines on a face.

'Do you mind if I smoke?' she asks.

'It's your house,' I answer, perching on the arm of a green armchair with wooden insets designed to rest a cup of tea on during peaceful retirement by the sea.

'Do you want one?' She holds out the royal purple pack of John Player Specials.

'Well, I'm not supposed to but I think I will. No, it's OK, I've got my own here.'

'You don't need to perch there, you can sit down.'

'Thanks.'

'That's no bother. I'm just glad you're here. I've been phoning and phoning the police and they keep promising to send someone round and they never do. They just think it's that mad woman again – she's just paranoid. Well I *am* paranoid because I don't know when it's going to happen next.'

I don't know what comment will do, so I just say, 'Well, I believe you.'

'And I have to go out to phone. But I've not been back long this time before you've come.'

'What have they took?'

A big sigh . . .

'I had a rental telly went – not even mine; money – I try to keep it all in postal orders for security but they go too. Jewellery, not much, but all I've got, all I had. They even took a frozen chicken.'

'Plus you have to go out again to phone the council to get them to come and put new locks on.'

'Yeah,' she says, meeting my eyes for the first time, like a daughter.

'How long does it usually take them?' I ask.

'They're quicker than you,' she flashes. 'Well, your colleagues, anyway.'

'Well, if I go across the road and say we've had a complaint . . . but then they can just say it wasn't them.' She looks down at folded hands on her lap, a cigarette smoking out of the top of eight knuckles. She's heard all this before, but I carry on, unable to think of anything better to say. 'And even if I got a warrant it may be that your stuff isn't there any more.'

She looks sad at the thought of her stuff off on a long junket. 'Or we could mark your property and next time they steal, we can trace it all the way back . . .' I trail off.

'Well, I appreciate you coming round anyway.'

We sit in silence for a bit. I watch our smoke form a hard-edged right-angle where it folds against the shaft of light through net-curtained window; light slanting down in the stare trajectory of those who watch and wait.

She nudges the ashtray towards me. I look around her room in silence.

Has she got any family? There's no photos anywhere. She is a woman alone in the world, and yet you always expect to see some photos. There aren't any.

'I'm John. What's your name?'

'Jill.'

'Hi Jill. Do you mind if I ask – um . . . er . . . I've noticed there aren't any pictures anywhere.'

She looks up again, levelly, defending her last patch. 'I've put them in a drawer. I don't want them seeing them when they break in, you know what I mean? Face-down in a drawer.'

I bought a six-inch wooden photo-frame the other day. Snappy Snaps. Saw it in the window. Shrink-wrapped with a photo of a model in place. A kind face, her light-brown hair blowing slightly over her face. She's grinning because we're halfway through a perfect picnic and she was right to fall in love. At first I left her in the frame as a kind of joke. But as the nights evaporated into chilly dawns, and the days blacked out again, I began to get a kind of comfort from her. Patron saint of a life we didn't lead, the path we never took. Smiling and waiting for us in some suspended-time parallel universe. Same sort of comfort I knew as a kid, staring at the kind woman on the sleeve of *Top of the Pops* compilation albums. Not the original artists. My friend. Looking at me with understanding and affection, big eyes in seventies black eyeliner, as she stood in string-mesh, hip-slipped bikini, the surf around her knees as the needle went *everybody was kung everybody was kung everybody was kung everybody was kung . . .*

'When did you last go shopping?' I ask embattled Jill, prisoner in her own home.

Everybody was kung fu fighting . . .

'Properly? Not for months. I have to live off junk food from the corner shop.'

'What, stuff that you can nip out and get in five minutes?'

'Crisps and bread rolls,' she says.

'Well Jill, I'm just coming to the end of my shift. Why don't you go shopping now? Proper shopping. I'll wait here.'

She raises her eyes to me. A smile sidles on to her face, turning up one corner of her mouth.

'No. Thanks, but I'd be gone an hour 'cos I'm gonna have to go to the Post Office first for money, and then I like Sainsbury's in Camden, and then the fruit market on Inverness Street.'

'Well, with any luck they'll try and break in.'

'No, they see who comes and goes. Are you serious?'

'Yeah.'

'You *sure*?'

Her eyes light up. She comes forward with her hands out two feet away from my face, stopping at the Manners force-field to mime cupping my nephew face in her hands. She goes into the hall to get her handbag and coat.

'Goodbye,' she shouts, slamming the door without even coming back into the room.

And now I'm alone in her flat.

Maybe she'll never come back. Maybe now I'm left with her life. Won't see her again. Cackling off into next week, like someone who's finally off-loaded a chain-letter.

I feel like one of those rota-system mourners at a vigil in olden days, someone trained to sit and wait for the tragedy to pass. I thought I'd be used to this, but no . . .

This is a purer vigil than my own. Here there's no chance of a phone-call or a letter from the Crown Prosecution Service. This is the control sample of my vigil. And now what?

I feel trapped. Cramped, stiff and aching like a cold-turkey addict in a holding cell, ready to confess.

There's a one-way window in Interview Room 1. You can step out the room and look through it at the prisoner. Innocent suspects pace around fretting, moving their lips; the guilty just rest their head on their arms: arsed, tired, bored.

Can't look out the window in case the kids see me.

A small lampshade hangs off the bulb in the middle of the ceiling. What they don't steal must feel as though they've passed comment on it: 'We've left you this because it's shit.'

This is hard waiting. Just me and me. Now what?

Oh no.

Oh no. Just *imagine* – oh no.

Imagine if – oh no, that would be terrible . . .

. . . if she came back and I'd robbed her!

I laugh out loud, giggling uncontrollably, trying to keep the noise down as if she were in the other room. In stitches, howling. How hideous that would be! I can't stop. My hahahas are deep and full-throated. Remonstrative echoes bounce off the bare walls of her quiet two rooms.

Or if I smashed up her flat! Oh no, that would be awful. Imagine if I wrote all over her walls! Tears. Imagine if she came back and I'd written JOHN 4 JILL in great big letters on the wall! My hand taps the marker pen in my jacket side-pocket and then I fold the flap over the pocket to seal the pen in. Or if I wrote FUCK ALL CUNTS and then completely denied I'd done it. Claimed I couldn't see it! Said it was there before!!! JOHN 4 JILL Great big fucking letters. Hahahaha! Hahaha! Oh man, that would freak her out. Oh dear, oh dear. Oh deary me.

She hasn't removed the boards over her back door since the last robbery (or the one before).

On her bedroom door is another notice in green felt-tip block capitals:

> THERE'S NOTHING OF VALUE IN HERE. KEEP OUT. I NEED PRIVACY! YOU KNOW THERE'S NOTHING IN HERE. THERE IS STILL NOTHING IN HERE.

I open the bedroom door tentatively as if in fear of someone being in there.

In the top drawer, under an old swatch of wallpaper, framed photos lie face to face. A tin-framed, just-short-of-focus colour photo on faded paper. Under battered polythene like an old savings book it shows a 1950s girl on a stripy pink deck-chair squinting with the small-garden sun in her eyes.

A black and white photo in a glass frame. A woman in a wide-lapel polka-dot blouse pretending a parked motor bike is hers. She stands next to it gripping the handles, leaning down as if doing ninety. She smiles into the camera. Perfect teeth.

I lift the heavy brown chest of drawers. The complacent dust shows that I've found something the burglars never did. A letter. I pick it up between the nails of thumb and forefinger like evidence.

Spindly handwriting on brown, lined paper. The coarse paper is porous and sometimes at the beginning or end of a word the ink expands where the thoughtful pen paused.

A love-letter.

> *. . . and already I miss you . . . tell me the name of that*
> *soap you use so I can go and . . . I wish . . . you left your*
> *. . . . when will . . . touching your leg under the sea . . . .*
> *and no one knew . . . pretending to fasten my brooch in*
> *the Sussex bar . . . all my love, xxx Maggie.*

I take several goes replacing the letter in its holding square of dust.

The cheeky cow has been out two hours.

How does Jill manage it here day after day? No telly, no books. And only some racy memories to keep her warm.

What can I do? Read the *Hornsey Journal* double-page spreads she uses for a tablecloth. *The judge ordered the jury to return a not-guilty verdict on the two men after no evidence was offered by the prosecution.* Shorthand for someone got at the plaintiff or the witness. Another judge gives weight to the fact that the accused showed no remorse . . . The story continues under an empty glass vase. Forget it.

Wonder how much Lee's fulsome knowledge of court procedure influenced his decision to have a go. He knew that if he'd gone to court for assaulting a policeman I wouldn't be able to mention what I was trying to arrest him for. The court wouldn't even be told that he had form. I mean, that might make him look like some kind of, well, *criminal*! And the CPS can't be having that.

He knew then that he'd only have to say he had no idea what I could possibly have against him. The fact that I am legally not able to specify it would leave me having to make vague grumblings about him being known to me. This, he knew, would reinforce the jury's unavoidable impression of me as having some sort of grudge against Mr suit-and-tie Andrew. All this was stuff he knew, and who knows what echo of it hummed down his synapses when he made that fatal decision?

There are occasional moments in history when the need for Justice with a capital J outweighs barrister etiquette. The Nuremberg judges, for example, never said, 'Now I want you to discount all you may have heard or read in the press about Mr Goering, Mr Goebbels and Mr Himmler. I am aware that many newsreels have sought to present the defendants in a bad light, but I want you all to strike all that from your minds. As far as you are concerned, they are innocent men.'

The daylight world's code of justice is as out of touch with the truth and reality of evil as we all are until it touches us. The public have no idea how fantastically quaint and naïve the idea of innocent-until-proven-guilty seems to a police officer or, for that matter, to anyone who lives on the same estate as the slag. They know he's guilty. I know he's guilty. He knows he's guilty. And he knows I know he's guilty. But the Crown – perhaps because of its ancient debt to robber barons – says he's innocent until he really, really wants to go to prison. Innocent until proven careless.

Sounds like an apology for verbals and planting, but it's not. No officer I know has ever done this. I think the reason for this is because you don't want to taint yourself with the evil. You want to keep definite lines between you and the bad. When you mess around with those lines, be it drink-driving, planting evidence, receiving seized goods, you open yourself to invasion by all the weird forces around in the night. Then again, maybe I'm not the sort of cop they'd tell.

Here in Jill's empty chamber is the first time I've thought about Lee Andrew for a long time. Then again maybe I've been thinking about nothing else. The Super never seemed totally satisfied with my description of how he died. Me neither. Gaps. There are gaps in what I can remember about the fight. Black holes that will tear me all apart? If I'm innocent then I should be able to just let memories about him and all just come, just come at me.

Lee. Lee Andrew. Lee and Tony Andrew. That balcony at the top of the tower with all the dishes and aerials. What was the name of the place? The something Estate or something Tower, something House. Tony razzing around in the white Hi-Ace. I think Lee had a black 4x4 Isuzi or some such shit. Not the language of remorse. Lee. First-name terms. Calling him Lee by an effort of will just now, I was hoping to key into or open the way to warmth, remorse. They didn't show, and without them 'Lee' just sounds sneering, patronizing, like he's my bitch. Breaconbridge. The Breaconbridge Estate.

That didn't go exactly as –

A loud rattling of bunchy keys in the lock makes the door frame shudder. (Still nervous after all these years hearing keys in the door in case it's Kenneth the coach-driver back late from the Stag's Head.)

'Give us a hand, there's some more outside,' she says.

A blue Sierra minicab drives off leaving two more stuffed shopping bags on the dusty pavement.

I put them on the kitchen floor next to a holder of rotten vegetables. She turns to me, saying, 'These are for you,' handing me a bouquet of damp daffodils wrapped in quality blue paper, and a chocolate policeman in a little plastic case.

Walking home. It's raining today and I'm as horny as all get out. A girl in a short black dress shelters under a news-agent's awning on Fortess Road. A nearly-pretty estate girl. Seventeen. The soft rain makes her bare legs intimate, her naked, sheltered legs. Indoors outdoors, inside out. Almost there.

It shouldn't be this way, dignifying shallow impulses with romantic ideas of being taken over by desire, carried away, awash.

Lust is really just a slight tingling in the testicular sub-basement. Yet despite this the *whole day* is National Horn Day. A State of Emergency is declared, democracy suspended, the rational debating chamber is shut down in favour of pumping rhetoric.

They don't know they're doing it, but men look at women in the street the way police-state cops look at civilians. You notice this particularly when a woman crosses the street swinging her bag or singing as if she owned the place, as if *she* owned the place rather than us men. You see it in the faces of men when a woman wears less than textile-regulation-minimum. Men think they're just staring, but it's that cautionary, chin-down, 'Are you sure?' type of stare; a devilling stare of warning and affronted authority. The stare that says, 'You may well have incurred a penalty ... or be about to.' Even though they don't know they're doing it, even though those aren't their thoughts explicitly.

Buddhists deal with pain by focusing on the fact that it is localized to one particular part of the body, and is not, though it feels like it, actually making the whole body throb. A bit of self-discipline, a bit of self-mastery is all that's required ... except we don't want to be masters of ourselves. Oh, the foolish, end-of-pier, grinning faces of men when you try to talk seriously about resisting lust.

Back here now after telling some builders off for whistling at a girl. Eating my chocolate policeman and watching telly with the flowers in my lap. The news.

A while ago they brought in performance-related pay for teachers and police. So what happened? Schools expel difficult kids, grades go up in the purged schools. Arrest rates go up because we keep arresting the same kids they threw out, who go out and re-offend 'cos they know there's fuck-all we can do to juveniles. But here tonight is your newsreader with A1 statistics and thumbs up when in reality things have got much, much worse all round.

Watching the news a cop wonders how each news item will tilt the ether, how it's gonna change the vibe on the street, the colour of the sky. It's beyond me to define, but there's an index-link between the share price and the knife in your back at the cashpoint. There is a connection somewhere between G8 handshakes and, say, the way graffiti migrates. First it was just white lorries and vans; then it moved to any colour lorries and vans, then it moved to white cars – which is where it's at now, in Holloway division at least. New crimes are round the corner, waiting like condensation for the right conditions. Kidnappings will be a major twenty-first century player; extortion demands will be nailed to the door of modest semis.

'*The government today pledged tax breaks for enterprise . . .*' says the newsreader. Now I'm independent, my instincts for detection swivel their gaze to new directions . . . Tax Breaks for Enterprise. Rearrange these letters and get Income Support for the Very Rich Paid For out of My Fucking Pocket. Rearrange and get No More Shekel for Dibble Choppers – my sky rocket – which will just have to rust and fall out of the sky into a parched and fenced-off Severn-Trent as we take points-failure-wounded from hozzy to hozzy on the rumour of a bed.

The Super was talking to me and Kieran once about her old nick in West Riding. She worked the Tobruk Estate, a satellite of what was once a mining town. Tobruk wasn't so bad until after the mines were shut down, after which it became The Estate That Time Forgot. From being a law-abiding community, she saw it go up 80 per cent in reported crime in the space of five years; as she said, 'It went from being a fairly decent community to a holding pen.' The kids break into boarded-up council houses and rip out copper piping to sell to the scrap-yard. These people have always scratched a living from the fossilized remains of a lost age. Only once it was coal and now it's copper.

'It's all to do with fucking shares, and the City, short-term profits. We should go into the City and nick the fucking lot of them!'

The Super looked at me in a curious new way, pleased, perhaps, to find I wasn't a mason.

People are always surprised when they meet you at parties that cops have political opinions (if they ever stop moaning about parking tickets long enough to find out). But most cops have seen something like what Sandra Rowse our Super has seen.

As a police-officer you're not supposed to express your personal political beliefs, which translates of course as being only able to express the personal political beliefs of the ruling classes: banks, big business, the MP for British Aerospace, the member for ICI. And so when we're on our own we love to talk about where society's gone wrong, and always in the head-shaking tone of the never-consulted, in-the-field expert. Not all of it radical, but not all of it bring-back-the-death-penalty either. (Not *all* of it.)

The way civilians say they don't want to be taxed, like there's a choice! There's always a tax. It's just a question of how you want to pay. Access Control Systems, Intruder Alarms, Automatic Porch Lighting, Home CCTV, Logic Control Entry Grilles, 24-Hour Monitoring Service.

All this crisis talk about the crime rate, but hasn't it always been this way? Bit more humane here, bit less there. Unsteady but holding. The first policeman was shot in 1798 during a riot by river smugglers on the Thames. In 1896 a Manchester teenager who murdered another in a gang fight was only charged with common assault. The average age of everyone ever hung in Britain is thirteen. There's less guns in London now than in the forties and fifties. There's less footpads around.

The government always go to the US to look at crime and the big-city solution. On police courses there's over-your-head projections from Greater Manchester DIs about 'the latest

American techniques'. But they never send fact-finding teams to look at how they *create* so much crime in America. To suss the latest house-on-the-hill techniques of crime creation before they happen here.

Oh fuck me.

Oh no. All these thoughts like – like I was still a part of decent people! Like I was still one of the good academically wondering how to make the world better, criticizing those whose views are harmful when I am not part of all that any more. I have made someone dead. I am on the outside of all that. Coming back from Jill's earlier, I stopped off to get some money out the Woolwich and the cashier woman said, 'Hello again, how are you? You've not been in for a while . . .'

And I thought, will she see my picture in the paper soon and know all about me? And I sensed how terrible it is going to be to lose that common connection with others, with strangers. What a terrible loss to be no longer part of everyone else. To be outside of fellow feeling. Not to be one of everyone any more. Upal the outcast. To sit in a cinema, say, and not to be on the side of right in the battle between Good and Evil.

And now here it comes again. Another night channel-scanning while I silently panic. Acute loneliness, a semi hard-on, searching and never resting. Thinking if only it wasn't too late to phone someone. If only I had someone to phone. If only there was a woman with me now to hug and to hold then I wouldn't feel so bad.

Everything seems distant or at one remove as if I had no body, no human self. It's been like this for years. Only then there was work. Working all the hours God gave me so as not to have to face the ones Satan gave me. Staying out long hours because I knew that when I came home late alone, Satan would be plumping up the cushions and saying:

Ah, there you are. I thought I'd wait up. So, um, on your own then . . . ? Oh dear, oh deary, deary me. Well, what am I gonna fuck you over with tonight? You wanna watch telly, eh? Go ahead. Put it on. What's this programme? 'Club Nation'. Yes, by all means put your hand down the front of your trousers if that makes you feel comfortable. Just look at all these girls, look at how they're giving it out . . . what's that? It does your head in, the aggressive competitive atmosphere of the club, the hard spirit, the revealing clothes that say fuck off and come here at the same time? Hey, never mind, let's channel-hop. A couple of hours of this and then you'll really feel like you've achieved something. Don't fancy it? Well, you can always . . . talk to me.

Frozen chicken sandwich. These days I can ignore sell-by dates, cooking instructions and star-marked freezer compartments. Pop pink bits of icy chicken in my mouth, knowing salmonella can't live in the acidic, black, molten lava of my dismal guts.

The porn channel. Glary American video. I hate American porn. There's something extra-mean about American porn. The men all have mean sadistic faces and say aggressive stuff like, 'You like this, don't you!' The women have to look distressed, they have to yelp like they're in pain if they want to work again. Or else they're kind of submissive-aggressive too in the declared war of American sexuality: '*Fuck me harder, fuck my bitch's arse!*' I hate it. It scalds my mind, and I've been putting in about three hours of this every night for months.

Phoned an 0898 number. All calls are charged international rate and women, love and comfort are a foreign country, half the world away.

Back out again now. The only thing that makes it better is the only thing that ever did. Back out again now. Tired (but my vigilance can seep with the night now only an hour or so away from first light and the dawn chorus of car alarms).

For the last ten minutes I've been trying to track the howl of a burglar alarm down to its source. Running. Maybe they're in the house and her screams are lost under the siren's wail. Still a few streets away the alarm cuts out. I stop. Hold my tarry breath. Listen. Nothing. Now I'll never know where it was. I wander round a few streets in the general direction, but don't find any broken windows, doors or a woman sitting on the front step of a private mews house, too scared to go in.

And now I feel wound-down, silly and pointless on my independent patrol. Like a sleepwalker who wakes to find himself outside Safeway in pyjamas holding a kettle. I must tighten up my procedure. I gotta think of something so I'm not just chasing burglar alarms. Not just walking around with a funny hat on.

Hornsey Road. Insomniac, in her thirties and a limp, white T-shirt wanders in a lit third-storey window. In a world without sound she has to guess when the kettle's boiled, and pours the hot water with the sad concentration of people that don't know you're watching them in their own home. She's like this every night. I take my helmet off so the badge doesn't catch the light.

scanner

It looks like a walkie-talkie. A chunky clutch of black plastic heavy in the hand with a rubber antenna. PRO-62 TRIPLE CONVERSION HYPERSCAN. 200 CHANNEL DIRECT ENTRY AM/FM PROGRAMMABLE SCANNER. Brand-name: REALISTIC. The volume dial clicks it on. I press PGM, ENTER, then MON. Press the down-arrow to scan south from 934.087 FM, listening in on random phone-calls within a two-mile radius. One of the two callers has to be within a two-mile radius. When I get below 911.000 it's just static and I press the up-arrow and go back to the top of the slide.

I listen in on home phones, payphones, mobiles, office switchboards and sometimes, strangely, *music*. Greek-Cypriot bazoukis and balalaikas, Hungarian folk zithers. Is this the head-height frequency of a coat-hanger basement station serving Green Lane's Azerbaijani community? Or did an Armenian folk troupe's minibus crash on the M25, leaving all the musicians in iron lungs and tetraplegic hook-ups, so that the only way they can jam now is on a six-way conference call? Whatever, however, I approve. It is a welcome light interlude when it comes. A respite.

Two hard-sounding estate girls:

> ' . . . *She's saying it's nothing to do with me, but I said no, she shouldn't be saying those things, and then when Darren come over, I said no, she should fuck herself 'cos it had been agreed, definitely agreed that she was gonna*

pay, but I just think if she was being like that then she's got to expect a slap . . .'

. . . *Blatant*, agrees her mate.

Many calls are reported speech endlessly tidying up estate-etiquette, self-justification, showing how last night's behaviour was totally to code, however whacked that code may be.

> ' . . . *I said to him "Do you know what my dog's like? Do you know what my dog's like? So shut the fuck up, then. Why am I even talking to you?" I told him, "Do you know what my dog's like? Do you know what my dog's like?"'*

Pressing up, down, up, down, all the time trying to home in on Slag Central. My own personal Control! To find out what's going down and where and when and who. Criminal intelligence.

I've never really believed what they say about fishing being the most popular sport in Britain, but here's the proof. Here's yet another call where two forty-year-olds are arranging to go fishing. Common to these calls is that both geezers always sound heavily reluctant. Like going fishing is the last thing they want to do, like they'd been given two hundred hours' community fishing:

> '*Oh well, . . .* [sigh] *What time, then?'*
> '*Well, I'm gonna have to get to you about five a.m., six at the latest.'*
> '*Oh no. Really?'*
> '*Yeah, if we wanna catch anything.'* [Sigh.]
> '*'Ow long's it take to get there?'* [Sigh.]
> '*Hour?'*
> '*Tench?'*
> '*Yeah. And pike.'* [Sigh.]
> '*And pike?'*

'Yeah.'

'Oh shit. [Sigh.] Yeah.'

'What if the weather's like this, though?'

'Yeah, then we can forget about it.'

'OK. But how will we know?'

'Oh.'

'I'll tell you what, I'll set my alarm for half-four, look out the window, and if it's shit I'll tell you don't bother to come over.'

'Yep.'

'OK, we'll leave it like that.'

'I won't answer the phone, if I hear it ringing I'll just stay in bed.'

'OK.'

Bought my control from Tandy in Camden High Street this morning. The way the law stands you can listen in but it's illegal to act on information received. A policeman may not use a phone scanner. But I can.

'Marky. What's up?'

'How d'you know it was me?'

'Your number comes up on my phone.'

'How you doin'?'

'Good, yeah.'

'Yeah, good. Er, have you got any of those, er, CDs left.'

'Yeah, they're here now. How many do you want?'

'Can I have two? And, uh, have you got any rock music ones?'

'Mm-hmm.'

'Can I have a dozen?'

'Yeah, yeah.'

'What are the, uh, CDs like now?'

'Did you like the last lot?'

> '*Well, I felt they were a bit sketchy, er, a bit too much treble in the mix type thing . . .*'
>
> '*Yeah, well you know the stuff from before, it's like that.*'
>
> '*Oh yeah, they were much more mellow, bit more bass in the mix.*'
>
> '*Bit more jazz-funk.*'
>
> '*Yeah.*'
>
> '*This is the same production values.*'
>
> '*You in now? I'm by yours.*'
>
> '*Yeah. All right. Bye.*'
>
> '*Yep.*'

No details. Inoperative. But I put the key-lock on that frequency so I can come back and visit them again.

The paranoia of the short-wave eavesdropper:

> '*He's under manners, don't worry abaht it, 'e's on his manners nahow, he's bin told, he didn't knah who you are, it won't happen agen, don't give it another thought. You go back there tonight, and you'll be whooshed strite through.*'

I'm sure they can hear me, or that their phones will register some interference. But no. A tentative heckle or two at first, followed by a pause. They can't hear.

> '*Where are you, Mummy?*'
>
> '*I'm up in Teesside.*'
>
> '*Where's that?*'
>
> '*You know, where your bedroom is with the Batman light? I'm there. Oh look, don't cry, I'll be back in a few days.*'

Having been in almost as many strange flats and houses as there are burglaries and domestics, I fancy I can picture the rooms that go with the voices. This last one recalls the desexed bedrooms of parents with young children which always look like store rooms, where their sex life has been packed away for the next five years somewhere among the battered cardboard boxes of breakables, kitchen implements, the iron and ironing board and the clothes-horse that used to be an exercise-bike. Refugee clutter from the spare room that became the baby's room.

> 'I'm afraid he's in a meeting.'
> 'Is that Lisa?'
> 'Oh, hi Ben . . . Do you wanna leave a message?'
> 'Yeah, if you could just tell him that they're saying we agreed on an estimate, but I'm saying yeah, but it's a sixteen-foot room and the estimate was for twelve foot. We're agreed however that it's twenty foot wide . . .'
> 'Hold on, he's free now.'

I scan up and down. Balalaika and wailing from another Moroccan pirate station with a coatwire aerial. A couple of calls I think I can locate for definite: this might be the pay-phones in the Magistrate's Court:

> 'I got two years.'
> 'Two years! What are you gonna do?' says his girlfriend or sister.
> 'What you mean, what am I gonna do? I'm gonna do fucking bird, inni'?'

And the background *bing-bong-beng* on this call must be Euston station. An Arab voice on a mobile with maybe his suitcase between his feet:

> ' . . . hadji, ach'um mhuna th, zim tadj un t'alla . . .'

Bing-bong-beng! Scanning now, a couple of calls just ending, someone's answering service saying *You have no more messages.* I scan all the way down and all the way up. I turn the knob that says 'squelch' and the static grates against the air like a harsh stylus bouncing on the rubber turntable. And then . . . It's the tone first; the tone that lets me know evil is here. The lack of complication in the tone, that costly simplicity of manner, the illicit ease.

' . . . *I've been trying to stop it,*' says the voice on the scanner. '*Trying to stop myself doing it for so long, but I can't. All this time waiting, waiting. Nothing happens. It's building and building. Holloway, Clapton, Tottenham, somewhere the bitch goes . . .*' The scanner keeps getting interrupted by bursts of static. ' . . . *at night . . . somewhere like that . . . the white van . . . or just get up behind the lamb . . . and teach that bitch manners . . . I don't care any more. Fuck the law, that's no justice . . . kill that bitch in the back of the van.*'

'. . . *The Repairmen! Hahaha!*'

'*You in?*'

'. . .'*Cept I got me case coming up.*'

'. . . *You don't have to do the killing, you can always say you didn't know I was gonna do it until I did . . . It's nature, innit? Instinct, blood rage, got to go with it or you get cancer.*'

'. . . *Do you know where the slag lives?*'

'. . . *No, but it's in the area. Get . . . in the back of the van and do it by – you know, by that place where we were that time – you know, that evil street? 'Cos I can't wait any more, I dunno where the bitch lives, but it's definitely in the area . . . and the stupid slag likes to wander at night, . . . He's on his own . . . We can get up behind the lamb, and do it quickly, blade, quick, in-out, yeah? . . . Hold on . . . What? No, chucked me fag out the window . . .*'

'. . . *mid-twenties?*'

'*Twenty-six, twenty-seven — won't see twenty-eight, that's for fucking . . .*'

The scan keeps cutting out. I freeze stock-still in the middle of the room. If you move when the signal's weak then the scan-search slides away rolling up or down to a solid lock. The squelch static wails away like sirens in distress.

' *. . . We did 'em in the slaughteryard, but not, not there . . . no manners, fuck it . . . put my face up close and say, "You know what this is for?"*'

'*Or by where you can't be seen because of the wall, by the railway, by that tag that says sensei —*'

'*. . . Either there or somewhere else. Check it out, but you never know who's gonna be passing.*'

'*. . . You still on the broken bridge?*'

'*. . . You know where it is, dontcha, yeah, 'cept there's no signposts anywhere . . . that derelict shop.*'

'*. . . Tonight . . . where are you?*'

'*. . . I'm the doorman at the end.*'

'*Promised land?*'

'*Yeah.*'

The call cuts out. Scramble-static. Blood pumping behind my eyes, thoughts like jelly, legs like thoughts, cold-neck fever. The victim — the innocent 'lamb' (wow, that's brutal to think of the target like that) is somewhere now, this very night, walking. I see her already with her hair up in a conical bun, a slow switching, dawdling step, high heels that mean she can't run. Her? Why am I saying 'the lamb' is a she? ' *. . . bitch . . .*' Maybe the intended murder victim is male. '*Kill the bitch in the back of the white van . . .*' To slags like this men are 'bitches' and women are 'its': that's inflation. Man or woman? Think now. Remember. Which is it? Shit. Wish I had my best mind. Wish I wasn't dopey with dead time, slugged by these nine months of mental sub-division. '*He's on his own.*' It's a man.

Now all the rights and wrongs of whether I should be out on unlicensed patrol or not don't matter, and all the slack time tight. The black clip-on tie seems to snap in by itself. I scramble, tipping black gloves out of my helmet to the floor, tunic still unbuttoned, running out the door.

Pounding through empty streets, running down the clues. '*You still on the broken bridge?*' Maybe a builder repairing a broken bridge. '*The repairmen!*' Pedestrian footbridge over a motorway? But that wouldn't be broken, without them closing the road, unless, of course, it just had a few steps missing. An estate bridge? Or the walkway on a derelict estate? Yes. Good. Possible. A rotten, planked-up, no-entry bulwark over a remote stretch of Thames or Grand Union? '*The doorman at the end*'. This is the killer's macho posturing, feeling so good to be holding the keys to life and death, coolly holding open death's door and saying this way please. To control the end of another's life. Yes, that's it. Weird: there, in his bow-tie and dress shirt, was a doorman without a door, at the beginning of my patrol, a patrol without a mission then; and now – '*I'm the doorman at the end.*'

Where am I going? I slow down to a fast walk. Accept nothing. Believe no one. Confirm everything. ABC. OK. Let's go.

'*The slaughteryard . . .*' Smithfield?

Move on.

A butt-end on the pavement. A derelict shop.

Bollocks. And this is imminent: '*I can't wait any more . . .*'

The murder is imminent. '*We can get up behind the lamb, and do it quickly, blade, quick, in-out, yeah?*' And I'm not getting anywhere. Ten minutes to midnight and the clock is ticking. *The end* could be a place. The end of a street, or a street called Something End.

The Repairmen. Electricians? Mechanics? TV-repairmen? A gang name?

In the area is in this area or at least a two-mile radius. One of them was within a two-mile radius. Right. Somewhere out there in this same night air.

Midnight by Caledonia Park. *The broken bridge.* Sometimes you get a folly bridge in nineteenth-century parks. That could be vandalized enough to count as a broken bridge. I climb the high Victorian railings of the padlocked park, and walk across flat blackness looking for shadows.

No, there's no bridge here, broken or humped. Folly. I stand in the park as empty and dark and useless as this place. Oh what the fuck am I doing? I am on a broken bridge myself. I track back over wet grass. Where's the way out? Which way did I come in? I see a bench. I remember passing one on the way in. Head for the bench. I'll be able to see the railings when I get there. It's not a bench. It's a bundle on the ground. Across dark grass in murder park I move towards it. A body. Still. I step nearer the clump of dead human very slow, as if it might leap up and devour me. The body stirs. I step back. A woman. Black. But . . . severe points of light flash on face, hands, arms, shins, bare feet. I go nearer, and moonlight reveals these flashes as bleach burns. She is wearing yellow plastic sunglasses. She lies on a bath towel, plastic bottles next to her. And now I know who she is. Violet MacKenzie – nutter of this parish, or Ultra-Violet as Kieran calls her. Heard about her but never seen her before. A mythical beast. Legend has it she sat in a bath of bleach as a kid and now moonbathes in the pitch-black, locked-up park. Every mild night she smears herself with Piz Buin and tries to catch the night rays – the famous Ultra-Violet MacKenzie.

She turns on her side, leans on her elbow, forearm pointing

up vertically and raises her head in the crook of her arm to stare at me.

'GET AWAY!' she shouts.

I panic but say, 'It's all right, Violet.'

'GET AWAY! I'LL SCREAM!' she screams.

'I'm a police-officer.'

'YOU'RE NOT!'

'Sssh! Look at me! Police.'

'I know what the police look like! I know what the police look like!'

'Maybe if you take your sunglasses off, madam.'

'I'm not taking any clothes off.'

I step back a pace.

'I'M NOT TAKING ANY CLOTHES OFF!'

'Sssh!'

'You're not police! You're not police!' On her brow, between her eyes the bleach-fried skin rumples in burnt black flesh-folds. Among the rustling leaves her rumpled dark skin looks like the deep ridges of oak bark. Then she mumbles, 'I know all about you and what you get up to when you think no one's watching. And what you did.'

'What did I do?'

'*You* know,' she says, turning her back on me. 'You know, you know, you know, you know, know, know, no, no, no –'

'What did I do?'

'GET *AWAY*!' she explodes.

'WHAT DID I DO?' I shout. 'WHAT DID I DO?'

'AAAIIEEE AAAAGH, AAAAIEYYAAGGH!' She gets up, screaming in her long skirt, bent double as if suffering stomach pain, like she'd just swallowed some more bleach in the dark. 'AAAIIEE, AAAGHH!'

'Stop screaming! Please stop scream–!'

'AAAAGH! GO AWAY!'

'STOP SCREAMING!'

'AAAAIIEEE!' She runs at me.

'AAAHH!' I scream. I'm stuck. I can't run. I'm stuck. I run scalded with terror. Hit a hidden litter-bin keep running. Is she chasing? Her breath is every swaying shrub, leaf-whisper and the blanched breath of my running. On, on. I rip my trousers on the wrought-iron railings. Mad fucking bitch! Back out on the road again, safe as houses, safe as factories with security spotlights, safe as all the signs and painted lines of the Highway Code.

Walking now. By making black white and white black, she can act like the past never happened – and see right through me in the dark.

the same force

Full headlights in a pot-holed, one-way gully searching for the *evil street*. Cold hands on the steering-wheel, windows all the way down the better to feel evil in the air. But this ain't the way. Too removed. It's not working. I can cover more streets in the car but can't sense what I'm looking for. Park up. Get out. Walking. Yes, this is better. I walk through a deserted estate car-park. On track. Walking now in the cold night air gives me space and rhythm to try and put my concept of evil into words. This will be a start in tracking the street that feels evil. Talking to others about good and evil makes you sound mad: you leave the narrow band-width of acceptable conversation, spinning into the static crackle of unresolved electrical energy in the night. Walking alone in the night air now, it seems to me that there's a kind of conspiracy behind what people talk about. Daytime conversations stick with the coherent, and yet most of our experience is incoherent. When you think of the complexities behind even the simplest human interactions you realize we're constantly receiving a whole spectrum of impressions but only talk on the narrow band-width of stuff that is coherent. And so the majority of our impressions, the incoherent, are outlawed from talk.

I cut through an evil alley streaked with reeky piss and broken bottles. They say you can pass a hundred negative ions through a thing and then just one positive ion and suddenly it's positive, the electro-magnetic charge reversed. On night patrol I always felt like I was the positive ion, a one-man

Reclaim the Night march – like those sisters did that time. This alley feels evil but it's not a street and they definitely said *that evil street*. Let it draw me to it, let it pull my negative ions. Where was I?

They way I imagine evil is like nitrogen or carbon and we are semi-permeable membranes for it. It's in the air, all around us. It enters us in different compounds. Little things we do can make its existence take or perish, and it leaks into us also through the system, spores grown in the shadow of big business, like industrial poisons leaked into the high-profit water supply.

One freezing winter's day I had to do Public Order outside an asbestos factory. Didn't really need to be there 'cos the demonstrators were peaceable, middle-aged mums lobbying about something this asbestos factory had done thirty years ago. Victolic Asbestos, the company was called. That's right. A truncheon charge being out of the question, I started chatting with the goodly mums. Back in the 1960s, they told me, before the effects of asbestos were made public, the asbestos factory used to leave piles of the stuff in the street. The children of the estate played in the white sandpit, silvery-white dust running through their fingers. Tyre-marks from Raleigh Choppers on its edges, rubbing white sand in the face of the new kid. Playing Best Man Dead clutching an invisible gun-shot wound to the chest, falling from garage roof on to ash-white, rough-cut powder. Clark's commandos jumping off the high wall, landing on all fours up to knee and elbow, puffed out clambering free. Breathing it every day. On windy days it hid in hair and knitted jumpers, settled on kitchen window-sills by food scraps left for birds.

Thirty years on, the prizes in the Best Man Dead competition go to silicosis, lung cancer and asbestosis. And this winter's day there were all these middle-aged mums demonstrating outside to get compensation and recognition for the fallen. Victolic Asbestos, meanwhile, were lawyered up and fighting the women's claim. And there was me, as usual, standing between protest and property.

Maybe evil's a bit like that invisible asbestos, in the air every day. Growing up on the Cromwell Estate, say, or Cannoncourt, there's more evil in the air, more evil in you being there: the greed of big business which insists on a system where profits are privatized and costs socialized. So they breathe the cynical air like asbestos. This may in a few cases lead to a powerful immunity, but in most it just means you're breathing in more evil every day. A force of its own, evil mulitplies like cancer cells, a force of its own, a rip-tide.

It would be good if we could see the swirls and spores of evil, if we could see evil in the air, how it forms and bonds on a sub-molecular level within and without us. To see how every time you go with an instinct it gets stronger; every time you deny an instinct it gets weaker.

A tiny hardening of the heart in a towel-flicking City boy as he gang-bangs the currency to free up some more chips for the Bundes-casino, the job-wrecker's allowance. Follow the swirls and spores down to the brown mould dotted with black on the filthy air-vent windows of the school, the dripping roof and the tattered books.

At my first nick in Liverpool they had helicopters with thermal-imaging night-sights. They felt they *could* see evil at the infra-red end of the spectrum, the robber hiding in a hedge, his ultra-scanned bad soul panting away in ultra-violet night. And that was what was wrong about the chopper cops. That's when I felt like one of those pathetic fucking brown-uniform shopping-mall security men. That's one of the reasons I transferred down to the Met. to join the scruffiest and the best.

When I'm walking the evil is out there; when I stop moving it's in me.

Across the street, a young woman hurries home with the intent purposefulness of lone women at night, leaning forward in the italicized body language: 'NO.' Behind her is a pub called the Lamb and Flag. I stare at the sign of a lamb holding a pennant in a raised front paw. *The lamb*. I stop. My heart starts bumping. *This* is what the scanner killers meant by 'lamb'. Not *lamb* as in innocent, unsuspecting victim. It's here. I walk up to the pub, shut now. A makeover ex-pub with a *cappuccino* machine and wine prices chalked on a blackboard for flash top-boys.

I cut through the alley beside the Lamb and Flag and find myself on the Rockingham. Grass sprouts through the slabs as council punishment for all the trouble they cause.

I hesitate when I see him. Me, not him. He looks at me curious. I carry on towards him. Heart beating some more.

'Mr Trevorrow.'

A pause, a puzzled look on his face. 'Mr Manners.'

'How are you?'

'Yeah, I'm fine.' He takes me by the arm, and leads me round a corner into a smashed chain-link five-a-side patch of crumbly, spent Tarmac.

'How ya doing?' he asks, looking right into me.

'OK.' A pause.

'Ah, um, are you allowed . . . I didn't know you were allowed to wear trainers.'

Oh shit. Through my rising neck-flush I manage to say, 'It's a new thing. They should be black though, you're right. I better go back and change them.'

'I suppose you wanna search me then?' he suggests, raising both arms to let the tailor take a chest measurement.

'Er, yeah.'

I run my palms over his skinny torso, under the back of his jacket, over his knobbly cotton spine.

Kyle checks left while I'm doing this. Nothing found. I step back, but he leaves his arms up scarecrow-stance. So I step forward again and pat down his pockets, only just remembering to mumble, 'Got any sharps?'

'Eh?'

'Got any sharps?'

'No. No sharps.'

At Hem Corner, however, I find a wrap. I slide my hand through the busted lining. (I know his coat better than my own, its stash-flaps and ripped lining.) A gram of charlie in my hand. A tiny, folded envelope cut-out from a colour A–Z.

Kyle lowers his arms. I look around. Look back at him. Look around.

'That's your car there,' he says.

So it is. The unmarked purple Astra. I've come round on myself. Full circle. And didn't even know it.

He checks over his left shoulder again. Can't see anything myself.

We drive. We drive right past the station. We carry on driving.

'Where we going?' he asks casually. Chipper.

He knows.

How long has he known?

He's known all along.

He knows.

'How come you got in the car?' I ask.

'Someone.'

'Who?'

'Someone just round the corner.'

'Who?'

'Tony Andrew.'

'How did you know he was just round the corner?'

'I just been round the corner.'

'Why? What were you doing?'

'I can't tell you that.' The car stops at the lights.

'No. OK. You were with him?'

'I said "Hello."' We both stare at the red light, waiting for it to change. 'I was glad you killed that shitcunt Lee Andrew.'

'I didn't "kill" him.'

'Well then they buried the wrong man.' Feel him look over at me a couple of times. Farringdon Road. 'I was there that night.'

'You saw it?'

'No, I was just in the mob that piled round right at the end.' Clerkenwell Road. 'Where we going?' he asks, mildly curious.

'Smithfield. I've got to check out a reference in someone's statement to what they called *the slaughteryard*. It might be around here, it might not.'

'The slaughteryard?'

'Yeah.'

'How do you know about that?'

'Eh?'

'That's what bouncers call the bit like the back-yard of a club where they beat up the other gang.'

'Who calls it that?'

'I dunno, it's lyrics, innit? Everyone. Many clubs. It's like, you know, *the slaughteryard*. I dunno, maybe they call it other things other places. You know about that! Ha!'

I follow the brown heritage sign for Smithfield.

'Yea-es,' says Kyle. I follow his gaze. A film-shoot. Or maybe a TV-shoot. Smithfield meat market is closed now but they are using its colonnades for a film. Blue light. A spray of fake snow on the cobbles. Trucks, wires, actors – ha! cops and robbers. 'We gotta check this out!'

'OK,' I say.

'*Go* dere!' he says, American.

Kyle buys two cups of tea from the catering truck.

'How many sugars is that?' I ask.

'I dunno – four, five.'

We sit on the steps shielded from everything except the film-set by a lorry on which *G.E. Stowell Theatrical Costumiers* is written heraldically.

'This is better, innit?'

'Yes, thanks,' I reply.

Actors with napkin make-up bibs sit around between takes. We stare at the sorry cop – all wrong – and at the woefully Pete-Tong black 'villain'.

'Dem ah fink we're *extras,* ha! ha! ha!' It used to piss me off when Kyle, a few years younger, used to talk Yardie shit, but now he's being ironic, or it's just an occasional trope.

I take off my helmet and put it between my feet on the step. Holding the hot cup with my fingertips, I balance my tea on the helmet, swivelling styrofoam cup on silver tit.

With a heavy smack it split-smashes on the pavement and my shoes. I groan.

Kyle gets up. I watch him stroll over to the catering van and sweet-talk *Miss Southend 1972* in the hatch. He ambles back and hands me the full, fresh cup wordlessly. He kicks the shitty split and spilt cup into the pavement, toeing it once, twice and into the gutter; wipes a tiny brown tea-splash from his Timberlands and throws the balled napkin into the gutter, where it lies at the mouth of the stained and disgraced ex-cup.

'Why did you get me out of the danger zone back there?' I ask. 'Why are you helping me?'

'No reason.'

'Right.'

'I dunno.'

'Oh.'

'I dunno, I seen you do a cool thing once.'

'Yeah?'

'Yeah. You was trying to calm down this old Jamaican drunk who'd been thrown out the betting-shop on, ah, Junction Road, and then this black like graduate-type comes by – little round, gold specs, you know, intellectual-brother-to-the-rescue sketch. "What are you doing with this man, I have a law degree, you know." Now when I've seen this sketch before, the dibble's got humpy and it's like, "Back out, this is none of your business." But you were like, "Oh, I'm glad you're here. Can you sort this out for me?" He starts talking to the old drunk feller and then you just like left them together.' Kyle started laughing.

'What you up to?'

'Me?' he asks. 'I'm fully changed. Well, maybe not fully, but I'm not – I'm at college and well into consciousness-raising.'

'Same course as Tony Andrew?'

He looks at me balefully. 'What – just 'cos I was talking to him? You can't just decide that you've thought better of the past and it doesn't exist. It's always there and looking to jib into your now, innit? It's like you can't give up smoking after fifty years and say, "Right, I'm a healthy guy now," you know? All the old years are still looking for their main chance in the present, in the now. Tony Andrew . . . I mean, I live on the estate, too, innit? But that's not – I'm not the person you think you know.'

'No?'

'Got fined and one year probation so I thought, "Well, which way now?" That was in August, and in September I signed on to a course. I'm doing Politics at North London University there. And I'm well into it, too. Bang into it. ARM. All that.'

'What's that?'

'African Reparation Movement. Moneys owing to us from all the years of slavery and exploitation, 'cos all the European and American wealth is built up on stolen labour and stolen land.'

'But it wasn't like *all* Europe . . . I mean, at the same time as slavery was going on you had your Lancashire cotton-mill workers who were slaves, white slaves, and children as well –

nine, ten; and you had the king's army wiping out all the Highland tribes in Scotland, and the Irish. So what, you gonna have everyone except –'

'You're saying it's not black and white – literally – but that's a white tactic – it's only *not* black and white because *you* throw in the grey to stop anything getting done,' he says as a grey four-a.m. dawn makes the lighting man stare up at the heavens with godless calculation. 'You can always say "What about? What about?" but two wrongs don't make a right and you start with the Big Wrong.'

'But if you say I can't say "What about?" then I can't argue.'

'Right! So shut up!' he grins. I take the lid off my tea. 'Careful now,' he says, 'you know what happened to the last one.'

'Yeah, yeah,' I murmur and am struck by how much I sound like old Duty Inspector Mickey. Now of all times when I'm not even trying. Now after all to be like my old sardonic skipper. *Yeah, yeah.*

They are breaking up the scene, gutting the arc lights and hushing the buzzing generator dead. They unplug and wind up cables, sweep fake snow into the gutter. Discussing and logging. A fit-looking young woman wearing a headset goes round speaking to all the cast individually to remind each of a small but important thing. She's told them all, and now she comes to a stop on her own; looks around for a bit, then falls into a trance.

'I dunno,' I pick up, 'my girlfriend Beverley – she has all these weird, strange angles –'

'And strange boyfriends.'

'Ex-boyfriend.'

'You an ex- everything!'

'I hear that man!'

'"*I hear that man!*"' he sneers.

'Well, this is it, that's just it . . . that's what Beverley's always saying. She says that white people, we love it whenever a black person gives us like a high-five or the black handshake or gives it, "You're broad"; We *love* that shit. We love all that stuff so much, she says, we love it so much you should start charging. And she reckons if you charged for it – you know, five quid for a "respeck" or a –' (I do the fist-thing) 'that would wipe out the poverty gap right there.'

'Ha ha ha . . . Yeah! In a day!' he says, '*She*'s broad.'

'Isn't she?'

Right by us two women push a clothes rail up a wooden ramp on to the lorry. A pair of blood-stained jeans, an empty police uniform in dry-cleaner's polythene, leather jackets, a clear, plastic bag full of old shoes labelled with cardboard name tags like corpses' toes. A man pulls up the battered ramp, jumps off the back of the lorry and drags down the shutter with a skiffly washboard sound. Sitting here with Kyle behind the wardrobe truck, it's like we met kind of backstage; like playing football between the trenches on Christmas Day.

'Why didn't you stop?' Kyle suddenly says. The silence kinks and sags.

'Oh . . . oh . . . Hmm.'

'What's going on?'

''Cos I knew I was innocent, and why wait, you know . . . I dunno.'

'Or 'cos you didn't know you were innocent,' he said.

The *Theatrical Costumiers* truck heaves up on its tonsil sparks, shudders all through and pulls off.

Suddenly exposed, we're backstage no more. First light.

Across the street are some faces walking from drum 'n' bass to a bagel. Just out of Turnmills or the EC1, probably.

Kyle and me stand up simultaneously. We don't know them, but they are the sort that we might. Might have. Once. We remember ourselves, we remember where we are. With the sudden frost of a film-set snowfall, we turn to face each other.

'Take care,' he says.

'Thanks. You all right to get home?'

'Yeah, yeah.'

I put my helmet back on. Looking down I tut bitterly at my wrong pumps.

We shake hands – in the European style, but with a Colombian joy buzzer palmed from soft, moist to hard, dry palm.

Kyle nods as if that's only right.

Driving home. I know Tony Andrew's after me, and I know that all the time I search for the murder of the lamb it puts me at risk of a beating from him, but that's never stopped me doing my duty before.

never walk alone

On Holloway Road every male I see in his mid- to late twenties I think, 'This could be him, this could be the victim.' Every male in his mid- to late twenties I think, 'This could be the killer.' Every male in his mid- to late twenties I'm almost 100 per cent sure is neither killer nor victim.

In spitting rain outside an Italian deli, I see a massive artic lorry with foreign number plates parked up for deliveries. They have rolled the lorry's black plastic side-panel all the way up to reveal a field of fresh-cut straw containing two hundred jumbo water melons, and a woman. The side-panel hasn't been opened since southern Italy and here's all this goodness laid open to a wet and blustery Hornsey. A melon in each arm, she rolls a third up her leg.

A lot of the time I'm on a pavement that I don't even realize is a bridge, like here by Kentish Town station. Anywhere with a high wall might be a bridge. I'm all confused again, like a divining rod twitcher in the rain. It's like one minute I'm led on by what looks like a bridge, the next I'm lurching to trace a street that feels evil, or even looking for a cigarette butt on the pavement. It's all crazy and insipid. I should settle on one thing per day or per hour. But it's hard to settle on one thing when the clues are so . . . nothing.

I've been walking for two hours with a lung-puncturing depression. I think I'm in Clapton, but then again, maybe that's just how it feels when you're this low.

Chilly sunshine on an evil street in a run-down meaningless council sprawl. The spirit of a place like this estate whose name I don't know gives me a crushing, ugly, reality overload that makes everything else look like padding, lagging. It makes everything else – music, Beverley, telly – all look like a precarious distraction. The denizens are mean and hard-faced and have glib rationalizations for the evil they do, like the glib tones of the politicians who rationalized *them*. Council semis sprawling over a few run-down roads. Half the houses are boarded up, one with a crater in the roof like a direct hit from aerial bombardment.

The only people who avoid us are the decent ones. That's how you know who's on the firm: there's no chance anyone would think they're informing, so they can come out and talk. But not the good people. A retired man up-ending the grass he's cut from the lawn-mower bucket keeps his head down. It doesn't do for him to be seen talking to me. What gives the estate a feel of evil rampant: the cowed, defeated faces of the law-abiding. Too scared to ask next door to turn down the banging techno, they try to concentrate on Gay Byrne on *The Late, Late Show* as if the noise from next door was just a fault with the transmitter in a poor reception area.

The centre of this estate is a large square of patchy grass, green and brown like army camouflage. Some scrawny white kids are sitting on a couple of comfy-looking leather armchairs liberated long ago from some derelict flat. The sunshine has dried the mould out of them.

'All right, cunt . . . stubble?' says one of the kids. I put both hands on my belly and move it up and down in a *Beano* ho ho ho. Already pissing themselves at the great pun, they continue to laugh as if my put-down was just me making a prat of myself.

I cross a huge, burnt-out patch of pagan cinder the size of a centre-circle: what mammoth bonfire was this? The super-lightness of silvery cinders on my boots (I remembered the right footwear today) is very satisfying – perhaps in contrast to the heavy adrenalin thickening my legs. I head their way. That's important: never obey their force-fields. IGNORE ALIEN ORDERS as the sticker on Joe Strummer's guitar used to say.

The way they're looking at me . . . To these kids the uniform's a joke. Fancy dress. Now I know why I don't feel mad walking around in uniform: the slags look at me EXACTLY THE SAME as they always did, when I was on home beat. A look that says: why the fuck is he wandering around in *that* fucking garb? Dispossessed youth look at *all* policemen as if they were unofficial. I feel exactly the same as when I was official.

I pass some teenage girls shouting on the top of garage roofs. Short skirts. They start throwing handfuls of gravel at me. 'Do you wanna shag her, you skinny fucking nonce!'

I keep my head steady. A gravel asteroid, clumpy with gooey asphalt, whacks me hard in the cheek. I walk on like it hasn't happened, but can feel how some gluey bits of dusty grit have stuck on my face.

'Ah, he's simple,' shouts one.

I walk on, unruffled by their laughter. I think I handled that quite well.

Fucking bitches! Losers! I earn over twenty grand a year! They've got nothing! Nothing! No future. Nothing! I wish I'd . . . I wish I'd coolly turned round and said, 'Oh, by the way, enjoy your lives of crushing poverty and being left on your own when you're up the stick at seventeen, won't you?' I've got a Dolce & Gabbana suit! I've got design furniture! I've been to university! I've got talent at my job! Fucking loser cow slapper slags!!!

Back on residential streets, a private-mortgage Georgian terrace. What a frustrating day. No progress made. No nearer to finding the street that feels evil or the broken bridge, and all the time the depressing sense that I might be walking through it all the time. And then those kids.

I overtake a middle-class mum belabouring her six-year-old son into wonder. 'Look at the beautiful bright-blue fence, Arthur. That's almost an azure, isn't it?' She's read all about how you have to talk to kids as if they're adults, and yet – surprise, surprise – the invaded boy is sullen and unresponsive. 'Do you want ciabatta for lunch?'

'Leave him alone,' I say in passing.

She looks stunned, shocked. And when I'm a few yards ahead I hear, 'I beg your pardon!'

I turn round. 'And give him a proper name, for fuck's sake – a kid's name.'

A red Sierra stops. The driver puts a clipboard on his lap to correlate some bullshit sales flow chart. He hasn't seen me and dumps a McDonald's carton and wrapping and thick-shake cup out the window on to the pavement. I scoop these up and throw them back in his window.

A few blocks later I have a terrible sense of winding down as the trail goes cold and I'm left in fancy dress.

The man drives an Isuzu jeep. Dry, brittle, light-brown hair in a side-parting. A bitter expression on his face. A young, black lad in an Escort hasn't noticed that Jeepster is trying to turn off the road. Jeepster moves his hand over the horn, changes his mind, mouthing curses instead behind silent glass: 'Fucking *nigger*.' The way his face settles back into the sediment of bile it lives in is truly bad. I know how his mind works: seeing evil in the everyday.

He finally pulls out on to Fortess Road, exasperatedly belabouring the power-steer, snatching the stick. Stepping into the road, I hold up my hand like a lord. Spot check.

'Pull in over there, please. Thank-you.'

205

'*What fucking now?*' says his giveaway face. Yes, that's right, life is designed just to thwart you. You with your money-for-nothing, beefy four-wheel drive.

'What? What did I do?' he asks.

'Turn off the ignition please, sir.'

'What, what for?' Wide-eyed, incredulous.

'Step out the car, please. Have you got some proof of ID?' Fawn linen suit, Pony sweatshirt.

'Yeah,' he sighs heavily, in the desert of his long and testing odyssey, his religious ordeal, the fucking muppet. His right hand goes to his jacket side-pocket. Peek-a-boo. He drops a black leather wallet back in his pocket again. Doh!

'No,' he says. That's me fooled! Smiling into his eyes to distract him, my left hand dips his wallet.

'No, this'll do,' I cheerily remark. No longer a question of *what* he's got that he shouldn't have, only of *where*. If I hadn't known it was there just now, I might have given up. But as seven fanfare trumpeters stand behind him and remove the bannered brass from their lips for the red-liveried toastmaster to announce: Possession of Controlled Substance, I take out all his business cards one by one until I find the wrap.

'Coke?'

'I don't know how it got there.'

'Oh, well on your way, then . . .' He actually makes to move. (No sense of irony!) 'No, really,' I say, grabbing his knobbly, hairy wrist.

Driving home in his car it turns out he works for a record label.

'This isn't a police station,' he objects, looking around my flat.

'It's a station-house.'

'I won't tell anyone,' he offers. 'If you let me go I won't tell anyone.'

'Sit down, please.' We sit down facing each other across the wooden table.

He looks around the room with fast, twitchy movements. I suspect he's recently done some of the controlled substance because he seems very paranoid, nervy, agitated, and as I stand up to put the kettle on he near jumps out of his skin.

If I'd arrested him before I was self-employed, I'd have had to process him under the statutory, recognized crime and let everything else go. I would've had to arrest Al Capone for tax evasion. Whereas in my present position as a locum, I am able to charge him with the real wrong-doing, the spiritual one.

'When you look at ancient paintings,' I tell him in a friendly village desk-sergeant manner, 'Tutankhamun, statues, Red Indians – their faces have got a calm pride, a dignified, placed bearing. But modern faces are all sullen and resentful – like yours. Which is why you're here.'

I've obviously hit a nerve here, as he puts the offending face in his hands and starts breathing heavily, trying to huff and puff off the capitalist mask.

And now his guilt seems to kind of turn this flat into an actual station house somehow anyway. 'And it would've been actually more polite to beep,' I point out.

'Yes,' he says, 'but you don't know what the reaction will be, do you? Everyone's ego's so brittle, all at snapping point.'

'Whose egos are these, then?' I ask. He only scowls. 'You're putting your problem – fear – on to him; you're making your weakness his fault.'

'No. Black people are under more pressure and they've been more devalued by society and friends of mine have beeped black people and paid the price, so it's not racist to assume . . . that it's not clever to bang the horn.'

'"*Fucking nigger.*"'

'What is this?'

'Expecting the worst from everyone and finding it. Seeing yourself, self-pityingly, as wronged – that's how malice breeds, that's how people like you –' My up-and-down hand gesture includes his suit, his middle-class, middle-aged face, the expression of self-righteousness which he wasn't actually wearing any more, to tell the truth, but which was why I'd arrested him. 'That's how people like you end up committing crimes. Most people who do wrong don't think they started it. They all see themselves as finally striking back. You only see what fits into how you see things. There they go, the avaricious, demonically energetic young estate criminals. The "new brutal breed". But maybe the lad just hadn't seen you, pal.'

He looked at his tea but didn't drink it. I suppose the drug puts you off hot drinks. I let him off with a caution and now that's done it's nice just to kick back and chat for a while.

'I've been thinking a lot about fear lately . . .' (He was a good listener, as it turned out. Nodding attentively a lot.) 'Well, being a policeman, it comes into your mind, just like in your job you probably find yourself thinking about, I dunno, er, drums or whatever –'

'Yes, yes, you're right, you're right.'

'Anyway, I was thinking about how, when you say, "It was one of those Friday nights with something evil in the air," it's not.'

'Yes, yes.'

'It's not different at all. What's *different* is that your cocoon against chaos and the ugliness of the world has got dislodged slightly, temporarily, and you get an inkling of all the wild forces of the world.'

'Yes, that's absolutely right.' He's saying this such a lot that it's embarrassing. But I smile, pleased that he's understood straight off without me having to go into a long, involved explanation. I suppose at the back of my mind is the worry that the ideas I've been brewing in long isolation might be eccentric. So him agreeing with me so readily is a good sign.

'You can go now,' I announce. He stands up and backs out nodding. Very respectful. That's nice, too. I smile, turning my hands up at the wrists and say, 'Just don't end up back here again. OK?'

control

Now he's gone I turn on the scanner while I fix a coffee. Someone dialling. I hear the eight-note chasing melody before the purr-purr, purr-purr, purr-purr. No one home.

I catch a couple of calls where the flickering signal's so weak it holds for just a sentence, a snatch: '*Hold on, I'm going under a tunnel . . . Hello? Hello?*' Static. Scan down. I hear the weary sighs of what I guess to be a couple of fat geezers. Heavy, burdened huffs and puffs, groans and tuts carry on throughout this call. Not the same blokes as before but it might as well be. All hail to thee, my old friends! The Brotherhood of Reluctant Fishermen!

> '*I just heard the, er, weather forecast. Said it's gonna be fine.*'
> '*What, tommorrer?*'
> '*Tomorrer . . .*'
> '*Sounds like we'll have to go.*'
> [*Tutting.*] '*It looks that way.*'
> '*Fuckin' tench, though.*'

I let the scanner run to automatic, flailing through the kilohertz until it picks up a strong signal. There's a woman up on some Sunderland estate talking to her man who's working down in London on the sites. Lonely, tearful, horny, she's worried about him meeting '*some fancy tart doon en Loondun. Just coom up now.*'

'*Oh, aye, I'll coom oop oan mi private jet ah've got parked opp at Heathrow.*'
'*Ah wish you fucking did.*'

Maybe I imagined *the end* and *the broken bridge.*

'*Take a sick,*' she says.
'*I hope you ent serious.*'

Was it Satan in my own echoey head urging me out on to the streets at night with all this chaos and rage in me, knowing more than I do about what I could do? Such a mystical landscape: broken bridges, the sacrificial lamb, the promised land – did I imagine it?

'*Just think of all the things ah cood do fah you in the mahnin' if you were heeah with me nahw,*' she tries, going all husky.
'*Just think of all the things ah* coodent *do fah you if ah didn't have a job.*'

Perhaps this voice so tired of waiting is the brother to a repressed, homicidal fury of my own. If Kieran was here he'd say that, dopey with redundancy, I needed a purpose and just heard something that wasn't there. Static crackle and fizz now. I watch LCD numbers tumble down the FM, looking for trouble.

'*We only seen him, but your phone was off – we followed as far as Holloway Road . . .*'
'*Did yer see where he lives?*'
'*No, I got fucking stop-and-searched didn't I?*'
'*Was you holding?*'
'*Yeah, but the dibble never took me cap off and it's always in the lining.*'
'*Keep it under yer hat.*'
'*Oh, something else altogether – is that your cap I*

found at mine with like the criss-cross-checks pattern inside?'

'Oh yeah, yeah.'

'I'll bring it round with the . . .'

'All right.'

'There's like a bloodstain in it and it's in like the shape of a tree.'

'Oh yeah, that's from – you were there – up the slaugh-teryard that time, remember, when –'

The scanner loses the wavelength in my shaking hand. *Holloway Road!* I was there yesterday! Maybe I saw the killers! Maybe I saw the victim. The lamb. No, not the lamb, that's a pub. The Lamb. The Lamb and Flag. Get it together. Stop your head reeling. Think. By following my divining plod and these strange, mystical clues I've scored a near-hit. I must be doing something right.

in a field of retired police horses

Don't want to get eyeballed by police or thieves, friends or enemies. But I can't stay out of relief now they're going to murder someone. I live walking distance from division. The scanner only picks up calls where one of the people talking is within a two- or three-mile radius. This means I traverse relief borders with my trail. What can I do? The Lamb and Flag is here, *the slaughteryard* is, I now know, thanks to Kyle, the back yard of one of the clubs in the area (although it could be a club in town where one of my two persons unknown works).

Other officers, the Super even, all warned me about living so close to work and now I see their point. Two close calls in two days. Yesterday on Willesden Lane I saw two cops across the street before they saw me. I ran towards them pretending that I'd chased someone out of my relief into theirs. 'He's gone down that way!' I yelled, 'IC1 male, twenties. Go round there!' They paused a second then gave it toes down the alley to head him off behind the deserted cinema. I ran round the block the other way, stopped, turned round and headed for Kilburn leaving the two officers to listen for the sound of one pincer clapping. Meanwhile *this* IC1 male in his late twenties stopped in Iverson Road, hands on knees, out of breath, and bitterly reflected that I was only there in the first place because I had had to take a tediously round-the-Wrekin route after I saw a parked-up patrol car effectively blocking the route I'd planned to the Lamb and Flag.

And this afternoon I was walking down Warren Street – and

I was only there because the two Kilburn cops had knocked me off course *again*! – when two vigilant WPCs came conferring and frowning towards me. I told them I'd just been giving evidence at Marylebone Crown Court. Oh right, sorry, of course, lovely day. We chatted on some more, whilst scanning the street, keeping one eye on the civilians, those *others*. I got in my car which was parked up by Regent's Park and I'm still driving. Everything seems to be conspiring to frustrate me in my mission. And as if time wasn't against me anyway!

Still driving I don't know where now.

An old Italian woman in black sits on her front wall on this A-road. Her brown, deep-lined, thin face looks baffled, lost. Growing up south of Basilicata in a one three-wheeled-van town this was what old people did. Sit out front in the late afternoon. But it ain't happening. Where's her knot of head-scarved widows? Where they at? Where's Hortensio the one-time *communista* mayor, now a smallholder with a scandalous love-life? All her *bella gioventù* this is what she seen the old folks do. After *grappa* and draughts you sit outside. Part of something. Not now, not here. Baffled as red, blue and pastel cars shoot the breeze from third to fourth. But the old Italian widow is made in the shape of her old life and knows no other. She is one of history's loose ends; history stared at her one sunny day in Calabria and still has her on his retina now that he looks at an overcast A1.

Beverley phoned last night. After a few seconds it was clear she doesn't know about my suspension and the man I killed. *Sub judice* has kept my name out of the papers. She doesn't know. It's weird her calling up and not knowing, like a late arrival ding-a-linging the doorbell at Cicelio Drive five minutes after the Manson murders, standing on the doorstep with a bottle of Liebfraumilch and saying, '*I hope I'm not too late?*'

I shan't tell her. It'll be nice to be the man I was. To be

innocent. To still look like a good man. For an interlude, at least.

Through the chain-link fence of a land-refill site I glimpse a half-buried strip of dirty white shirt tugged at by the breeze, the gentle wind toying with a project of excavation.

I've been wondering where I'm going exactly as suburb leads to dual carriageway, but driving up a slip-road and on to a bridge now, I know that I'm headed for the field of retired police horses.

On one of our first dates she drove us ten miles to the field of retired police horses at whose fence I'm standing now, the light failing in the chilly sky. Last time I was here, when I came with Beverley, there were a dozen horses. Now there's only one.

There is an unexpected beauty here about this field with its lone retired police horse near a big roundabout junction off the M1; the huge horse and a moon loitering in the day sky having missed the shuttle. Massive reddy-brown horse with a stiff, matted, off-white fringe. A long white tail which is ginger again at the end like it had grown out its blond roots. A bathtub in the middle of the green field is his trough of nettle-soup.

I vault the gate and go up to the horse. Now the low orange sun makes an acid bath of the trough-water. 'Where the others? Where your mates, eh?'

It's fucking enormous. Nine-foot tall with a tyrannosaurus head. I have a stab at patting the side of its big suede jaw. There's meant to be some way of doing this, isn't there? What is it? From the side so they can see you? I try it. Pat pat. He flinches, then throws his head right up. Maybe it's not from the side, after all. I mean, you're very close to their eyes like that and that's got to make them nervous. I'm nervous too. He can smell it. Wheels away. Canters off ten yards or so. I turn and walk back from the middle of the field to the fence. He follows. Catches up. Drops his muzzle – bang – right on my shoulder. I jump and yelp. He wants to bite my ear off. I run a few steps. The horse runs a few steps. Overtakes. I change course. Don't want to be behind his Wang Chung hams. Head out the field another way, walking but sharpish. He blocks my way, standing side on. Immovable object. I try patting his side. We've got off on the wrong foot; here, let's be friends: guy patting horse in field. OK? He thrashes his head at me in furious zig-zags. I jump out of my skin, screaming, 'Fuck off!'

I start trotting towards yet another part of the fence, even though it's furthest from my car. He gallops off to a neutral corner. Relief. I've got the whole thing wrong – he was just feeling frisky and playful but my nervy sudden arm movements made him nervous. He turns. Homes in. Charging. Is he playing? I run for the fence like a bullfighter. He gets there first. Cuts me off. Drops shoulder. Late swerve. His wheeling bulk at forty-five degrees to the steaming grass. Charges straight at me, high-stepping, front hooves as high as my neck. Head going up and down like crazy, nostrils flaring, gob dribbly. Throwing everything into it I punch the suede cheek block. His yellow, rotten teeth come right by my face as he rears up. His front legs in the air, I shoulder charge his stomach. We fall together into the threshing machine of his legs. Upturned hooves kicking out, his writhing rear legs make his hips slither like an 'S' on the grass. Both of us wild flailing and writhing and wrong-side-down. Is he fighting or just trying to get up? Am I fighting or just trying to get up, get away?

Apeshit. Eyeball to frenzied eyeball. His eye like an anchovy caught in amber staring with terrible knowledge, drawing me in until it becomes a rock thrown in a brown pond, and then a kaleidoscope as he makes a strange noise that I've never heard a horse make before. Like a human voice on film rewound, a whale yawn, low walrus whine.

The yellowy lights of the North Circular pass over my

windscreen. My car has been accepted among the traffic like any other car. Thank-you. Mud or blood on my face and hands. What happened I don't want to know. I'm driving a car. The radio broadcasts comforting words from the known world: Viking, Cromarty, North Utsire, South Utsire, Dogger Light Vessel Automatic. A terrible dread: what do those hot entrails tell me about the future?

Two a.m. All is quiet on this tidy, seventies, rabbit-hutch council estate. At this time of night it rests as peaceful as the one-inch scale model in the council-planning chamber. You see what the architect had in mind. You can see the plastic model poplars of the optimistic T-board. There is a copse in the drop off this cement walkway: concessionary trees and bushes give up their surplus scent in an end-of-day clearance. Expansive as the scent from council shrubs and trees, I shout, 'Two o'clock and all's well!'

I thread through Dalston Lane and veer off towards Shackle-well. It's safer for me to patrol the no-go areas. No chance of getting eyeballed by other cops.

Three a.m. The pool room empties. They're surprised to see me here.

'Want some gear?' asks the big feller and they all fall about. Stripy, jumbo strides and plenty architecture (that sovereign ring will hurt). I'm pretty sure the voices on the scanner were both white but you can never be 100 per cent and as Kieran always used to say, 'If in doubt rule it out.' (We always got stuck in, and he called other beat officers who didn't ball-watchers, farts in a trance, spectators.)

I lift each baseball cap, check inside as if for controlled substances, looking all the time for a bloodstain shaped like a tree. They stare in shocked silence, which helps me concentrate. Maybe, like a Rorschach ink test, it won't look like a tree to me? I put each cap back on their heads one by one so as not to put the wrong cap on the wrong head, and look incompetent, occasionally stopping to count how many I've done so far so as not to miss one out or do the same head twice at the risk of annoying anyone. Nothing doing. Clean. A sixth sense tells me that to say, 'Thank-you very much, gents,' would break the spell and lead to trouble, tells me that the silence is somehow a magical force-field for me, so I just turn away and head up Lower Clapton Road.

The deserted streets look as innocent and expectant as a film-set, as if tomorrow everyone might wake up, having slept on it, and do the world all different.

Four a.m. I'm somewhere near Euston.

A six-foot wall hides a seventy-foot drop on to railway tracks. I climb over the wall and drop ten feet on to a ledge. Someone has tagged the word SENSE in hip-hop silver. Below me a nuclear slow-train tiptoes through the night, taking the points warily. On the cylindrical container carriages is the zig-zag in a circle code-sign which means radioactive material in transit, as only the MOD, emergency services and Mr Sands are meant to know. I throw a rock which whacks the cylindrical hull with a bang.

drifter

I've walked through the whole night and now day comes to relieve me. Miles from home.

I sit on the edge of a canal-cut section of the Thames, thick with green flotsam. A hot sunny morning burns through dawn mist.

A lean young man cycles to work on a mountain bike. He seems surprised to see a cop sitting down on the tow-path, contemplative. Stops and asks, 'Are you OK?'

'Fine thanks, just tired. Lovely day . . .'

'Yeah it is!' he says. Puts earphones back in and cycles on with a smile. (I've probably conformed to some crusty notion of how even fascist pigs can be chilled out by a beautiful day. Yeah, tell your friends.)

In the new-issue shadows cast by tow-path on river, a blackened three-litre oil can or a block of slimy wood or something bobs towards me, very, very slowly.

My arse aches bonily from the cement. I feel tired now as the sun warms my back. Think I'll get up soon and find somewhere that's open for coffee. Yeah. Coffee and a sausage sandwich. Mmm.

I watch the bobbing object. Bulky, weed-covered oblong. A piece of material snagged up with it, floating four feet behind like a trailer. The driftwood moves towards me as imperceptibly as a minute hand. Sometimes it seems it isn't drifting towards me at all but is static. I'm imagining a current that isn't actually there. The tiny, white, duck feathers and little white gobbets of moorhen spit in the green flotsam right near me don't seem to be moving. Maybe the driftwood isn't moving either.

No, it is definitely drawing nearer and flowing ever-so-slightly swifter now; perhaps because it has found a fast-track current in the nearside shadows of the canal, or perhaps it can move easier now that it has resolved what it is: a dead man floating face-down.

Let him come to me. Neither of us has any reason to rush. I wait maybe three more minutes for him to nudge my DM dangling in the sun above the scuzz of thick jetsam.

I get on my knees, lean over and pull at his collar. It's all I can do to lift his upper body a foot out the water. His slack neck whacks his head against the cement back with a sickening force which would've killed him if he wasn't dead.

I turn him round so that his head and shoulders are at right angles to the edge and haul the waterlogged dead feller out the water. His pockets are inside-out, jacket and trousers dark with canal water.

What to do? What do I do now?

The dead old man's watery-blue and bloodshot eyes look past me at Kieran who hovers high against the sun with his familiar twinkly self-confidence. 'Wait till someone comes along: it doesn't look suspicious if no one can see it, and as soon as someone does come down the tow-path then you can get them to call an ambulance,' he says, vanishing.

Yeah, why not wait? No pressure in waiting if there's no one else around to see, is there? And as soon as someone else is around then I'll have help.

I wipe the gunk off his face. He doesn't look at rest, he just looks bone-tired, face slack with exhaustion, his drained mouth falling open in last gasp. Still knackered after death. I close his eyes which squelch water out shockingly.

I look up. Fifty yards away, a woman is watching me while her dog makes elaborate preparation before taking a piss. The dog, a lurcher, is on one of those extender leads and she has another lurcher trotting free.

I clear my throat and hum a single note with my mouth open to make sure I'll be able to talk normally when she gets in range.

Her brown hair has streaks of blonde highlighter and is tousled from sleep. She has a River Island sweatshirt on and grey jogging pants. She hasn't put any make-up on yet. She is a breakfast-sexy, slightly overweight council housewife in her mid-thirties.

'My radio fell into the water when I dragged him out. Can you call an ambulance, please.' She pulls a mobile from her pocket and holds it out to me. 'Just call an ambulance, please,' I repeat (not knowing where the fuck I am). I busy myself in trying to close his mouth while she makes the call, but it won't stay shut unless I tilt his head back.

'What happened?' she asks, slowly pushing the aerial back in with her cheek after she's made the call.

'Dead tramp. They fall in the river at the Embankment and they fetch up anywhere.'

'Poor soul.'

'Yeah.'

'Will you be able to find out who he was?' she asks. I put my hand in his inside pocket but it's empty.

'No. Probably not.' I stand up. Smile. She smiles weakly back, impotently commiserating. I get out my notebook. 'I just need your name and address, please.'

'But I haven't seen anything.'

'Well, it's only –'

'I can't tell you anything,' she says.

'Well, obviously any dependants of his are gonna have to come and stay at yours now.'

'I'd help if there was anything to do, but what do you need my address for?'

'It's just to corroborate what I'm gonna write up.'

'But you're a policeman. You don't need me to back you up.'

'Yeah, but suppose I'd killed a string of tramps . . .'

'No, no, sorry,' she says, walking smartly away and making hand gestures like she's erasing herself out of the scene. She leaves the tow-path and disappears into a cul-de-sac, shouting at her lurchers.

I prop the man against a brick wall among nettles that have no sting for him now. We wait for the ambulance.

I once heard someone describe seeing their father in his coffin at a wake. I remember the thing which seemed to upset them most was that the undertakers had combed his hair into a side-parting and that wasn't, they said, how he used to have it. The greasy water has plastered his hair forward in a centre-parting over his face. I clear the wet hair out of his eyes. And recognize the face.

'Where's your smarts, old friend, eh?'

His rotting woollen coat has been pulled and sagged by this long-cycle rinse. The buttonholes have shrunk. The top button of his coat is wedged tight. Hard to unfasten, but now it comes. And there is the bow-tie and frilly dress-shirt of the old Irish down-and-out, the doorman I saw at the corner of Marylebone High Street, the boxer who refused to go down. 'Stay standing and wait for a change in the world, Pops?' I gently smooth his hair back, now that I know how he used to have it.

His clothes have soaked into mine. We both smell of river. A kind of musty algae, diesel and mud smell. The sun has warmed his face and hands. My legs ache from his dead weight but I'm not moving him again.

Earth spins from dark to light, a siren flashing in space. I look at my dead doorman. '*Time to go back now,*' says the ventriloquist's dummy. Time to go back. This is the end.

How did I get here? I've got to stop and go back now. Got to go back now. Over.

Making my fingers into a comb I slick back his ruddy-brown hair some more, running my fingers through silty strands, smoothing it, slicking it back, smoothing and smoothing it down.

The dead old doorman's clothes leak river on to me, but it's cold and external unlike the hot leaking of the sunken, melted old woman. The ambulance is taking him to St Jude's Morgue in Teddington. I start the long walk home as the hot day begins. I've come to the end of something. Wet trousers chafe my sore legs like scurrying back from the Drum Club that time. Can't say why exactly, but it's like certain options have gone, and as I walk the long walk back to mine it feels like a summons.

A sore throat arrives. One minute I'm just thinking how it's only a few more blocks and I don't have a sore throat and the next I do. It's starting to hurt every time I swallow, every time I move my Adam's apple which I need to do a lot now with my mouth being so dry. I feel very cold, but I'm too tired to tuck my jumper in. Trying not to throw up.

I rush into the flat like sickness was my secret lover and we couldn't wait to strip and jump into bed, hot and trembling for it and my head is down the toilet.

Lying with my head on the lip of the bowl – like in the club urinal that time – every shitty thought I have makes me groan, like the memory of dicky mussels when you've got food-poisoning. Solid chunks of fake belief come up like undigested poison; every repeated little mantra hurts my head like a sudden stab of brain knock in septic migraine brine. It's them, the big undigested slabs of rotten phrases that course jaggedly round my skull: conversational stock phrases I've been repeating long past believing. All the wank and the shite and the spume and the spout. Out, out, out, out, out. And all the incoming too, all that hurts my head: *a bowl of Fruit and Fibre's doubly ace, apples, hazelnuts, bananas, raisins, coconuts, sultanas, when we're on our hols we eat it by the case. The promised land at the end.*

After sweating the night in bed I am this morning a tad shaky on my pins.

Hollowed but happy, I sit out on the low wall in front of my flat and feel a sense of stillness and clean slate. The birds twittering on the green awning of the shop next door are unhampered by my ideas of birds twittering. Lived here, what, three years? – but I've never noticed before how pretty these street-lights are: little perspex cylinders topped off with a black hot-pot lid. Telegraph poles radiate wires to each house like bunting or rigging. It's a gently ruffled, mild, post-rain day and the air smells like essence of everything. A portly, blonde, red-faced woman walks past with her daughter. For some reason they both smile and say, 'Hello.'

Hello.

a leave-taking

I sit out on Beverley's fire-escape, my back against the brick wall. Out here I share the black iron platform with chunks of broken sink, a stack of plant pots, a set of rusted gears off a bike with a pile of nuts and bolts beside it. Washing hangs on the railings next door and down one.

The sky is still and gently fading. Lilac-grey clouds are static against a hard, flat, black-and-blue sky. Past the city's edge a spent mauve sunset flares and sputters over the hills and far away.

'Blackcurrant bracer,' Beverley says, setting a steaming mug next to my hip. She perches side-on to me, her feet on the top step.

In a garden down below, collapsed apples decompose in unmown grass, making the dusk dew a turned cider. The last squirrel of autumn pops out, stops, strobe-pumps its tail. Its movements are the usual melodramatic farce I've come to expect from squirrels. Frantically late! Fugitive! Fuck off, squizzer. Who still eats you anyway?

'I'm glad you were in,' I say at last. 'I tried to phone to confirm but there was no answer.'

'They cut me off again.'

Paul Weller's 'Above the Clouds' tails off midway as if Weller has spotted someone bad come into the room, or has suddenly become preoccupied with something else.

'What happened to the music?' I ask.

'The volume control's fucked,' she tuts resignedly. 'It plays all right for a bit but it keeps falling.' I can just hear the tin-tin high bits like when you're on the tube a few seats down from a personal stezzy. We go into the front room to inspect. The sound is nowhere but the orange graphic-equalizer bars still flicker up and down like a fake fire on one of those plug-in heaters with plastic coal and ember lookalikes.

She tries another tape and ups the volume. We go back out on the fire-escape. I move the stack of plant pots so I can sit with my legs out. We listen to the music while it's there.

'This is beautiful, what is it?'

'*Le Mystère de Voix Bulgare*,' she replies.

'What?'

'*Le Mystère de Voix Bulgare*.'

'Is that the song or the name of the, er –?'

'No, the song's called "*Kalimankou Denkou*". I just got it.'

A still ecstacy settles over Beverley and me. We don't need to ask each other to know we are both being taken somewhere by this, or taken back somewhere, resonating to something strange and anciently familiar.

A hush settles over the blood. My arms lie still at my side like they have been turned to stone and yet at the same time I feel more alive than ever and my arms feel very strong, like I could do many things with them. I realize my forehead has been in a type of frown for the last however many years. I put the muscles of my face back how they were again for all that time and the unconscious expression which was mine seems very strange.

It doesn't sound Bulgarian, it sounds Middle Eastern, or maybe Russian or even Red Indian, and sometimes like classical choristers. The music is like another culture calling to those bits of us not activated in this culture. The music switches on our capitalist souls' silent areas, sets them vibrating because we're all the same and we always knew this, even though we forgot for a long time and will forget it again.

It sounds like a hero has died and they're singing an upbeat lament for the body. A requiem, maybe; or as if he's riding away to certain death and this is a blessing upon his head. A mixture of mourning and of strength and vindication got from his passing. And though I know the way I apprehend this music has all sorts of Western cultural grit in it – Charlton Heston riding out strapped to the saddle in the last frames of *El Cid* is at the back of my mind, probably – yet, listening to this music, there are things which seem beyond all those cultural motes in your eye. Whatever iron heaven I imagine my life under, I now know that it is a kinder place; that the store of human sympathy is greater than I imagined; that there have always been these women, representatives of the cloud of witnesses that look upon us with only love wherever we've been. The mixture of anguish and benediction in these women's voices knows my extremes. '*Aaah Kaa-li aach.*' All the chatter and inane babble of papers and daytime TV and magazines and evening TV fall away like dead grass on the wind. Fall under a shadow, back to the shadow world they came from and always were.

I feel strong and confident. I see where my body ends and the world begins. My whole body feels stony, placid, and yet my heart more open. Not with the tizzy of emotiveness that lasts the seven-minute song, where gangsters and dictators weep at the opera; no, more generally open and with a sense of what a fucking idiot I've been all my life.

Kalimankou Denkou. I don't know what the words mean and I don't want to know. That would just get in the way. And at times the women aren't singing in words anyway, more like the ululating wail from the minaret during Ramadan when consonants are not allowed. *Aie – ohhhh – ah – aiie!*

It's taken me a while to realize that it's just voices. One woman sings while the other women back her with sustained notes held like long, drawn bows on a 'cello, like low oboes, and then like flutes which hover high and still as a kestrel. A younger woman's voice rises full-throated above the others only to drop down enfolded by the other women's voices, as they come together at the end of a phrase like slow violins. Each time they go away it's like they might not come back – like Beverley's stezzy is playing up again. But again the singing returns, this time crashing in as a wave of passion rides the woman on her own and now all the other women rise up to join her, all rising up together like a Zulu woza!

Gathering and releasing, gathering and releasing. They are mapping a complex path. Not only listening to each other while they're singing but also, it seems, listening to the experience to make sure they describe its contours and the way through the Kalimankou desert, the way of making meaning of the pain and goodness. Navigating without words because we don't have the words in any language, but describing the shape of the experience in sound and emotion. A gorgeous spasm now, a strict compression as Ofrah-Hazi wail is reined in hard to sudden, choral control: the fiery sandstorm and the settled mist; the broken bridge you thought you'd never find and the power which carries you over.

At the same time as I feel removed I feel more here. I am aware of Beverley's flat. Of the light and shade on the brick wall – a lovely balance. Of the spinning, plastic air-vent set into the window whose slats, now I turn, are brown with the wind and its messages and contamination, spinning prettily and helpfully. Now almost stopping, then, on a whim, set whirring fast again.

The sound has fallen away totally this time. Beverley gets up and presses the stop-start stezzy and the women resume normal service. I'm not surprised by where they are when we come in because I know what they're describing, have a vague imprint of its shape. Even though the women went away they were still always there.

Maybe a quarter-mile away, dot children in white kit reach the cotton-twine finish tape of a hundred-yards dash. Last event of the school sports day.

The women slip away like Radio Free Europe fading down prior to announcing a State of Emergency . . .

Clothes are picked up, parents disperse and the school is emptied in dribs and drabs.

'It's like I don't know what *Kalimankou Denkou* means and I don't want to know,' I tell Beverley. 'I didn't know what they were singing, what the words mean, and I didn't want to know because they would only get in the way.'

A look of mischief on the Bevster's face: 'I know exactly what it means 'cos I read it on the sleeve.'

'Don't tell me!'

'OK,' she says and smiles mysteriously.

'All right, tell me.'

'*Kalimankou Denkou* is the name of this Bulgarian betting-shop and the women have all just spunked their kids' college money on Frankie Dettori. And that's why they're so up-set.'

'Fuck off,' I say, affectionately, because there's a sort of care in her saying this. So off the mark that it still protects us from the intrusion of words. Not like the vindictive, prick-your-bubble tone with which, say, Heavy Polly would have resent-fully, impatiently belaboured me off my high horse, and would have made a *point* of getting me off it, as it would have been her ancient duty to stand by a carousel and shout at children, 'It's not a horse! They're not horses!' (Maybe this spell is not so ethereal as I thought with all this hate left for Polly.)

'It doesn't sound Bulgarian, it sounds sort of Middle Eastern,' I go.

'Yeah. No they're these plump, middle-aged peasant women in headscarves and this comes out of them.'

From somewhere down below we hear but can't see a collage of three, maybe four police sirens. Sounds like a couple of ARVs, a Trojan Land Rover and maybe a squad car. Must be something special for the armed response. An end-of-day armed robbery perhaps. They'll have been on since two so maybe they were just beginning to wane into mid-shift boredom. But now they are minutes away from a Beretta in the face. It could even be a named op that's been months in the planning. This is it and if it doesn't come off some DS will get carpeted and told how many tens of thousands of public sovs he's spunked. The multi-layered, four-track sirens fall out of earshot.

'What's it feel like,' Beverley asks, 'now that you've left, now that you're not part of it no more?'

'Just a real sense of failure and I can't even think about it.'

'Mightn't you go back after the trial then?'

'No . . . if they ever did have me back now I'd just be a shiny-arse, sitting in a roomful of VDUs at the nick, until the day I die and my arse outshines St Peter's Pearly Gates.'

'But you were a good cop and that.'

'"Were"?'

'Well, it's like for you the job is like drugs – it only ends up exacerbating the central problem.'

'Every time I hear a siren or see a cop in the street I feel ashamed. Ashamed that I wasn't up to the job. You know, every time I turn the telly on it's a cop show or there's a crime story on the news, or there's a policeman outside Number Ten. Jesus, you realize how much mention there is of the police.'

'That's how I felt when you left me.' There is a beat while we let the silence absorb this. 'You know,' she says, 'you going out on your own . . . all the people you've told me you homed in on, it's like you were depositing all these different bits of yourself before you could move on . . . to the next stage or something. I felt like that when you left me: it was like you were leaving the bit of you that you couldn't handle any more or that you couldn't be any more, like for safe-keeping . . . No, no, like disowning. Disowning.'

'Yeah, it's like now I can't believe it was me doing that, something so . . . nuts . . . but it didn't feel mad when I –'

'Yeah, but you're doing it again. Now you're disowning that part of you that went out in uniform. "Oh, I was mad, it wasn't me." But it was you and it's still you 'cos you've always – and it's something I've never understood about you – you expect the job to be about right and wrong.'

'Why's that strange?'

''Cos you go on about how there's no morality, only market forces, and yet you expect the job to be the one area in society where that's not true.'

'No, I don't. I know the laws were made by landowners and tycoons –'

'But you don't, 'cos you get a cob on about it. I think you were taking a stand but now you're saying you just had a funny turn.'

After a while I say, 'I'd forgotten that I was this familiar with anyone, and that someone else knew me this well *and still liked me*! Despite my faults.'

'Or because of them, even.'

'Yeah, you're right – and maybe they're not faults . . .'

'No, no – they're faults,' she says with a little chuckle.

There is a sense of things having been said. Done and dusted, laid to rest. Spells of conclusive silence. Words seem like an effort. An intrusion.

This calm, however, is interrupted now and then by a sense of looking at her through the wrong end of a telescope, and by the walls of the room tilting away from me.

She fills a black bin-liner with cast-offs for the Spastics Shop. The pizzas arrive.

'Are you allowed to have cutlery in your hand?' she asks.

'Yes.'

'Oh no, it's OK – phew, they've got *plastic* knives and forks.'

'Phew.'

'Are you allowed to eat cheese?' she jests.

'Yes, yes, that's fine.'

'And you're – there's no reaction on olives?'

'Well, they haven't specifically said anything, so I'll . . .'

'You'll risk it.'

'Yeah.'

She gets up and comes back with a half-dead bottle of red and one glass from which she sips before sitting down.

'Are you allowed to drink wine?'

'Fuck off.' I grab the bottle and fill my mug.

Beverley sits on the floor of the darker room with her tucker on the coffee table. I chomp away at our cheese-dripping discs on the couch.

'What are you gonna do now?' she asks, gob full.

'I don't know.'

'I'll let you know if I hear of anything going. Would you be into that?'

'Yeah, anything. For now.'

Ha! Working alongside Beverley as a roadie only not for a band but for venues and festivals. Knocking up the lighting rig, rolling in the amps, laying the steel-tread hardfloor over the grass!

On her wall, the size of a phone box, is a poster of a bearded but still young and red-shirted George Best, off-the-ball in pensive-stroll mode. There is a crowd in the background, but there are no other players on the green grass.

'Where d'you get that?' I ask.

'Skanked it off a venue wall.'

'It's fierce.'

'Yeah.'

'Do you like George Best?' I ask her.

'I was talking to someone the other day, and I was saying, you know, how everyone goes on about what a waste he didn't play longer and that, you know, "what a waste of talent". Well, I was saying he was so beautiful that if all he'd done was train and play then that would've been a waste as well. What about his talent as a drinker, and a party animal, talent for socializing and having a laugh or shagging. Maybe he was a brilliant pub talker. You know, just 'cos you can't put a pound sign in front of those skills or whatever like you can with football, doesn't mean to say they're not equally valid.'

'Well, that's, er, certainly an unorthodox view,' I reply.

Ugly furniture came with the flat. She has a navy-blue bedspread as a throw cover for the couch, but it keeps sliding down every now and then, exposing the stained white of the real sofa. I get up from the couch to pull the blue bedspread up again.

I tidy away the pizza boxes, ketchup, plates.

I stare out the black window. My stiff-faced, candle-lit reflection hovers out in the cold night above towerblocks, lights and cars. I can hear her tidying away a few things behind me. Now she draws the red-velvet curtains over the hovering ghost. The tall red curtains are unhemmed. Long black thread unravels at floor and ceiling, like human hair.

A half-hearted siren goes by somewhere. Doesn't sound like such a big deal now.

I'm relieved as we sit on the sofa to have a certain blurring of the physical-contact rules, to be able to sit with my arm round her feeling her bulging midriff with its familiar goose-pimples naked under my palm in the gap between her jeans and her top. Not to be slammed out.

My head lies on her black denim lap. It's only about ten but

I'm falling asleep as she strokes and strokes my hair back, her hands still damp from washing-up, and her lemfresh thumb makes the sign of the cross on my forehead.

I awake on the couch at six a.m. under a sleeping bag and my trousers still, alas, on.

I watch a programme for the deaf with the sound down. I write her a little note on the back of an unopened British Telecom red bill envelope.

> Dear Bevster,
> Thanks for a beautiful stay. Feels like I've been away days. Give us a call when you get reconnected.
> Lots of love gorgeous girl,
> Johnny xxx.

I open her bedroom door and look in on her. Her face is sulky in sleep. Looking in on the sleeping woman I feel half like a fond parent and half like a home-invader sex criminal. I soundlessly shut the door.

I borrow her crushed toothbrush and catch myself in the bathroom mirror. Something's changed. A friendly face. No longer an inspection parade. This must be what most people see in the mirror all the time. Hello John. Hello you. We had a good time, didn't we, John?

Outside the front door the keen morning wind finds out my unwashed face. A white car starts up and drives away, its exhaust blowing out visible smoke like my breath on this chill morning.

At the end of her street I feel a strong urge to go back to her house. I turn and look at her flats once, and then a few steps on, I turn and look a second time. But now I can't tell which door is hers.

'Birmingham New Street, please.'

Leaning across, the cabbie speaks in a quick, hushed, undertone like he's not supposed to be doing this, or as if someone else was listening. 'Yeah, alroit, yeah.'

At the traffic-lights on Mosely High Street I see a kid trying to ponce some money off an old troubled cove. The kid gives up trying to cadge a dollar off him as we move on. Maybe if something had happened I might have tried to intervene and cool things off just like any good citizen might. But it feels good to drive on by and leave the scene. Now that I'm not personally responsible for every evil act committed.

Before I used to say about the job, 'There's nothing else out there, there's nothing like the buzz.' And as Beverley herself might say, when people talk about there being nothing out there they mean in themselves.

The murder would've happened by now anyway. Or else the killers have changed their minds, called it off, just given him a slap instead. Whatever.

Builders sit around waiting for my train to go. The 07.15 Birmingham New Street to Euston is the last train to leave before the station's closed for renovations. As my train pulls out and eases round a curve, hardhats who've been sitting vacantly on the roof drop down pulley-ropes. On the concourse a scaffold tower is wheeled into position.

The train accelerates. A sudden slew of rain falls across the city like a veil. I pull in my head.

We slip clear of Birmingham. Streets, houses, pubs and shops seen from the wrong end. Presenting themselves to each other but not to us passengers. Up and beyond and looking down from another tack. It is good not to know, in this strange town, what happens where and all that.

The rain stops or we've gone beyond it. The countryside now lies under a sharp, polished sky. Steam from the earth's crust escapes up through sheep-bitten turf. A transmission aerial with its precarious guy-ropes; pretty, pattern fields; brown power stations curved in the middle like clay thrown on a potter's wheel. All our weedy, brittle structures on nature's unimaginable violence.

A crooked stream in a crack of earth between two green pastures. Rivers are beautiful to everyone except police frogmen. As the train curves away from the stream, light catches its surface and it becomes a shining hard top of silver-plate.

I borrow a *Mirror* off the chap sitting on the other side of the train, facing forwards too. He's drowsing in the heat of the bright windows, though it's chilly out. I hand it back before Milton Keynes, page open on George Best's column.

'Thanks.' I tell him. 'You know, they always go on about George Best wasting his talent because of drinking and dancing and socializing, but maybe he was a great dancer and a great drinker. Perhaps he had a real talent for socializing, and it would've been a waste if he hadn't devoted himself to that, too.'

'Ye-es,' the suit replies uncertainly.

I lean back against the headrest, smiling like the advert, as a simpler country slides past.

I was stuck, and time is now moving. The fever has broken. I'm out of it. There's the trial still, but as for staying on the force, well even if they had me back I'd be shiny-arsed for ever. I know that now.

I am no longer a police-officer. Of course not. Not now I think about it. All that remains is one final duty. A funeral to attend.

boxer beat

If it wasn't for me phoning the morgue, getting the number of the hostel and then phoning the hostel, he would've been cremated with no one there. And now I know his name at least. A name like a boxer's: Ray Dunney. No middle name and no fixed abode. No middle name and no hot water to shave by. It's like his parents knew there'd be nothing down for him. After all, you're only given a middle name to stop the bank computer confusing you with another investor. John Steven Manners – so I was one up from him.

I wear full uniform out of respect. Cap not helmet.

I am the sole mourner in the modest, 1970s Catholic crematorium brick-built like a kiln. I'm wondering whether the priest will drop the liturgical, declamatory style, seeing as it's just the two of us and I'm just the copper who found him. He doesn't. I'm glad. The cadences carry us through.

'And it is certain we leave with nothing,' intones the priest. He had nothing to leave, but the Thames turned his pockets inside-out to be certain.

There's a danger in sentimentalizing tramps, of course. When you've had to deal with a few you see their vagrancy more in terms of the merciful release their present lifestyle must be for the family they terrorized, rather than seeing the tramp as victim. Still, I shouldn't be having these thoughts here.

The priest commits Ray Dunney to the trundle-trundle curtains trundle-trundle fire. He smiles a puny-in-the-face-ofeternity smile at me. I get up and walk down the little aisle to his lectern. I tell him thanks and we shake hands.

'You were the officer who found him?'

'Yes,' I say, like it's as cut and dried as that.

'Did you know him before?' he asks, and suddenly I feel like he knows some guilty secret of mine. But why this shame about admitting I only saw him once, in the street?

'No, well, yes, I saw him once before, just on the street.' The priest turns his gaze sharp on me, like I've let it slip in Interview Room 1. He doesn't say anything so I have to fill in the silence. 'He used to wear a bow-tie and a dress-shirt and, you know, dress smart,' I say, touching where a bow-tie would be on me. 'Not like . . . I suspect that was his old job, he was a doorman or something once.'

He thinks he knows now and says, 'Yes, there's a sort of mental block that stops us, most of the time, from being able to simply get our heads round the fact that down and outs don't want to be down and outs. And I think this is because to accept the idea that *they* don't want to be there means accepting that we're *all* just a run of bad luck away from our own cardboard box in a doorway.' He thinks he knows but he doesn't, and now I can't bear things being cut and dried.

'Father, I need to talk.'

'A confession?' He is late twenties, early thirties (they seem to get younger all the time!). He has big expressive eyes, a lively, open face and a one-piece eyebrow. Irish, fey. When you 'fess up to the priest, though, you don't really want to sense his human delineaments. You don't want a 'smashing feller' or a 'great bloke'. You want him to be possessed of more than mortal knowledge, you want a heavenly father.

'No, not a confession.'

'Shall we go to the pub, or . . . ?'

'No.'

We walk the mile or so to his church. On the way he passes

parishioners he knows just like I used to on my beat and stops and chats just like I did when I saw a known face. But banter with the civilians he knows is tinged with good, whereas talk with the faces I knew was always tinged with evil. He gets to look for their better selves and wait for them to do the good he's always known they could. Me, I had always to keep in mind their worse selves and wait for them to do the bad I always knew they might.

He has a little office (is it called the vestry?) off the altar. He goes into a kitchenette to fix us both a coffee. Spotless white surplices hang from a row of pegs and some more hang from the door. They remind me of the brilliant white space-suits which forensic officers wear at a murder scene: white gloved and white booted, eyes behind the perspex visor like astronauts in raw evil and me standing on the other side of a knotted blue-and-white plastic tape that says, POLICE LINE DO NOT CROSS POLICE LINE DO NOT CROSS POLICE.

Mine is a Power Rangers mug and his is a Lourdes mug.

'Do you know Paul Kenealy?' he asks.

'No.'

'He's an Inspector at Kentish Town station. Lovely bloke.'

'Well, that's another division, not my nick.'

He can tell by my curt reply that I want to cut to the chase and he gives me a high-quality silence.

'Is this all confidential?' I ask.

'Yes, of course.'

'Even though it's not a confession?'

'Mm-hm,' he nods.

I tell him the worst. We finish the coffee and go on to a well-expensive brandy and I'm still talking. I finish by saying, 'I don't know why I've come to see you.'

He ignores this and thinks for a while with his little finger in the side of his mouth. Who is he? Who have I just told everything to?

'If for some reason they defrocked *me* tomorrow, I would still be a priest – I just wouldn't have a ministry. I would still be a priest because nothing would've changed in terms of having devoted my life to the service of God. You are a policeman in terms of having devoted your life to justice, and, uh, as you say, to fighting evil. You just don't have a beat or a division – and this is, I suspect, why you felt that affinity with Ray Dunney still in *his* uniform, as it were. Although in another way you do. Your beat is wherever you encounter evil – and it may be that the frontline is within your own soul. Your division.'

'I don't think I'm a particularly bad person though.'

'That's not quite what I'm saying. Jesus says we should *love one another as ourselves* and that second part is often forgotten: we are told to *love ourselves*. I was once like you in that I didn't love myself as a man, only as a priest.'

I sigh noisily, a big huff. He presses on through the gale. 'You have – John? – put *yourself* in the way of perdition, by going out on this . . . long walk. You have opened the door to all the terrible temptations which accrue when we set ourselves up as more than human.'

'No, I'm not, that's not what –'

'You're marching around town stuck in the past and going nowhere really,' – careful son, I'm a killer – 'because you won't go on the *real* journey to find out who you are as a man rather than as a policeman. You are being asked to go on a real journey on behalf of the Holy Spirit, but you think there's nothing worth finding at the other end.'

'No, there's not a plan. I don't believe in a plan.'

'Nor do I. I'm not saying it's part of a plan.'

'Well, what then. What?'

The length of time he takes before answering is in proportion to how het up my last remark was. And three, and four. Just like a cop that, calming down a drunk outside the betting shop. Very good, padre. And nine, and ten. And now continues: 'I was speaking only last Sunday about phrases which have fallen out of use or out of fashion without our noticing. Phrases like "putting yourself in the way of perdition", or "to enter a world of cares" – people don't say them any more. And I was asking why is this? Why is it that we don't hear them nowadays? Why *is* this? I was wondering. Why is there no longer a sense of every action having a consequence? In the past, in what I call "the old days of belief", people had a clearer sense of every action having a consequence. To the simple believer this was seen in terms of punishment and reward, but even the undogmatic, the secular souls, understood that if they put themselves in the way of perdition they must expect certain woes, or to enter, as the old-fashioned phrase goes, a world of cares. Simple wisdom. Homely prudence.

'Belief is a map, a map of the spiritual landscape, I was saying, but the ancient signposts have gone so that now we only recognize a place when we're in it. That's why people are always surprised by how they feel. They're *surprised* all the time. That's what was in the back of my mind when I wrote this particular sermon: most of the people who come to see me are *surprised* by how they feel: "Father, why do I feel so empty?" They're baffled, everything seemed so tickety-boo. You know what I mean?'

'Yeah,' I say, a tad pissed-off. Yeah, I'm just trying to do good and everyone's having a pop at me: him, Beverley. Why is this, I wonder; why *is* this?

'There's no sense of everything you do being connected because . . . because most people's jobs are . . . you can't see how what you're doing at your desk, in an office or a bank or wherever, is connected to the whole. And our jobs aren't connected to the past and the future either because we may be sacked tomorrow or next year. There's no sense of the inter-connectedness of our actions, because we don't *live* integrally, we are literally "without integrity" in how we live together. The rich live there and the poor live here, polarized cities full of strangers, commuters, the submission of morality to market forces . . . And the end of it is, the end of it is, is this, is that the loss of a sense of the inter-connectedness of our actions means that whether we do good or evil can sometimes feel like a matter of etiquette.'

'One simply isn't the sort of person to beat up a Paki.'

'Er, yes. We choose what things we're going to take the trouble of being conscientious about, rather than having a fixed conscience that informs and shapes everything we do according to its own template.'

I take a sip more brandy. 'None of the other officers want to talk about evil. They deal with it. Black humour and strong whisky.'

'You keep talking about evil but that might not be it. Uh . . . it might be your own despair you have to police. Let's put it another way – it sounds to me that with these vigilante antics of yours you have stripped your job down to its spiritual essence; that is, down to why you became a policeman in the first place.'

'Hit me.'

'To prevent the evil you say you feel so capable of.'

'No, I just want to get back to the job! I wish I was still doing it. To be able to do something about it was the best thing. To take prisoners. That sort of reversed the charge of all the bad stuff coming in.'

'Well, did it? It did a bit, I suppose.'

'I just want to do the job!'

'Yes, I know, but I'm saying, I'm wondering whether you haven't been feeling the loss of something else for much longer.'

'What?'

'Faith.'

'Oh right. I came to you man to man, and you just wanna recruit!'

'No you didn't.' I go quiet at that, lean forward in the red, polypropylene stacker chair and rest my arms across my knees, looking sideways to the door. 'This brandy is the business,' he says. 'Will you have another?'

'Yeah,' I laugh, straightening up. I look for my glass but he finds it first and tops me up. And then, as casually as if he was saying 'Lovely weather for the time of year,' he says, 'We cannot conquer evil in the world, we can only resist evil in ourselves,' then leans back in his chair.

'And just let the bad guy run around town all night doing what he likes, then?'

'No, what I mean is that joining the police-force or becoming a priest gives us a grafted-on, fake identity. Now you have to let the old self die, for a new one to be born.'

I can't agree and so, in imitation of an absent friend, I nod earnestly and reply, '*Yes* . . .'

He gives me a look, then adds, 'But instead of letting the old self die you're just trying to get yourself killed.'

'What can you have faith in? There's nothing that can't be destroyed. Faith is lying to yourself –'

'Oh no,' he said, shaking his head like this was a venial one. 'Oh no, no, no, no, no.' The lowest notes in his dulcet Dub accent.

'Yeah, people who can believe the lie are happier, but it's still a lie.'

'Faith is not some abstract tenet of the Catholic Church, it's what stands between you and despair. It's having a pattern, a frame – in the way that work used to be for you – and this frame, this bigger picture, faith, means that when things hit us they are easily absorbed by the frame and don't strike us nearly so hard. It doesn't have to be Catholic or even Christian. In fact – and as it's just the two of us and strictly off the record – I've been wondering lately whether it even has to be what we usually mean by religious. Although it is religion in another way.'

'Is it all right to smoke? Ta. There's the devil, you see. When people are drunk or high on crack or all lads together in a crowd at night, that's when the devil can enter them. But more than that, there are certain things you say – like what you'd like to do to a nonce – and as you say them you feel engorged, carried along by something else . . . oh, I dunno.'

He says nothing.

'That's all I see all the time, those moments when they're taken up by that. I mean, most of the time it's just petty shit: a metal bin through the window of McDonald's, or the lies, but it's the same force, the same feller, and it's just as soul-destroying as the big stuff. All those scuzzy little lies. But, the point is, because I see this all the time it's so hard to believe that the opposing forces are any more than isolated incidents . . . Yeah.'

'"*Wherefore*,"' he says, smiling while quoting like he doesn't really believe, like he's embarrassed to be quoting scripture, what with it being so, well, priest-like, '"*seeing we also are compassed about with so great a cloud of witnesses, let us lay aside every weight, and the sin which doth so easily beset us, and let us run with patience the race that is set before us.*"'

What's he on about now? He stares at me from under his beetly brows without blinking his brown eyes. Poufter, I think, forgetting to put that thought in a TSG voice.

I look up at him, then down at the floor, then up at him again.

'A cloud of witnesses?'

'*I* think there is,' he replies, and stands up with a secular, game-over smile.

'Yeah, but if you asked them to come forward, they'd say they didn't see anything!'

He drops the smile and says, 'Well, they did in your case that night.'

Walking back through the spitting rain on to Kentish Town High Street, an empty Royal Variety Sunshine Coach drives past. Suddenly it seems like all those unsound jokes me and Kieran told are real weights on the scales of justice, of whether I'm a good man or not.

I wait patiently at the lights to prove to him that I'm not trying to get myself killed. I stand at the pedestrian crossing with people who are by chance all about a foot shorter than me, which makes me feel a bit heroic. I wonder whether I am, like he said, a representative of some sort. Was that what he meant or am I putting a vainglorious Ben Hur gloss on it? Let me think. How did he put it?

A Metro with two cops in crawls past in the thick traffic.

Something is being asked of you, he said. The demand of not being able to take prisoners, of not, then, being able to reverse the charge, the electrical charge of all this bad stuff coming in. Is that what he meant?

The two cops get out the Metro and walk up to me putting on their caps. 'Hello,' one of them says.

'Hello.'

'Where's your radio?'

'Division.'

'Where's that?'

'E.H.'

'East Holloway. What are you doing out here?'

'I've just been to a funeral.'

'I'm sorry. Who was it?'

'Some tramp.'

'Right.'

'A tramp?' says the other one, the passenger.

'Yeah, I found the body.'

'Right,' says the other one and looks at his mate who asks, 'Do you wanna lift?'

'No, I'm gonna walk home. Think,' I say, pointing at my head.

'Is it far?'

'Not really. Well yeah, actually, Archway. But I'm OK.'

'Look,' he says, changing stance so he's standing side-on to me. Hendon, Week One: harder to push over. 'I don't want to be rude but you understand, I'm sure, and would want to do this yourself in my position ... Would you mind just showing me your warrant card, please?'

My skin turns cold. 'Which relief are you from?' I ask them.

'Kentish Town.' The other officer moves round so he's just on the edge of my field of vision. Trouble brewing, eh, lads?

'Oh, do you know an Indian DS called, um, oh ... what is it ... um, Nanda, yeah, Nanda?'

'No.'

'Oh, maybe he's somewhere else then.'

'Your warrant, sir.'

'I haven't got one.'

'Are you impersonating a policeman?'

'No, I'm suspended.'

'For what?' asks the passenger.

But then the main man clicks his finger and points it at my face. 'John Manners.'

'Yeah,' I croak.

'Oh Jesus,' he says. 'Get in. We'll take you home.'

I want to say something funny like 'I'll drive,' but I start crying. My crying sounds loud in the cramped Metro and I'm saying 'Sorry' over and over. I keep thinking I've stopped crying but then I find I've just eased up to resume crying in another key. There are no paper hankies in the car and I get snot all over my sleeve.

new dawn fades

Big Stuart is in the car park and radios Mickey down for me. Mickey says I'll have to see Sandra Rowse the Super, but first he agitatedly leads me upstairs, downstairs, along corridors, looking for an empty office where we can talk. Eventually he settles for two plastic chairs in the corridor quite near the Super's own office.

'What were you thinking of?' he asks, perched sideways on the chair.

'Well, I'm sorry, sir, I know it's strictly out, but it was just because it was ceremonial. It's not as if I was making an arrest or anything. I just wore the uniform as a mark of respect for this down-and-out who I knew from the beat. He was quite a character –'

'Whoah, whoah! Stop! Slow down! Didn't catch a word of that. I can't understand you. Just start again. Slowly. Take a deep breath.'

'Well, all I was saying was that it was a one-off which I won't repeat again. I mean, I was the only mourner, and I just felt it gave things a –'

Mickey tightly pinned my upper arms. 'Stop! Stop! Stop! It's no good. Calm down. Do you feel all right?'

'Oh yeah, I feel very well actually.'

'What was that? Can you understand me?'

'Yeah, of course.'

Mickey breathes out heavily. 'OK, just stay there. I'm gonna go in and have a word.' He gets up and knocks at the Super's office. She tells him to wait a second. I hear her saying exciting stuff that makes me wish to be back in the force again: 'Was it the same man who spoke to you? . . . No, no, but they're all the same – all public school straight into MFI and they think we're just street sweepers . . . Eh? Did I say MFI? Yeah, I did. Ha ha. Well, I think I'll make that same mistake on purpose next time he deigns to call me. OK. I'm needed – we have some crime in this division, unlike you . . . Ah no, that's where you're wrong, we're eighteen per cent solved on Eagle Eye and the target's only thirteen. But don't worry, they'll all start going to you 'cos it's easier. Sorry, gotta go. Bye.'

Mickey disappears into the Super's office and I hear only mumblings. But I'm worried all the same that they'll think I'm eavesdropping, so I tum-te-tum drum on her wall as I sing this tune I'm making up as I go along.

The Super comes to the door with Mickey. Her hair is darker now. It used to be blonde and shorter, but now it's chestnut brown. Dry, thick brown hair, which doesn't go quietly into hairgrips. Her face still has that same look of concentration and focus, however, which always made me want to copy it – as if that would somehow double my own powers of observation, awareness and energy, make me as sharp as her. She shakes my hand, briefly, scrutinizing my eyes closely.

'That's something I've never been able to do,' I start trying to tell her, 'you know, to actually be able to tell, you know, from someone's eyes . . .' I stop. I give up explaining how, whenever I've tried looking into someone's eyes to gauge something, all I see are the concentric circles of inscrutability, like when you throw a rock into a lake.

She looks at Mickey – 'What's he saying?' – and then back at me. 'John, I want to be able to have you back after the trial.'

'Yes, ma'am.'

'Is there anyone you can go and stay with?'

'No.'

'No one at all?'

'Well, there might be, ma'am.'

'Mickey thinks you should take advantage of another couple of counselling sessions and I agree.'

'No, that's fine, ma'am. I spoke to her the other day but it would be, you know, still good to, you know, have a couple more, yes certainly.'

'I didn't catch a word of that. John, you've got a very strong future in my opinion, you've just gotta sit tight, yeah? And don't get me wrong. Even though I have every respect for you as an officer, if I don't think – if I honestly don't think you're fit to return I'm gonna say so. All right? That's all.'

I nod. I try to say 'ma'am,' but for some reason can't get the word out and a strangled lowing noise comes from me. 'Mmmmaaaaa! mmmmmmaaa!' Braying like a crushed donkey.

I walk away with Mickey.

'Right,' he says, 'this is how it is. You go home now, bring back the car and the uniform. You understand why we've got to have them back today, don't you?' I nod. 'OK, see yer in a shiver.'

'Hey, Mickey, tell me that story about the iron bar again?'

'No, John,' he says, slowly shaking his head. 'No. No. No.'

There's a sort of charisma about the slow way he shakes his head, and so I start doing it too.

I make my own way out the nick. Weirdly, I don't see a soul right until I'm almost outside. I open a door with a poster on it warning about walk-in thieves in the workplace.

It's not the usual front desk: building renovations mean that half the station, including front desk, is in Portakabins. Uncle Jess is on the desk.

'Hi John,' he says, before disappearing under the desk burrowing through folded blue jumpers, helmets, phone books and scraps of paper. Even though him doing that is just a coincidence, of course, it reminds me of how in gangster films the barkeeper ducks down below the optics when there's a hit on.

'Hi Uncle,' I say. Meaning 'Bye.'

And with that, I'm out the front in the chilly sunshine.

A 134 at the bus-stop. I get on. Take me home. We putter up the high street. I stand up for home. Ding-ding. Round twelve. A father-and-son team get up ahead of me. The kid is only about twelve but sports a cloth cap. I think that's pretty individual of him. Only twelve but with his own style. No Nike or Arsenal cap for him. A flat cap. Our eyes meet briefly as we queue in the stalled gangway before the bus docks. Only twelve, his dark eyes are old with brown bags in the sallow skin beneath them.

I step off, concertina doors hiss shut behind me. A little way away the boy waits while his dad takes an empty Evian bottle out his canvas haversack, puts it in the bin, and then rejigs the haversack on his shoulders. It was hot on the bus, and here in the cold outdoors the boy removes his flat cap to scratch his bald head. Leukaemia. A novice in the Order of Chemotherapy. Here and there is a frizzy twist of light-brown nearly-hair, like settled dust. He presses his cloth cap back in place on his dome, smooths it down with the junior hollow of both palms and rejoins the pedestrians.

My keys still work in the front door. Chewing the edge of my bus ticket I get changed. Mickey'll be impressed seeing me all laid-back in natty threads. Grey cords, baggy V-neck, loafers. But I'm sorry, Mickey, I can't take the uniform back. Not today. Just the car for now, Mickey.

I park the purple Astra in the pound for the last time

and walk in through the side door. A loud voice familiar and unexpected as a positive thought. 'Johnny!'

'Kieran! All right mate?'

An arm around my neck, and a stubbly kiss on my cheek.

'Ma pigga!'

'What's that?' I ask, looking at the hypo in his hand.

'Fuckin' druggie cunts,' he says. 'Becca's pulling out the kiddie seat from the back of the car, and she feels something down the back of the seat, puts her hand down and she finds fucking this. Could have been there for weeks or months, baby could have got fucking junkie AIDS.'

'Jesus.'

'How you doing?' Kieran asks gravely.

'Not very well . . . I'm like some kind of . . .'

'. . . Not-doing-very-well-at-all . . . person.'

'Yea-eh.'

'I feel bad about not being in touch, but, you know –'

'We shouldn't be talking now.'

'Fuck it, this is the nick.'

'Yeah,' I smile, looking at the floor.

'I should've –'

'I know.'

'Yeah.'

'You don't need to –'

'Johnny! Johnny!'

'Ha!'

'Hey, we took those fruit and veg. men a few months back.'

'Shit! I'd've loved that one!'

'Well, you were there, when – you know . . .'

'Yeah, but . . .'

Shit, the fruit and veg. men. I put a lot of work into that and I wasn't there for the pull. I'd missed out on the fruit and veg. men. Fuck. Eagle Eye, too, so double-plus points from the bosses.

'What are you doing now?' he asks.

'Well, I've just returned my car. I think I'll check it now before I take the keys to Uncle.'

'Well, I'll see you down there.'

'OK.'

I buy a sausage roll and a mini Malvern water from the deserted canteen. Munching away in the car park, I put the rest of the sausage roll on the car's roof. I clear out my A–Z and an old Lucozade bottle from the glove compartment. I run my hand carefully down the back-seat groove. Loose change, a neatly folded empty crisp packet, and then . . . seven tiny half-gram sealed-up polythene sachets of smack . . . and then a gun. I carry the sachets straight in to Uncle Jess, who bags, tags and signs for them in triplicate. The Uncle must be something like sixty-five. Everyone knows he's way past retirement, but they bent the rules and let him stay on because he lives alone and there's nothing down for him beyond the job. I give him the sachets but all the time I wear the gun down the small of my back, stuck in the belt. He goes away to put them in the drugs cupboard. Kieran comes back in and Jess says to him, 'You didn't last long without your needle.'

'I need it back, Uncle. I'm hurting, man.' The Uncle cackles like a miser and disappears into his back office.

'Listen John,' says K., 'look, just come round on Sunday for dinner.'

'But I can't.'

'Fuck it. We're on our internal honour. As long as we don't discuss the case.'

'Thank-you. Thanks. But no, I can't do that.'

Kieran nods, and looks at me. ' "*Cuppa tea*?" '

' "*Yeah, awright geezah*" ' I manage.

I was worried that we'd bump into Mickey on the way and he'd ask why I hadn't brought the uniform back. The canteen was empty, and me and Kieran sat on the edge of two freshly wiped tables facing each other.

He looked at me, raised his eyebrows. 'You're not looking your best.'

I grinned and said, 'I dunno, K., it's like the job slowly strips everything away, you know – first you can't have friends outside the job – that goes – and it's like layer after layer – then your idealism, and Beverley, and then –' But thinking of his settled drum with Becca and the kids I changed tack. 'Or maybe not the job – it's like there's some force that's singled me out, and it's been steadily dividing and sub-dividing me, reducing me to some central – I dunno, it's like I'm locked into some process of stripping everything away until there's just the thing that needs to be . . . met.'

'Yes . . .' he said, non-sarcastically, for once. And yet somehow the fact that he was being sincere made me feel even lonelier. As it would if he'd ended a letter to me with 'yours sincerely'. I looked down. Time passed. I heard him move. His arms were round my shoulders. I leant into him and stood up. We both stood up, him still hugging me. I buried my face in his shoulder, my crinkle-cut eyelids stinging, but not crying. I wanted this hug to last, but as his hands went from my shoulders to my back, all I could think of was that I didn't want him to find the butt of the gun sticking in my waistband. I stepped away. And looked at him with the strange force having sub-divided me one more turn. And I knew he knew that I'd been going out in my uniform and wanted to ask, but he wasn't going to say anything until I did, so I said I had to leave to get a solicitor sorted out and that I hadn't got a solicitor because I was waiting till I had a date for trial before bothering.

'No, no. If you'd had a solicitor he could've *speeded up* the trial date.' Then he paused, and I knew he was thinking that maybe that was why I hadn't got one before now. He turned his radio up to listen to something. Then turned it down again.

'What was that?' I asked.

'Oh, machine-gun maniac on the rampage just outside, killing everyone,' he said and sat back on the edge of the table. Not going anywhere.

'Well, see you then,' I said. He looked at me and frowned quizzically. 'I better get off.'

'Yeah, all right, John,' he said, disappointed. 'All right.' Then, 'Make sure you stay the course.'

Walking back from the nick in plain clothes now I'm worried that everyone thinks I'm a dangerous criminal maniac. Nothing to do with the gun. I've always felt like this in civvies, but I've only really been aware of it since suspension, like a rattly roof tile you can only hear once the factory has shut down. My walk is different in civvies. In uniform I just move my eyes and keep my head still; now my head rubber-necks and rolls.

I hail a Joe Baxy. Sitting in the back of the black cab, I notice the driver has a colour photo of his wife and kids stuck to the dash by a magnetic bulldog clip that also holds his chits and shit. I tap the pane and say, 'Excuse me.' He leans back with his head to one side and slides the perspex panel open. I have to shout a bit to be heard. 'I'm not being funny or anything, but do you have that picture of your wife and kids there to remind you what you're going through all this ache for; or is it really there in case you get a violent bloke in the back of the cab and you hope that it will deter him, like a sort of human shield?'

He swings the cab over, flashes his headlights at a parked cab, gets out and walks round the bonnet. As the other taxi-driver gets out of the other cab, he says to me querulously, 'Out you go! Get out son! I'm not taking you!'

I'm so angry I shout at them both for a bit. I walk off still staring at them and nearly get run over.

Taking a short-cut through the estate playground, a couple of little girls sit on the swings, drifting the heels of their roller-skates, and every twitching net-curtain thinks I'm a nonce. Perhaps it's because my stroll is aimless where everyone else has some project or purpose.

I pop into the corner shop for a Coke and worry that the Muslim woman thinks I'm about to rob the gaff: sees me time-coded and fuzzy, leaning over the scarred counter, smashing the till.

And when I wear civvies at night it seems lone women are particularly scared of civilian me. Do they see something feverish, vengeful in my steps? I try to correct my walk but only the attacker *tries* to look harmless.

There's an upside though to being in civvies. Today a man in a parked van and me walking past – we smiled at each other. It happens sometimes, doesn't it? Some meteorological kink in the air, some pocket, some loophole, a temporary cessation of hostilities . . . and two strangers smile. And the beauty of it was that it wasn't a black–white thing, it wasn't a gay thing or a guy thing, it was just like we'd both caught each other off-balance, open, or had recognized that we were both harmless or I don't know what, but there it is, a smile between two strangers for no reason in London.

It didn't feel at all odd to be in uniform even though I wasn't meant to be. Certainly no more absurd than when I was a community policeman looking for a community that wasn't there – just getting my tithead bashed in the cross-fire of its corporate destruction, in fact. You can build a little community centre and have meetings, but it won't ever be a community, no matter how many of your neighbours you say 'hello' to, because all that really links us is that we're all fighting each other for cash. That's why the word 'community' always sounds so fucking forlorn. The council puts up painted diagrams outside every estate. Something about these field maps outside every council estate in Britain suggests a general and a baton-pointer for the flashpoint battle-zones of the cash war.

Law-abiding citizens think the uniform means you're less likely to get hit when something kicks off. In fact, cops get hit more than anyone except women and children. There's a crowd of thugs fighting outside a club, oh everything's all right here comes someone wearing a blue jacket with brass buttons. When you go to arrest a slag, the look they often give you is a fight threat. *Come on then*. And sometimes a freaked cop won't make the pull. He'll back down from the arrest. Cops are just like everyone else: how important does any job become when it looks like something might happen to your face? Though the general public see the uniform and not the face, that's not true of the slag. He's having a good look at your face: your jaw, your nose, your neck, and checking your eyes for weakness, for fear.

But there's a twist here, isn't there? It never felt like just a uniform to me. For me, the uniform did make the biggest difference, change my face, my eyes, cancel my weakness, my fear. (Some officers wear the uniform like a council bib or like protective goggles: something you *put on* rather than something you *wear*, or *are*.) And it felt like me or a better me. It felt like how I would've been all the time if every detail of my upbringing had been positive. And I always have the trousers tailored down to a drainpipe cut (rather than the frumpy pegs they expect you to risk your life in, ducky).

Why did I keep that gun? Why? Now I'm home it has no words on it. No idea what make it is. Big and heavy with a revolving chamber and six bullets. Empty the caps and hide them in the bottom of a flowerpot. There is one central hole in the bottom of the flowerpot and five in a circle. I insert a bullet into each as if the up-ended pot were a chamber itself.

magnet

Don't put on your uniform. If you're spotted this time then you'll have finally fucked up your life. The chin-strap sits snug under my chin. Don't go out the door. Keys in pocket.

I cross over the road. I'll know what I'm looking for when I find it. I have a sense that a futile gesture is important. What am I about? I'm not doing a penance walk any more, not looking for *the end* either. (They've probably got to that poor bastard by now anyway. Hope they didn't kill him.) No, I'm just looking for some kind of end to this patrol, maybe.

Walking through an industrial estate I see a picket-line outside the Magnet kitchens factory. The pickets see me. Shit. Now I'll have to do what a policeman would normally do so as not to attract their suspicion. I take up position on the other side of the entrance. How long will I have to stand here before I can go and do this thing which I will know what it is when I get there? The pickets give it some booing and muttering. A middle-aged Hindu woman with a red dot on her forehead is walking towards me holding up two leaflets. She has a strange smile as if I'd just dropped the leaflets myself and she is returning them to me. Over her sari and under her sky-blue raincoat she has a T-shirt with a compass print on her chest. A detailed compass design like you get on old, seafaring maps: all points and cogs within cogs. At the top, instead of an N, there's a B. She goes back to the lines. The pickets give a little sarcastic clap when I start reading it.

I read how the dispute has wrecked the homes of those who

make kitchens for dream homes. I look at model kitchens in the factory showroom window. At least Pol Pot actually offered his punters the real agricultural idyll, not just phoney farm-house kitchens in the mass-production age. The pickets all start booing and shouting and blowing whistles as if they've just heard my last thought, but when I look up I find that a big artic. lorry is turning into the entrance. The driver has fucked it slightly though, perhaps in guilty haste to get by the picket-line without meeting anyone's eye. He reverses out slightly with his lorry making its loud reverse beeping. Not my concern. I go back to the leaflet: *'After all the years of hard-working, loyal service I've put in, they turn round and tell me I am expendable. The year since the sackings has been very hard on strikers' health and morale. Men and women who have worked all their lives must now face each day without any structure, shape or purpose apart from the struggle for full re-instatement.'* The lorry revs up noisily, disturbing my read. I look up. The driver looks well-vexed as he starts his second attempt to drive through the entrance. He checks his side mirror, works it out, front bumper clean through now. He's got it right this time and gives me a conspiratorial wink.

I put my hand up. He doesn't stop at first so I bang the medicine-cabinet-sized wing mirror. He stops, still revving. I walk round the front of the cab, ignoring the pickets as best I can. I tell them to step back. They're not happy about that, but do as I say.

'Turn the engine off, please.'

He looks in the wing mirror. 'There's a car behind me.'

'Just turn the engine off, please, sir. Thank-you.' He jerks back his thumb, but it falls away like the ghost of hitch-hikers passed. The engine shudders down to a big stop. The pickets use the silence to orchestrate their jeers and shouts into a unified chant of 'Scab! Scab! Scab!' I feel a delicious transfer of pressure from me to driver man. He is carrying so much pressure! A car up his arse, living in the hate of the common people, and now me ducking down under the wheel arch. I kick his tyres. The more pressure he gets the more I'm floating on air.

Standing up again I lean into his window, saying, 'There's not enough tread on these tyres.'

'I only had it serviced a few months ago!'

'Well, I'm telling you there's not enough tread on these tyres.' I go and check the back ones. A car is hooting behind him. I give the car a calm-down gesture. They give me a nod back. 'The others are all right,' I come back and tell the lorry driver, 'but this front offside is no good. You're gonna have to go to the nearest garage.'

'It's not my lorry. It's the company's.'

'Well, it's your responsibility. You're the one breaking the law driving this lorry.'

'OK. I'll just go and do my pick-up first.'

'No, I'm afraid not.'

'But I'm here now. It's madness not to!'

I shake my head. 'Start it up and then reverse slowly out.'

'But they'll be closed the night then!'

'Well you must have been very wicked in a past life,' I chuckle, banging the door panel twice. 'See ya!' He gives me a look of disgust as the window moves away and the lorry starts its beeping. He reverses out. Tricky: the lorry's rear-end wobbles like a south-pole magnet approaching repellent north. Finally straightened up in the road, he gives a digit to the cheering pickets, handbrake hisses in impotent hydraulic fury and lorry snorts off down the road.

The pickets are giving it a round of applause and cheering. I steadfastly ignore them, and take up position where I was. The gates swing closed electronically. I'm hoping things can go back to how they were but now an old feller picket with a Japanese headscarf starts them all off singing. '*He's our friend, he's our friend, he's our friend,*' they chant to the tune of 'Here We Go'. Hot-faced, embarrassed, I pretend to have just heard something over the radio and wander off. I stop, go back and climb the ladder to the security man who sits in a little conning tower pressing a button to let the gates swing open for the lorries, only it's not a button I see now, it's a key in a panel of controls. I tell him I have to talk confidentially on my radio. He doesn't notice that it's really a scanner. He steps out and goes a couple of rungs down the ladder so I can just see the white-banded cap on his Group 4 head. I look down at all the executive cars parked in named places. I pull the key out the panel. The gates will stay locked. The executives will be staging an unofficial sit-in tonight. Banged them up goodstyle! 'Cheers mate,' I say to the security guard as we swap places at the top of the ladder, and give him a wink like the lorry driver gave me.

Strong legs pump my way home. I feel super-charged and whole, like I've squared some circle. Like I've locked on to the magnetic north in all my wandering and whatever bad things happen now are at least framed. I have a compass. Now I'm more than halfway home, though, my legs have started to feel lodestone heavy.

Home, I take off my helmet and put it on the table. I fold my jacket and put the helmet on top of it. I sit in the chair and wait now for the bad thing to come.

The door buzzes. I've left it open. I stay in my chair. They'll be in in a minute.

'Hello?' calls a voice. I hear footsteps, I see faces. Two young CBOs. They hold themselves very distant, wanting to have just enough for canteen chatter but not wanting to breathe the air of a hell that might be waiting for them too. 'Because you didn't bring the uniform in, I'm afraid we've got orders to come and take it from you.'

It's been a while now since he said that. They're still here. My hand rises, eventually it reaches my throat. I unplug the black clip-on tie and lay it on the table. In a disconnected trance I undo the top button, staring into space where perhaps their heads may be. Slow fingertips find the next plastic button down. I unbutton this one too. I bring my other hand up to help me do the third button. My hands fall softly down. Slowly I raise my arms out to the sides. Without a word the two CBOs come forward. Gently, they unfasten all the buttons of my shirt and the two buttons on the cuff of each sleeve. One of them positions my arms straight up. He slides the shirt off over my head. Fingertips are undoing the laces on my black shoes. They undo my belt. Very carefully, they stand me up and slide my serge trousers down over my legs. Words now. 'Lift up,' murmurs the voice belonging to a hand at the back of my knee. A horse's leg in the blacksmith's hands. 'Other leg.' They sit me back down. I hear them empty the pockets. Lowered keys settle on the table as quietly as if they were being lifted. Loose change is stacked. I hear them folding the heavy trousers. I see a hand lifting a folded blue tunic. I hear the black handcuff wallet put inside the upside-down helmet, hear them tread quietly away and the door close.

I don't know how long I've been sitting here in boxer shorts and socks. It's very dark now. And cold. I reach out and pick up the scanner. Switch it on. Nothing, no one. Radio silence. The only man in the electrostatic of the night sky, looking for a friendly word in space. Somewhere to snag and hold, to stop me boosting into space.

peeled

Chain-smoking like a lab. beagle on Charing Cross Road. I think I've set my lungs on fire. Feel lungs smoulder like the start of a sofa fire. If I breathe in will I fan the embers? An open-topped, sash-staircase tourist bus goes by. A Japanese tour guide with microphone stands on the top deck. I strain to hear what he's saying over the bus-chuga-drone and the amp-waving, blustery wind. 'He's on John Manners Patrol, heh-heh,' he says. 'He's on Manners Patrol!'

In Leicester Square – ach! all the ugly tension of the pulling vibe. All the violent dissatisfaction. All the short-changed mullahs and northern ale lads not ready to give it up and go home. On the steps of the closed Underground, late-night maintenance workers in grimy orange jackets look on at the crowds, enjoying a reprieve from the Speak Your Worth machine of Friday nights. A life-size cut-out of Laurel and Hardy in the window of a hardcore porn shop. 'I'm frightened Ollie!'

Too much to look at. My eyes swivel and sway, spin, fidget and flicker. Head up, down, around, neck screwing tight into the base of my skull. Brain emulsifies to fatty droplets inside my forehead. Oh no, not this again. I try breathing slowly. Feel like I'm running out of air when I let the long breath out. Feel like I'm gonna pop my lung seams when I hold the big breath in. And inhale. And exhale.

*

In the rocking compartment I saw a man look at her funny, so I'm following this woman out Belsize Park tube. She regrets the mini-skirt now. A creeping silver car slows. The fat bastard at the wheel has been in the minicab business exactly fifteen seconds. Sees me clocking him. Drives by. '*You're certainly getting the results, John.*' Cheers, Mickey.

Ten feet ahead of me she turns off into a dark street. I hesitate. Without the uniform this is tricky. What do I do? I hate this. She fears me. I'll go away. But then, but then suppose something happened up that dark street? (I mean that's where it would happen, after all.) What would happen if I wasn't making sure it didn't? If I wasn't doing my job? I clear my throat and start singing a hymn.

A little look over her shoulder as we turn off Rosslyn Hill. I try to look like I'm not following her, but then that's just like someone who was following her. She's worried *I* might be a stalker! I try to reassure her by singing a bit louder. She's out of range so I shout the hymn and get closer. '*Do but themselves confound . . .*'

She drops her keys at her front door, then gets in OK. I take the scanner out of my pocket. Switch it on. '*I'll see you when I see you, then . . . All right, bye then, bye.*'

I cut through the Breaconbridge Estate. I remember Kieran pointing out the top of Breaconbridge Tower. The Andrews had taken over the whole top floor and lived in separate flats. Two balconies at the top of the tower bristling with giant dishes, telescopes, and an aerial. Check for probable nominals. Eagle Eye. Yeah, yeah. It'll come to me when I get there. I'll come to it. It'll come to fit when it is what it is. '*I'm nearly at the door now, pet.*'

Making sure this female doctor gets home safe from the Whittington nightshift. Hornsey Road. Mustard door. I feel a connection between us. Wish I could tell her that we're both in the emergency services, kind of. If we lived in a village we'd be friends, but the world being as it is, all I can do is look out for her, watch her, check up on my old mate from behind the glass of a parallel universe. And see she gets home all right.

> *'We know where he lives, saw him in town and followed him home, Tone, and it's only by . . .'*

It cuts out. Furious, I'm about to throw the scanner on the floor when the signal comes back again. I freeze. Scanner still poised behind my head spear-chucker style.

> *'Right, I'll burn his fucking house down for starters. I know how to get his phone number off it so we can let him know we're on our way.'*
> *'When's it on?'*
> *'I'm at the end, tonight.'*
> *'Now?'*
> *'Yeah, . . . But tomorrer. Set up an alibi. Dawn's or whatever. Fuck it, whatever. S'y'later!!'*
> *'S'later!'*

No internal rhythm, brain spinning so fast I'm all a hollow echo-chamber of soiled phrases and shop-jingles, echoing in a vomitorium. Brain whirring too fast to think. It's them. It's on. It's all still on.

Through Highbury Fields, on to Highbury Crescent, an avenue of handsome sycamore trees along the path through the park. Bark peeled in patterns off the sycamore trunks reveals smooth, bleached patches in the dark. And then, strangely, just as I'm thinking about Ultra-Violet MacKenzie I see her walking slowly, slowly down the street, studying the pavement a few inches ahead of her careful feet. As I draw near hoping to scrape past without her noticing me, she looks up as if I'd just walked into her office. In a tiny, placid voice, and like we're in mid-conversation, this intimate nutter stranger says, 'The social services are saying I can't have home visits, I said you weren't a policeman, why can't I have home visits if the social says I can?' She glides calmly away, having forgotten entirely that I'm there.

Where was I going again? The broken bridge estate. No, I've just been there. Lost my way. I'll stop and have a coffee somewhere. Yeah, coffee, sit down, bifta. I'll find somewhere near here soon. That Tex-Mex over there.

remote

Channel-trawling with the remote. Keep coming back and coming back and coming back to the same scene. There's other more innocent, more rewarding things to watch: an alligator documentary, *To Have and Have Not* – all good for the soul perhaps but I pass them by. Keep coming back to where there's this man bound and gagged. He is tall with slightly balding fair hair. He winces every time a gun is levelled at his battered head.

Hopping through the fifty-one channels I fancy I can still hear his muffled whimpers through the skirting boards of *Tom and Jerry*, or under the newsreader saying it's the *worst* snowfall (why not the best?), round the cape of QVC diamond sales on The Shopping Channel, and orbiting back through *Countdown*, *Fifteen-To-One*, *Jeopardy!*

But none of these can compete with the sensationalist thrill of seeing a man in fear of his life. I don't think I'm alone here, but *why is it* that this stuff is more exciting? Why don't we strive harder to get on to less zappy but more subtly rewarding planes of experience?

Coming back from the kitchen with these questions in my head and a plate of chicken sandwiches in my hand, I notice the tall, balding trussee slithering across the wooden floor trying to escape, the stupid fucker. I put my plate down on the coffee table, careful not to put it on the edge because if I accidentally knock something over I find I get really angry. I have to be careful about that. I walk across and kick him in the stomach.

Weakly he tries to call for help, of all things, but his shout-volume is fractioned by the gag: the long-division sign in his maw.

I politely tap him with the steel gun on flinching cheek. He has the bruised and bloody face of a slow learner.

'Now each time you make a mistake,' I say, 'you will hear this sound.' I pull back the ratchet of the hand-cannon.

uncouth behaviour

They were loud. I don't care for loudness in public places.

I had gone to eat alone in a large and noisy Tex-Mex.

Sitting in my padded green bomber-jacket, eating alone. Tough among all the happy eaters to get my food down even though I hadn't eaten for two days and nights.

I was on a small table for two. Five feet away was a long table with a bunch of City boys. They were making the shit jokes posh people make and think is wit. They were singing songs – *our* songs, working-class songs – they had no business singing. *Celery, celery* . . . Fuck off, you Norman cunts. City boys' night out. Celebrating what exactly? Maybe a new contract won – but these City-types can never go out without behaving like they are celebrating their fragile economic supremacy, the rout of all else. And I do not care for loudness in public places.

Under the din I rested my eyes on a small point of calm. She had delicate Jewish features, olive skin and straight black hair that was perhaps a bob when not behind her ears for work. Petite with very large breasts which she'd tried to hide behind a baggy black cardigan. Walking or standing the waitress was foal-footed on the wooden floor: not sure of her right to a place on earth, not sure it'd hold her tiny weight. There was something oddly assailable about her. For some reason she lacked the usual human force-field. As she stood near waiting for my selection from the easy-wipe menu, how easy and natural it would be, I felt, to reach out and put my arm around her tiny waist; or just pick her off her uncertain ground, sit her on my table like a child and have her carry on with her order pad as if nothing had happened. Maybe it's good, I was thinking, that I'm at least aware of these bad ideas.

Tried to ignore the roar from their table by watching the waitress, chewing the cardboard nachos very slowly. Living in the corner of her eyes she ignored the noise from the big table behind her while she attended some middle-aged, portly man who leaned back sweatily in his open shirt, leaning right back in his chair looking up at her as if she was holding grapes or her tits over his beaming boat. It being unconscious, this openness vibe, it must have driven her to confusion that she got in so many tight corners. If she did. Yes, she probably did. A legacy of sexual abuse? They say abusers often marry abusees. Or abusees marry abusers. What did that make me, staring at her now, I wondered.

A crust of bread landed on my table. I stared at it. Then, without looking at the City boys I threw it back and carried on eating my indigestible dip.

Same crust came back again. I looked up. A tall, muscly cove with thinning blond hair met my stare. Pointing at the crust, I slowly mouthed three words – 'pick it up!' – like I was helping him cheat in an exam. He got up and came over to me. 'Whooo's from his mates at the long table. And then it happened again. This thing that happens in these situations happened then, in the face-off with this man who could no doubt have creamed me – he hesitated. I felt that same beatific eagerness spreading over my face, like everything I ever wanted had just happened. Not a hard look, not a look of menace or macho aggro-geezer, just a sort of serenity. I was at home here (thanks, maybe, to Kenneth the coach-driver) and he hesitated, then decided not to do what he came over to do. He just broke out in a face-saving leer and took the crust away.

The others must have been surprised when he backed off

instead of getting it on with neat, skinny me. On his way back to the table, one of the sweaty others held up an empty lager jug and bellowed, 'Go and get the waitress!' Still standing, he raised index-finger in a 'Right-ho' gesture, set off . . . and came back moments later with the waitress over his shoulder. Her head by the small of his back, her arse where his radio would be if he was me and I was still what I was. Roars of approval from his mates, round of applause. Then mock slapping-forehead Inspector Dreyfus-type gestures, with 'Uh-oh,' and 'Did you have to?'

He set her down.

'Don't mind him,' said a short scrum-half in yellow tie and red forehead. 'Don't mind him – he's completely insane!' Yeah. Crazy. A madman. A wild force of nature, him. A total madman. Wild. Demented. Psychotic. The scrum-half gave her a tenner which she slipped quietly into the big pocket of her wrap-around white mini-apron. Smoothed the whole thing out, hadn't he? Yeah, it's all straightened out now. Tenner, that should cover it.

Pretending to have laughed it off, she quickly took their orders.

The situation had passed. They didn't know how close they came. I pushed my plate away and stared at the table.

It doesn't matter, said a voice in my head, *they've said sorry. She doesn't seem too shaken. What am I like when I'm drunk? Am I so much better?*

I've never done this, said another, louder voice, *and they think this makes them great fucking lads. They'll retell this one. Look at big cunt now with his beaming face soaking up the plaudits. Hero of the Night. Hero of the Fucking Night.*

It's nothing. They were quite polite with the girl, really. They all said sorry. It was just high spirits and everything was smoothed out. It's just 'cos I'm on my own in a crowd. Right. Right.

Wandered off for a few blocks out in the night air. Heading back fast to the restaurant I told myself I was just checking nothing else had gone off. Seeing him alone at the cash-point I told myself this was his Last Supper and nicked him at gunpoint.

We got into a scuffle getting into his car. At the front door he was like a horse refusing the starting stall. Someone had spelt 'MURDERAR' wrong on my wall. I had to use the pistol-butt once maybe two times. Twice at most.

And then with him sitting on the wooden floor at gunpoint I began: 'You know why you're here?'

'No.'

'You were uncouth.'

'I didn't break any law. I'm law-abiding.'

'Which law is this?'

'The law.'

'You let evil into you. If a kid from the Cannoncourt estate let the same amount of devil into his soul, it would be a recognized crime. Sliding scale, it's a sliding scale. Why should he be hit harder than you, eh? Why? You never wanting for anything your whole life.' Just to freak him out a bit I put on like a mad face. Did a sort of nutter face.

'I know how it is . . .' he said, winding up some pathetic bit of preppy psychobabble.

I inclined my head as if to say 'I think not, El Cunto,' and he gave up the gambit. 'Your only way out of this,' I said 'is if I see a particular look on your face. Now I'm not going to tell you what that look is, you're going to have to arrive at it, to achieve it yourself.'

He didn't look up or say anything. Smiled to himself, got up saying, 'Fuck this.'

I got up and grabbed him.

'Get off!' he shouted. I smacked him in the face, ran him to the wall, his head banged against it. An arm went up to his head I punched him twice more left and right and he went to the ground with a little blood and not much fuss.

Once he was sitting on the wooden floor with his wrists cuffed behind him I brought him the picture of me in uniform with the Home Secretary just to impress upon him the gravity of his situation; to make him think this was a special underground department. I trussed his legs with washing-line and put the telly on.

I felt very calm. And that in itself meant a lot to me: to punish him or not to punish was one of those decisions you won't know is right until you take it, until you take it and feel a rewarding gladness descend upon neck and shoulders, gut and heart.

I could have done without him being there when I got back from my walk. I put the telly on again, though, and zapped channels with the dibber. Coming back with a chicken sandwich and crisps, however, he is slithering to the door, trying to escape. Not yet. Not nearly yet. No-oh-oh-no. But what? What then? Now what? What is it? What?

'It would be so easy now,' I divulge, making a slow gun explosion noise with the catarrh part of my mouth whilst miming the last shot. 'So easy now,' I say, lifting the gun up slowly to his chemical-film eyeballs. What would it be like to shove gun metal into the pond? Wonder if you'd go straight in; or would it be unexpectedly hard and resistant like a horse's eyeball to the thumb? Or perhaps the barrel would skid up into the upper socket part. Don't seriously think of doing it though, not really.

It crosses my mind to hit him with the gun. I click into place what I'm pretty sure is the safety catch. Pause. If I'm going to do this thing it has to be right. I'm glad he is quiet now because it lets me think it through . . .

Sickening to think of myself as one of the bad. What's going on? What then? Now what? Where do I go from here?

The phone rings. I jump. He jumps because I jumped with the loaded handgun. The phone is ringing in my room. Not on the scanner, but live and direct on my phone. I sit on the floor next to him and let the message run on to the answerphone where it says:

> *Ready for death?*
> *Are you*
>   *ready*
>   *for death?*

The charged flat is twice as silent now, like the caller might talk again without the phone even ringing. '*Ready for death?*' When I look round the hostage is staring at me, breathing heavily. I look at him, but don't see him. The voice was disguised. Tony Andrew? But then why would he have to disguise his voice? I've never heard him talk. Maybe it's just the Assistant Commissioner checking to see how I am! I hear a grunt. Oh, him. You're still here, are you? I unclink his cuffs, unbind his legs. He disappears fast as a salamander into the skirting board. Unbelievably fast. Whoomph. Out the door. Gone. The letter-box flapping like he's coming round for tea.

I wish he hadn't left me. Now he's gone there's so much I wish I'd said. I wish I'd told him that what shocked me was when she stopped struggling. What shocked me was his air of 'captain's privilege' with her. I wish I'd never let him go. Especially as now he knows. Especially as now someone else knows that I wanted to shoot him and then shoot myself and then be nothing.

I lie on the floor crying, hot tears run into my ears.

What am I gonna do now? What am I gonna do? What am I gonna do now?'

him or me

Now I've let the hostage go I'm full of terrible dread. Not that he'll go to the police. (Unlikely.) But just . . . but . . . where do I go from here? I know now that I am not a killer and never have been a killer. Not something I can do, it turns out. But at what terrible cost? What reckoning will I have to pay now? What lengths I've had to go to and how painfully to learn this about me. All the time that I've wasted, to have walked so far in the wrong direction, because I never had any faith or knowledge of myself.

To attempt anything constructive feels like flicking a light-switch after smelling gas. A shower, a shave, a coffee all pass without a breakdown.

Wearing combat trousers, Ben Sherman and bomber jacket my reflection in the mirrored rear-view of a passing cash dispenser says I look normal.

This is Holloway Road seven p.m. A low-slung sun, with the streets exhausted and relaxed after business and the first steel shutters rattling down in the still air frame the quiet.

Three beefy white men in their late thirties are chatting by some railings: 'So I've got him like this and I just went –' he mimes one fist holding a neck, the other fist judiciously popping him in the face, once, twice, then skipping a beat to pick his spot for the third.

I pass the open door of Ladbroke's. In a white tunic with green epaulettes a medical orderly stares up at the overhead screen with professional scrutiny.

I pass some pinch-faced 'under-5's' drinking outside the George. I can't hear what they're saying but it's the same mime. All these men talking about violence. Fear-management.

A man drunk and woozy with a new bandage, sleeve ripped to the shoulder and blood all over his shirt weaves his way home. Tall with thinning blond hair, he sways into the traffic, reeling across to the other side of the street.

Two Hare Krishnas barefoot across the ped-X at Highbury Corner. I turn my eyes away from the topknot guy walking along with clipboard, orange robes, turquoise socks and grey nylon trackie bottoms. Fuck off looking at me. If they see the emptiness in my eyes I'll come quietly, led by the hand into a little room with orange vinyl chairs where I sign over pension and possessions to the Maharishi.

A side road bending round some deserted depots, business units and a fleet of BT vans is a dead-end. Walk back the way I came. Feel myself winding down. Must keep going. Keep going.

At some lights by Seven Sisters I feel myself winding down again. Less and less to hold me here. I stop. And stand still. People are going in and out of the Seven Eleven, they're crossing the road, going into a pub and a minicab office.

I empty out my pockets of money, keys, everything. I sit on the fibreglass bit from a traffic-island which rests on its side by a pile of boxes and bin-bags on the pavement. Eventually I walk on about a hundred, two hundred yards, think better of it, come back and pick up my shit. It's still there. No one's dared touch. Or no one's been unkind enough to touch it.

the day the world turned sad

Everywhere, people sigh to a stop, empty their pockets of the dreck and coins and crumpled nowhere tickets and lie down: Birmingham's Bull Ring, in leafy suburban avenues, or on Hungerford Bridge over the static Thames.

Pouring a pint the landlord lets the liquid overflow his hand awhile. Bored with the sticky stink he lets the straight glass drop and smash. Beer pours from tap to floor, foam jizzing in the broken glass for a bit then stopping.

The surgeon's finger doodles in blood on anaesthetized flesh; he pushes out his bottom lip, breathes in the smell of exposed organs palpating tinily, purposefully.

Phone receivers dangle in boxes, with or without people underneath them.

The builders and engineers give up on the bypass, leaving scattered cable-drums, muddy yellow pipes and earth-caked cement blocks to litter the slipway. The rain blurs JCB tracks on the dirt ramp while the Portakabin subsides.

There's hardly anyone on our cracked and rubbly, weed-sprouting motorways these days anyway. And no one cares when the car in front just stops. Come to think of it, it had become too big an effort of will to keep foot down, even 5 m.p.h. For the same reason we all use bumpers not brakes now. Saves having to move your foot from one pedal to another.

Somewhere behind a car revs up, but not impatient or aggressive. The fifty-year-old woman is just seeing how without you doing anything there's nothing and the universe pours over you. Her foot and the engine sound, or just her foot. Her foot and the engine sound, or just her foot. Or just her foot.

No one puts down the ferry gangplank. The passengers just sit there, as the ferry drifts back out again with the engine cut.

When one person starts crying in the high street that starts us all off. The out-of-focus newsreader tells where it was worst – when he doesn't have his head on the desk. But there's no sound anyway. The soundman didn't make it in today. Third day running.

The TV chef tears sliced bread from its Mother's Pride bag, but he can't find the marg. When he steps out of focus the cameraman doesn't pull to follow him.

On stage actors say, 'that all the world might stand up and blah, blah, blah, blah, blah, beeurggh, beuurgh, wer . . . and he comes in, and he kills him, the end. Bravo.'

The homeless are standing up from their dishevelled cardboard boxes. Only they are alert, wired and full of energy. They can sense their meal-ticket going down the toilet. A homeless man says to a pedestrian, 'Hey, hey, hey, what's going on?' Then he recognizes a glazed look – 'Oh that,' and goes back to his box. Hard to tell nowadays who's homeless from who isn't, who's homeless from who's dead.

Watching telly the young couple piss their pants on the sofa with about half an hour separating them.

Liverpool *v.* Everton. Some players have forgotten boots or shorts or that today's Saturday. Lying down the keeper pulls at Anfield dandelions, crumbles brown leaves to dust in his hand. A couple of them punt a ball for a bit, then it goes past one and rolls to a stop among clover. Wasn't properly inflated anyway. They sit or lay down for a bit, but despite the long coats it's cold and so after a while most go back inside.

A Party Political Broadcast ends with, 'Whoever you vote for, it doesn't make any difference, we're all just the same in the end.'

They held a press conference but nobody came, not even the speaker. The neglected audio rig howls and howls, bellowing its empty feedback round the vacant room with its rows of chairs. A giant slogan says, *Time For Ac–*, followed by a downslide of paint-splurge.

What are we gonna do now? What are we gonna do? We think, gathered to watch the lights which change from green to amber to red to red and amber to green. What are we gonna do now? We think, knowing one day they'll stop.

An ex-policeman is helped into the back of a paramedic van. The windows are brown.

another kind of section house

The wooden bench is colder than the air. Its back legs sink into soft mud under the long wet grass. I'm leaning back now and it's not sinking further.

A scruffy, overweight, black man stands over me. Hot and bothered, out of breath. 'Are you playing ping-pong or what?' he demands, waving a red table-tennis bat. I look at the wet green lawn, at the cold, orange-streaked sky. What an absurd question! Then I look down and see that I'm also holding a red table-tennis bat.

Mine is a thick, maxi-ply, smooth one, his is a flappy, bobbly-surface thin one. If only we could swap bats then I'd feel all right. I lunge for his bat. There's a bit of scuffle. He walks off. My ear's burning but it's not on fire. No, definitely not. And even if it was I'd have patted it out by now. It is unusually hot. For an ear.

I can hear fast cars whoosh-whoosh-whoosh. All I can see of the distant dual-carriageway is a bit of concrete bridge through thick, black evening trees beyond the fence. The more I listen the more the hum and fall, whoosh, whoosh, whoosh is sound shapes, then words. What are they saying to me?

'*Wary. Don't now! Wary – don't now!*'
'*Wary – don't know.*'
'*Well – I don't . . . know*'
'*Whenseet cooooming?*'

'*Whensit cooom?*'
'*Wah!*'

No, that's not it. So what is it?

'John,' calls one of the nurses who's also called John. 'Come on, John, you'll get double pneumonia.'

'NNOOOO!!!!' I scream, 'I'm concentrating!!!'

'John! Come on.'

'Tell *me* what to do! Fucking tell *me* what to do!' I shout, meaning don't.

'It's eight p.m. and me and you have got an agreement, haven't we?'

I respect his appeal to my better nature, and get up to go in.

I can't remember what the agreement is exactly.

Then again, I think a lot of the car sound shapes had to do with patting my ear. The further I walk from the bench, the more all I can hear is the patting hand on my sore lug. Poor lug.

Red pill, yellow pill. John the nurse keeps them in his palm or in a tiny, tinted, plastic jar with a crack in it sometimes.

Red pill, yellow pill.

Aching arms, no breath, dry, dry mouth. Drinking water all the time. My hands smell of piss, lots of drips, dripping with drops on them. Wipe, wipe, wipe, but now my clothes smell of piss. Wash hands. Tap water in toilet smells of piss.

Red pill, yellow pill.

I'm worried that if I keep taking the pills then I'll never get better, never improve, always be here.

I'm worried they've given me the wrong pills, wrong label, someone else's.

I'm worried the pills are making me slow.

I'm worried the pills are killing me.

I'm worried the pills will give me a heart attack.

But most of all, I'm worried the pills will run out.

Did I just get up or am I just getting to sleep?

A black Mondeo leaves the crumbly asphalt drive. My mother is leaving without saying goodbye. A sky-blue Escort leaves the crumbly asphalt drive. My mother is leaving without saying hello.

The number plates of all the cars in the car park are:

N234 RST

F502 BUR

M520 BRO

P60 GYP

N614 WPP

A white hand-towel brittle with starch falls apart in my hands like a horse's spine.

There's a young woman who avoids me. Hiding something. She knows I know. Looks horrified when she sees me. I follow her out the TV room. Stop and search. Running my thumb bone up inside her dress, between her rigid legs, over her naked arse. Everyone's shouting and pulling me to the floor and Lee Andrew's sitting on my chest but he's not going to kill me this time and it's John the nurse not Lee, and it's John the nurse not me.

I've got a little equation I say to myself in secret so I know I'm not mad. Or maybe a saying or a little phrase.

The grey wall-phone. Its receiver hanging down. I pick it up. Kieran's voice.

'Johnny? All right Johnny? Was that one of the nurses answered?' So I hadn't just picked up the phone by chance after all.

'Hello?' I croak.

'Listen, good news: because you're nuts the trial's been dropped. They've thrown away all the charges!'

I hear him. But I want to hear the words again. I cover one ear against the silence and say: 'Sorry, it's too noisy here. What did you say?'

'They've dropped the whole case! All you gotta do is pretend to be sane and you're back to work!'

'Yeah.'

'Yea-es!'

'Yes!'

'It's all over. I'd visit but I've –'

'I've got to go now.'

'What?'

'Bye.'

Never known a week like this: snow, sleet, stick trees with no leaves. Sun, heat, trees in white, bunchy bloom.

There's a male nurse here who's called John as well.

'You were lucky,' he says. I look down and see him leaning a red bat on a white ball on the ping-pong table. 'You've been getting sneaky practice in.'

'John, when can I go?'

'Well, you're voluntary entry. If you've never been sectioned you can go when you feel up to it. Unless there's – you can go when you want.'

'Only my mate Kieran phoned the other day and said that I could go back to work when I was better.'

'When?'

'When I want.'

'No. No, when did he phone?'

'I can't remember.'

'You said the other day.'

'Yeah, the other day.'

'When he phoned you and said the charges had been dropped?'

'And that I could go back to work, yeah.'

'That was . . . March.'

'Where are we now?'
'July.'
'July, eh?'
'Yes.'
I try and respond before it turns into August: 'Lumme!'

gutted

'I hope that's not your house, is it?' says the taxi-driver as we pull up in the cab.

'No. Thank god!'

'Well, that's a relief. Imagine coming home to that!'

'Yeah, after a long journey – heh-heh, you know, when you just want a shower . . .'

'Yeah, that's right – have a shower or a bath, put your feet up, put the kettle on, tea and biscuits, but instead you have to go through all that.'

'Yeah-heh!' I had just enough money left to pay him and tip. And then maybe a few shekels left for the phone.

Wooden boards over floor and window. The brick is black but holding where fire couldn't take.

The POLICE LINE DO NOT CROSS plastic banner tells me it was arson. Lee Andrew's brother Tony – with his '*Ready for Death?*' catch-phrase? The City boy? Who cares? What does it matter now? What does anything matter now?

I knock next-door and ask for a wrench. The babysitter stands in the corner of the front room, holding the baby towards the wall. She slowly points back to the kitchen not saying anything (probably a foreign exchange student or something). Best I can find is a steel thing for sharpening knives on.

I leave through her kitchen door, climb over the garden wall and into my back yard.

Can't wrench my new, six-ply back-door board off. I stomp

my luggage to fuck, treading the overnight bag until I hear the biscuity crunch that says Walkman, camera, credit cards are all destroyed. At last.

I stand on a pile of charred timber and glass, wedge the sharpener in the top of the eight-foot six-ply board, and hang down with all my weight and strength on the handle. I crawl my feet up, until I'm hanging like a vexed chimp and bounce. The board and me rip down together into the glass and timber pile.

A musty, stagnant cloud gusts out.

I step in. Gutted. A black mist of moist ash shreds my throat in seconds.

Piss-taky charcoal swirlings on the smoke-patterned ceiling. Tide-marks from the fire-fighters' foam.

What fire hasn't destroyed it's thrown around. Though there's less in the flat there's more on the floor. A face-down cupboard all crashed and burned. Piles of ex-books and the *Pompeii News*. Under ash, smashed plates litter the five-foot-high floor. Shards of shattered, blackened striplight curled at the edges. Pretty. A clump of CDs smelted down into one solid wadge. How would this condensed version of all my music sound if you could play it? Under the bubbly casing I can still see a burnt-out Beatle and bits of prismatic discs. *It won't be long, yeah, yeah* . . .

Weirdly, some things seem untouched and lie pristine on top of Armageddon: a set of vinyl playing-cards must have spewed from the bottom of a drawer in the last of the fire roar, flecking the devastation like calling cards.

It takes a while to see what's missing, to remember what was where.

The perspex door of the microwave has popped into nothingness, leaving only melted resin in the buckled groove of the blackened gaping panel. Snapped and soldered copper pipes litter the pile.

Brittle, black blocks of flaky stuff I don't recognize. Exposed grooves where the kindling wires and cables once ran. The brittle, black blocks of flaky stuff are, I see now, chunks of plaster fallen from ceiling and wall. Terracotta powdery bullet-holes in the wall from where the loaded flowerpot exploded.

Most depressing, for some reason, are door knobs on the floor under the ash. *It won't be lo-ong, yeah, yeah, yeah, yeah . . .*

The exact same listlessness that I always used to feel here now makes it impossible to lift a melted, buckled TV aerial. You can destroy the structure but not the spirit! Charred it looks more like home than before.

I kick the blackened shell of a kitchen cabinet. It flings back vicious slake and I'm bent double in the garden coughing up a soot-storm, red eyes streaming.

In no mood to get on the case. To go all the way to a phone booth. To have to go and borrow some money off the corner shop, in case I need to make more than one call. Who to? Address book in the fire with all my phone numbers.

Spent, fucked over, all fight gone, down and out. I go back into the flat.

I sit down on rubble where the chair used to be. Maybe I'll bed down here the night and then hassle out the organizational stuff later. The repairs.

Hanging ash scours my eyes and stubble-burnt throat. The stink clings to skin and filthy fingers, soot fuzzy-felts my lungs. A singeing in my nose. I can't even sit five minutes in this chimney.

I find the scanner in the sooty jumble rubble of my old waste site. The black box in the plane crash. Except it's broken and useless, too. I'll take it. I pick up a rolled-up curtain that was lying with other debris in the garden.

Standing in a phone box of shattered glass, staring at the blood on my fists and trying to remember what happened.

Walking round the block I pass all the homeowners crossing to the other side of the street going home from work. I find a space in an alley behind some shops to sit down and cry.

Pride keeps me from a night in the cells.

Walking and choked-up walking. I still have the bag I've brought with me with spare jeans and jumper and this curtain with weather-whitened ridges in the cloth.

Walking and walking in a daze as far and wide as Lincoln's Inn Field. The homeless are all behind a mesh fence like a refugee compound. All around are offices of barristers, solicitors and judges, and here they are camped in the middle of all the bad laws that brought them here. With the grass and all I'd hoped it'd feel more like a camp-site than it does.

It takes me ages to walk back. Lost.

Lost now. So difficult to think where Pentonville Road is. Where's Euston? Euston Street? Euston Road? Euston? Which way is the centre? The centre of London? How do I get more central than I am now? Which way is it more built up? That way will be more central probably. I'll just be walking. Yes. That's the thing. I'll just walk until I hit a sign or something familiar.

It all looks very unfamiliar.

Embankment. The same Embankment where I policed demos (feeling schizophrenic if the cause was just. But then it was a double-time and I had nothing better to do.) Cold piss-stew stings my eyes.

Some crazy, ginger-beard tramp is stealing a sleeping bag with menaces. I caution him. He hits me while I'm trying to tug the sleeping bag off him. I hit him back. He kicks off with all the fury of a decider for the last two places in the pecking order of All-England. I run away and now I'll only be able to police the cardboard hamlet when he's not around or not watching.

Night comes down mercilessly. I go up to a young, scraggy,

scouse couple. They both have sandy hair. I buy their cardboard den off them for the ten pound in my pocket.

It stinks. They didn't look that smelly, but maybe they weren't first-time owners. Ah shit, maybe it's not even theirs. I lay out my curtain for a blanket, neatly folding the spare coat which will be stolen by morning.

lying in a stone cattle trough

Now that I'm immune to piss-haze and the stewed, body-rot stench, other smells are detectable: the graphite smell from cars up on the street above, diesel gusts off weary trains hobbling in to Charing Cross, and the greasy, nettle-soup river smell.

A withered blue balloon floats over the river. One end like a scraggy blue belly-button, the other like an old woman's wrinkled pap. The knackered, light-blue balloon – hooked by the Thames breeze – is carried high, high, high in the sky until a dot and then just flotsam in my eye.

I am becoming invisible. My body is blinking like a tired bulb in a deserted hallway. Today, for example, the silver-haired cockney on the Embankment souvenir stall can't see me. Yesterday he shouted at me when I stole a plastic bobby's helmet. But now as I walk right past his stall (it's on my beat) he can't see me. He still can't see me now even though I'm standing right in front of him, arms behind my back in the too-small helmet, looking down at mini red phone-boxes, distant Dinky red buses, tiny black taxis, and small brass Houses of Parliament. He busies himself with trays of football scarves, muttering to himself. Alone. A woman comes up and wants a light. He won't give her one, so she has to buy a souvenir lighter. I'm right in his sightline when he gives her the change, but he looks through me.

I'm becoming invisible like an old and unimportant memory: the face of the corner-shop keeper two addresses ago. Sometimes standing by the fire, I lift my jumper and pat my bare tum to see if I'm still here under this dead man's overcoat. When I start a-pat-pat-patting I can't stop. I strip off to look at my skin, patting and rubbing, until all the dossers start caterwauling and throwing bits of wood. So instead I've taken to crossing the road very, very slowly. I like to stop halfway and listen to the horns a-tooting: a sweet sound that says I can be seen. Beep-beep! And last night when they were a-beep-beep-beeping I saw the ghost of Lee Andrew, smaller and scruffier now he's in the after-life. He was behind the wheel of a white van with *Repairs and Alterations* written in black on the side-panel over a cartoon tailor holding giant shears. Stepping out the van the phantom said, 'Ready for death?', ignoring the hooting traffic in that way ghosts do, because they can walk through things and that.

'Yes,' I nodded, pleased that my contact had got in touch. Smaller now than he was, though, eyes popping with supernatural knowledge.

The ghost's familiars bundled him back into the van. 'Later, later,' they said, their hands going right through him time after time, but eventually closing the red-tail-light doors on him. I was on all fours on the central reservation with blood flowing from my nose and the traffic moving on.

In a locked-up deserted forecourt I find an old friend. What's it called now? It's not ragwort, what's it called? I used to put it in my bike pump when I was a child and fire it – pop! Groundsel. Is what it's called. It's called groundsel. Must remember that so if anyone asks me, 'Oh, John, what's the name of that weed that looks like a plant with little capsule-like buds, yellow-tipped, and with very fine fluffy bits like on a dandelion puffball?' I'll say, 'That'll be groundsel. Lots of people get it confused with ragwort, but they're different.' Must remember that. My memory's not what it was. Down among the groundsel just now I found a crumpled bit of purple card. Promised Land at The End it says. Capital Tango, capital Echo. I know this has to do with something. Or did have.

It's dark as I near the Embankment. Almost there when a black kid crosses the road tidily and comes up to me.

'Mr Manners.'

'Mr . . . Trevorrow.'

'OK,' he huffs, holding up his arms out to the side like I just asked to search him. This confuses me. I stare at him for a bit. I put a hand down his back and run the other along his sleeve like we're about to tango. 'Tony Andrew knows where you are,' says my dancing partner softly. 'You gotta leave here. He knows you're here, he's seen you.'

'Tell me, what do you make of this?' I ask, looking for the flyer. 'Fuck it! Where is it? Here.' I hand him the flyer. It says:

Promised Land at The End.
Techno + trance
Billy Nasty, Sabresonic
10 p.m.–4 a.m. Nearest tube Embankment.

'*Yeah*, that's where he works,' says Kyle. 'Now, you gotta –'

'Where who works?'

'What?'

'What's his name?' I ask. He stares at me.

'You know his name,' he says. 'Tony Andrew. He's on the door and, you know, all what goes with it.'

'The doorman at The End.' A tango echo.

'Tony Andrew's coming for you. Him and his team. Here's me car there.'

'What?'

'Just get in!' I stop at the black VW Golf. Pull back. I give him a look to say: 'You may think I've lost the plot, son, but I got enough wits about me to suss a trap.' He clocks this and just says, 'You've got to trust me.'

'So you can drive me to him?'

'No. *He's* coming *here*. Tonight. Tonight! Soon as he's finished at The End.'

'You want me to get in the car?'

'Yes. Please.' He holds the door open for me.

We're driving somewhere fast. It's cold out yet he has the window wound down and all the air blowers on. Strange . . .

'Satan?' I ask. 'Are you Satan?'

'No,' he says. He raises a riot scarf up like he was a-ram-raiding. 'Where else is there?' he asks from under the black cloth. 'Where else can you doss down? Is there a hostel or anything?'

'Arlington House.'

'Camden?'

'Can't remember. That's the problem I can't remember.'

'Yeah, it's Camden, Arlington Road. Arlington House, Arlington Road. I know it.'

'You got a licence?'

'No,' comes the muffled voice from under the black cloth. We stop at a red. I'm about to ask Kyle why he's got his scarf up when my shanks sting with sudden shame.

'I'm sorry,' I blurt, 'the smell . . . It's not me, really. It's where I've been. Sorry.'

'Well, the good news is,' he says, scarf sucked into his mouth as he speaks, 'I thought I'd lost me sense of smell with all the bugle but now . . .' He breaks off. I look across. His head's turned away. Follow his gaze. A squad car beside us at the lights, the cop staring in. Kyle drops the scarf too late and says, 'Fuck!' The cop points at Kyle, drops his own window and leans across the empty passenger seat.

'It's all right he's with me,' I say to the cop, lifting the helmet off my lap and pointing at it by way of explanation. He stares at me blankly for a bit, blinks, slowly shifts his gaze back to Kyle and now points to the side of the road.

Kyle pulls over and switches the engine off. I look at him.

He's thinking. I'll start thinking too. The cop gets out of his car. Yes, thinking is good. Thinking, thinking. If word gets out where Kyle was and who with then that will go bad for him with the ghost and his familiars. This copper's on his own. He walks towards the driver door. I open my door a tiny, tiny crack. His serge trousers arrive Kyle-side. I jump out the car and give it toes.

I don't know where these streets are. It's like I've been beamed down from another point in history. I see as if for the first time that I am just in one particular space at a particular time, with its own peculiar noises, roofing styles and design of bottle. It's as if I've just landed on planet earth and am seeing everything fresh, and sort of *objectively*.

An old Kentucky box balanced on the rim of the green, plastic bin. I open the carton. Its bones have been sucked white. A fellow traveller must have been here before me. No one with a roof over their head ever sucks this shit clean to the bone. I'm glad I saved Kyle from trouble with his friends.

I hunt down a street name: Arlington Road. Ahead of me is Arlington House. I walk right past the lit door. The clever moth.

On a wall I find a nearly full bottle of Appletize, with the lid on. I sniff it to make sure it's not piss and empty the lot in two camel gulps.

Behind sandy polythene night-shift carpenters are fitting a shop. One of the fitters sings, a good voice like an old-style crooner. His steps on the concrete floor, the slide of one plank on another, his catches of song – each sound is distinct. So too the smells of wood and of sawdust burning on the worklight.

I turn off into a pretty, little curving road of four-storey Georgian houses with pillars and wrought-iron railings. A step ahead of me a black cat with white paws and white-tipped tail jumps through iron railings into a basement flat's 'area', activating an automatic security light. Like a magician's wand the cat's white-tipped tail turns the dark recess into a bright and beautiful garden: terracotta pots of sunflowers, hanging twirls of ivy, a curly bay tree in a wooden barrel and the grey stone statue of a cherub.

I pass a house which has a hand-painted 127 in the glass above the door – painted door-number 127. The two has come out really fat and so they've tried to make the seven and the one fat as well but they just look like blobs. And now here's 144. Same sort of home-made crisis in the glass above the door – *real* trouble. When it comes to '4's you're better off getting a professional in. The next time someone says to me, 'Oh, John, I'm not sure whether to paint my door number myself or get a signwriter to do it,' I'll say, 'What number do you live at?' 'Flat 144.' 'Get a properly trained professional signwriter in.'

I check the locks of offices and shops. Looking through their back doors I see a right old mess. Stacks of scattered yellow post-its, a fanned sprawl of phone books, telephones whose wires aren't quite long enough to reach the desk and have to go on the floor, botched splodges of polyfilla. A good-humoured voice in my head draws my attention to this (and to the botched door-numbers, too). All the time I spent thinking that everyone else has got life down pat except me. But, see, says the voice, it's not just you, is it?

I can hear a voice in my head now that's always been there. Through all my careering this sure voice has always been there, just as the liver and kidneys still function in a panic attack with slow mineral knowledge down where profound patterns are simple and complex molecules made easy. I half expect this voice to be angry with me for ignoring him so long when he's been the true measure all the time. But he's not angry. The voice speaks with patience, he knows how it is, this never-fazed voice, father to myself.

On Albany Street now I find a stone trough carved with the legend: Metropolitan Drinking Fountain and Cattle Trough Association. I sit down on the ancient tub. Where was I?

Is it a voice or is it more like a face? A calm smile, a steady elephant eye on the slowest of slow-exposure time-settings and a step back from all my peaks and troughs. Only not the pitiless eye of time – which is where I started this journey – more like the partisan who knows I'm secretly stronger than I go around thinking. The easy, half smile of a logical man. Below petty rages, this sound inner core of sense is always level like a ship's compass. A good-humoured, benevolent voice. And all my hard rind of concerns and opinions I find are not actually shared here at my inner core by this lateral thinker. A still centre. Patient and encouraging, the voice suggests it might be more comfortable to lie down in the disused, stone cattle trough. Empty but for some mouldy leaves and sieved grit. I lie in the trough. Rest my feet up on the ledge like I'm in the bath.

Exhale, the unfazed father suggests. I exhale. By following this core voice it speaks stronger in me. It feels good to rest my legs.

All my long walking has been to hack a knowledge of what I *did* that night out of who I *am* (and to know now that I'm not a killer.) Through knowing who I am came knowledge of what went on with me and Lee back there. Before the long walk I felt that everything I'd seen was nothing I knew. Stranded from reality, God, and nature, they tell us, we stand alone in a pitiless universe from which nothing can be known separately from our perception of it. (Who ever wanted to know anything separately anyway?) It's all in our heads and nowhere else. But in the autopsy room at the Middlesex I saw a human brain once. Smooth as sea-snails its wibbly-wobbly foldings were the funny shape of ridged coral turf, shared the same intelligent pattern of sea-anemones. Our brain and its perceptions are shaped by the same intelligence that puts the finishing touches on a lamb, or decides when to rift a valley. Because the shape of my skull is a cast of my mother's uterus I know that the universe isn't mere crunch or spread but that it has the self-organizing suss of cells, spunk and shrimp's eggs, and the revealed pattern of dissolved air on the surface of the Thames, a pattern which intricately repeats to the end of space.

My eyelids are heavy. When I close my eyes I can make it night and when I open them as now I make it day! Pink light is reflected on high white walls. A sweet-cidery taste in the mouth. My face feels like malty, baked bread, leavened, rich, toasted. I haul myself up to prop my arms on the side of the stone trough. One streetlight hasn't been turned off like all the others and burns yellow in daylight through the green leaves of a tree.

I climb out the trough and sit on the edge. I pick a few crackly brown leaves off my shoulders and out my hair and rub them into dust in my hands.

Every lie I ever told myself and others folded matter in on itself and things were not what they could have been. How could I ever have thought any different? To think that I could ever fold my soul and expect the world to be the same! Not just my perception, but the very medium I lived in was changed by every falsehood. All the energy I've wasted. All that hard this-is-me chatter and rind of opinion and fixity. Ach!

I flick brown dust out the lines on my palm.

Why have I never tried to be as virtuous as I could? Well, says the voice now, because I didn't want to miss out on anything and be less happy, when all the time I might have got the whole concept of virtue wrong anyway. Because in our time there's always someone who comes up and says, 'No, you've got it all wrong'. Because it looked like real virtue might be a looser affair: you know, all that intelligent stuff about how you might actually be a better person morally by being less rigidly upstanding. Why didn't I just go ahead anyway? In the olden days, your togaed nobleman's lifetime's project was to build an inner temple by living according to his best instincts. I can't think of an actual example, but a sort of ancient Greek on a mountain path thinking about other people, transcending lust in a grey beard and sandals, a temple in himself just for its own sake, or maybe because he lived when there was a cult of being in yourself as high a testament to human nature as possible. But I lived in a time when goods were made to be obsolete in a year or so. Because there was no audience and so no one would know. Why, though, wasn't it enough to have my own secret project? Because the world might end? Because no one else was doing it? Because I got the idea that everything you know is wrong? And the idea that who you think you are is always wrong, and therefore if you think you're living soulfully you're wrong? And besides, who you are is always changing, and so there's no stone to build on?

Sitting on the edge of the disused tub I run my fingers over the letters carved into the stone. Each preserved cattle trough has a name. This one's called 'Florence'. I get up.

Goodbye cattle trough. Now here's a thing: revelatory peace doesn't come round often, and yet now it has I'm about to leave it quite casually, like I'll know where to find it again. When you're in peace, it feels like it was never far. But when it's gone it's a world away. So why don't I hang around here some more? Why leave peace and the truths it reveals? Well, it's a bit of an ache hanging on to it, slightly boring in fact. Not our natural element. Time for a walk.

This is better: watching *Tom and Jerry* outside the window of a closed shop. One of those off-licences that are just three cans of Red Stripe and a wasp. Jerry ties anvil to Tom's tail. Runs round corner. Whistles. Tom chases. Jerry disappears into hole. Tom brakes, slides on polished floor. Stops. Anvil hits back of his head. Face shape of anvil.

From now on I will be the best I can be in all things and not pretend I don't know what the right way is. Forget what other people are doing: it's not like it's *their* conscience I'm trying to live by anyway, is it?

My feet are sore. I've been heading somewhere definite but now I can't remember where. Bone tired. *I have been to the wild woods, mother, make my bed soon, for I am weary wi' hunger and fain would lie down.* In the last few years I've noticed the following: my tears have been about knowing that as I've got older my heart has seized up more and more. Sometimes it is right to die young, if life gets you there naturally, old friend, but only then. Sometimes it might even be a sin to die old. I would like to be released now, but among other things I am paying for my impatience. I couldn't wait that suspension out and tried to bend time to my will. Now I must be patient. Because your soul is deeply involved with time, not totally apart like that crazy priest believed. I must be as patient as this column of traffic headed by a big, white lorry that waits for a little red car which is attempting to reverse into a parking space in front of the lorry and the helpful queue of cars and vans behind it. I hear sparrow natter and look up. Birds congregate on a wire and, when their number reaches a certain density, they have their instructions and are off all together. Sore feet and heavy legs like I've just walked all the walking I ever did. But I do not will things to be one way or the other.

Mazy King's Cross. Which way shall I go from here? Which way now? York Way looks beyond my strength, another uphill climb. Will it just get steeper and steeper? Euston Road to the left and Pentonville to the right? Will it ever be better up there? My memory's not what it was but I don't fancy either. Gray's Inn Road is downhill at least.

last tour of duty

A sunny day. You can go right down on to the little mud and shale beaches of the Thames because no one else is interested in them. Here I wash my face and arse in the river. Then wash my tanned hands and wet my hair down. It's grown out its spikes and feels clumpy when I slick it back out of my eyes.

I sit on the wall by a crazy iron fish wrapped round a lamp post. There was some reason, something Kyle said, why I wasn't supposed to come back here. Sitting here on this granite wall, though, the Embankment doesn't feel evil. He's crazy. Nowhere feels evil any more. If it did I'd have done what the man said. Stayed away. He's like I used to be, Kyle, thinking this place is evil and that place is good. Crazy. Next time I see him I'll be sure and tell him nowhere's evil.

'Here y'are, uncle.'

I look round. It's the young scouse couple I bought the cardboard den off. 'We knew you'd forget it's Tuesday,' says the girl, handing me a big paper cup with a wrong-sized lid on.

'Soup van. Gotta dobble-'elping dare,' says the lad, in a punchy friendly tune. 'Oh, and – ' he takes a spoon out from under his coat and hands it over. 'Cootlery.' They both smile at me, like parents with a little kid, or kids with a forgetful dad. She's wrong. I do know it's Tuesday. I know it's Tuesday because they've brought me some soup.

'Thanks.' I put the blazing spoon on the sparkly mica-granite wall and sip the soup while they tell me their plans again. Interrupting each other and then looking back and forth at each other like no offence and none taken. I smile and look at the magnesium river, so shiny but after a while my eyes adjust to see its subtle rippling pattern, repeating, feinting. A mesmerizing riddle. It's so mesmerizing because there is some answer there. The pattern isn't just on the surface, the same pattern is under the surface as well, but only takes the shape it does when it gives way to the air.

You know you're being initiated into the secret of the river when you start to smell it. That means you've been staring at it long enough. The secret's open to you with only the smell of algae dripping off the rotten slime-ropes and the smell of mud on the river beach. The *strength* of the river! All that melted ice-age tonnage powering through the present. The light that couldn't join in the river's pattern blazes back and now I look up at my two friends I can't see them, they have become hovering dots of light, shards of faces in white light, half a nose and an eye. Teeth, cheek, hair, all separated. But they're there because I can hear them behind the glittering.

' . . . And we've been there two days, they're all sound, and if we just stay in the squat for six weeks then we'll get money from the social and go down to Brighton, me spar's down there, says there're jobs on the deck-chairs no probs.'

'And we can jib on the train if . . .'

I got caught in the rain the other day. Now they're dry my sky-blue trainers have come up looking nearly new. The white flashes and laces have come up whiter too. I swing my feet a little and the spongy heels bounce off the wall. They were a size and a half too big before but now they're just right, even when each bounce off the wall bangs the heel right into the back of them. Just right and twice as bright.

I hope she says 'six weeks' again. They way she said it – sicckhsss hoowheeechchkkss – was like spinning a bright copper wheel or cog.

'. . . And he's worked in hotels, him –'

'Yeah,' he says, 'that's how come I'm here. Listen to this right – worked in a hotel. Seventy-five a week. They took seventy for food and lodging and so I was left with a fiver. Fucked it off but couldn't get Housing Benefit 'cos I'd left me last job and that's how I'm here.'

' . . . And we'll get a jacket and he can start going for interviews then, 'cos they need more staff in the summer, and it's all hotels right along the south coast . . . I mean, you can't *move* for hotels, innit!'

'Or bar work. I've worked in bars – optics, "*Who's next?*", touch-tills, all that.'

'Who's next?' doesn't sound like it'd take a long time to learn, but to stack hope on such a reedy plank probably does. I like to hear their plans.

'And there's lots of shelters there, night shelters, until – if we don't, you know, straightaway, aren't straightaway –'

' – Successful,' says the girl, finding the word he superstitiously avoided.

I like to hear their plans. It's like they think I'm their bank manager or something and any minute might just give the OK to their future. And so, in a solemn wish that I could be, I simply say, 'Yes, that all sounds in order. I'll give you the go ahead on that.'

They start laughing at this. 'I'm buzzin' now,' says the boy. 'Laters, uncle.'

'See youse,' says his bride, then pauses. 'You never remember me, do you?'

'Yeah. Yeah I do. I remember you every week.'

'OK. Never mind.' She walks off sad like she didn't believe me. I should have put more into it. *Yes, I remember you, you're the girl that brings me soup with your boyfriend every week.* I'll say that next time she comes, which will be next week when they bring me soup. Two good campers.

I get up and wander under the bridge. Peel some strong black tape off the hinges of what was my cardboard den. Someone else's stuff in there now. Using the gaffer tape I lash top and bottom of the cracked, collapsed, stoved-in scanner to the day-glo lime-green shoulder of my cast-off black jacket. I think it's a seafarer's coat. Or the navy. Sergeant stripes on the arm.

And still it holds: looking around me each object seems more individual, separated out. The spear-railings painted black, the sweep of the white lines in the road, the metal instructions on the water-hydrant pavement flap; a bush in the park that seems to hover out an inch high over the grass – you can almost feel, touch the one-inch-high shadow.

Yet at the same time as each thing and being is more individual, each seems more part of the same whole, part of one thing. And I am part of all this, and everything is part of me. How long did I spend not knowing that I am part of everyone else and they are part of me? At night the freezing, far-off stars or the warm red hum of the Oxo tower, and today the swipy, thin clouds and swirl of the sky, the perpetual-motion trees, the crisp-walking woman in smart suit and set face, processing encounters of the day before or her day ahead, and the crazy red-beard tramp now lumbering my way.

'Some lads eh took this, but I took-took eh back, said it's youren, took eh back off 'ummmah.' Having mutter-growled his piece, he hands me back my souvenir bobby's helmet and walks away before I can thank him. I put it on. Thanks tramp. The cold, plastic chin-strap cuts into the curve between bottom lip and bristly chin. Ceremonial.

Time for my last tour of duty.

I walk up on to street-level, and all of a sudden know why this is the last tour of duty: I've waited a lifetime to see this, and now at last my work is done.

On Hungerford bridge a girl walks along with a gaping

tartan duffle-bag on her shoulder: wallet, keys, mobile all open to the air. She smiles safe in the knowledge that dipping and snatching are things of the past.

In Villiers Street I see the manager of H. Samuel crouching in the doorway. He is peeling the electric strip off the tinted glass door, while behind him a fiancé stands on the pavement examining the sapphires in daylight before deciding to buy.

In Golden Square a woman lies sunbathing on the grass with her Walkman beside her, eyes closed and legs raised as if she was in her own back garden.

Tickets are handed in to the empty kiosk at Embankment tube, and I see a ten-year-old girl with a kid's random selection of teeth smile and safely accept a lift from a stranger with a bag of Liquorice Allsorts on his dashboard.

On the white floor of Charing Cross station bags are left unattended while their owners have coffee or lager in The Traveller's Rest.

A car has broken down jamming the merge of two lanes of traffic where the Embankment underpass rises to Piccadilly. Drivers are friendly towards the traffic-cop. They grin and wave, shouting, 'Well done!' or 'Thank-you!' as I first stop one lane and then wave the other on.

'Yes, OK,' I say, still beckoning the lane. 'Keep it coming.' I look down the underpass and, where dark ceiling meets curving tiles, see in rows the jet-engines which turbo the earth around the day and night as dusk turns to dark now.

'You're making my job look easy,' comments the motorbike cop just arrived, as he puts on white gloves and takes over the waving.

'I always did, son.' A few motorists clap as I walk away. I turn back to the cop. 'Follow that,' I tell him, pointing at my fans.

In an alley off the Strand a double-parked car is left unlocked with keys in the ignition in case anyone needs to move it to get out.

Returning to his open-topped army jeep, a young, black man with designer dreads picks his Ray-bans from the dash, puts them back on and turns the waiting key.

On Camberwell New Road at the Speedlink cashpoint no one looks over their shoulder. Free to day-dream as they walk away towards the low hum, tinkle and pop of late-night picnics in Kennington Park.

A young woman, alone in a white minidress, cools her feet in the pond. She looks up at the city lights reflected in the black night, miles away, her shoes and bag safe behind her, twenty feet away on a bench.

A foursome of pensioners stroll through an unlit alley with the slow, swinging gait of an afternoon in the botanical gardens. Still chatting they stop while one of them, a white-haired old man, knots his jumper over his shoulders. And in that moment I saw they had forgotten fear.

Now at last my work is done.

May I remain only as a spirit, a force for good in the world, a presence on the ether.

Back at the Embankment I stand easy under the bridge.

I take off my plastic helmet and put it under my arm. And wait. Inhale.

Whatever it is within me that needs to be done I find already taken care of. That's good. Taken care of now.

. . . And exhale.

Wait.

I pat the cracked and knackered hollow scanner taped to the day-glo shoulder of this old, navy jacket. A few last bits of wire on a cracked half of green circuit-board poke out from melted black plastic. The breeze blows a little dust and grit. And now, what's this? What's this?

Music. A single bar, and then whistling static. A couple more bars. Women singing. Static fizz. Fade out. If I stand still will it bless me? Nothing. Comes back. Holds this time. Snagged on the scanner and me not moving. 'Aaah Kaa-li aach . . .' Ah, just as the spring coil of a busted sofa in the yard picks up stray kilohertz and foreign chatter on the wind, so now, in the gentle, gentle night breeze, the shattered scanner mumbles stray music. I know this. *Kali-man-kou* means I am part of people I have never met and they are part of me.

The music whispers up into my ear while I stare ahead. A little white van with no lights drives slowly, very slowly through the cardboard camp. A tiny, glowing, red fag-end floats inside the black windscreen as if being smoked by the Invisible Man.

Repairs and Alterations.

It stops.

Four men get out. They've come for me at last. The Repairmen.

The Repairmen are holding the screwdrivers and spanners we will need to unbolt the casing that has kept me here. To free me to become a spirit in the air, a force for good. It will be hard work because these rivets were put in years and years ago and I've expanded since.

'Aie – ahhhh – ah – aiie!'

The pace of the spirit as he walks towards me and the fury on his face is good. You don't want to be botched, half-finished and left even more trapped in the body than before.

One of the Repairmen is the ghost of someone I saw die, as though whoever the Repairmen work for is telling me, 'Don't worry because you go on, you see, you go on in spirit. Don't worry even though it's tough to unscrew, unbolt, prise off and free you from your casing.'

Kicks and punches and stabbing prods. The ghost's screwdriver has a blue handle.

The ghost looks like he's trying his best to get the job done. I can't speak any more because I'm already half spirit, but if I could speak I'd say, 'Don't worry because I know.'

The body I'm about to lose, meanwhile, is using the bits that still work to howl and howl. But that's only right.

I'm all over the place, falling and moaning – all disorganized-looking. I wish they knew how I'm not really.

Exhaling, blowing out, expelling. There's so much to puff out, out and out.

Lying panting, wheezing, gurgling. Presences in the air above anoint me with flecks of water.

A kick in the head. Face smacks groundswell pavement. The join of concrete wall and asphalt pavement. Dried and flaky piss.

Sitting up. Falling into him, he props me up with the sole of his boots.

Stand up. Yes, good. Stand up.

I'm standing, standing on premises. Hands behind back, but I can only get one arm behind.

'Jesus Christ,' says the priest.

Eyes open now. Eyes open again. Was it like this for you, ghost? That time? The hosts hover, sway and spin.

The ghost is looking at my neck. OK. Neck. It's the neck. Neck next.

Everything's quiet now. I find I'm kneeling with my head against the sore wall. My slow hand gropes for something that isn't there. I thought there'd be a big blue handle in my neck to lift myself up with. It has floated downstream in the hot flood. I follow down to soft pavement.

Exhale.

Now at last I'm going to remain. Right. Silent and remaining. To remain here. But silent.